Dead man on the porch

Hoppy was snuffling at a man who lay on the floor of the summer porch by the Hoosier cabinet. The upper and lower cabinet doors were wide open, and Jaymie swiftly shut the bottom one so she could get at the fellow. A cardboard box rested partly on his bleeding head, broken china on and all around him. Jaymie tossed the broom away and knelt by him, pushing the cardboard box away.

"Becca, can you take Hoppy? There's broken china all over the floor," she said, pushing the little dog aside and brushing the shattered pieces and whole teacups and saucers from the injured man, a tinkle of porcelain echoing in the quiet night. Was he breathing?

Rebecca cried out, picked up Hoppy, then grabbed the cordless phone from the wall mount in the kitchen as Jaymie reached out and tried to help the man roll over. He didn't budge, despite her efforts; he was dead weight.

"Hey, mister?" she said, staring at the still man. He was a well-dressed fellow, wearing khaki slacks and a polo shirt under a cable-knit cardigan. Besides the gash on his head and the blood that oozed in a messy stream from it, his nose was also crusted with old blood. Jaymie, dizzy and a little nauseous, wondered what the heck he had been doing on their summer porch. She glanced up and saw that the door was wide open and hanging drunkenly from its hinges, which explained the night air drifting in. In the distance someone's dog was barking, which started a chorus of howls from the other dogs in town . . .

A DEADLY GRIND

VICTORIA HAMILTON

BERKLEY PRIME CRIME, NEW YORK

THE BERKLEY PUBLISHING GROUP
Published by the Penguin Group
Penguin Group (USA) Inc.
375 Hudson Street, New York, New York 10014, USA

Penguin Group (Canada), 90 Eglinton Avenue East, Suite 700, Toronto, Ontario M4P 2Y3, Canada
(a division of Pearson Penguin Canada Inc.) • Penguin Books Ltd., 80 Strand, London WC2R 0RL,
England • Penguin Group Ireland, 25 St. Stephen's Green, Dublin 2, Ireland (a division of Penguin
Books Ltd.) • Penguin Group (Australia), 250 Camberwell Road, Camberwell, Victoria 3124, Australia
(a division of Pearson Australia Group Pty. Ltd.) • Penguin Books India Pvt. Ltd., 11 Community
Centre, Panchsheel Park, New Delhi—110 017, India • Penguin Group (NZ), 67 Apollo Drive,
Rosedale, Auckland 0632, New Zealand (a division of Pearson New Zealand Ltd.) • Penguin Books
(South Africa) (Pty.) Ltd., 24 Sturdee Avenue, Rosebank, Johannesburg 2196, South Africa

Penguin Books Ltd., Registered Offices: 80 Strand, London WC2R 0RL, England

This is a work of fiction. Names, characters, places, and incidents either are the product of the author's
imagination or are used fictitiously, and any resemblance to actual persons, living or dead, business
establishments, events, or locales is entirely coincidental. The publisher does not have any control over
and does not assume any responsibility for author or third-party websites or their content.

PUBLISHER'S NOTE: The recipes contained in this book are to be followed exactly as written.
The publisher is not responsible for your specific health or allergy needs that may require
medical supervision. The publisher is not responsible for any adverse reactions to the
recipes contained in this book.

A DEADLY GRIND

A Berkley Prime Crime Book / published by arrangement with the author

PUBLISHING HISTORY
Berkley Prime Crime mass-market edition / May 2012

Copyright © 2012 by Donna Lea Simpson.
Cover illustration by Tim O'Brian.
Cover design by Lesley Worrell.
Interior text design by Tiffany Estreicher.

ISBN: 978-0-425-24801-0

BERKLEY® PRIME CRIME
Berkley Prime Crime Books are published by The Berkley Publishing Group,
a division of Penguin Group (USA) Inc.,
375 Hudson Street, New York, New York 10014.
BERKLEY® PRIME CRIME and the PRIME CRIME logo are trademarks of
Penguin Group (USA) Inc.

PRINTED IN THE UNITED STATES OF AMERICA

10 9 8 7 6 5 4 3 2 1

ACKNOWLEDGMENTS

The road is long, with many a winding turn . . .

Once upon a time there was a little girl who read her mother's Agatha Christie and Dorothy L. Sayers mysteries and dreamed of growing up to become a mystery author. She took a few side roads and detours along the way, but today, she fulfilled her childhood dream.

So many people to thank, so little time!

Thanks to the Berkley Prime Crime team, among them Andy Ball, Lesley Worrell, and cover artist Tim O'Brian. Special thanks to Michelle, for loving the Vintage Kitchen Mysteries!

Thanks to my mom, who loves mysteries, and let her kid borrow them all.

And to all of you out there who dream of writing your own mystery . . . my wish for you is that you have someone who believes in you every step of the way, because that—and the willingness to work and learn—is what it takes.

❧ One ❧

NO ONE WOULD expect to find a new love at an estate auction, but Jaymie Leighton just had; her heart skipped a beat when she first saw the Indiana housewife's dream. She wasn't in Indiana and she wasn't a housewife, but those were just details. Tall, stately and handsome, if a little the worse for wear, the Hoosier stood alone on the long porch of the deserted yellow-brick farmhouse. The hubbub of the crowd melted away as Jaymie mounted the steps, strode down the creaky wooden porch floor and approached, reverently.

"You are so beautiful!" she crooned, stroking the dusty porcelain work top and gently fiddling with the chromed latch of the Hoosier cabinet cupboard, handled by so many generations of housewives before her eager, yet inexperienced, hands touched it. It was a *genuine* Hoosier, if the metal plate affixed above the top cupboards of the cabinet was to be believed, and she had no cause to doubt it. The latch of the long cupboard popped and the door swung open to reveal an intact flour sifter, mounted on a tilt-out pin.

"Wow," Rebecca, Jaymie's older sister, said, as she approached from the lawn below the porch railing.

"I *know*," Jaymie said, standing back and tilting her head to one side, gazing at the piece with admiring eyes. "The latches work, at least the ones I've tried, even if some of them are rusty. And the darn thing still has the flour sifter intact! Do you know how rare that is? Most times someone has stripped it out to make more storage space. And it's never been painted! Original oak. Someone really treasured this piece."

She stepped back up to the cabinet and fiddled with the tambour door, a section that looked like the rolltop on a rolltop desk; it was near the porcelain work top and should have rolled up to reveal a storage area where glass spice jars, as well as baking tools and other cooking necessities, were kept. But the tambour would not budge. It was either jammed or broken, or moisture had caused the slats to swell, making them stick. That could be fixed, but it would temporarily keep her from finding out if it had more original parts hidden. "Isn't it beautiful?" Jaymie said, glancing at her sister and stepping back so Becca could get a good look.

"That's not what I was going to say, but . . . okay."

"I'm going to bid on it," Jaymie said, jotting down the lot number on her pad.

"What? Why?"

"Why?" Jaymie stuck the pad back in her purse and stared down at her older sister in disbelief. "Becca, *look* at it!"

"I am," she said, eyeing it, a dubious expression on her round face. "It's dirty and damaged. The side panels are chipped, the porcelain work top is scarred and the legs have water staining. It looks like crap. As far as vintage pieces go, I'd give this one a two out of ten."

Jaymie marveled at how differently she and Becca could

see things. Her sister was fifteen when Jaymie was born and almost seemed like a second mother at times; the message was always the same: *I am so much older than you,* she implied time and again, *that I know more and my ideas are better!*

Becca was logical and pragmatic and had a numerical grading system for everything in life; two out of ten did not cut it. Anything worthwhile, from food to men to antiques, had to be a seven or better. Jaymie preferred to look beneath the surface to the heart of a piece, and this one had a heart of solid, twenty-four carat gold. "It just needs a little cleaning up. I love it, and I'm going to bid on it."

"And put it where?" her older sister said, crossing her arms over her ample bosom, sensibly covered by a burgundy sweater to ward off the chill of approaching evening.

"I'm not sure yet," Jaymie said, rubbing her bare arms. May in Michigan is changeable and moody, sun shining one moment and dark clouds scudding across the sky the next. Seduced by the heat of the late-afternoon sun, Jaymie had optimistically pulled her canvas sneakers out of the closet and had neglected to slip a sweatshirt or sweater over her pink T-shirt. The auction didn't start until five p.m., and would likely run for hours; it would be dark and cold by the time they left, and she would be freezing. She shrugged, both at the cold and her sister's gloomy assessment of the Hoosier. "I'll find a place for it."

"Jaymie, get real," Becca said, still staring over the porch railing at her from the lawn. "The kitchen is packed enough as it is with all your crap. Vintage tins, old pots and pans, Pyrex bowls, bowls, bowls and more bowls *everywhere*! How many bowls can one cook use? The last thing we need is another big piece of furniture."

"Do I call all your china and teacups '*crap*'?" Jaymie shot back.

"My china and teacups are not cluttering the kitchen. I'm just saying there is no more room for another scrap of furniture or cooking junk!"

"You only live at the house every other weekend, so you don't have to worry about it," Jaymie said, going back to examining the Hoosier. Though they jointly owned the family's nineteenth-century two-story yellow-brick home in Queensville, she was the only one who lived there full-time. It was truly a family heirloom, and had been deeded to Jaymie and Rebecca by their parents, Joy and Alan Leighton, who preferred the Florida heat and humidity to Michigan's variable temperatures: too hot in summer, too cold and snowy in winter, and iffy in between.

"What do you think Mom would say about all that stuff crowding her kitchen?" Becca pointed out.

Jaymie sighed. Becca could be so controlling, a trait she had inherited from their mother. She thought—again, because she was so much older than Jaymie—she had a right to tell her sister what to do, but Jaymie was thirty-two, not ten, so the fifteen-year age gap was not such a big deal anymore. "Okay, first, it isn't her kitchen. She always hated it anyway. Thank heavens she didn't modernize it in the eighties when she wanted to." She shuddered, and continued. "But I know exactly what she'd say: *'Jaymie, you can't possibly like all this clutter!'* She would mutter something about 'hoarders', then Dad would tell her to butt out. It isn't their house anymore, and they shouldn't care one bit what I do to it." She gave her older sister a defiant look.

Becca couldn't deny that; though Joy Leighton had come to the home in Queensville as a young bride in the sixties, she had never been fond of the old, yellow-brick house. In fact, when the Leightons did come back north, in the sultry heat of midsummer, they were more likely to stay at the family's cottage on Heartbreak Island, the heart-shaped island in the middle of the St. Clair River between Queensville, Michigan, and Johnsonville, Ontario, the Canadian town named in honor of President Andrew Johnson, back in the eighteen hundreds.

Heartbreak Island, split in two by a navigable channel,

was shared by American and Canadian cottagers, a compromise reached in the early eighteen hundreds to settle ongoing land disputes that lingered after the War of 1812. To Jaymie, that compromise was symbolic of the ongoing friendship between two sovereign nations that shared the world's longest undefended border. In honor of that unique friendship, Queensville and Johnsonville shared holidays. This late-May Friday ushered in the first Canadian holiday weekend of summer, the Victoria Day weekend. On Sunday and Monday Canadian visitors would flock across the St. Clair River to Jaymie's hometown—Queensville, Michigan, was named in honor of Queen Victoria—to attend the long-standing traditional "Tea with the Queen."

But still, while Jaymie lived in Queensville year-round and adored her touristy little village home, Rebecca Leighton Burke ran her own company, RLB China Matching, out of her home in the nearby southwestern Ontario city of London, halfway along the highway between Detroit and Toronto and perfectly situated for business. She had settled there when she married a Canadian, and now, even after the divorce, stayed to look after their grandmother, who lived in London, too.

Becca bought and sold old bone china and made a good deal of money doing it. If someone had broken an antique Spode platter or Minton teacup, Becca could sell them a replacement . . . for a premium price. Perhaps it was unfair, as they shared ownership of the family home, but Jaymie felt that, since she was the one who cared for it most, she should be able to do what she wanted, as long as she consulted Becca on any substantial changes.

"Look, Jaymie, I can't discuss this right now," Becca said, her glance returning to the back lawn of the old house, where the flatbed stage was set; the nattily dressed gentleman auctioneer was mounting the steps as they spoke, so the auction must be starting in minutes. She glanced down at her notebook and said, "I only came to tell you that I'll be bidding on an assorted box of teacups and saucers—that'll be for the Tea with the Queen fundraiser Sunday and Monday, in case we run out—the complete set of Crown Derby, the Minton tea set, and the box of Spode completer pieces." She checked each one off as she named it. She looked up at her sister with a worried frown. "Oh, and, uh, Joel and his new squeeze are here. I just thought I'd better warn you." She began to walk away, but over her shoulder she threw, "And don't you dare bid on that Hoosier!"

Jaymie stood frozen, her hand on the dusty porcelain work top of the cabinet, as she overlooked the green lawn, dotted with buyers and gawkers threading back through the tables of auction lots toward the stage. Joel was at the auction? And he was there with Heidi? Crap! As she stood there, silent, undecided on whether to flee or stay, she listened idly to a murmured conversation taking place around the corner of the old brick farmhouse, one of many, no doubt, as couples and groups decided on their bidding strategy.

"Look, I'll bid on it," a man said, "you just stay in the back and make sure no one *else* bids."

"How am I going to do that?" a second voice asked.

"I don't know! Be creative."

"But where *exactly* is the button?" The second voice was a mere whisper, too soft to tell if it was a man or woman, but the tone was urgent.

"Never you mind," the first speaker said. "Do you think I'm gonna tell you?" There was a moment of hesitation, then, "Look, if I knew, I'd already freaking have it. It's in there somewhere; we'll figure that out once we get out of here. Just do as I say."

The second person said something, but too quietly to catch.

"Yeah, well, too bad if you don't trust me, you're just gonna have to. We're in this together, I told you, just you and me. Don't attract attention. I don't wanna tip anyone off that we know where the button is." The voices faded.

Jaymie shook herself and focused. The little snippet of conversation, weird and out of place—the voices were silent now, so the speakers must have moved off toward the auction stage—brought her back to the reason she was there, the auction. She had driven her van over for Becca, who was acquiring stock for the business, but also to look around for herself and her own collection, vintage cookware and old cookbooks. She was bidding on a couple of lots of both, so she had better get going.

And yet . . . she stood, looking over the lawn from her sheltered, quiet spot on the long wood veranda on the back of the big house, shaded by vigorous trumpet vines that coiled up the supports and along the railing, overhanging the roof. The auctioneer was taking the podium, delivering his rules on decorum at the auction. Lesley Mackenzie of Mackenzie Auctions, a gentleman in his seventies, was recognizable as a "character," and he prided himself on it. He wore a pinstripe suit with a string tie, a black bowler hat and handmade spats. When he walked, he did so with a cane, but it was pure affectation, for he was as vigorous as a thirty-year-old.

Was bidding on the box of vintage Pyrex cookware and the collection of old cookbooks worth facing Joel and Heidi? Joel, who had hurt her by leaving so suddenly? Heidi, who as a svelte twenty-seven-year-old was a few years younger and quite a few pounds lighter than Jaymie?

What hurt so much about their pairing, Jaymie supposed, was not knowing. Had she done something to make Joel fall out of love with her? Why hadn't he talked to her before leaving? Still . . . it had been six months since Joel moved out of her home and directly into the arms and house of his new girlfriend, Heidi. It was past time that Jaymie moved on, too. She tilted her chin up and decided; Joel Anderson was *not* going to chase her away from this auction.

She walked along the porch to the steps, descended and strolled across the soft, thick grass in step with a tall, ele-

gantly dressed woman who appeared out of her element at
a farmhouse estate auction. But maybe the woman was after
the same Royal Crown Derby china as Becca; Jaymie hoped
not. Her sneakers soaked from the dew that was already
beginning to dampen the grass, Jaymie squeaked on and
joined the crowd in front of the auctioneer's stage. Lesley
finished his speech with a flourish of his cane, saying no
one would be allowed to dally or delay, rudeness or bullying
would not be tolerated, and his decision would be the final
and binding one in any dispute. He played fair, and expected
them to do so, too. It was a sizable crowd, some seated on
chairs near the stage but most milling about behind and
around the chairs.

As the sun descended behind the pines that lined the farm
laneway, a fresh breeze rustled through the green spring
leaves and blush-pink blossoms of the stately plum just
behind the auctioneer's trailer stage. The enormous tree was
long past the age of bearing good fruit but still bloomed and
grew vigorously, shedding a last shower of pastel petals as
a vigorous breeze swayed the branches.

Lesley, as stalwart as the noble plum tree, began the bidding, using the assorted box lots to get the crowd focused
and going. This was the time to get some stuff cheap, and
Jaymie pushed through toward the front, picking a spot
among those standing to the left of the stage. She glanced
around and instantly caught sight of Joel, his arm around
Heidi, standing on the other side of the seating area, but
Jaymie took a deep breath and ignored him.

She was going to bid on a box of assorted cookbooks,
and another box lot of vintage cookware that had some nice-
condition Pyrex glass refrigerator dishes, melamine dishes
and a few random cooking tools, as well as some odds and
ends. She and Becca, by previous arrangement, ignored each
other. It was too easy to get distracted by chatting while the
auction was going on, so they stood several yards apart,

Becca waiting patiently for the lots she was interested in, referring to her notes and the photos on her digital camera.

Lesley had his youngest grandson, a boy of about eleven, hoist the box of cookbooks up. "Lookee here, now," Lesley said. "A whole carton of cookbooks! Food's the same no matter the century, so snap 'em up and get into the kitchen. And I'm not just talking to you ladies," he finished, with a saucy wink.

He started the bidding at an optimistic ten dollars, but Jaymie held back, waiting and watching. No one bid.

"C'mon folks! Whatta we got here . . . let's see." He reached in and flipped through some of the cookbooks, rattling off titles, but the crowd was getting restless, so he restarted the bidding at a buck. Jaymie stuck up her hand. Someone else halfheartedly bid two, but when Jaymie went to three dollars the other person dropped out. She wrote her purchase down in her notebook, lot number and final bid.

Lesley, a longtime friend of one of Jaymie's favorite neighbors, septuagenarian Trip Findley, winked at her. "Now there's a catch, lads!" He pointed his auction gavel at her. "The girl's pretty as a picture—blue eyes, brown hair up in a sweet ponytail, rounded in all the right places—and she can cook, too!" he crowed, as laughter rippled through the crowd.

Jaymie wanted to sink into the ground at Lesley's ill-timed witticism, and even more so when she saw Joel smile and bend over to listen to Heidi, as she cupped her hand around her mouth and whispered something in his ear. Jaymie took a deep breath and once more turned away, ignoring them.

Several more lots of household items went for bargains, and finally the box of Pyrex dishes and cooking utensils came up. Jaymie crossed her fingers as the bidding started at five dollars. Soon, it was just her and another bidder still in it. She scanned the crowd as she bid, and when she saw

her competitor was DeeDee Stubbs, another friend and
neighbor from Queensville, she called out, "What d'you
want in the box, Dee?" There must be one specific thing she
was after, because DeeDee was no Pyrex collector.

The plump woman, the same age as Rebecca, peered
through the crowd, shading her eyes from the slanting sunlight. "Jaymie! It's you I'm bidding against? I only want the
Partridge Family lunchbox!"

"Let me have the lot and I'll gladly *give* you the
lunchbox."

"Done!" DeeDee called out, "I'm out of it, Les. Jaymie
can have it."

The old man had a look of mock severity on his face as
he glared at Jaymie. "You're cutting into profits, young lady!
Not the done thing, and you know it." Another ripple of
laughter flowed through the crowd at his chiding.

Jaymie shrugged. "Sorry, Les! But nobody *else* wants it;
I'm just speeding up your auction." Another wave of laughter followed as she got the box for twenty dollars, and the
auction moved on, fast-forwarding through several more
lots.

The jewelry, art, antique furniture and anything more
valuable from the estate dissolution was going to a big auction house in Detroit, but somehow the entire collection of
Royal Crown Derby had been spared, and Becca successfully bid on it, spending a rather large sum to get it. Jaymie
knew that her older sister would triple or quadruple her
money on the Crown Derby set by breaking it up. It seemed
to Jaymie that the family china of two generations ago
should stay together, but Rebecca pointed out that nobody
wanted it that way. Her buyers were replacing individual
pieces that had been broken over the years, or were acquiring place settings or missing serving pieces to add to their
own sets. It didn't do to get sentimental about business.

The crystal lot came up, and then some silver plate, so
Jaymie tuned out, melting back among some taller folks and

watching. It was an oddly assorted crowd. She recognized some people: the local farmers there to bid on the farm equipment and antique tools; DeeDee, who attended to beef up her inventory of fifties, sixties and seventies kitsch and TV tie-in merchandise for her online selling; and a few more. Joel and Heidi bid on a vintage fur jacket and a steamer trunk, then drifted away.

But the strangers were fascinating, as always. There were young couples buying up the necessities of life: pots and pans, small appliances, and lots of cheap dishes. And there were those who were clearly there for just one item; the non-functioning grandfather clock, old paintings—smoke-stained and grimy, but potentially worth money if you had a good eye and a willingness to gamble—a set of six farm chairs. If she'd had room, Jaymie would have bought the sturdy farm chairs herself, but their Queensville house was fully furnished—overstuffed, actually. Despite Becca's admonition, though, she *was* going to buy that gorgeous old Hoosier kitchen cabinet, so she'd stick around until its lot number came up.

But who, Jaymie idly wondered, were the two people talking about the mysterious and valuable button? She scanned the crowd. Was it someone she knew? Hard to tell just from a whisper. There were lots of folks she recognized; with DeeDee was her son, Arnie, and her brother Lyle's latest girlfriend, Edith. Jewel Dandridge, owner of Jewel's Junk, a funky little shop in Queensville, was scouting the auction, too. She had just bid on a lot of five boxes kindly described by Lesley as "unique, undervalued treasures"; in other words, broken junk. In her hands they would become weird and wonderful works of art. Bill Waterman, a local handyman, had bid and won a lot of obscure tools, to add to the collection he kept in his barn, on display. He was in the process, he'd told her the summer before, of writing a history of the handyman, and the vintage tools were to be photographed to illustrate his book. As a collector herself,

Jaymie knew most of the other people in the village who were fellow collectors.

But there were many more at the auction she didn't recognize. One fellow was notable because he did nothing but wander aimlessly through the crowd. The second time he squeezed past the same people a couple of them gave him that irritated look one does when impatient with someone, but not ready to confront them. He, however, appeared oblivious and kept wandering.

A middle-aged couple, wealthy-looking and faintly bored, stood watching the action. Jaymie had spotted them outside the Queensville Inn just that morning while she was shopping across the road at the Queensville Emporium in advance of Becca's arrival. The dark-haired woman, elegantly dressed in a black suit with a black-and-white silk flower pin on the lapel and diamond earrings, was the one Jaymie had walked beside back toward the auction site when she'd left the porch. The couple whispered to each other but didn't engage with anyone else in the crowd, keeping themselves separate in some miracle of aloofness. There was an actual personless circle around them, as if they had a commoner-shunning force field. The husband, a distinguished-looking silver-haired gentleman, bought a small painting, but if they bid on anything else, she didn't catch it.

There was another fellow in the crowd she recognized by sight; he was staying next door to her, at Anna and Clive Jones's bed-and-breakfast. He was handsome in an overly clean-cut way, perfectly groomed, almost beautiful, with dark collar-length hair and a chiseled jaw. He turned as she eyed him, caught her look and smiled. Jaymie, mortified that he had caught her staring, turned her gaze to the front, feeling the blush rise in her cheeks.

"Lot number one-sixty-eight," Lesley intoned, looking down at his pad as his grandson held up the cardboard box, "is a mixed batch of sewing paraphernalia: rickrack, needles, bobbins, thread, a large jar of buttons, assorted other sewing oddments. Who numbered this junk lot to come up so late?" He gave his grandson a mock-severe look, then turned his gaze back to the crowd. "Who'll give me five dollars?"

Buttons! Jaymie slewed her glance around. No one looked interested, but that didn't indicate anything at an auction, where a poker face was an asset. "One," she said, shooting her hand up, wondering if this was the lot that held the potentially valuable button. Someone else in the crowd bid two, she bid three, then several others joined the bidding. She tried to see her competition, but she was placed badly and could only see hands. She was curious enough, though, that she went to fifteen dollars, at which point she won the box and glanced around for disappointed faces. Nobody appeared disappointed or upset; most looked bored. If it was what Lesley said it was, she had overpaid. She added it to her notebook.

The sun was sinking, the shadows lengthening, and it was getting colder. A stiff, earth-scented breeze swept across the newly sown fields and tossed the stately pines that lined the long driveway. As the bidding continued, Jaymie rubbed her bare arms, glad that the crowd kept the breeze from making her even colder than she was. Becca bought a box of antique linens, and another of inexpensive china teacups and mismatched saucers, useful for the 'Tea with the Queen' fundraiser they would be helping with Sunday and Monday, an annual feature of Queensville's Victoria Day weekend celebrations.

It was a long-standing tradition in Queensville. After church on Sunday, old Mrs. Bellwood, gowned in a black bombazine dress and jet jewelry, her gray hair done up in a bun and adorned with a lace-edged mantilla and a jeweled coronet, would majestically rustle over to Stowe House to preside over the birthday tea as Queen Victoria. She would repeat her performance on the Canadian holiday Monday, for the benefit of their visitors from Ontario, who would come across on the ferry or by water taxi for the day. If the weather was nasty, she would ride in a carriage provided by Mackenzie Auctions, and the tea would be held in the parlor of Stowe House, the oldest house in town, now owned by wealthy micro-systems inventor Daniel Collins. If the weather held, though, tea would be served on the lawn. Becca was in Queensville for that very reason: she supplied all the china.

Jaymie's wandering attention was reclaimed by the auction as the Hoosier finally came up, carried to a spot on the grass below the stage by two burly fellows.

Rebecca approached Jaymie. "C'mon, sis, I'm bushed. Let's cash out now before the crowd so we can get home," she said, pulling her checkbook out of her bag.

Jaymie didn't answer, listening intently as Lesley Mackenzie described the Hoosier as a "housewife's dream," the most modern convenience of the housewife's world in 1920.

"The woman who first bought this—probably a Bourne wife—likely paid for it on the installment plan, a dollar a month. Its arrival from the *original* Hoosier Manufacturing Company in Indiana would have been a major event in this young married woman's life and would have made her the queen of the county, with the very latest in kitchen conveniences at her fingertips. Her friends would have gathered 'round it *ooh*ing and *ahh*ing!" He looked around at the crowd, squinted, and said, "This item has some damage, but many original parts, so I'll start at a hundred."

No one bid.

"Jaymie, come on," Becca said, checkbook and pen in hand.

Jaymie ignored her, waiting, gritting her teeth as Becca started to tap her pen on the checkbook.

"All righty, then, fifty," Lesley said, "but not a penny less! Suitable as a desk, or for its original use; just needs a little TLC, folks." He glanced around, and said, "I've got fifty, do I see sixty?"

Jaymie shot up her hand.

"I've got sixty," Lesley said, then, sensing the warming crowd interest, went into his auctioneer's singsong spiel.

"Jaymie, you are *not* bidding!" Rebecca hissed, glancing around. "Are you nuts? Let it go. We don't have room."

"Maybe '*we*' don't, but I do," Jaymie growled, throwing up her hand to indicate ninety, as someone else in the crowd shouted something. "You go on and cash out. I want that Hoosier."

Becca shook her head and shrugged. "Okay, but I guarantee you won't find any room for it in the kitchen! You'll see what I mean, and then you'll have to get rid of it for a quarter of what you paid. Waste of money."

"I'll *make* room," Jaymie softly said, as her sister threaded back through the crowd and DeeDee approached. Jaymie put her hand up for $120.

"You go, girl," DeeDee said, looking over her shoulder at Jaymie's older sister's retreat. "Rebecca always was too bossy for her own good, even when we were kids together. It's about time you stood up for yourself. You live in Queensville and look after that house, not her."

Jaymie appreciated the support, but didn't answer. Someone else in the crowd—or some*two* else in the crowd—was/ were bidding, but she couldn't see who it was. The cost climbed until she was up to $250, and she was thinking she was going to have to bow out. She mentally tallied her savings and what she had already spent, plus the buyer's premium; she could go higher, she decided. DeeDee, at her elbow, was cheering her on.

Lesley kept on, and Jaymie heard a commotion in the back of the standing crowd as the bidding reached $270, and Jaymie bid $280. Someone screamed, and most of the crowd turned toward the source of the trouble, surging back to see what was going on. Lesley kept right on, though, as if he hadn't heard, and no one else upped the bidding as a noisy fracas broke out.

Winding up, Lesley, with a big wink at her and pointing his gavel, launched into his final patter; "Going . . . going! Fair warning, folks . . . and *sold*! To the little lady in front, Miss Jaymie Leighton!" He brought the gavel down on his podium for her price. DeeDee grabbed her and they both jumped for joy as the yelling in the crowd reached a height.

A screech of fury erupted, then a muffled voice rang out from the crowd: "Hey, I was going to three hundred!"

Jaymie held her breath as she and DeeDee clung to each other, watching Lesley.

"Too late, fella," Lesley said, squinting into the growing gloom.

"I'll go three twenty," another voice chimed in.

"You old fart, open up again," the first muffled voice shouted. "I go three forty!"

Someone in the middle of the crowd hollered, "Don't you talk that way to Les, you jerk."

"That's Joel!" Jaymie said, recognizing her ex-boy-friend's voice as Lesley's defender.

"I'll say whatever I wanta say, asshole!"

A scuffle broke out, just a little pushing and shoving from what Jaymie could tell, as the crowd egged the combatants on, but there was a shriek and it swiftly ended. Jaymie's cheeks burned a little; she was proud of Joel for standing up to the rude guy. He always did have a quixotic streak in him.

"Done deal!" Lesley crowed. "Your bid, Jaymie," he said, again pointing his gavel at her. "Go and claim your prize." He surveyed the crowd, arcing his gavel over them in a semicircle. "Any more outbursts like that and I will finish this auction here and now. We'll now move on to the farm equipment!"

Jaymie felt a spurt of elation. Now to claim her prize and pay. "I wonder who that was who put up a fuss?"

"I don't know," DeeDee said. "That tall couple was in the way, and I couldn't see. That's Lynn and Nathan Foster," she said, pointing at them. "They're staying at Lyle's inn," she said, naming her brother-in-law, who owned the Queensville Inn.

Dee, as always, was ready with gossip, even stuff that wasn't particularly interesting. "I'd better go cash out and face the wrath of Rebecca. Come with me," Jaymie said, putting her bare arm through the crook in DeeDee's sweater-clad elbow, "and get your *Partridge Family* lunchbox."

"You mean defend you against your big sister," DeeDee said, with a warm chuckle.

"That, too," Jaymie said, smiling. Old friends were the best kind, it's been said; they know all the old jokes and where the bodies are buried.

❋ Two ❋

TWO STURDY FELLOWS who worked for Lesley Mackenzie loaded the Hoosier into the back of Jaymie's beat-up white-and-rust Chevy van as darkness set in, while another wheeled the boxes of goods she and Becca had both bought on a hand dolly. Fortunately, the top hutch section of the Hoosier unscrewed from a bracket and came away from the wider bottom cabinet.

Jaymie watched the guys move the Hoosier easily. "I just hope we can get it out of the van once we get home. Do you guys come with the package?" she joked.

The brawniest smiled and winked at her, flexing his biceps, and Jaymie's face heated as DeeDee nudged her. He thought she was flirting with him! She *never* flirted; she just wasn't good at it.

"Nope, you'll have to handle that on your own," he said, pushing the heaviest lower section a little farther into the van.

The feet screeched across the metal floor and Becca grimaced as she gingerly lifted the box of newsprint-wrapped teacups and saucers and set it in the van.

"Lesley Mackenzie is my granddad. We're only here because there's been some trouble this week," the muscular guy said. "Some lowlife broke into Bourne House, probably hoping to steal some of the more valuable goods once the auction was announced. Gramps was worried. We're security, making sure a thief doesn't take off with the coins or silver plate while no one's looking." He rolled his impressive shoulders.

Becca fussed over the placement of the boxes of china, insisting that the "eyesore," as she called the Hoosier, was going to crush the boxes of fragile goods. She dithered as a young fellow, yet another grandson of Lesley Mackenzie, loaded the other boxes into the back.

"Oh, for heaven's sake, Becca, just put the best stuff at your feet! Look," Jaymie said, leaning into the back of the van, "if we wedge this stuff in with blankets, nothing's going to move." She tucked in the blankets she kept in the back around the boxes of teacups, crystal and silver, and had the box of Crown Derby, the most valuable lot, moved by the cute bicep guy to the passenger's side of the van so it would ride at Becca's feet.

Jaymie thanked the auction helpers and climbed up into the driver's seat, but just as she slammed her door shut with a resounding creak of rusty hinges, she saw Joel and Heidi stroll past, arm in arm, toward the parking area, a fallow field just beyond the line of pine trees. Impulsively, she leaned out of the van window saying, "Way to go, Joel! I heard you shut that guy up, the one who was harassing Les Mackenzie."

Joel tugged Heidi along across the gravel drive and they approached the van. He looked up at Jaymie, a smile crinkling the corners of his blue eyes. Those eyes, and the way they crinkled, were his most attractive feature, but the whole package wasn't bad either. "He was outta line. He and another guy were arguing, and he lost track of the bidding on that Hoosier, so he lost out! It happens . . . no need to be a jerk about it." He tossed his lank blond hair out of his eyes.

"That's a nice piece you bought, Jaymie, that big Hoosier," Heidi said, softly, from the shelter of Joel's crooked arm.

"It needs some work," Jaymie said, glancing over her shoulder at Becca, who sat stiffly in the passenger seat, not acknowledging Joel or Heidi. Sometimes Jaymie thought her sister took Joel's defection harder than she did, but that was because she was a protective big sister, even though Jaymie was in her thirties and didn't need to be looked after anymore.

"But it's got some original pieces," she said. "I looked it over earlier. My grandma has one, and some guy offered her two thousand dollars for it."

"Really? Two thousand dollars!" Jaymie gazed at Heidi, a sweet-faced blonde dressed in designer jeans and a blue cashmere sweater. Her curling hair reached down below her shoulders and silver chandelier earrings dangled from her petite ears. She seemed genuine, her blue eyes innocent of any hidden meaning in her steady gaze.

In the six months since Joel left her for Heidi, Jaymie had pictured the woman, a migrant from New York, as a stuck-up Paris Hilton wannabe because she wore designer jeans and carried a Louis Vuitton bag. That wasn't exactly a fair assessment, since Jaymie didn't know Heidi except to see her. She was going to try to be nice, she decided. "I don't expect the Hoosier to be worth anything—it's got some damage—but it'll give me something to work on this summer, fixing it up. I just kinda fell in love with it."

"Jaymie's crazy about anything old; that's why she went out with me," Joel joked, then his expression fell. "I didn't mean *now*, that she still is . . . I meant . . ." He trailed off and shook his head.

"Joel, you're an idiot," Rebecca said, leaning around Jaymie to stare out the van window at him.

"Becca!" Jaymie said, with a look of warning to her older sister.

Heidi squeezed Joel's arm and rolled her eyes. "Was he *always* this quick-witted?" she said, her pale brows arched.

Jaymie laughed and found herself warming to the younger woman, whose remark had gracefully deflated the bubble of tension that was building. "We have to get going. I just wanted to say, way to go, Joel, for telling that creep off."

"And for jabbing him in the nose when the jerk shoved me!" Heidi said.

Jaymie felt a pang of sadness; well, then . . . that explained Joel's chivalrous response more completely. Beyond what the creep was saying to Les, he had insulted and threatened little Heidi. She was the kind of woman men instantly wanted to protect. Jaymie sighed. Joel had always said that Jaymie was too self-reliant, that she never asked for help or appeared to want it. It looked like he'd found the kind of woman he was looking for all along so he could be the knight in shining armor. "We have to get back to Queensville," she said, pushing down the clutch pedal and putting the stick into neutral.

"See you around?" Heidi said, staring up at Jaymie, punctuating her remark with a question mark.

"Yeah, of course. Are you coming to the Queen's Tea on Sunday or Monday?"

"Both days; I've got a part!" Heidi gave a little hop of excitement. "I ordered a dress from a costumer in Stratford." Stratford, Ontario, across the border and several miles north, was a world-renowned center of Shakespearian theatre, and so had a specialist or two in historical costuming willing to make a buck by sewing costumes for the public. "I'll be there dressed as Queen Victoria's daughter, Princess Beatrice."

"Of *course* you'll be dressed as a princess," Becca, beside Jaymie, murmured.

Jaymie threw her sister a warning glance. She had to live in Queensville; Becca didn't. She forced a smile. Why hadn't anyone told her this interesting piece of news, given that she would be working the tea all afternoon both days as a server, *and* everyone knew Heidi was the girl who'd stolen Jaymie's boyfriend away? She swallowed hard. "We'll see you there, then!" she said, waving as she shifted and reversed, backing down the farmhouse lane.

She needed all of her concentration to drive the gravel lane toward the county road that would lead to the highway that ran between Queensville and Wolverhampton, the nearest larger center, and Becca, fussing about the box of Royal Crown Derby Old Imari at her feet as they traversed the rugged country road, was silent.

Once they were on the smoother county road, paved but still narrow, Jaymie said, "Why didn't anyone tell me about that? I don't understand. I'm on the planning committee, and no one thought to say that Joel's girlfriend is playing one of Queen Victoria's daughters?"

When Becca didn't answer, Jaymie slewed a glance sideways at her sister's profile in the dimness of the van, then returned her attention to the road. "Don't tell me you *knew*?"

"Of *course* not! I'm out of the loop, living across the border in Ontario. I'm not even on the committee anymore. You *know* I'd have told you." She paused and glanced over at her younger sister's face. "But I do understand why the others didn't."

"Why?"

Becca was silent for a moment, clearly choosing her words carefully, and Jaymie wondered if she was so fragile, or appeared to be so fragile, that folks couldn't be honest.

"Well, you were so hurt when Joel left you—"

"Do you blame me? He didn't say a word, he just walked out of my house two weeks before Christmas and right into another woman's arms!" She grimaced and shook her head. That sounded *so* melodramatic. She read lots of romance novels, and no good writer would ever have that phrase coming out of a heroine's mouth. But she clearly wasn't the heroine of this story; she was the scorned ex-girlfriend.

"It's not about blame, sweetie, but everyone in Queensville loves you—you're one of them—and no one wants to hurt your feelings. So they just avoid the topic of Heidi and Joel with you."

Jaymie was silent, making the turn onto the highway, squinting into the rearview mirror at headlights that followed them in their turn. "I didn't realize everyone was tiptoeing around me," she mused.

"That's natural the first few months after a breakup," Becca said. "Trust me, with two marriages on the rocks, I'm familiar with it. Usually that fades and, six months in or so, after the bust-up, people get back to normal. But you do wear your heart on your sleeve, little sister," Becca said, reaching over and rubbing Jaymie's shoulder. "They all know how hurt you were by what Joel did."

Jaymie sighed and checked the rearview mirror. The vehicle was a little close for comfort in the dark like this, but not unusually so. If she hadn't been driving a van full of fragile cargo, she wouldn't have been unnerved, but if she had to brake suddenly, that car would not have time to stop and would crash into the back. China and crystal everywhere, not to mention how the unsecured Hoosier would fare!

"I'm pulling over to let this guy pass," she said, slowing and pulling to the shoulder. "He's a bumper-hugger, and if he's so in a hurry, I want him to go." The car shot past them, and Jaymie pulled back onto the highway.

She and Rebecca discussed the weekend. Daniel Collins, the multimillionaire who owned Stowe House—the location of the Tea with the Queen fundraiser—would have already arrived or would be arriving early the next morning. Committee members, including Jaymie, would oversee the placement of the tables on his lawn Sunday, while Rebecca was responsible for laying the tables with linens and cups and saucers. The committee had been busy baking scones and tea cakes, and would brew the tea on-site.

Mrs. Bellwood, the Queen Victoria impersonator, would be escorted by Trip Findley, who would play her consort, a rather elderly Prince Albert. He was seventy-four and had been playing Prince Albert for thirty-five years. Even though Prince Albert had died at forty-two, no one on the committee had enough cruelty in their bones to tell Trip he couldn't play the part anymore.

But who really cared? It wasn't as if they were truly going for historical accuracy. The servers and historical reenactors would be garbed in Victorian clothes, but the paying customers would be dressed in everything ranging from skirts and blouses for the ladies and sport coats for men, to tank tops and cutoffs for the most casual tourists.

They sped past the Motel 6 on the highway—travelers who weren't able to find a room in one of Queensville's five bed-and-breakfast establishments and two inns would soon fill the motel—and approached the turnoff for the village. Jaymie slowed gently, not willing to take the corner too fast with the weighty piece of furniture in the back, and another car zoomed up behind them, almost running into the back of the van.

"Jerk," she muttered, as the car careened past. "What is up with drivers tonight?"

The road into the village was better lit than the highway, and Jaymie sighed with relief, easily navigating the corners and heading toward the lane that ran behind her house and the other homes on Maple Street. It was an old-fashioned village, with lanes running *behind* the houses instead of laneways *beside* each house. In years gone by the carriage and horses needed stabling, so each home had a shed or barn on the lane, except for some who had torn down a barn in favor of more lawn space.

Somebody with their headlights on high blinded her for a second, the reflection beaming into her eyes from the side mirror, but she turned without incident and cruised down the back alley, shutting off her lights and backing into the spot behind her and Rebecca's house. Becca's Lexus had the place of honor in the drive shed, which shared a structure with the gardening shed.

"What is it with drivers tonight?" Becca said, echoing Jaymie's previous comment. "High beams in a village? Some people have no common sense."

"Maybe it's a late arrival to Anna's B&B," Jaymie said of their next-door neighbor, as she unbuckled her seat belt. "She's got a full house for the weekend. I saw one of her patrons at the auction."

"Can you get the back door, Jaymie?" Becca muttered, hefting the box at her feet. "I want to get this Crown Derby up to my room right away. I didn't say anything before— didn't want to advertise the fact—but there could be eight thousand dollars' worth of china here, if I'm smart. Maybe even more."

"Wow." Jaymie shuddered. "I'm glad you didn't tell me that while I was being tailed by that creep on the highway!"

"Exactly! Why do you think I didn't say anything until now? I have a half dozen customers panting after good condition Old Imari. Now, go ahead of me and open the back door and do *not* let Hopalong trip me!"

Jaymie did as she was told, and both of them heaved a huge sigh of relief once the weighty box of china was safely stowed in Rebecca's room. They made two more trips up the stairs to Becca's room with the boxes of fragile but nicely packed French crystal and Spode china. When they returned to the van to figure out how to move the Hoosier, Hopalong, Jaymie's three-legged Yorkie-Poo, pranced along with them while Denver, her sleek, green-eyed tabby, slunk into the holly bushes that lined the backyard, creeping along until he got to the blooming forsythia bush. He parked himself under it and glared out at the world. Denver had a perpetually gloomy worldview and seemed utterly amazed when anyone stooped to pet him.

Standing between the open back doors of the van, Rebecca crossed her arms over her bosom in her customary stance and glared at the two pieces of the Hoosier. "*Now* what?" she said.

Jaymie stared up at the cabinet. It looked bigger, hulking in the dim interior of her van, than it had on the porch of the old farmhouse. "I can handle it," she said, trying to muster up the confidence.

"You can *not*! I will not let you be crushed by that . . . that eyesore. Why don't you go ask Clive if he can help?" sensible Rebecca suggested, naming their neighbor, Clive Jones, who owned the next-door bed-and-breakfast with his wife, Anna.

"He's not arriving from Toronto until tomorrow," Jaymie said. "He has to work late, and the last ferry runs from Johnsonville at eight, so he's going to come first thing in the morning." Clive worked in Toronto during the week, then made the long trek to Queensville to help his wife on weekends, supporting her dream, the bed-and-breakfast. With that and a toddler, their time was fully taken up.

"Can I help?" came a voice out of the dark.

Both women jumped, but then a fellow emerged from the darkness.

"Pardon me," he said, "but I overheard your dilemma, and I'm here to offer my services. Brett Delgado . . . I'm staying at the Jones's bed-and-breakfast. Since Anna's husband is not available, may I help?"

"I saw you at the auction this evening," Jaymie said, looking him over. He was the fellow who'd caught her staring and had smiled at her. But he was excessively well dressed to be hauling a dusty old piece of furniture out of the van. He smelled strongly of cigarette smoke, which explained his late night stroll. Anna did not allow smoking in the B&B.

"Yes, we did exchange glances, didn't we?" he said, smiling at her, the dim lights that lined the back lane glinting in his blue eyes.

"Did you buy anything?"

He shook his head. "I didn't see anything I really wanted.

But I see that you did!" He eyed the hulking cabinet in the dark interior of the van.

"We would be delighted if you would help," Rebecca said, smiling over at him, her head cocked to one side.

Jaymie rolled her eyes at Becca's flirtatious glance; Brett caught Jaymie's expression and winked at her. She hid her grin. Her big sister did not like to be laughed at. "First we have to dispose of these boxes, then we can carry the Hoosier into the kitchen."

"What did you call that thing . . . a Hoosier? As in, Indiana basketball team, or inspiring sports movie starring Gene Hackman?"

First Jaymie removed the box of teacups and saucers and handed it off to Rebecca, who toted it through the back wrought-iron gate, along the flagstone path and up to the house, where the summer porch and kitchen lights shone a path out the back windows and door. Then she explained what a Hoosier was, and what it was used for, a modern cooking center for the early nineteen-hundreds woman. "This really is a 'Hoosier' brand cabinet, but there are other brands, like Knechtel and Sellers. Napanee. A few more."

"What's in this box?" he asked, as he pulled out one covered in a tea towel.

"Um . . . I don't know. Let me see." Jaymie looked under the tea towel. "Oh, that's the box of sewing oddments."

"What the heck did you buy that stuff for?" Rebecca asked, returning to their side and peering into the box. "We already have enough junk like that to sink the *Titanic*!"

Jaymie was about to explain the conversation she'd overheard about the valuable button, but something made her shut her mouth. She shrugged, and said, "I just felt like it. There were some interesting vintage trims."

Brett and Jaymie conferred over the Hoosier.

"Where do you plan on taking it?" he said. "I don't think I'd want to carry it up too many stairs."

"Well, no, it's going in the kitchen."

"And that is . . . where?"

"Right in the back of the house."

He hoisted himself into the back of the van and pushed the bottom portion of the Hoosier as she grabbed the end and pulled; it groaned and screeched along the metal floor the whole way, as befit anything almost a hundred years old. When it was at the edge, he hopped down and helped her lift it out, down to the ground, while Hopalong danced around, wiggling and pleading for Brett's attention.

"He's a cute little guy," Brett said, bending down and scruffing Hoppy's neck while he caught his breath. In the dim spill of light from the lane lamps, the little dog did the insane eye-rolling/butt-wiggling "I *never* get this kind of attention" thing dogs do, and flopped on the ground, rolling around like a Pentecostal adherent seized by the spirit. "Is he your only dog?"

"Yeah, he's it. Don't mind him," Jaymie said. "He's *sooo* neglected."

"I can tell," Brett said, straightening. "So, ready to go with this thing? It's heavier than it looks. You don't have an alarm system on that back door, do you?"

"Nope. No alarm, and we've already got it open, anyway."

She and Brett carried it along the path, stopping once to put it down and huff and puff a little. Something was sliding around inside one of the drawers, something heavy that made a heck of a lot of noise. They awkwardly manhandled the lower cabinet up the three steps to the summer porch, an airy room the width of the house that was used for sleeping during hot summers gone by, before air conditioning. It was lined with enormous screened windows that were still covered in storms—storm windows—this early in the spring, and the solid wood door was still in place. Taking down the storms and removing the solid door was a task Bill Waterman, their handyman, would undertake before Memorial Day. They set the Hoosier down.

"Do you really want to take it into the kitchen right now?" he asked, panting. "It's dusty. Why don't you store it out here until you get a chance to clean it up?"

Jaymie nodded. "Good idea. Let's just line it up along the wall between the door and the kitchen window so we can still get to the couch and chairs beyond."

They returned to the van and retrieved the top section, carried the much lighter part in one trip, and set it gently on its metal brackets over the porcelain work top. "I won't bother screwing it down, because I'll just need to unscrew it again when I take it apart to clean it."

"This is such a lovely house," Brett said, looking around the screened summer porch while he dusted his hands off. He swung the door back and forth on its hinges idly, and said, "Ted and I admired it when we checked in to the Shady Rest. Do you own it?"

Rebecca joined them from the kitchen, and said, "We both do. Our parents deeded it to us equally when they moved down to Florida."

"Oh, do you live here, too? Just the two of you?"

"Not exactly; Jaymie's the only one who lives here full-time. I come down some weekends from London . . . that's London, Ontario, not England."

"Becca, can you grab one of those boxes I toted into the kitchen?" Jaymie said of the boxes of cookbooks, vintage cookware and sewing oddments. "I'll get the others. I don't want to trip over them in the morning, so I think I'll leave them on the Hoosier until I get a chance to look at what I bought."

"Can you come in for a cup of coffee? Or tea? Or maybe a glass of wine?" Becca said, eyeing their new acquaintance.

"I'd better be getting back to the room. You two must be tired. Early to bed, I'll bet!"

"Not that early," Becca said, with a laugh. "We don't mind the company."

"I'd better get back," he repeated. "I didn't expect to be gone more than ten minutes."

"I'm so sorry to have kept you!" Jaymie said, at the same time as Becca said, "Oh, come on, a few more minutes and a glass of wine won't kill you."

"Becca!" Jaymie said.

"Jaymie," Becca replied, giving her a wide-eyed look that meant "Don't interfere."

Brett glanced back and forth between them, and said, "No, I really do have to go. Ted gets wound up if he starts worrying."

"Your friend will be fine for another couple minutes," Becca said.

Jaymie bit her tongue and clamped her mouth shut, as she set the box of teacups on the porcelain work top of the Hoosier, pushing it back, tempted almost beyond standing to tell Becca to leave the poor guy alone. Just because he was good-looking, nice, well dressed, well spoken . . . didn't mean he should be mooned over by every single woman he came across. Besides, she knew something Becca didn't.

When he firmly but politely said no and bowed out of the invitation, then left, Jaymie got the dog and cat inside and locked up the screen door and the inside panel door, turning the lights out on the summer porch. She looked out the window for a moment, as Brett walked down the lawn to the back gate and pulled it closed behind him, then paused and looked back. He was dimly lit by the faint alley light. She waved, and he waved, then turned away. She returned to the kitchen and put on the kettle for tea. "Becca, you didn't have to plague the poor guy to stay."

"I didn't plague him; I just repeated an invitation." She washed her hands at the old porcelain sink and dried them on the tea towel that hung beneath it.

"Three times! Couldn't you tell he was just being polite?"

"He's a really good-looking guy. And nice. And not wearing a wedding ring. No harm in trying," Rebecca said with a smile, waggling her eyebrows.

Jaymie laughed, pouring boiling water over a Tetley tea

bag in her Brown Betty teapot, then carrying it to the long
trestle-style table. "No, except you were barking up the
wrong tree. Anna told me that Brett Delgado and Ted Abernathy are up here from New York to get married. They're
going over by ferry to Johnsonville next weekend to see a
justice of the peace about the ceremony. Canada doesn't
require residency to marry there," she added, helpfully,
"even for a gay couple."

"Are you sure that he's the guy? I do not think that man
is gay."

"I know it's him. Can't you just admit for once that you
are occasionally wrong?" That was her sister's one problem:
she always thought she was right.

"I didn't get that vibe at all, and I usually pick up on it.
Not to stereotype or anything, but in my business, I meet
my share of gay men." Becca shrugged. "Oh well. I can
admit I'm wrong, despite what you think, little sister," she
said, leaning across the table and tapping Jaymie on the
shoulder.

"I didn't mean that crack to sound harsh. Sorry."

"It's okay. That's a long way, though, just to get married.
Couldn't they have married in New York, or just go to Con-
necticut? It's been legal there for a while, I think."

Jaymie shrugged. "I don't know . . . marriage and hon-
eymoon all at once? Maybe they're doing an antiques tour.
He was at the auction."

Rebecca yawned. "I am *so* tired. I was up at dawn doing
stuff, then drove here and went to the auction. I'm going to
look over my Crown Derby and go to bed."

"I'm not far behind you."

Once Becca was gone, Jaymie went back out to the summer porch and stood looking at her new acquisition. Despite
her confidence to Becca, it was going to be a tight squeeze
putting it in the kitchen. She'd manage, though. She pulled
open the drawers one by one, wondering what had made
such a racket as they moved it. Something was in the bottom

drawer, and she reached in, lifting it out. Heavy little devil, whatever it was. Aha! She knew exactly what she held the moment she looked at it, and it gave her hope that the piece would have other original pieces with it.

The complicated piece of machinery was a grinder, used to grind meat and vegetables and made with a screw clamp on the bottom. In the dim spill of light from the kitchen, she knelt by the Hoosier and affixed the grinder to the porcelain work top, screwing the clamp on at the side where there were notches in the wood slides under the work top. The grinder was made of steel and had a hopper at the top, a handle to turn to make the auger move and various round disc plates that would attach to the auger output with a wing nut; the auger chopped and pushed food through the discs, which determined the size of the chunks of meat or veggies that came out.

She sat down on the summer porch floor and sighed, gazing at the grinder attached to the Hoosier. The piece was even more perfect now; nothing could spoil this love affair with her new Hoosier.

She returned to the kitchen and closed the door to the summer porch. The house gradually fell silent as Hoppy curled up in his basket near the stove, and Denver slunk away to whatever hidey-hole he brooded in. Jaymie drank her tea, then cleaned up the table and counter from their hasty lunch/supper earlier, before the auction, washing the dishes in the long, deep porcelain sink, and putting them on the drain board to air dry. The kitchen, newly renovated in 1927, was her favorite room in the house. She sat down at the long, well-worn trestle table that centered the room and took a moment to let the busyness of the day drain away, to be replaced by the peace that the kitchen brought her.

It was the center of her home enterprise, for one thing, this kitchen. Here she tested vintage recipes, pored over old cookbooks, experimented and perfected. She was no gourmet chef, but someday, maybe, she'd have her own cookbook to add to her shelf. She gazed affectionately around at the room in the butter-yellow light from the single fixture over the sink. She loved the house so much that coming back to it after university had been an experience she had never forgotten; she felt like it had welcomed her with loving arms, folding her to its bosom and whispering that she was home again, at last. She had never left again for any length of time.

It was old, a big, two-story yellow-brick built in the 1860s to replace a log home. A long central hall was flanked first, at the front of the house, by the living room and parlor—the parlor smaller by quite a few feet because the staircase to the second floor took up some of the left side of the house— then, beyond that, by the library and a guest bedroom, and beyond that were the expansive kitchen and summer porch that were both the width of the house. The kitchen was the home's heart, and her haven, lined with that ultramodern invention—in 1927—built-in cupboards; it still had ample room for a pie safe, a big gas stove and modern side-by-side fridge/freezer, as well as a worktable and long, beat-up trestle-style table with benches along both sides and arm-chairs on both ends. The items lined up on the top of the cupboards reflected Jaymie's love of all things antique or vintage—*junk*, as her mother and Becca called it—with old biscuit, honey, cocoa and mustard tins competing for limited space.

The deep porcelain sink, a molded piece complete with porcelain backsplash, was topped by a window that opened onto the summer porch and overlooked the lawn through the big windows that lined the porch. She always left the dim light on over the sink. She finished her tea, rinsed the mug out and put it on the drain board with the other dishes, then drew the curtains, a tatty lace café-style set that was out of keeping with the vintage kitchen. She intended to replace them this summer, so maybe the vintage trims in the box of sewing oddments would come in handy after all.

Time for bed. She climbed the stairs, followed by Hoppy

and the silently reappearing Denver, and stopped at Becca's bedroom door, still the same room she had inhabited as a girl, though the décor had changed. It was now clean and simple, Becca's preference. She disliked fuss and had a modern sensibility, so the room was decorated in white and ice blue, her childhood furniture painted with a stark white melamine. It was the opposite of Jaymie's room, which was painted in warm butter-yellow and with an antique iron-frame bed covered with a quilt handmade by Mrs. Bellwood. Jaymie had won it in a church raffle and treasured it as a piece of local history.

Becca looked up from the box of Royal Crown Derby Old Imari dishes. "Aren't these gorgeous?" she crooned, her voice hushed with reverence.

Jaymie joined her, sitting cross-legged on the bare wood floor and taking a dinner plate in her hands. Old Imari is gaudy, rich reds and blues ornamented by gold trim in an elaborate formal design; surprising that Becca liked it so much. Jaymie turned it over.

"Careful, *careful!*" Becca cried. "That plate is worth a few hundred dollars."

"Wow. Not my taste, but it's nice stuff."

Becca shook her head and took the plate back. "Nice? *Nice?* I just can't understand why you get so enthused about a box of old Pyrex and melamine dishes and a cocoa tin from 1938, but aren't crazy about something as fabulous as this!"

Jaymie shrugged and struggled up off the floor. "To each his own, I guess. I love all the stuff that housewives used, and the cookbooks. It feels like real life to me. I imagine the hands of the woman who used them, how she pored over the cookbooks, carefully washed her Pyrex, handed out quick meals to her kids on melamine plates." She hesitated, but then plunged ahead, saying, "Becca, I've written a cookbook."

"You've what?"

Now she had her sister's undivided attention. Becca's eyes were round with wonder. "Grandma Leighton's old cookbooks were up in the attic, and I brought a bunch of them down last winter. I started looking through them and just loved the recipes. I asked her about them, and she said they were family recipes passed down. So . . . I started compiling them, altering them for the modern kitchen, and some worked really well. Remember her buttermilk biscuits? And her sage and sausage stuffing?"

Becca regarded her with interest, staring up at her younger sister in the dim light. "How did I not know this? Why the secrecy?"

Jaymie shook her head. How could she remind Becca of the number of times she had ridiculed "little sister's" ideas? Jaymie had learned to flesh things out and have a solid plan before telling Becca anything. In a way that had been a valuable tool, forcing her to become more critical of her own, sometimes impulsive, ideas and intentions. "Grandma Leighton and I talked about it. When I came up at Christmas and was so blue—about Joel and Heidi, and everything—she and I got to talking about the recipes. I had just found the box of cookbooks up in the attic at that point."

"I didn't even know they were there. I thought they were long gone."

"I got fired up after talking to Grandma, and in January started working on them. Some of them had no real instructions, and for some, the instructions were so outdated, I had to rewrite them for a modern kitchen. I did that all winter, along with some research, then wrote some intros to the recipes. When I was up last month, Grandma looked at my final copy and loved it. So . . ." She took a deep breath. "An editor is looking at the proposal for *Recipes from the Vintage Kitchen* right now."

Becca stared, her mouth open, and shook her head. "I had no idea!"

Warming up to her topic, letting her enthusiasm build,

as it always did, Jaymie said, "And now I'm researching other recipes from vintage cookbooks, looking for ways to update them. If it works out, I'll have enough for a second cookbook. I like using the real thing when I'm cooking, vintage Pyrex or Depression glass mixing bowls, old egg-beaters and wooden spoons. I want to use them for photographs to accompany the recipes, too."

"That's a really good idea!" Becca exclaimed. "When will you hear back from the publisher?"

Jaymie grimaced, rocking back and forth on the wood floor, listening to the hardwood creak. "I don't know. I started out so green, but since then I've done a lot of research; it's a long process. I'm just going to keep working on the new cookbook and not wait. So that's why I want to set up the Hoosier and use it as a woman in the twenties and thirties and so on would use it. I want to *experience* how the kitchen of those days worked. I think it will help me get in touch with the recipes, understand them better. I'll update them, but I still want them to have the feel of the old days and old ways."

"I get you," Becca said, nodding. "Wow, my sister, the cookbook author!"

"I hope," Jaymie said, crossing her fingers.

"I'll be visiting Grandma Leighton on Friday, probably." Their grandmother had returned to Canada, the country of her birth, after their grandfather died thirty years ago, and lived near Becca in London, in a comfortable retirement home. "Can I talk to her about the cookbook?"

"Sure. Cat's out of the bag now," Jaymie said, with a half smile. She had been so nervous about telling Becca, but this had seemed like the right time, and she was glad she'd done it.

"But I still say you won't find a spot in that overcrowded kitchen for the Hoosier."

"Just watch me," Jaymie said, as she exited and padded down the hall to her own room. "I know exactly where I'm putting it," she said aloud, as she stripped off her clothes and pulled on her night attire, a T-shirt and shorts, tossing the clothes into the hamper by her wardrobe.

Sleep came quickly. Much later she began to dream, the auction replaying in her sleep. Someone kept whispering in her ear that her button was undone. Then she drifted into a dream of her Hoosier; it kept falling over, hitting the floor with a loud bang. She awoke with a start, her heart pounding. It was the dark and silent hours of the middle of the night. The loud bang had not been a dream, she thought, but something falling over downstairs.

She heard a shout from below and, groggily, not quite sure what was going on, she yelled, "Denver, get down off of the counter!" Darn cat; he'd broken a nice teapot once, in one of his nightly rambles on the kitchen counter. She swung her feet over the edge of the bed, and put her foot down on Denver. Hoppy stood half-in and half-out of his basket, head cocked, listening to something.

So it was not the cat who was responsible for the noise, nor was it Hoppy, who took off and trotted out the door toward the staircase. Cats and dogs did not shout anyway, she realized as her mind cleared of its sleep fog.

"Jaymie, what was that?" Becca called out from her room, her voice thick with sleep.

At that same moment Jaymie heard another scream and a crash. She bolted to the head of the stairs, grabbing a potted ivy off the plant stand on the landing as she went, and was joined by Becca. Hoppy staggered down the stairs ahead of them, barking his little head off.

"What *was* that?" Becca repeated.

"If I knew, would I be standing here whispering to you, holding a potted plant as a weapon? I'm going down," she said, and began down the stairs. "I don't want Hoppy getting in trouble if it's a burglar."

"You and that damned dog!" Rebecca whispered, following.

❋ Three ❋

THE HOUSE WAS dead silent again, but there was another muted tinkle as Jaymie tiptoed through the hall, checking the den and guest bedroom as she crept toward the kitchen. Becca was behind her.

"Where's Hoppy?" Jaymie whispered. "Why did he stop barking?" Panic surged through her and she hastened her pace.

"Turn a light on!" Becca whispered.

"No way. Not 'til I know what's going on." Jaymie threaded her way through the kitchen and around the trestle table, setting the potted plant down as she passed. She heard a noise and a muffled expletive from her older sister—and a scratching noise from the other side of the kitchen.

"Dammit, I stubbed my toe," Becca muttered. "If you'd just turn a light on . . ."

Jaymie ignored her, cautiously approaching the door to the summer porch. Hoppy scratched and pawed at the door, so that answered where he was, but the door was still closed and locked. The dim light over the sink didn't reveal anyone moving. When she unlocked and opened the door to the summer porch, Hoppy darted past her and a cool night breeze wafted through the kitchen. That wasn't right. The solid back door of the summer porch had been shut and locked before she went to bed.

Pausing, she listened, grabbing Becca's arm to keep her from going farther. Absolute silence, except for a wheezing, snuffling sound. She released her sister and moved stealthily forward, grabbing a broom as she passed the corner by the kitchen cupboard.

Reaching out with her free hand as she moved to the door, she finally flicked on the overhead light. What she saw made her cry, "Becca, come here! Someone's hurt."

Hoppy was snuffling at a man who lay on the floor of the summer porch by the Hoosier cabinet. The upper and lower cabinet doors were all wide open, and Jaymie swiftly shut the bottom one so she could get at the fellow. A cardboard box rested partly on his bleeding head, broken china on and all around him. Jaymie tossed the broom away and knelt by him, pushing the cardboard box away.

"Becca, can you take Hoppy? There's broken china all over the floor," she said, pushing the little dog aside and brushing the shattered china and whole teacups and saucers from the injured man, a tinkle of china echoing in the quiet night. Was he breathing?

Rebecca cried out, picked up Hoppy, and then grabbed the cordless phone from the wall mount in the kitchen as Jaymie reached out and tried to help the man roll over. He didn't budge, despite her efforts: a dead weight.

"Hey, mister?" she said, staring at the still man; he was a well-dressed fellow, wearing khaki slacks and a polo shirt under a cable-knit cardigan. Besides the bloody gash on his head and the blood that oozed in a messy stream from it, his nose was also crusted with old blood. Jaymie, dizzy and a little nauseous, wondered what the heck he had been doing on their summer porch. She glanced up and saw that the door was wide open and hung drunkenly from its hinges, which explained the night air drifting in. In the distance, someone's dog was barking, which started a chorus of howls from the other dogs in town.

"C'mon, guy, please . . . wake up!" she said again, beginning to shake, and feeling weirdly unreal. Becca was babbling in the background, giving their address and details over the phone.

Jaymie looked up and out toward the backyard again, breathing deeply to quell a rising tide of dizziness; someone had pried the screen door off the hinges and popped the lock on the inside door to break in, and this guy was either the one who'd done it, or had tried to stop someone who did. She didn't see any tool around that could have been used to do such damage to the door frame. Jaymie settled back on her heels, wondering what to do; was this guy friend or foe? Should she even be trying to revive him? Becca had set Hoppy down, and he came back and sniffed at the man's loafer-covered feet, then nudged Jaymie's hand as Denver slunk out to the summer porch and approached them.

"Jaymie, they want to know, is he conscious?" Becca asked, the receiver to her ear.

"No," Jaymie said, her voice strange and hollow. "He's . . ." She bent over to look at the man's face. He was pale, too pale for life, and still, no movement of his chest. "I . . . I think he's dead," she said, her heart thudding and her stomach roiling.

"Jaymie, are you okay? Jaymie!" Becca cried, standing at the door with the phone to her ear. "My sister doesn't look well," she said to the 911 operator.

Jaymie felt herself sway, and sat down with a thump on the floor, staring at the still figure. "Becca, I'm okay, I just . . ." She retched and coughed.

In another moment Clive Jones, wearing just boxers,

strode up the three steps to the summer porch. "Jaymie!" he yelped. "You okay?"

Jaymie looked up, as Becca babbled in the background to the 911 operator. She gazed steadily at Clive's face, his dark eyes wide, the contrast between his white striped boxers and dark skin stark in the spill of light from the kitchen. "I think so." She took a deep breath, calmed by his presence, and said, "Yes, I'm fine. But this poor guy isn't. Clive, is he . . . is he dead? Can you tell?"

Composed as always, Clive immediately knelt down by the fellow, holding one long finger to the carotid artery and compressing lightly. He stilled for a long moment, then looked over at Jaymie. "He's dead," he said, his expression somber.

"Should we . . . should we try CPR?" Jaymie asked.

"Let's try," he said. "I don't think there's much hope, but . . ." He turned the guy over onto his back and began chest compressions, counting out loud. Then he bent over and tried to breathe into the guy's lungs. When he looked up again, his cheek smeared in blood, he asked, "What happened here? Was this a break-in?"

"I wish I knew," Jaymie said. She dashed back into the kitchen and got a tea towel, saying, "He was like this when we found him." Apply pressure to the wound, first aid advertisements always said. She knelt at his side and put her tea towel to his head wound, looking away, trying not to notice the red sopping into the towel.

It seemed obvious. The busted door, the box of broken and spilled teacups and saucers that used to be atop the Hoosier: this guy, or someone else, had broken in to rob them, and the falling box had killed him. Or . . . she sharpened her gaze and stared at the dead man. He had been facedown with his head turned to one side. Shattered china was everywhere, but the blood dripping from his head wound indicated that something much heavier than a box full of teacups had hit him. It couldn't have been that! But what?

Clive kept working, and put his finger to the man's throat. He shook his head and stood. "He's long gone, Jaymie. There's no bringing him back," he said, stepping in to the kitchen to the sink and washing his hands of the blood that had stained them from his efforts at lifesaving.

Sirens wailed in the distance. Jaymie stared and stared, unable to form complete thoughts. The guy was dead, but how? There was nothing but shattered teacups scattered around. Death by Doulton? Murder by Minton?

The police and paramedics arrived at about the same time, sirens and lights creating a chaotic barrage of sight and sound in the narrow back alley. Two uniformed cops, a man and a woman, were first on the scene, then the paramedics. Paramedics went to work on the fellow, nodding as Clive told them what he had done to try to revive the man. More cops arrived, and Jaymie heard a female voice give orders for them to fan out in the neighborhood looking for an assailant and the weapon. So Becca must have gotten the full message through to the 911 operator. It was as obvious, then, to the police as it was to Jaymie, that the dead man had been hit by something heavier than a box of teacups.

When it became obvious to the paramedics that there was no helping the fellow, the police took over, sending Jaymie into the kitchen to stand with Rebecca and Clive. The three stood for a while in a huddle, silent at first, and Jaymie held Hoppy in her arms to keep him out of trouble. He was quivering with excitement. Denver had disappeared back into the house, unnerved by the commotion.

"Who do you think he is?" Rebecca asked. "Have you ever seen him before, Jaymie?"

She shook her head and shuddered. "He's so pale, and the blood . . ." She could smell it, the metallic tang, the organic scent of death, filling her nostrils.

"Why would someone break into your place?" Clive

asked, his arms over his bare chest. He lifted one bare foot and pulled a sliver of china out of it. Frowning at it, he set it on the kitchen counter. "And what is that all over the floor of the summer porch?"

"That is the remains of a box of teacups Rebecca bought yesterday," Jaymie said quietly, flicking a glance at the clock. It was almost four in the morning. "They were supposed to be for the Tea with the Queen fundraiser tomorrow afternoon. She brought enough, but when she saw the box at the Bourne auction it seemed like a good idea."

"If not for this year, for next year. I can always use more teacups and saucers," Becca said.

"This is your first year in Queensville for the Tea with the Queen," Jaymie said to Clive. He and Anna had just bought the bed-and-breakfast next door, the Shady Rest, in January, to run as a family business. "Customers can actually buy the teacup and saucer set that they use, if they like. We get a few every year who do, as a souvenir."

"Are they valuable?"

Becca snorted. "No, they're mostly Royal Albert or Royal Vale . . . junk, in the china world."

"But pretty," Jaymie said, defending the shattered pottery. She thought for a moment and glanced toward the door where officers examined the summer porch and the backyard beyond, the wide arc of flashlights cutting through the night blackness. She could hear an officer upstairs searching; she and Becca had, of course, given the police permission to investigate the entire house, though it seemed obvious to her that the burglar had not made it past the kitchen door, which had still been locked when she'd come down. With the banality of their conversation, her mind was beginning to work again.

Something wasn't right about the scene, other than the obvious: a dead guy and smashed teacups. The other boxes she had purchased were off the Hoosier as well, the cookbooks scattered across the floor and the box of sewing oddments on the top step. Why? Who had moved the boxes from the Hoosier, and for what purpose? And why were the Hoosier's cupboard doors open?

"Sir, look here!" a female officer shouted. She played her flashlight around the shadowy corners of the summer porch. "Could be the murder weapon!"

Jaymie bolted forward with another uniformed officer and followed the beam of light. On the board floor of the porch, in the shadows between windows, lay the heavy steel meat grinder she had loosely attached to the Hoosier work top. As the beam of light settled on it, Jaymie could see that it was smeared with dark fluid . . . the victim's blood.

"No!" she whispered, and turned away.

"Jaymie come back," Becca said, grabbing her T-shirt sleeve and pulling her away as the police crowded around.

Her sister made her sit down in one of the kitchen chairs, an old wood farm chair that had one wobbly leg. That is where a police officer found them. He was a tall fellow with a grave expression on his clean-shaven face. "Sergeant Mac-Adams," he said. "May I ask you folks a few questions? Who lives here?"

Jaymie and Rebecca both put up their hands. The officer established their co-ownership, then asked to speak with them all separately, Rebecca first; he led her to the library and, after ten minutes or so, he came back to get Jaymie. She followed him through the kitchen door to the hall and into the library, still furnished for its original purpose, with tall built-in bookcases lining the walls and a cushioned seat set into the window. She put Hoppy down and wearily sank into a chair by the fireplace. Hoppy demanded to come up on her lap, so she cradled him again as he curled up in her arms, trembling.

"Do you know the deceased?"

"No. Who is he?" Jaymie asked, sitting back in the chair and petting the Yorkie-Poo's head.

"Could you just take me through what happened?"

Jaymie thought a moment. "Well, Becca and I went to bed about eleven or eleven-thirty, I guess."

He jotted down notes in a coil-bound notebook. "That's your sister?"

"Yes. We had come back from the Bourne estate auction near Wolverhampton, and we were both tired. I woke up to Hoppy barking and a shout and a crash—"

"Hoppy is your dog?"

She nodded.

"In what order?"

"Huh?"

"Was it in that order, the dog barking, then a shout, then a crash?"

Jaymie stopped and stared into the fireplace, the original coal fire grate from when the house was built. "No, that's not quite how it happened." She was silent for a moment, organizing her thoughts. "I was sound asleep but heard *something* that woke me up. A shout, maybe?" She mused. "Or maybe the sound of the back door being pried off its hinges? I don't know. I think it was something banging, like falling down. Anyway, I thought the noise was Hoppy at first, but Hoppy and Denver—Denver's my cat—were both in my room. Then I heard a shout, and *then* the crash."

"And then?"

"We met in the upstairs hall, Becca and I. She asked me what the noise was, and I said I didn't know. I grabbed a potted plant as we came down the stairs. Hoppy had bolted ahead of us and started barking. We followed Hoppy's noise into the kitchen. I went toward the back door."

"Why?"

"Why? The noise I'd heard came from the summer porch."

"Everything was dark?" he asked, pencil poised over his notepad.

Jaymie nodded, but got what he meant. He wondered why she hadn't turned any lights on as she went through the house. "I never turn lights on when I come down at night. I've lived here my whole life, and I could find my way through it blindfolded, but Becca stubbed her toe on the table leg, I think. Anyway, I was worried about my dog, but if there was a prowler, I didn't want them to see me."

"So you went toward the back door?"

"Yeah. I don't know what I was thinking. I should have headed out the front door, but, like I said, Hoppy had darted into the kitchen, and I was worried about him. Anyway, when I got into the kitchen I could kind of see, by the light over the sink—I leave that on all night, but it's only, like, fifteen watts—that there was no one in the kitchen. In fact, the door between the kitchen and the summer porch was still locked."

"So you are sure there was no one in the kitchen?"

"Yep. As I passed the kitchen table I put down the plant, grabbed the broom, then opened the door from the kitchen to the summer porch—"

"Why did you do that?"

"I don't know," she said. "Stupid thing to do, I guess, but I just wasn't thinking. It was a false alarm, I thought, something falling over on the summer porch. I hadn't processed hearing a scream and all that. I was woken up from a dead sleep, so I wasn't really coherent."

"How long did all of this take?"

"Not as long as it's taking to describe," Jaymie joked, but the officer remained stoic, staring at her. She sighed, and said, "Just a couple of minutes. As I opened the back door, I finally turned on the light, and that's when I saw him; Hoppy was sniffing him. I said something to Becca, and she came up behind me."

"Did you touch the deceased?"

"Well, of course! I didn't know he was dead then." She swallowed and took in a deep shuddering breath, battling the memory of that moment. "Look, officer, are we safe? What happened? Did someone kill him, or was it the box . . ." She trailed off and shook her head. "But it can't have been the box."

"The box?"

"Oh. I didn't say that yet, did I? When I came out onto the summer porch the box that held the teacups—that's the china that's shattered all over him—was on him, on the dead guy. And the Hoosier cabinet doors were swung open. I closed the bottom door and pushed the box of teacups off him so I could get at him," she continued, as the officer jotted swiftly. "I think I tossed a teacup and a couple of saucers aside and brushed china shards off his face. I saw the blood, and I felt sick. That's when Clive came up to the back steps. I think that's how it all happened."

"Clive Jones? Your . . ." He consulted his notes. "Your neighbor?"

She nodded.

"Why was he there?"

She looked at him in surprise. "Well, he must have heard the commotion, I guess. There's a wood fence between us, but if he had his bedroom window open . . . Hoppy had been barking like mad, remember. He had stopped by the time I got to the man on the floor. But Clive may even have heard the shouts and the crash that woke me up. You'll have to ask him." She realized Clive must have arrived at the bed-and-breakfast in the middle of the night, meaning he must have come by way of the bridge at Port Huron, and not the ferry, because he hadn't been around when they unloaded the van the night before.

"And then?"

"Clive knelt down and checked the man for a pulse."

"How did he do that?"

"He put his fingers about here," Jaymie said, putting her fingers against her carotid artery, "and lightly pressed, then he looked at me and shook his head. I think I knew he was dead, but Clive confirmed it."

"Where was your sister while you were doing this?"

"She was in the kitchen on the phone with the 911 operator." Jaymie yawned, weariness settling in, and, still cradling Hoppy, rubbed her eyes. "I said, shouldn't we try to revive him, and Clive started CPR, and I got a tea towel and applied pressure to the wound on his head. As best as I could, anyway." Her breath caught in her throat, and she said, weakly, "He was pale, and there was so much blood!"

He asked a couple more questions, then let her go, asking her to send Clive Jones in, just as someone banged on the front door. Jaymie set Hoppy down, and he followed her to the front door, yapping crazily. She flicked on the dim hall light, an original Tiffany pendant that had been restored when the electrical had been updated, and opened the door to find Anna holding her daughter, Tabby, on her hip. The woman looked frightened, her red freckles standing out against the pale skin of her face.

"Where's Clive?" she asked, shivering with terror, tears coursing down her cheeks, while her daughter sobbed and buried her head in her mother's neck. "I can't get anyone to tell me anything! He heard something, a crash and a shout, and rushed over to your place and then there were sirens and the police came banging on our door, my guests are all upset, and I haven't seen Clive since he—"

"Anna, take it easy," Jaymie said, putting one hand on Anna's bare arm. Anna was dressed in a mauve shortie set and was shivering with fright or cold or both. For her daughter's sake she needed to calm down. "Clive *is* here, and he's fine. We . . . we had an incident, and Clive stayed while we sort things out."

Just then Clive followed the officer into the library, but he leaned back out to the hall to say, "It's okay, Anna. I'll be out in a few minutes."

"What's going on?" Anna shifted Tabby higher on her hip. The baby had calmed, and reached out, touching Jaymie's cheek as Hoppy danced around their feet. "I should have brought Clive a T-shirt or something; I hope he's not cold. What happened, Jaymie?"

Jaymie kissed the baby's hand and shook it, and said, "Becca and I heard a noise and found someone on our summer porch."

"Found someone? You mean . . . ?" She mouthed the word *dead* as Tabby reached down toward Hoppy, screeching with laughter at the dog hopping and dancing on his two hind legs.

Jaymie nodded.

"Oh no!"

In a hushed voice, Jaymie told her neighbor what happened, then Clive came out of the library and joined them, putting his arm around Anna's shoulders.

"The police want us to go to the station and answer questions," he said wearily, passing one long-fingered hand over his eyes.

"But we've already done that!" Jaymie said.

"I think that might be code for the fact that they wish us to be out of their way while they investigate thoroughly," Clive said, his dark face splitting in a blinding white smile, his Jamaican accent marking his words with precise diction. He took Anna and Tabby into his arms, kissing the top of his wife's head.

"Who is the guy, Jaymie?" Anna asked.

"I have no idea. I've never seen him before in my life."

❧ Four ❧

"WHOEVER HE IS, his passing is a terrible thing," Clive said, hugging Anna and his baby daughter even closer. Anna buried her face in his shoulder.

Jaymie watched, not without envy. Anna and Clive were new to Queensville, and there had been whispering over the fact that she was white and he black, but that lasted only a couple of days. Clive and Anna were a splendid addition to their cosmopolitan little village. Queensville, with its blend of small-town charm, a marina serving both Canadian and American boats, and upscale shops selling everything from homemade jam to Piaget watches, was accustomed to an influx of newcomers—Americans, Japanese, Europeans from every nation—so Clive's Jamaican roots, accent and cooking became interesting topics of conversation for all but the most reserved. He was one of the good guys, loving, hardworking, dependable . . . all the things Jaymie yearned for in a man, and had seen in Joel, at first. With the distance of a few months now, she wondered if she had just imagined in Joel what she wanted to find.

The police let Clive go home and dress as Jaymie provided a safe haven for her pets in her bedroom, with Denver's litter box and bowls and Hoppy's favorite blankie. She changed into jeans and a T-shirt—Becca did too—then an officer collected them and took them to the Queensville Township Police Department, a modern glass-and-steel building on the highway out of Queensville.

For a couple of hours Jaymie sat alone, in a dull beige box of a room. What was going on? Why couldn't she sit with the others? A female police officer leaned her head in and asked if Jaymie would like coffee, and she said yes, but the brew was strong and bitter. She wasn't willing to ask for tea instead; that would be too much to ask of a uniformed officer of the law. It wasn't a tea shop, after all. She gulped some down, and the bitter taste remained on her palate.

Finally, a tired-looking man in a suit and tie came in, carrying a clipboard and sheaf of papers. "Ms. Leighton? I'm Detective Christian. How are you this morning?"

"Not so great since I found a dead body on my summer porch."

He quirked a grin, and she examined him with interest. He was good-looking in the traditional tall, dark and handsome vein, about six foot, thick hair, a little mussed, and with a lean, hungry look to him. Excellent romance-novel hero material, if you liked contemporaries, which she didn't. Give her a historical romance anytime. On the other hand . . . she cocked her head to one side as she listened to his lovely baritone voice. Put him in knee breeches and a cutaway coat, and give him a sword . . .

She shook her head to clear the cobwebs. "I'm sorry, what did you say?" she asked, realizing she had zoned out for a moment. A blush climbed her cheeks as she thought about how she had been viewing him. But anything was better than thinking of the body that lay on her summer porch floor that moment. She shuddered and met his eyes.

"I said I'd like you to go over what happened again for me, a step at a time. I know Sergeant MacAdams already went through this with you, but I'd like to hear your story myself."

Over the next hour, Jaymie answered the same questions she had already answered and a few more regarding the boxes on the summer porch, her usual habits and the summer porch door. Did she recognize the victim? No, she'd never seen him before, she was pretty sure. Not positive, but close. He asked about any strange occurrences over the last while, and she found herself even talking about the auction, buying the Hoosier and the rude drivers on the highway and in Queensville the evening before.

What about the grinder that they suspected was the murder weapon, he asked; where was that?

She took him through finding the grinder in a drawer late the night before and screwing it loosely to the porcelain work top.

"So it wasn't just lying on the work top, it was screwed down?"

"But loosely," Jaymie replied. "I just wanted to see if it fit. I don't know why I didn't take it off and put it back in the drawer. I . . . I wish now that I had!"

He didn't comment, just went back to questions. Why did she think the man broke into her house? She mused about the summer residents' perennial problems with break-ins and the issues they'd had in past years with the family cottage on Heartbreak Island. She talked about the stuff she had bought at the sale, the Hoosier, china dishes and sewing paraphernalia, the linens and the valuable Royal Crown Derby. But she also noted that the guy on her porch was well dressed. He sure didn't look like some transient thief, trying to find something he could pawn for a few quick bucks.

"Why our house?" she said. "I don't understand."

Detective Christian left the room, telling her he would be right back, but he was gone for quite a while. She had a lot of time to think, sitting alone on that ugly, uncomfortable cracked plastic chair in the drab, uninspiring room. Why *her* house, she wondered again, if the dead guy, and/or whoever had killed him, were thieves? Among all the summer houses of folks who weren't even in Queensville yet, people who had stashes of jewelry and loads of other expensive treasures, why *her* house? Had other houses been broken into? Her neighbors on the other side, for example, hadn't arrived for the summer yet. Their home was locked up tighter than Mrs. Bellwood's Royal Doulton figurines. Locked, yes, but still, with no one home it would have been less risky than breaking into *her* house.

Was the dead guy a thief specifically targeting stuff they had bought at the auction? The cookbooks were everywhere, and the carton of sewing stuff and the box of vintage cookware were down on the floor. But that was all crap, worth only a little more than she had paid.

The only thing worth anything was Becca's Crown Derby. He was a very well-dressed thief, and might have recognized the value of that box of china. Becca's professional evaluation of it was eight thousand dollars—a lot of money.

The detective finally came back. "All right, Ms. Leighton, your story checks out."

"Well, of course it does," she blurted out, startled. "What, did you think I killed him?"

"Did you?" he said.

"Of course not!" She stared up at him, disconcerted by his blank expression.

"No problem, then, is there?"

"No, no problem at all," she retorted. "Detective, assuming the killer used my grinder to kill the guy, why did he do that? If we assume the guy who was killed broke into our house, then he must have used something strong to pry our screen door off; why didn't the murderer use that? And who *is* the victim?"

"First, you're making a lot of assumptions that we haven't established yet as to why and how the victim was in your house. And we don't know the victim's identity; he didn't have any identification on him."

"That's unusual, isn't it?"

"You'd be surprised how few crooks want us to ID them," he said, with deadpan irony.

"He was really well dressed; that can't be normal for a thief. He was wearing a cable-knit cardigan, for heaven's sake."

"Maybe he forgot his black cat burglar suit. Ms. Leighton, as I said, we can't assume anything at this point. You can go home now. We'll be in touch if we have more questions."

He shook her hand and left, and an officer was assigned to drive them all home. Jaymie saw Clive folded into his wife's arms, as Tabby toddled about near them on the sidewalk in front of the Shady Rest Bed-and-Breakfast. She unlocked the front door to their home, trailed by Rebecca, who looked gray with weariness. The body had been taken away, and the crime scene had been investigated thoroughly, she had been assured.

But what to do about the scene of the crime, her summer porch? The sun was high in the sky as she and Rebecca walked into their house and looked around with trepidation. But their beloved home was just as it always was, calm, quiet, bars of color from the stained glass sidelight slanting across the front hall's hardwood floor.

"Guess it'll be okay," Becca said.

"It will be," Jaymie said, linking her arm through her sister's. "Life goes on. It was awful, but we'll be all right. We still have the Tea with the Queen tomorrow to prepare for."

"I'll help later," Becca said on a wide yawn. "Right now

I'm so tired I could drop. I'm going to *try* to get a few more hours of sleep. You should, too."

Jaymie nodded. "You go ahead. I'm too wired on bad coffee to sleep. I'll get the summer porch cleaned up."

Rebecca stopped at the foot of the stairs and touched Jaymie's arm, watching her eyes. "Jaymie, no. Let's call in a professional. I asked the cops, and they said there's a company in Detroit that specializes in crime-scene cleanup. I got their card. Let's call them; we can do that now, then get some sleep."

Crime-scene cleanup! Jaymie hesitated and glanced toward the back of the house. She didn't even know what to expect. "These crime-scene-cleanup people . . . could they come right away?"

"Probably not."

"I don't want that . . . that *awfulness* to sit there for days . . . or even for hours!"

"We could go stay somewhere else for a few days. Dee would take us in. Or we could get a room at the Inn."

Jaymie shuddered. "It's only going to get worse, Becca. Think about it sitting there for days and days. This is our home. I can't stand the thought of that . . . I just can't stand it."

"I can't let you handle that alone, but I will *not* go back there right now," Becca said, her voice tight with nerves. She didn't like blood; even a scratch on her arm made her queasy.

Jaymie took a deep breath and gritted her teeth. "I'll clean it up. It's just blood. I think. I hope." She shuddered internally, but trying to rest while knowing blood was seeping into the boards of her beloved summer porch was an absolute no go. Surely cleaning it up quickly would be best all around.

"Are you sure? Look, rest now, and I'll help you later, I promise."

"No, Becca, it's okay," Jaymie said, reaching out and

hugging her sister. It was a magnanimous offer, given how she felt about blood. "I *want* to do this. You know me; I like a little solitude and a boring task when things get crazy." She pushed Rebecca toward the stairs and said, "Go! Come down when you're good and ready."

Without further protest, Rebecca went. But if Jaymie thought she'd have solitude, she was wrong. All she had time for was letting Denver and Hoppy out of her room, when the steady stream of gawkers and neighbors and concerned citizens began. She turned them all away as politely as she could until DeeDee Stubbs trotted toward her up the walk.

She carried a pail with a lid, gloves and a bottle of bleach. The very first things she said were, "Are you okay? How's Becca?"

"I'm all right. I think," Jaymie said. "Becca went up to bed. She's exhausted."

"Meaning she can't deal with the blood. I've come to work, not just gawk," she said, reaching down to pet Hoppy, who was begging for attention. "If even a fraction of what I heard is correct, you'll need some help cleaning up your summer porch. That's where it happened, right?"

"Yeah, that's where . . . yeah." She shuddered. "But Dee, you didn't need to come over. I could never ask your help for something like this. You really don't know what you're signing up for."

"I think I probably do," she said. "Maybe more than you."

On that cryptic comment, Jaymie looked up and down the street and ushered DeeDee into the house. "Okay, but *I* don't even know yet what I'll find," she admitted. "I haven't gone to the kitchen or the summer porch. All I've had time to do is let Denver and Hoppy out of my room. Now I have to go and look at the damage, and I'm kind of spooked."

"We'll face it together, kiddo," DeeDee said. She linked arms with Jaymie and tugged her toward the back of the house. "Let's go."

The animals followed them down the hall toward the

kitchen, Hoppy with the mindless happiness he always seemed to proceed through life exuding, and Denver slinking along with an attitude of surly suspicion, *his* customary outlook. Jaymie, with her older friend, held back one moment, then took a deep breath and stepped into the kitchen. The police had closed and locked the door between the kitchen and summer porch, so Jaymie walked slowly through her favorite room of the house, but quailed just as she got to the porch door. The memory of the dark and the body and her fear flooded her.

"Jaymie," DeeDee said, gently, touching her arm, "it's okay, hon, I'm here."

"And I'm glad," Jaymie said, covering DeeDee's hand on her arm with her own. DeeDee had the motherly vibe that Rebecca occasionally emanated, but in a far different sense. Where Becca could be harrying, pushier toward Jaymie than their mom had ever been, Dee had kids, one just a few years younger than Jaymie, and knew how to be encouraging without being aggressive. Jaymie took heart and opened the door, staring aghast at the mess, which looked even worse in the light of day. For one thing, the summer porch door was still hanging from its hinges, though someone had put a piece of wood over it and nailed it on. For another, dark smudges covered so many surfaces: fingerprint powder, dusted over everything!

But worse than that was the stuff spilled everywhere: cookbooks, teacups, shattered china. The grinder, thank heavens, had been seized for examination; she didn't know if she could ever even look at it again if it turned out it was the murder weapon. Worst of all, though, was the rucked-up, bloody rag mat and the pool of dark, congealing blood. A spray of blood spattered the door to the summer porch. Jaymie turned away from the sight.

DeeDee had already plunked down her bucket and had the water on in the kitchen sink. She fished around in the cupboard under the sink and got a roll of paper towels out.

She returned to Jaymie's side armed for a cleansing battle. "Honey, in case you don't remember, when I married Johnny Stubbs, the best man in the world, I was a surgical nurse, and for a time before that a nurse in emerge over at Wolverhampton General. I can see you're a little green around the gills at the blood, but to me it's just so much red paint."

She shook out a red garbage bag. "Blood and other body fluids need to be handled correctly. I'll mop up the blood, you just concentrate on the china and books." She pulled on the rubber gloves, squirted some detergent into the pail, poured in some bleach and filled it with steaming water.

"I remember your nursing days," Jaymie said, heartened by DeeDee's no-nonsense company. "But I would never have assumed it meant you could face this."

"No sweat."

DeeDee and Becca had known each other for years, since high school at Wolverhampton High, but it was only in recent years that DeeDee had become Jaymie's friend, too. In the past their fifteen-year age difference had meant they had little in common, but lately, their mutual love of "old stuff" had helped cement the bond of familiarity into friendship.

"Not much difference between a crime scene and a fight between siblings," Dee said, with a chuckle. "When I quit working and started popping out babies, I thought my days of scrubbing blood were over, but having five kids just means the blood oozes out of someone you love." She knocked the nailed board off the back door with one well-placed kick, and got down to business. First, she held up the bloody tea towel. "Do you want to rescue this, honey? Wash it?"

Jaymie shuddered. "No. Trash it."

Dee then pulled up the bloodstained mat, tossed it into the garbage bag she had brought with her and vigorously scoured the blood spatter from the door. Then she got down on her hands and knees to clean, her wide bottom moving in rhythm as she scrubbed, first the door and legs of the Hoosier, and parts of the wall, then moved down to the floor. It looked like the shiny gray paint that coated the board floor had resisted any of the blood soaking in. That was a relief.

Jaymie stood and stared for a moment, then got her broom and started rescuing those cups and saucers that were intact, sweeping up the rest of the chips and chunks. They were silent for a long while, scrubbing and sweeping, but finally Jaymie needed to move her mind away from grimness and blood. She was tired to the bone, but wouldn't give in to her weariness. "DeeDee, why didn't anyone on the committee tell me Heidi was going to be playing a part in the Tea with the Queen?"

"Yikes!" DeeDee sat back on her haunches and cast a rueful look up at Jaymie. "We didn't know how, hon. Heidi comes along—she's not such a bad kid, really—and she offers to donate a big whack of money if we let her play a part. Greed overcame good sense; I wasn't at the meeting, nor were you, apparently. I think you were up in Canada visiting your Grandma Leighton. Later I raised hell. I thought there must be a reason why Heidi was at one of the only meetings of the year you weren't at, but the others said no, it was just chance. Then I said, we've never done anything like that before, let someone pay their way onto the committee or the tea. Bad precedent."

"I didn't ask why you all *let* her, I asked why no one told me."

DeeDee began scrubbing again. She carefully disposed of the cleaning cloths and soiled paper towels in the garbage bag. She had already explained that they would be taken to the hospital; it was vital that they be disposed of correctly by someone experienced in handling bio-waste.

"No one would volunteer to hurt your feelings, hon," DeeDee said. "We were going to get Becca to do it—God knows she doesn't have trouble hurting anyone's feelings—

but she never came to town, and it wasn't the kind of thing we wanted to do over the phone."

She had to stop mooning around Queensville, Jaymie decided, because if people thought she still carried a torch for Joel six months after he'd dumped her, she was risking looking like an idiot. She swept the shards of china up and disposed of them, then knelt down by the cookbooks. As she stacked them back in the box, one in particular stood out; it was a small vintage book, grease-stained, with a line drawing on it of a church. "The Johnsonville United Church Ladies' Auxiliary—1953. That's interesting," she said. She plunked her butt down on the wide board floor of the summer porch, trying to ignore what DeeDee was doing, and leafed through it. One recipe jumped out at her. Queen Elizabeth cake. Hmmm. She held it up to show DeeDee, and said, "This must have been made to honor Queen Elizabeth's coronation in 1953."

DeeDee bent forward and stared at the recipe. "Maybe, but my grandmother swears that recipe was around during World War II; says it was a favorite of the Queen Mum, and that's why it was called Queen Elizabeth cake."

"Oh, right! I forgot her name was Queen Elizabeth, too. I'm going to try this recipe for the tea tomorrow," Jaymie said, beginning to feel better just focusing on something other than the dead body. "If I ever get this stuff cleared up, that is."

"Who do you think he is . . . was, the dead man, I mean?" DeeDee asked. "Hoosier dead guy?" she said, laughing. She wrung red water into the pail from her cloth.

Jaymie looked away, queasy, but tried to smile at DeeDee's joke. "I don't have a clue. Why did he break into our house, of all places, with all the houses that are empty and loaded with expensive stuff? I don't get it."

"Maybe he wasn't the robber," DeeDee said. "Maybe he saw or heard something, came up to investigate, caught someone *else* in the act and got whacked."

"At our back door?" Jaymie considered it, but shook her head. "He'd have to come through the gate and down the path and up to the house, and he'd have had to be walking down the back lane to see anything going on. Unlikely at three or four a.m."

The whole thing was unlikely, though. Who was he, and what had he wanted? And why had he lifted all the boxes off the Hoosier? She glanced over, and her eye was caught by the box of sewing stuff; she remembered the random conversation she'd overheard at the auction about the valuable button. When she bid on the sewing stuff, it was really to see who else would be bidding on the box, hoping she'd see who was after a valuable button, but she'd gotten the whole box for fifteen bucks.

Surely someone wouldn't have followed her home for *that*? She'd never been broken into until the night she brought stuff home from the auction, though. It was something to consider. She packed the cookbooks into the box, piled the sewing box on top of it, and piled them on the Hoosier. She was going to take it all up to her room to sort, at some point, but not until after the tea.

Even as she made plans and tried to forget the awfulness of the last several hours, the problem still plagued her: who *was* the dead guy by the Hoosier?

❧ Five ❧

DEEDEE AND JAYMIE finished up the cleaning, working together on the fingerprint dust with dish detergent and cloths, which seemed to cut through it and remove it well, even off the Hoosier, which, it seemed, had been dusted more than anything else. The kitchen and summer porch finally had no visual or olfactory reminders of the terrible death that had taken place during the night. Instead, it smelled of bleach, pine cleaner and window spray, overlaid with the fresh spring air that poured through the open door. Her older friend snapped a lid on the bucket of blood-tinged water, tossed the rubber gloves in the red garbage bag, and said she would take care of them both; she still had connections at the Wolverhampton General Hospital, and they could properly dispose of the bio-waste. She hugged Jaymie tight, told her to take it easy and try not to think of what happened too much, and then trotted away to her car, parked out front.

Jaymie went back through the house and stood staring

out over the backyard as Hoppy sniffed around the perimeter, along the line of holly bushes and down to the forsythia.
Did he smell the victim's and the murderer's scents? She
had heard somewhere that a dog's sense of smell was a
hundred thousand times better than a human's; what would
that be like, being able to scent out the villain? So much
information that no human could access.

A breeze raised goose bumps on her bare arms, and she
shivered. Somewhere out there was a murderer, a cold-
blooded killer who had not hesitated to dispatch another
human life, extinguishing it like it was a candle to be
snuffed. It was a horrible end for the unknown man, whoever
he was. But the freshening breeze reminded her that she
needed to get on with things, among them, fixing the broken
back door. She'd make a call to Bill Waterman, their local
handyman.

But first, she wanted to make sure there were no shards
of glass or china to get stuck in little paws. She got the
broom and swept the whole long porch, edging past the
wicker furniture on one side, just past the Hoosier: dust
balls, some shards of bone china, random pieces of dried
plant material, and a triangular corner of some piece of
paper were all she swept up. She bent over to look at the
triangle of paper, then picked it up. It had typed print on it;
it looked like it had been torn from something, a receipt,
maybe, or perhaps it had fluttered out of the box of cookbooks when they'd been dumped, so she stuck it in her jeans
pocket to look at later, then dumped the rest of the stuff in
the trash.

"Hoppy, come on in, fella," she said, clicking her tongue.
He turned and stared back at her, but with a puzzled look
in his eyes. She never denied him time in the yard. Denver
prowled up behind Jaymie and stood with her, looking out
over the yard, a long rectangle rimmed with a battered
wooden fence, old forsythia bushes and the line of holly
bushes Jaymie had planted just the month before. She loved

her backyard. It was an oasis of calm, an untidy strike at a world enamored of right angles and hard lines. The frayed edge of her lawn, where it tattered along the wrought-iron fence and hard-packed dirt of the back lane, was perfect in its imperfection.

This was her home, and it made her sick to the pit of her stomach that someone had died right near where she stood. She looked over her shoulder at the Hoosier, with the boxes now tidily loaded back on top of it. After the night she'd had, she was exhausted, but she wasn't going to sleep yet. Instead, she would find refuge in the warmth and comfort of her kitchen, and the recipe for Queen Elizabeth cake she had found in the old cookbook. If it worked out, it would be part of the Tea with the Queen fundraiser the next day. More importantly, maybe cooking, her familiar work, would erase the horrible scene that was imprinted on her home like a pheromone scent.

But to bake, she needed to shop. With a list of ingredients in her shoulder bag, Jaymie set out, Hoppy tugging her along, bobbing on the end of the leash with his bouncy gait. The only thing better than the backyard for the lionhearted, three-legged little Yorkie-Poo was a walk. First stop, Anna and Clive's bed-and-breakfast, the Shady Rest.

She strode up the short walk to the Queen Anne–style home that had been converted to a bed-and-breakfast ten years before. Clive and Anna were the third set of owners since the conversion. "I'm going to the Emporium. Can I pick you up anything?" she asked as Anna opened the door to her brisk knock.

Tabby was on Anna's hip, as usual. "Jaymie, you are a lifesaver!" she said, glancing over her shoulder as the phone began to ring. "After that awful night and his long drive, Clive's sleeping. The house is a mess, and I haven't even started cleaning the room for today's arrival! Wait a sec while I answer that and get my list." She thrust Tabby into

Jaymie's arms and dashed back into the house, leaving the door open.

Jaymie bobbed Tabby on her hip while the baby cooed and laughed at Hoppy's antics. The little dog was running in circles, then, loose for the moment, dashed into the house trailing his leash. He sniffed around the base of the stairs, yipping excitedly and looked up at Jaymie. "What on earth are you on about?" she asked.

Anna came back to the door and reclaimed her child, handing Jaymie a list in exchange. She leaned forward and said, in an undertone, "Could you pick up something at the pharmacy, too? I wouldn't ask, but I can't get away right now, and if I don't get it, we may have an unexpected bundle of joy in nine months' time!"

Jaymie laughed. "I can pick that little item up for you, though if not getting it resulted in another one of these," she said, chucking Tabby under the chin, "it wouldn't hurt my feelings."

"Not just yet," Anna said, with a harried laugh, "not until we get this place settled a little more."

"It's the least I can do after standing you up this morning; I was supposed to help with breakfast. I haven't forgotten!"

"You were slightly distracted," Anna replied.

Jaymie set off with Hoppy leashed again, and only then looked at the list. "Wow. I didn't know she needed so much stuff!"

The walk was short, but it kept her mind from wandering to the dark night and the dead body. She mounted the creaky porch of Queensville's general store, a place that stocked a weird assortment of everything from batteries to beach balls to baklava. She put Hoppy in the "puppy pen" that the Klausners, the elderly Queensville Emporium owners, provided on the side porch of the store (fresh water and companionship for Hoppy, who immediately met one of his closest pals and rivals, Junk Junior, a bichon mix with no snooty attitude), and then entered. It had been a general store since the mid–eighteen hundreds, so the floors creaked and groaned like an elderly aunt settling down into a too-comfortable chair. There were always folks inside, though some were not buying but "chatting" with Mrs. Klausner—gossiping—and if you needed the local news, this was the place to stop.

She was greeted by name, and though curious stares followed her past the register, nobody said a word about the murder. They probably already knew as much as Jaymie did, and perhaps more. Along the back wall there was a pharmacy, a postal outlet and a Sears catalogue depot, all manned by one person, Valetta Nibley, a sour-faced spinster of an astonishingly sweet disposition. Jaymie took a spot behind Valetta's one customer, a tall gentleman who was explaining that he couldn't possibly sleep without his pills, but had run out, or hadn't brought enough from home.

"I thought I brought enough with me, but I seem to have misjudged my needs." He pushed an empty prescription bottle across the counter to her. "It's very strange. I don't think I've lost any, but they are gone, nonetheless."

"Certainly, Mr. Foster," Valetta, a registered pharmacist, said, writing down his doctor's name as he spelled it out. "I'll phone his office about your prescription, and he can fax the okay to me. We do this all the time for visitors."

He said he'd be back later, and ambled off down the aisle. Jaymie recognized him; when she had last seen him, he and an equally tall and stately-looking lady were at the auction.

"Jaymie, how are you? Are you okay? I was going to call, but then I figured every other person in town had already called you, and you'd need a rest." Valetta glanced around and then leaned out the little window. "Are you and Becca all right staying there? You can come bunk in with me, if you don't mind sharing a double bed in the guest room."

"I appreciate the offer, but I think we're going to be okay. Whatever the thief wanted, he's dead now."

"Yeah, but someone killed him. *In your house.* Aren't you scared to death?"

Jaymie shrugged. She was terrified, but she was not going to admit it. Folks were already feeling sorry for her—she was really going to have to address her prolonged mourning for her love life—and she was not going to give them more reasons to tiptoe around her. "It'll be okay. The cops are going to be watching the house for a while."

A customer edged closer, probably to listen in on their conversation. Valetta said, "What can I do for you?"

Jaymie quietly explained what she needed to pick up for Anna Jones, and Valetta promised the prescription would be waiting for her when she was done with her shopping, but as Jaymie turned to retrieve one of the tiny shopping carts reserved for serious customers, the woman added, in her normal voice, "Folks are saying that the fella who was murdered was looking to hide drugs in your place. That true?"

"Wow," Jaymie said, turning back to her. "Wherever you got that from, the person is badly misinformed. Who told you that?"

The woman squinted and cocked her head to one side. "Can't remember. It was before the woman who told me the guy was an international terrorist, but after the one who said he was trying to sneak in to steal your panties."

Jaymie felt the heat flush her face. "I'd be grateful if you'd tell anyone who speculates that no one knows who the guy is, why he broke into my house, or who killed him. And he didn't make it past my summer porch!"

"Yeah, well, I knew he wasn't the panty thief, 'cause I know who that is, and he doesn't break into houses. He only steals panties left on clotheslines to dry."

Jaymie bit her lip to keep from laughing, the incongruity of Valetta Nibley talking so matter-of-factly about a panty thief was too funny. "And you've never turned him in?"

"The police know too, but you'd have to catch him in the

act, or with the stolen goods, and he *wears* the stolen panties, then tosses them out." She wrinkled her nose. "Yuk."

"I think I have too much information now," Jaymie said.

There was a twinkle in Valetta's gray eyes that indicated
she *might* be joking, but one never knew with the woman.
"I'll holler when I've got the item you need," Valetta said,
winking at her and turning away.

She was a good friend, Jaymie thought, as she collected
the dates and cream she needed to try the Queen Elizabeth
cake recipe. Valetta Nibley, a "spinster"—that was her own
name for herself—was likely trying to raise Jaymie's mood
in the wake of the murder. So far, she was holding up. Jaymie started on Anna's list. Bananas, apples, milk, flour,
baking powder, cereal . . . on and on. "I should have brought
the van," she said aloud, trying to imagine carrying it all
with Hoppy tugging at the leash.

"I beg your pardon?"

Jaymie looked up from the list to find Mrs. Bellwood,
the annual Tea's short, stout Queen Victoria, staring at her,
thick dark brows drawn down over beady eyes. "Sorry, Mrs.
Bellwood, I was thinking aloud."

"Bad habit. I do it all the time."

Jaymie was about to move on, but the silver-haired
woman grabbed ahold of her sleeve with a firm grasp.

"Is that outsider in Queensville yet?" she said.

Jaymie effortlessly translated the woman's reference. "I
don't know if Daniel Collins is here yet, but I sure hope he
is. We need to get into the attic to get down the tables for
the tea." The tables for the Tea with the Queen had been
stored in Stowe House attic for thirty-five years, ever since
the first event.

"Weather channel says rain for tomorrow," she replied,
obliquely.

"I hope not," Jaymie said. "We can't get nearly as many
people in the house as we can when we hold the event on
the lawn. And Canadian tourists won't come over on the

ferry if it's raining." Jaymie suspected that Mrs. Bellwood would love the chance to lord it over a tea table in the parlor, which Daniel had not changed since he bought the house with the furniture three years before.

In those three years he had spent, probably, less than a month total in Queensville, and many of the locals resented an "outsider's" grasp on the oldest and most prominent house in the village. Lazarus Stowe, builder of Stowe House, was an important local figure, the man who had brokered the agreement to split Heartbreak Island between the neighboring countries of Canada and the US, avoiding an international incident in the 1840s, when feelings were still running high in Canada after a rebellion in 1837. It was rumored that Sir John A. MacDonald, the first prime minister of Canada, had spent a few days there once as Lazarus Stowe's guest, before Canadian confederation, that momentous uniting of various parts of the northern nation into one dominion on July 1, 1867.

"Trip Findley told me that there was a car outside that house all night long!" Mrs. Bellwood said, her voice low. "Probably another outsider!"

"How did Mr. Findley know the car was there all night?" Jaymie asked, vaguely moved to defend Daniel Collins, whose only discernible flaw was that he had bought Stowe House from underneath the nose of the heritage committee.

"Trip walks every morning at five a.m., and he goes past Stowe House. He feels that since Collins is so seldom there," she said, her chins wobbling with indignation, "it behooves those of us with a stake in Queensville to keep an eye on the place."

Jaymie resisted the urge to retort. When the place had gone up for sale three years before, Mrs. Bellwood and Trip Findley had spearheaded a movement to buy Stowe House and convert it into a Queensville historical museum, but the plan had fallen through, the victim of not enough cash and a lack of local enthusiasm. As good an idea as it was, local people felt it would be a money drain, and probably foresaw decades of pleas for more money to repair and maintain the building as a museum. The local economy was not that strong and folks' pockets not that deep.

Even after the plan died for lack of interest, when the irascible pair of oldsters learned that an outsider had bought that precious piece of village history, they became incensed and never forgave the buyer. Daniel Collins seemed happily oblivious to Mrs. Bellwood's frosty stares and cutting re-marks. In truth, Daniel, whom Jaymie had befriended, had perfectly good caretakers who checked daily on the house. He had installed an expensive alarm system and fire protec-tion, and even though he was seldom there, was an excellent guardian of that bit of village history.

"So, what did Mr. Findley see?" Jaymie said, urging the woman (who was staring down her mortal enemy, Imogene Frump, in the pet food aisle) to continue. Anything about a stranger in town was interesting, given what had happened at Jaymie's house.

Mrs. Bellwood looked to the left and to the right, then leaned toward Jaymie. "There was a car with out-of-state plates sitting outside Stowe House." She flashed a look at Imogene Frump, then leaned over even closer and whispered to Jaymie, "And there was a *man* asleep in the backseat!" Mrs. Frump was edging closer down the crowded grocery aisle, and Mrs. Bellwood straightened, and said, in a ringing, carrying tone, "And that's all I know about that!"

The two old enemies nodded and drifted past each other, like great sailing ships signaling their presence in murky fog and thus avoiding a catastrophic collision.

"I'll see you at the tea tomorrow, Jaymie dear," Mrs. Bellwood cried. Her position playing Queen Victoria in the annual tea had been her victory decades ago over Imogene Frump, and the root of their enmity, since she took every opportunity to remind the other woman of her triumph.

"Jaymie, parcel pickup," Valetta called just then.

Jaymie, musing about the new information Mrs. Bell-wood had given her, finished up her shopping, got Anna's birth control from the pharmacy and left the store with much to think of, not the least of which was how was she going to handle four bags of groceries and a prancing little dog all the way back home. She released Hoppy from puppy prison—Junk Junior was already gone, so Hoppy was the only little dog in the pen—and put her bags down on the creaking stoop while she snapped on his leash.

"Hey, Jaymie!" a voice called out, fighting to be heard over the roar of an energetic engine.

She looked up as Daniel Collins himself cruised up in front of the store in his battered Jeep Wrangler. "Hi, Daniel! I was just talking about you. Were your ears burning?"

He grinned and unfolded himself from the driver's seat, hopping out and strolling around to greet her. "I was talking about you, too. I met your new neighbor, Anna Jones, when I went looking for you. I figure everyone is probably freak-ing out that I haven't gotten here yet."

"A little," Jaymie admitted. "Hey, can you give me, Hoppy and this mountain of groceries a lift back home?"

"That's what I came here for! Anna said she hadn't real-ized you were walking and had given you her whole shop-ping list." He slung her bags in the back, as Jaymie climbed in the passenger side and belted herself in, holding Hoppy securely on her lap.

The ride back to her home took less than three minutes, but it saved her a lot of time and trouble, and Jaymie told Daniel so. There was something different about him this time, she thought, glancing over at his beaky profile, tousled sandy hair dancing in the wind and flopping over his high forehead. He was smiling more and seemed unusually animated.

As they pulled up in front of the B&B, Jaymie said, reaching behind for Anna's grocery bags, "I heard there was someone sleeping outside of your house all night. What's up with that?"

Daniel reached over to help her retrieve a runaway apple as Hoppy leaped into the back of the Jeep and chased it. "Bad timing is what's up with that. That's Zell McIntosh, an old college buddy of mine. We're having a reunion of sorts this weekend through to Memorial Day weekend next week. Just the three of us: me, Zell and Trev Standish. Frat buddies."

Jaymie tried, and failed, to imagine Daniel Collins—serious, (generally) bespectacled and levelheaded—as a frat brat. "Were you supposed to be here earlier, or was he the one who got the timing wrong?"

Collins nodded. "Perspicacious: that's what my mom would call you. He's the one who got it wrong, because I texted him three days ago that I'd be here Saturday morning. I was early, got here at seven a.m., so I don't know why he arrived last night." He paused one beat, then said, "Hey, I heard there was a fracas at your house last night, but nobody would tell me what happened. What's up?"

"Hold on, and I'll get rid of these bags and tell you," Jaymie said. After she unloaded Anna's groceries and helped her harassed neighbor get them into the house, Daniel and Jaymie went into the Leightons' front door, just as Becca came down the stairs yawning and stretching.

Between them they told their village neighbor what had happened as Jaymie unloaded the groceries. He exclaimed at the awful event and regarded Jaymie with great seriousness for a few moments over his glasses. "Are you all right? Really?"

"Yeah, I am. I'm just fine," she said, wondering at his expression. Becca was watching him with raised eyebrows.

"And I'm okay too, in case you're concerned," she said, after a moment's silence.

"Right. Good. Hey, can I see the Hoosier cabinet?"

Jaymie led him back to the summer porch and pointed it out, and watched while he looked it over.

"A real Hoosier, right?" he said. "What are you going to do with it? You putting it in the kitchen?"

"Eventually," she said, "but not until it's cleaned up some." She shuddered and turned away, not able to look at it without thinking of the man dead beside it, or the grinder that had been the murder weapon.

"Oh, I'm sorry!" Daniel said. "It was . . . it was right here that it happened, wasn't it?"

She nodded and went back to the kitchen table; the police hadn't warned her against it, but she was not about to reveal to anyone else what they suspected about the grinder.

Daniel then told them his plans for the next while. He and Zell—and his friend Trevor, if he showed up in the next few hours—could handle getting the tables down from the attic. His lawn service was mowing that very moment, pruning the forsythia that lined the south side of the house and trimming the spirea on the other side. Tables would be set out the next morning, and he and Zell and Trevor would be available to move them into place. Becca, naturally bossy, said she would be there to organize them.

There was silence for a moment, and then Daniel slapped his open palms on the trestle table and stood. "I guess I'd better get going. Zell wants to see the sights, and I said we'd go across the river into Canada for dinner." He pulled his cell phone out of his pocket as it buzzed. "Damn!" he said, reading the tiny screen with a frown. He pushed his glasses up on his nose. "Looks like Trev's going to be late."

"Your other friend?"

"Yeah, Trevor Standish. He's the one who organized me and Zell and him getting together, and now he's going to be late." Collins swiftly texted an answer and slid the device back into his pocket. "How late, he didn't say. Typical Trevor. I'll let you both get back to . . . to whatever you were doing," he said, with a shy look at Becca.

And he was gone.

Jaymie and Becca had some lunch and then, to relax a bit from the horrors of the night, Jaymie began her Queen Elizabeth cake, turning the sticky dates into a newer glass bowl, boiling the kettle and pouring one cup over the dates and baking soda, which fizzed up. She would never pour boiling water into a vintage bowl; an unseen hairline crack could cause it to shatter. Nor did she ever use her vintage bowls in the microwave. That would be like putting her grandmother in a rocket ship to the moon.

"What is *that* all about, boiling water and baking soda?" Becca asked, looking over her shoulder.

"I think you do this to soften the dates, so they blend well with the moist cake batter," Jaymie said, lifting down her favorite Pyrex bowls, a vintage "Primary Colors" set, from the open shelf over the sink. She set the oven to preheat while Becca sat down at the kitchen table to make a list of things to do before the next day.

There was silence for a moment, other than the sounds of Jaymie mixing and Becca scratching items on her list.

"I can't stop thinking about that poor guy . . . the dead man," Becca said, tapping her pen against her pad of paper.

"I know," Jaymie said. She worked the moist ingredients together in the red bowl, the second smallest in the graduated nesting set, while her sister watched.

"Who can he be? Do you think the cops know and just aren't saying?"

Jaymie shrugged. "The detective told me that they didn't know yet. That was hours ago, though."

"I should have stayed up to help you clean, Jaymie," Rebecca said, looking toward the sunporch. "You did a great job. I was almost afraid to come down, but . . . it's like it never happened." She was silent for a moment, then said, "I'm not sure about sleeping here tonight, though. There's a murderer running around out there."

Jaymie had been trying not to think about that all day. "I have Bill Waterman coming to fix that back door later," she said, in an oblique answer. "I want him to take the storms off the summer porch, too. I was going to call him this week about that anyway. The police did say they're going to cruise by often for the next while, and even have someone sitting out back, until they figure out who did it. Bill's going to put in motion detector alarms."

"I know. Still . . . it freaks me out."

Jaymie set the bowl aside for a moment, pushing thoughts of the blood and violence out of her mind. It wasn't easy because, as tired as she was, it was looming, like an awful weight on her shoulders. "Anyway," she said, brusquely, "about the cleaning . . . DeeDee showed up to help just after you went upstairs. She dug right in and did the stuff I couldn't face—you know her; blood doesn't faze an ER nurse—so don't worry about it, sis."

Becca smiled and put one hand over Jaymie's and squeezed. "Old friends are the best kind. Anyway, to change the subject to something lighter . . . I bought a gross of white polyester napkins that look a lot like damask. You know how every year some idiots steal the vintage ones, and we can't replace them. Polyester'll make it a lot easier to wash out the jam stains."

"Let me see them." While Becca was gone, Jaymie finished the cake batter, poured it into a round pan and popped it in the preheated oven.

Becca plunked a shopping bag with plastic sleeves of the white polyester napkins on the table, and Jaymie slipped a set out of the plastic and shook one loose. She handled it, the cheap fabric catching on a ragged fingernail and the rough skin along her thumb. "Becca, these are awful! They don't feel anything like real damask!"

"Good enough for the masses, Jaymie. They'll steal them anyway, and I won't care because they're only fifty cents apiece and replaceable, instead of real damask or linen at five bucks."

"But . . ." Jaymie stopped, dismayed but unable to fight

her sister on it. Becca was right in one respect; folks did keep filching the vintage linens, as petty as it seemed, as a souvenir of the tea. But polyester! She looked down at the textured striping meant to simulate damask. "We use real china and real linen tablecloths because we're trying to create a Victorian ambience. This doesn't really go along with that."

"I know," Becca said. "But it's like trying to feed foie gras to a five-year-old. They don't appreciate the real thing anyway, and when they steal one of these, the last laugh is on them, not us. You *know* I'm right."

As uneasy as Jaymie was with Becca's sweeping statement, she was right about the polyester napkins. This was a fundraiser for the Heritage Society, and losing vintage damask or linen didn't help the bottom line. "Counterfeit damask. What'll they think of next?" Jaymie said, and rose to pull the cake out of the oven. She had already boiled the odd "icing"—it was made of brown sugar, coconut, butter and one other ingredient she had had to guess at; she hoped "top milk" meant cream—and poured it over the cake. It pooled, so she got a nutpick out of the drawer and poked holes in the top, letting the brown sugar mixture ooze into the cake. She then stuck the pan back in the oven, watching it carefully so she could tell when the coconut had browned slightly.

"People will counterfeit anything!" Becca said, bundling up the bag.

When she pulled the cake out of the oven, she stared at it, unsure what it would taste like. It was a lovely golden brown, and smelled divine. "Yeah, but counterfeit damask napkins? Sheesh!"

❈ Six ❈

BECCA HAD A million things to do, she said, not the least of which was a visit to the Queensville Methodist Church to see how preparations for the next day's affair were going. She bustled off, happy to have someone to boss around, Jaymie thought with a smile. Maybe her sister needed that activity to get her mind off what had happened in the night. No matter what Jaymie did, the questions continued to hum in the back of her mind: Who was the dead guy, and who'd murdered him? And why? And why in their home with that darned grinder? She had a headache that probably wouldn't go away until she got some sleep.

After washing and pairing up the china teacups and saucers that hadn't been smashed in the murderous melee, and setting aside the strays—cups or saucers that didn't have mates—Jaymie packed the sets in a box to be taken along with the ones they had already chosen for the tea, as well as the boxes of serving pieces, and set them in the hall near the front door. The Queensville Methodist Church Lady's

Guild, in support of the Queensville Heritage Society, would be using their own giant urns to hold boiling hot water from which they would make pots of tea fresh, as needed. Tea was a delicate thing, and one could not make an urn of tea and expect it to be palatable, not on the ladies of the Guild's watch, anyway! Coffee would also be available for confirmed tea haters, and the ladies themselves, most of them in their seventies or eighties, would be up on the wide wood porch manning the urns, teapots and serving tables while the nimbler women, like Jaymie, DeeDee and others would be doing the table-to-table serving.

In costume. *Ugh*, Jaymie thought. She had a black dress made a few years back for her first time serving at the Tea, and it was authentic in most details, sewn of "stuff," that ubiquitous scratchy cloth considered adequate for the serving class in Victorian England. Black didn't suit her, magically draining all the color from her pink cheeks and making her look like a superannuated spinster. In the historical romance novels she read, the servant girls (usually earls' daughters who felt compelled to escape evil guardians, or who wanted to earn their way with honest labor, rather than living in the luxury to which they had been born) always managed to look fetching and piquant in black maids' outfits and white lace mobcaps. But Jaymie knew she looked frumpy, especially when compared to Heidi, who would be decked out in a gown fit for a princess. And Joel would certainly be there if Heidi was. She sighed, resigned to her fate of looking like Heidi's dowdy older sister.

She returned to the kitchen, avoiding looking through to the summer porch, the spot where the poor unknown man had died in the night, and examined the Queen Elizabeth cake, with its coconut and brown sugar drizzle. It didn't look particularly inspiring, but hopefully it tasted better than it looked. Maybe there was a way to jazz it up, make it more appealing. She cocked her head and stared at it; cream cheese icing, maybe, instead of the coconut and brown sugar? There was no cake in the world that cream cheese icing couldn't improve. It wouldn't be authentic to the vintage recipe, but sometimes you just had to go for flavor.

She'd have to taste it later, after it cooled, to see if it was good enough to consider adding to the treats offered to the Tea with the Queen customers. As she stood brooding at the kitchen counter, Denver rubbed up against her ankle; she dished him out some kibble, then made a cup of Tetley (bought across the river in Canada) for herself and took it into the backyard with a cookbook, followed by Hoppy. Jaymie sat in an Adirondack chair in the shade of the maple and stared up the lawn at her tainted summer porch. Becca had questioned whether they should spend the night, but Jaymie figured, if they didn't, when would they come back?

What if the murderer was *never* discovered?

She shook off the heebie-jeebies and turned her mind back to the Tea with the Queen event. Tomorrow was the first day, and it just had to go well! The previous year's affair had been a bit of a disaster. It had been unseasonably hot, no one had wanted to drink tea and the cakes had gone gungy and dry, with colored icing melting off the tea cakes in the heat. One of the older Guild ladies had fainted, and 911 was called. An ambulance and paramedics don't make for an elegant tea atmosphere, they discovered. The woman recovered swiftly and was horribly embarrassed that she had spoiled the event, though no one among the heritage committee members even whispered such a thing.

This year would be better if the weather held. A light breeze fluttered through the leaves, and a robin sang his throaty love song, liquid and melodic. The day had already seemed endless; she was exhausted and fretful, but had no inclination to nap yet. Denver stretched out in a patch of slanting sunlight, while Hoppy intently sniffed one particular spot in the hedge of holly bushes.

"What is there that fascinates you about that spot?" Jaymie said to her dog, as she set aside the cookbook she had on her lap and got up to have a look. Hoppy bounced around her as she leaned over and peered into the holly. Denver also shook himself awake and strolled over to see what she was staring at.

It was a small, square pavé pin, with a checkerboard pattern of black and clear stones set in gold. She picked it up and turned it over. The pin would have had a "clutch"— the back of a tack pin, in jeweler's parlance—to hold it in place, and the absence or loss of that was what had caused it to drop in her hedge. Tangled on the teeth holding the stones in place was a white thread.

Who had lost it? And why in her garden? She had just planted the line of holly bushes in April, and the pin was perched on *top* of the soil, unaffected by the rain that had puddled the earth into mud just the weekend before. Had it been dropped by the murderer?

Jaymie shook her head and stuck it in her pocket. That was just ridiculous. How many murderers wandered around wearing diamond pavé pins? She should put up a notice at the store, because the pin looked really quite valuable. If someone claimed it, they would have to explain how it had gotten in her hedge.

She sat back down in her chair and picked up the cookbook. Was there anything else she could make to add to the treats at the tea? She leafed through, but shook her head. Nothing suited. She was only a beginning baker, and the bar was set high, because the baked goods on offer were extraordinarily good. Violet Nibley, Valetta's English sister-in-law, who lived across the river in Johnsonville, Ontario, was an amazing baker, and churned out dozens and dozens of scones, Eccles cakes, tea cakes, and the more mundane items folks seemed to expect, like muffins, cookies and cupcakes.

But lots of other ladies would be providing whatever items were their specialties. As a fan of history and a lover of the romance of past ages, Jaymie wanted to try to bring some sense of authenticity with her offerings, and had suggested clotted cream to go with the scones and jam for a proper cream tea, but real clotted cream was not available.

She had made some headway, though; Victoria sponge and a tricky-to-make but lovely-to-look-at Battenberg cake (when cut, the cake displayed a pink and yellow checkerboard effect) were both on the menu. That delicacy, the Battenberg, had reportedly been named for Queen Victoria's granddaughter's husband, Prince Louis of Battenberg. Over the winter she had researched the Queen's family history and knew far more than she would ever need to know.

Jaymie dreamed that, one day, the annual Queensville Tea with the Queen event would be famous worldwide, as celebrated as high tea at the Empress Hotel in Victoria, British Columbia. But she had to admit that some treats, while not traditional afternoon tea staples, were too good to leave out. Most Americans, especially, had never tasted an honest-to-goodness, runny, delicious Canadian butter tart, and that deficiency would be filled by Tansy's Tarts, Tansy Woodrow's bakery on Heartbreak Island. She donated dozens of the gooey, sweet, drippy treats, like a savvy drug dealer giving out freebies to hook customers. Once someone tried a Tansy butter or butter-pecan tart, there was no going back. Tourists would gladly pay the water taxi to ferry them over to the island so they could buy a dozen of the pricey diet-busters.

At last Jaymie returned inside, blocked the back door as well as she could until Bill fixed it, and made some calls. Then she locked the door to the summer porch and retreated to her bedroom. She stretched out on her comfy bed, Denver curled up at her feet and Hoppy took to his big pillow under her side table. She tried closing her eyes, but they popped open. She was alone in the house, and felt it, every creak and moan making her edgy. This wasn't going to work.

Was Becca right? Would they have to abandon their home for a while?

She got up, made the circuit around the house—which was still vacant of thieves or murderers—then returned to her room. Opening her window wider, she listened for a moment to the sound of a distant lawn mower. This was her house, her *home*, she thought, sitting on the edge of her bed. It was safe. The murderer, whoever it was, was probably long gone after the violence of the night. There was no way they would hang around Queensville just waiting to be discovered.

But what if it was a local, someone she knew intimately, someone who smiled at her every day, and said, "Good morning, Jaymie"? It just couldn't be. Queensville, her beloved little town, didn't grow murderers.

She lay back down and finally fell asleep. Weird dreams threaded through her slumber, of different houses, shadowy assailants, broken teacups, barking dogs, a meat grinder and a river of blood. Some time later she drifted up to awareness of the downward progress of shadows on her bedroom wall and the uneasy sense that night was approaching, like fog, on little cat feet. Or maybe that was Denver approaching on little cat feet, prowling along her body and sniffing at her mouth.

Startled awake, she pushed the cat away. Doors locked? Dog safe? Yes and yes, she thought. But she felt alone. Where was Becca? Alarm coursed through her and she bounced up to sit on the edge of the bed, shaking. "Becca?" she called, still groggy, her voice thick with unshed sleepiness.

But her sister didn't answer. When Jaymie swiftly descended to the kitchen, she found a note on the trestle table with some keys weighing it down: *Bill has fixed the back door; new keys. Motion detectors have to wait. I'm at DeeDee's for dinner. Come on over, Dee says! Want to stay there tonight? Becca*

No, she didn't want to stay anywhere but their home. And she had taken enough time away from real life. This was

Anna and Clive's first season as proprietors of the Shady Rest, and the initial run was this holiday weekend. They were fully booked, all three rooms taken for the Victoria Day weekend, and Jaymie was working for Anna, or was supposed to be. After that disastrous morning, who knew?

Hoppy was overjoyed to get outside, and not so happy to be called in after only his necessary jobs were done. But Jaymie had to get next door if she was going to help Anna prep for the next morning. She locked up and trotted toward her neighbor's home.

"I've come to help!" she said, when Anna let her in the front door.

"Have you had dinner yet?" the young woman asked.

"No, but I'll come back after you guys are done, if you're eating."

"Don't be silly," Anna said, grabbing Jaymie's arm and hauling her down the hall toward the back sliding doors off the kitchen. "Clive's got some jerk chicken on the grill, and we're celebrating the first full day of the season with some wine. Come on, eat with us. He made lots, and bought potato salad, too," Anna added, to forestall any objection. "Tabby's in bed, the guests are all out for dinner or whatever, and it's just us."

"I came to work, you know," Jaymie said, following Anna down the long shadowy central hall of the Shady Rest, through the bright, modern kitchen and out to the elevated deck in back.

"And you will, don't worry!"

"Jaymie!" Clive said, from his position near the grill. He waved his spatula in greeting, looking relaxed and handsome in dark shorts and a golf shirt that had his company's logo stitched on the pocket. He wore an apron over it all that said, "Grill or be Grilled." Chicken sizzled and spat, and he turned one leg quarter over, then pointed his tongs at the table under the awning. "Sit. Drink. You look like you need a glass of wine as much as I did."

"I lay down for a couple of hours' sleep this afternoon and woke up shaking," Jaymie admitted, as Anna pushed her to sit and filled an acrylic wine goblet with a fruity merlot.

"After what you went through? Poor pet," Anna said with a quick look over at Clive. "I'm freaked about a murderer in the neighborhood. Who could have done such a thing?"

"I've been thinking of nothing but that," Jaymie said. "And who was the poor guy who died?" She shivered, and resolved to call the police the next morning to see what they had found out.

The sun was descending as Clive and Anna served up dinner. They chatted, but came to no conclusions. Dinner had been cleared and they were just enjoying another glass of wine when the tone triggered by the front door sent Anna through the house. She came back a moment later with someone Jaymie recognized.

"Jaymie!" Brett Delgado said. "What a pleasure to see you again." He took her outthrust hand and held it between both of his own. "How are you? I heard about the awful events of last night."

"I'm better than I was." Jaymie gave him a small smile.

"Sit and have a glass of wine with us," Anna said, filling another acrylic wineglass and pulling out a chair.

Brett sat, and said, with a worried frown, "Anna, I forgot to take my cell phone with me when I went out; I should check it, I suppose, but I was wondering, has Ted phoned here at all?"

"Ted? Why would he phone here?" Anna asked.

The man shrugged in discomfort. "We had a quarrel this morning, and he took off."

"Took off? What do you mean?"

"Got in the rental car and took off. He's done it before. He's such a moody little brat sometimes," Brett said, gloomily swirling the wine in his glass.

"Where did he go?" Jaymie asked.

Brett shrugged.

"When was this? I wonder if he saw or heard anything that happened next door?"

"Oh, I don't think so. I think it was well before the trouble at your place," Brett said. "How are you dealing with that? Was it a burglary? Was anything taken?"

"No, nothing was taken. It seemed like a burglary interrupted by a murder."

He shuddered. "A murder, right next door! I heard the commotion, and then the cops showed up."

"Was Ted already gone?" she asked.

"Yes. Didn't I say that?"

The inevitable possibility occurred to her. "What does Ted look like?"

"The police asked me the same thing," Brett said. "Don't worry; your dead body is not my Ted."

She relaxed, relieved.

He took a sniff of the fruity wine, then wrinkled his nose and put the glass down. "I'd better go up and check the voice mail on my cell phone," he said, rising.

"What did you fight about?" Jaymie asked. She rarely pried, but it seemed odd that the guy had taken off so abruptly.

He shrugged, tapping his fingers on the tabletop. "Just . . . nothing, really. We fought for hours, though, actually, from the time I got in until . . . I don't know what time. I was afraid we'd kept others awake," he said, glancing over at Anna, who shook her head. "Anyway, he was angry over two things, that I stayed out so long when I said I'd be back in ten minutes, and that . . . that I still smoke. I told him I'd quit, but I still sneak out for a ciggie once in a while."

Jaymie said, "Any nonsmoker would smell it on you the minute you stepped back into the room, you know. I smelled it on your clothes last night."

"I just can't kick it. Anyway, you know how quarrels go. We started with that, but then everything else blew up, and we fought about it all. He's been so tense lately about the wedding. It's no big deal. I told him we could put it off if it was stressing him, but then he accused me of wanting to break up." Brett took in a long, shaky breath and looked away, squinting. "Maybe he's called my cell phone."

"What did you do after he left?" Jaymie asked.

He stared at her, his expression one of puzzlement. "I went to sleep. Why?"

"Just wondering."

He gave her an odd look, then said, "I'll retire for the night."

There was silence for a long moment after he left.

"Did you hear them fight?" Clive asked Anna.

"I heard *something*. Loud voices. But I wasn't sure who it was. Your friends, the Carters, got in about ten and went straight up, and you got here at what . . . two or three?"

He nodded. "I didn't want to wait," he said to Jaymie, "so I came directly from work; took the Blue Water instead of parking the car in Johnsonville and waiting for the morning ferry." The Blue Water was the bridge between Sarnia, Ontario, and Port Huron, Michigan. "I heard voices when I came in, but I lost track of that when I came to bed," he added, covering his wife's hand.

"I heard someone fighting," Anna said, "but I didn't know if the quarrel I heard was Jack and Elaine Carter or Brett and Ted. The Carters both told the police that they didn't hear anything, so I guess I should have figured it wasn't them."

"If it was over and Ted was gone before the murder, they didn't really fight 'all night long,'" Jaymie pointed out.

Clive shrugged. "Just an expression, I suppose."

"And you really couldn't tell who was fighting?" she asked Anna, who shook her head and shrugged.

"Sound is weird in this old house," Clive said. "It's hard to tell. And we were . . . a little distracted. We'll have to remember the sound issue if we fight. Or do anything else."

Anna blushed bright pink and touched her husband's hand.

"I'm just glad you heard the commotion at our place and came over," Jaymie said. She felt like a creaky third wheel and got up. "I'm going into the kitchen, Anna. I'll cut up the fruit for tomorrow morning's breakfast buffet and make the muffin batter. And I promise, I *will* be around tomorrow to help."

"But you have the tea to worry about tomorrow!" Anna said.

"Doesn't matter. A promise is a promise, and I'll have loads of time. The tea isn't until two in the afternoon. I hope you're going to bring Tabby?"

"I am. She's looking forward to it; I bought her a new dress and promised her we're going to play tea party with lots of people. We've been practicing."

❅ Seven ❅

JAYMIE RETIRED EARLY and avoided thinking about
the dead man on her summer porch by reading herself to
sleep with an old Mary Balogh, but the historical romance spell
only lasted awhile. She awoke when she heard Becca come in
a half hour later, and went out in the hall to talk to her. Becca
had waited awhile at Dee's to see if Jaymie was coming over,
but then returned home, worried about her little sister.

"I just can't abandon our home," Jaymie said edgily, hugging herself and shivering in the dim hall light.

Becca went to her and hugged her close. "I'm in the room
right next to you. If you have trouble sleeping, come on in.
We can huddle together like we did when you were little
and had nightmares, remember?"

Jaymie, in her sister's embrace, inhaled the familiar scent
of Becca, who only ever used baby powder. When she was
three or four, Jaymie had gone through a bout of sleepless-
ness, and sometimes crawled into bed with Becca, who was
in her late teens and seemed almost like a second mother.

"You told me weird stories, I remember, with fairy princesses named Rebecca and Jaymie who ruled the world and ate homemade fudge every day!"

"I wanted you to be happy. That was while Mom and Dad were going through a rough patch, and I knew you heard them fighting. But if I could get you giggling, I felt so great, like I'd accomplished something."

"You did," Jaymie said softly. "You got me through it."

"And they stayed married," Becca said.

It would be okay, Jaymie suddenly felt. Everything would be all right. They'd hang tight and get through it together. "Good night, Becca," she said, hugging her sister hard. "You are the best sister in the world. See you in the morning."

When she returned to her own room, she glanced over to her dresser. Darn it! She had meant to show Becca the pavé pin and ask if she'd lost it, but it would have to wait until the next day now. She tossed and turned for the rest of the night, getting up to test the doors half a dozen times, followed by an anxious Hoppy, whose little lion heart would not let her go into danger, real or imagined, alone.

Finally she rose at six and her day got off to a running start. Becca was still sleeping when she left the house, so she left her a note, promising to meet up with her later. They had survived their first night in the house, and the next would be better.

First, Jaymie helped Anna with breakfast for her B&B guests, and did up the dishes for her. Though she was a competent woman and a great mom to Tabby, Anna was surprisingly tentative about her chosen business. Should she serve all kinds of fruit, she had asked Jaymie, or only what was in season? The notion of what eggs to serve had given Anna nightmares for three weeks; should they be ordered as the guest liked, or available on a hot plate, served only one way? Multigrain, morning glory, or muesli muffins? Why Anna had wanted to run a B&B if she couldn't decide on even the breakfast was a mystery.

Jaymie had tried, for the three months leading up to the Shady Rest's grand opening, to help Anna, to the point that it seemed that most of the final decisions about the *breakfast* part of *B&B* were Jaymie's, even down to the china pattern for the dishes that Anna ultimately chose and sourced through Becca, a lovely robin's egg blue chintz pattern that echoed the wallpaper in the entryway. As much as Jaymie liked Anna and Clive, she was going to have to put limits on the amount she helped, since it was just beginning to occur to her that Anna would take as much help as Jaymie would give, and always need more.

Jaymie then returned home to find that Becca had left a note: *Gone to help Dee and the others move boxes of china and coffee urns to Stowe House—come as soon as you can. We need all the help we can get!*

She had to get moving, but first things first. She called the police department and was put on hold, shunted through various departments until she finally got Detective Christian's voice mail and left a message. He called right back, just as she was making something to eat.

"What can I do for you, Ms. Leighton?"

"Any news?" she asked, trying to keep her tone light. She got some eggs out of the fridge and cracked a couple in a bowl. "An arrest?"

"Not yet. We're working on it."

"Do you know who the dead guy is?"

"It takes time to run his prints through the database."

"I notice you dusted the Hoosier."

"The big cabinet? Yes, the victim's prints were on it, but they were on every box and some of the other things, too."

"What about the grinder?"

"No comment."

"No hint as to what the victim was looking for?"

"I'm afraid not, Ms. Leighton."

He sounded distracted, and she knew he wanted to go and do his work, but she had one more question. "I've been thinking," she said, "and I'm wondering if the guy who died broke into our house by mistake. The house on the other side of ours, the Watsons' home, is empty right now. They won't be up from Florida for a few weeks."

"We'll look into it. Is that it, Ms. Leighton?"

"I won't keep you. You must be busy," she said.

"We had an unusually active night last night," he said. "Lots of calls about prowlers."

"I suppose folks are nervous about the murder. I sure am. So, you still don't know who the dead guy is, and don't have any leads on the murderer."

"We're working on it. You can call or drop in at the station anytime, and we'll let you know what we can." He paused, then said, "Is everything all right there? We had an officer stationed outside your house last night."

She sighed. "It would have helped a lot if I'd known for sure you were going to do that," she said.

"My apologies. An officer will be there again tonight, just so you know, but I doubt we'll be able to keep someone there indefinitely; limited manpower. You understand. Is there anything else?"

In other words, let him get back to work. "No, nothing else."

After she hung up, she thought of the diamond pavé pin she'd found in the holly bushes, but that didn't seem like the kind of detail the detective was looking for. She shrugged, and made some scrambled eggs. After a quick brunch, gulped in mouthfuls while she changed into her dreadful maid's outfit, it was time to get to Daniel's house to help set up. Jaymie patted the last hairpin in place, finishing her transformation into nineteenth-century servant, and glared at herself in the cheval mirror in the spare room, where her Victorian maid's uniform was kept, and where she changed into it.

There was no getting around it; she looked awful! Black was most definitely not her color, and her gold-flecked brown

hair—a bit unruly at times but her most attractive feature—
was pulled up away from her too-round face into a matronly
bun with a lace cap pinned over it. Blush and lipstick would
have helped, but she was determined to be as authentic as
possible. Many of the other servers—all would be wearing
maid's outfits—didn't bother with historical accuracy, but
it didn't feel right to Jaymie to go all out and then not finish
with the details. So she would just have to suck it up, she
thought, taking a deep breath and nodding to her disgruntled
reflection.

She had to walk through the village in her outfit, since
Stowe House was just a few blocks away. It was a glorious
May day, though, the liquid song of robins and orioles flut-
ing through the air as the birds flitted back and forth in the
maples and poplars above her, their songs contrasted by the
discordant screech of blue jays. Chipmunks darted in and
out of the shrubberies, cheeks full of sunflower seeds from
the bird feeders.

She focused on all these things as she strolled past Queen
Anne–style brick homes bounded by picket fences that
enclosed burgeoning gardens, and smaller cottages surrounded by split-rail enclosures. More modern homes were
confined to the perimeter of the village, away from the town
center. The swish of her long skirts around her ankles took
her back; she wondered about life in her riverside village in
the eighteen hundreds.

The name *Queensville* was chosen for the former hamlet
of Stoweville in 1864 in honor of Queen Victoria and fifty
years of peace between Canada and the United States. Canada was moving toward its own celebration of national independence by then; since Confederation, the two towns
celebrated each other's national days with a joint week of
festivities. At first it was all about the villagers of the two
towns, but now it launched the summer tourist trade.

Heartbreak Island, split between the two friendly (most
of the time) nations, was used as the launching point for

fireworks displays. Detroit had the sponsorship to put a barge in the middle of their own river for fireworks, but Queensville had to make do with the island.

Jaymie would have to get out there soon to make sure Rose Tree Cottage was fitted up for the first summer guests, who arrived for their annual visit in mid-June. The rental and maintenance of the Leighton family cottage was her responsibility. With her various other part-time jobs, it gave her a sparse income that would hopefully be supplemented by income from her cookbook-to-be. There were seven regular guests over the summer, staying a week or two each; they all liked the island's isolation, and yet also its proximity to Lake Huron beaches; Stratford, Ontario's Shakespeare festival; Detroit's shopping and the annual Queensville/ Johnsonville regatta and race in the St. Clair River.

She rounded the corner of MacDonald and Maple and noted that Stowe House was already abuzz with activity, even an hour before the two p.m. start of the Queen's Tea. Jaymie stood for a moment on the road, watching before diving in to help. Stowe House was a Queen Anne mansion built by Queensville's most prominent citizen, Lazarus Stowe, in 1882 to replace a more modest house since torn down. It was typical Queen Anne, with multiple cupolas, a sweeping porch with a large rounded section to the left front and a widow's walk up at the peak of the turreted section.

The lawns were broad swaths of emerald grass bounded by hardy China rose hedges and wrought-iron spike-topped fencing. Mrs. Bellwood's fear that Daniel Collins would ruin the property with newfangled notions like central air had not come to fruition, and in fact he was likely a more sympathetic owner than anyone else, other than the Heritage Society, would have been. Even the Heritage Society would have had to do things like put in a modern fire-alarm system, install exit signs and make lots of other modifications, if the home was to be used as a public facility. Strange for a microcomputer millionaire, but Daniel Collins seemed to have a genuine appreciation for history and had saved Stowe House from its inevitable fate, being cut up into offices or apartments.

Why had he bought the house in the first place? Jaymie realized she had never even thought to ask him.

An assortment of round and square tables dotted the lawn, and up on the porch, in the shade, were the tables that held the coffee urns, kettles, teapots and trays of goodies. In accordance with health regulations, a couple of small refrigerators had been pressed into service to hold the milk and cream, so gaudy orange outdoor extension cords snaked along the porch and into an open window.

Jaymie took in a deep breath—"girding her loins" as Grandma Leighton called it—and entered the property through the open wrought-iron gate and proceeded up the stone walkway. Several others were dressed as she was, in the black stuff maid's outfits, but the ladies of the heritage guild, in deference to their age and fragility, sat up on the porch in the shade. They wore their usual Sunday church dresses and hats and presided in august splendor. One of the elderly husbands was just setting up a card table at the gate and fanning out glossy full-color pamphlets explaining the Tea with the Queen. Folks would be directed to pay up on the porch and get their tea tickets, and from there they would be guided to a table by the "servants."

"Jaymie!" Becca called, striding across the grass toward her, carrying a box, face flushed and in full panic mode. She paused, directed Daniel Collins in the placement of what looked like the last table on the lawn, then continued on to Jaymie, plunking a big cardboard box labeled "Linens" at her feet. "We need to get these tables dressed. We only have a half hour or so to go before the first guests arrive, and you're the only one of these women I trust to do it right!"

Daniel glanced toward her, waved, but then continued working to level the table with a chunk of brick under one leg. Jaymie got busy laying tablecloths and setting out the dreadful polyester faux-damask napkins. Some tables would fit six, some only four, and one long one, suitable for twelve, was for strays and the truly sociable. Before long guests started arriving, and then it was time for the grand entrance of the Queen and her retinue. Jaymie and the rest of the "servants" formed a respectful line near the gate.

The Queensville Heritage Society must have decided at one of the meetings Jaymie had missed to have Mrs. Bellwood arrive at the tea in grand style, by carriage, even in good weather. Perhaps it was in deference to her age, and the fact that she wore a thirty-pound black bombazine gown underpinned by a tight corset, and topped her ensemble with five pounds of jet jewelry. The Mackenzie Auctions open landau and team of black carriage horses had been pressed into use. Mrs. Bellwood (Her Majesty, Queen Victoria), Trip Findley (His Royal Highness Albert, Prince Consort), and Heidi (Princess Beatrice) were comfortably resplendent. It was a wonderful sight, despite MACKENZIE FAMILY AUCTIONS emblazoned in gold lettering on the side of the shiny black coach.

The tourists were eating it up, Jaymie noted, glancing around at the number of Canadian tourists, American visitors and dozens of locals standing opposite the "servants," near the wrought-iron fence, snapping the scene with digital cameras and disposables. Weather was always a concern at the Queen's Tea; May was fickle . . . it could be balmy, sultry or even frigid. It could rain, snow, hail, or the humidity could be so high—like it had been the previous year—that folks would be rushing to put in air conditioners and open pools. But this day was perfect: cerulean sky, white puffy clouds, a light breeze and nodding gardens full of perennials and even some early roses.

The queen and her husband and daughter—Jaymie had to admit that Heidi looked lovely and regal in an ivory off-the-shoulder gown adorned with silk roses, meant to resemble, perhaps, Princess Beatrice's wedding gown—took their places at the center table and were served by DeeDee, in her modified Victorian maid's outfit. Jaymie got busy. For a while, all she could think of was pouring and bussing and carrying trays of goodies, directing people to pay at the table on the veranda, and smiling at people's cracks about her outfit. Sticky-handed children, cranky elderly folk, and the odd dissatisfied customer contrasted sharply with most guests, who were polite and complimentary.

But eventually things calmed down and she got to serve a few of the locals: Valetta Nibley, her brother, Brock, and Anna, Clive and Tabitha Jones among them. Of course the murder victim was a hot topic.

"I figure that to know who the murderer is, we first have to know who the dead guy is," Jaymie said.

"So, who is he?" Valetta asked, her gaze steady on Jaymie's face.

"That's the problem. I have no clue," Jaymie said.

"You saw him, though," Brock said, his beady stare boring into her.

"I did," she said, pleating the tablecloth between her fingers, trying to erase the bloody image from her mind. "He was . . . I don't know, maybe mid-thirties, nicely dressed, sandy brown hair." She shuddered at the memory of the blood clotting his thick thatch of hair.

"How was he killed?" Brock asked.

"Don't remind her of that," Valetta said, giving her brother a dig in the ribs.

"You started it," he retorted.

"No, it's okay," Jaymie said. "He was hit over the head with . . . with something," she said, unwilling to go into her supposition that the weapon was her vintage grinder. "I've been racking my brain since yesterday trying to figure it all out. I just checked, and the police don't know who he is yet."

"That means his fingerprints aren't on file," Valetta said. "So he's not a federal employee, and he's never been in the military."

"They took all of our fingerprints—mine, Clive's and Becca's—I guess to eliminate them from the ones they lifted from the summer porch," Jaymie said. "But neither the dead guy nor whoever killed him made it into the house. Who's missing in town? Guess that would be a good place to start."

Anna, at the next table, leaned over and said, "Well, Ted Abernathy, our guest."

"One of the gay guys staying at the Shady Rest?" Brock Nibley asked, from his seat to the left of his sister.

Anna blushed crimson and glanced over at Tabby, who, in her pretty dress and last-minute addition—fairy wings—was wholly entranced with pouring imaginary tea down her doll's throat. Clive put one dark hand over his wife's, and said, "Yes, Mr. Abernathy is one of our guests, Brett Delgado's life partner," he affirmed. "But Brett and he had a disagreement, and Mr. Abernathy left in a huff. No mystery; just a lovers' quarrel."

"So the guy says! Maybe he killed his lover." Brock had a dim view of anyone outside of his immediate circle of acquaintances, so an "outsider" was immediately suspect.

"I don't think so," Clive said. "Besides, the deceased is about five foot ten or so. I saw him too, remember. Mr. Abernathy is, from my understanding, a good four or five inches taller and somewhat older, with lighter hair, graying at the temples."

"We've checked with the other B&B owners in town; no one else is missing anyone," Anna said.

"Daniel Collins' friend, Trevor Standish, hasn't shown up when he said he would," Jaymie chimed in. "But he texted Daniel to tell him he'd be late, so I guess you can't count him missing."

"Why are we even thinking the dead guy is someone local or staying in town?" Valetta asked, glancing around. "He's probably some stranger passing through."

"But how did he get here, then?" Jaymie asked, tucking a loose lock of hair behind her ear.

"There aren't any strange cars in town," Clive said, "and no one was noticed hitching anywhere near, or so I heard from one of the officers on the case."

"Someone could have come over from the island or from Canada on the ferry, though," Jaymie said, as it occurred to her. She shifted from foot to foot. The black shoes she was wearing were beginning to hurt her feet on the uneven lawn.

Valetta nodded. "It's too easy to walk on the ferry in Canada and walk off here, and just not go back."

Brock said, "That's how all the illegals get here!"

They ignored him. Brock got that reaction a lot. He was the voice of truth, Jaymie had heard him say once, only people don't like to hear the truth. She privately thought he was the voice of idiocy, but out of respect for Valetta, she kept her mouth shut.

DeeDee, who was passing with a tray full of dirty teacups, paused. "You all talking about the mur . . . uh, the unfortunate occurrence?" she asked, modifying her wording as she caught sight of Tabitha. She leaned in toward them and continued, "Lyle says one of his guests hasn't checked in for a few days, but the guy has been staying at the inn for weeks and sometimes goes off on jaunts to the city and over to Canada."

"What's his name?" Jaymie asked.

"McIntosh. Somebody-or-other McIntosh . . . a strange first name. He hasn't been around a lot, Lyle says."

Jaymie stopped and thought, then said, "McIntosh . . . Why does that name sound familiar?" She shook her head; it would come to her. "Dee, maybe that's him. Have the cops been around to ask about guests at the Inn yet?"

"Lyle wasn't in when they came 'round. He's supposed to go to the police station to check out the photos, see if he recognizes anyone. Do you think it could be that guy?"

"It wouldn't hurt to check."

"I'll call Lyle as soon as I get home today." DeeDee bustled off with her tray.

"Well, until we figure out who the man is," Jaymie said, with a sigh, "I don't suppose they'll be able to figure out who killed him, or why."

"But why was he breaking into your house?" Anna asked.

"Hey, are you the girl with the murder? I heard about you!" a passing fellow said, stopping and staring at Jaymie, pointing one long finger at her. "You're the gal Dannyboy is hooked on."

❈ Eight ❈

SILENCE FELL AMONG her group of friends, and Jaymie found herself the object of the stranger's regard. Color rose in her cheeks. Darn, she wished she'd stop blushing like a romance novel heroine!

"Dannyboy . . . who is Dannyboy?" Becca chose that moment to happen along and joined the knot of conversationalists.

"And you are . . . ?" Jaymie did her best "Mrs. Bellwood as Queen Victoria" impression, freezing the fellow with a cold look.

"I'm Zell McIntosh. Dan Collins' buddy, from Ball State in Indiana?" He was tall and lanky, dressed in striped trousers and a cutaway coat, kind of faux-Victorian garb. He had a black-and-white checked tie that flopped around in the breeze. It could have benefited from a tiepin.

"McIntosh? DeeDee was just saying there's been some guy with that last name staying for the last while at the

Queensville Inn," Jaymie said, as Becca and Valetta whispered together behind her, and Anna and Clive looked on. "Is that you?" But no, she had heard his name before, and it suddenly dawned on her who he was, just as he spoke.

"I just got here yesterday morning."

"Yesterday morning?" This must be the fellow Trip Findley saw sleeping in his car outside Stowe House at five a.m.

"Yeah, I'm staying here," he said, waving toward Stowe House, "with my old frat buddy, Danny. Our other pal, Trev Standish, is coming, too, but he's been held up." He shoved his hands in his pockets and rocked back on his heels.

"I know about that. Is that usual with your friend, Trevor? Him not showing up when he says he's going to?"

"Sure is," Zell said. "He always has some half-baked get-rich-quick scheme that needs attending to. When he called me to arrange this week, I agreed. Figured there's probably some catch. He likely wants to sell us insurance, or a time-share condo, or something, but I figured, hey, I'd hook up with our rich buddy, Danny, and stay on his dime for a while. Y'know?"

He moved closer and put his arm over her shoulders, drawing her away from the tables. "Sooo, my buddy says you bought some kinda old cupboard. He called it a Hoosier. I'm a Hoosier by association, you know? Going to Ball State and all? Maybe you want to take me home, too?"

She ducked out from under his arm, and said, "I don't think so."

Becca, standing by Valetta, was watching, her eyebrows high in surprise at the sight of her sister being hit on.

"Aw, c'mon," he said, smiling down at her. "I'll hold your dishes, and anything else you want me to hold."

"Excuse me, I have to get back to work," she said.

He was still watching her with a baffled expression on his face as she went back to serving.

"Who is that?" Becca asked, following her little sister.

Jaymie paused in her task of clearing an empty table, and explained. "What kind of guy acts like that?" she asked. "He says Daniel likes me, then tries to pick me up himself."

Becca shrugged. "Some guys are competitive with their friends when it comes to women."

"Yeah, well I find it creepy. And he compared himself to my Hoosier!" She shuddered. "My Hoosier would be a more entertaining date, I think."

ANOTHER HOUR TO go. Jaymie's feet were killing her, so she took a break, sitting on a stool in the shade of the sweeping bridal wreath spirea that edged the veranda. Watching life from a safe distance was fascinating, she had always found. Trip Findley, the septuagenarian Albert, Prince Consort, was circulating among the tables and chatting to any and all who would listen. He liked to tell tales about Queensville's storied past, but alternated them with tidbits from his character's life. At the main table—the "Queen's" table—Zell McIntosh had moved in on Heidi, pulling up a folding chair to sit by her, chatting animatedly while Mrs. Bellwood, in full, frosty, Queen Victoria "we are not amused" mode, glared at his back. Heidi, unlike Jaymie, seemed to be enjoying the conversation with Zell; she tossed her clustered ringlets back and smiled up at him, laughing at his jests and touching his arm.

Even with Zell fawning all over her, no amount of attention seemed enough for the girl. When Daniel passed by, Heidi tried to draw him in, too, touching his arm and tugging at his shirt, but he just smiled and wandered off. Jaymie bit her lip and watched, trying to figure the girl out. She knew a fair bit about her, having become slightly obsessed over the long winter with finding out all she could, after Joel had bolted straight out of Jaymie's home into Heidi's slender arms.

Heidi appeared to be independently wealthy and had

bought her modern rambler-style home on a quiet street in Queensville as an outright, cash purchase. Her family, went local gossip, had made their millions in real estate, and Heidi was said to own a midtown Manhattan block, as well as some frontage on Chicago's pricey Lake Shore Drive. She spent a portion of her time in New York, presumably with family. No one was quite sure why she had come to Queensville, except for the interesting morsel of gossip that her grandfather, Homer Lockland, had once owned Lockland Hardware on Riverfront Drive, now an Ace Hardware store. Homer had ambition, though, that far outstripped a little town in Michigan and had left after some scandal, making his millions in New York. He never returned to his family's roots.

Sometime during the previous autumn, blonde, beautiful Heidi Lockland drove into Queensville in a baby blue Porsche Boxster, saw a house for sale and bought it on a whim, and just as whimsically stole Joel away from Jaymie. Well, okay, so that was hardly fair, Jaymie gloomily thought, since she didn't know the woman's motivations.

But why did Jaymie always have to be so fair anyway? What had it ever gotten her? Sighing deeply, she rested her elbow on her knee and her chin in her hand and watched the pageant of Heidi's indubitable charm that even nineteenth-century accoutrements could not conceal. With all she had, why did Heidi seem so darned needy?

Valetta Nibley and her brother had gotten up to leave, and she spotted Jaymie sitting alone. She came over and put one sympathetic hand on her shoulder, then looked over at Heidi. "He's not worth you worrying about, kiddo," she said.

"What?"

"Joel. If *that's* the kind of girl he likes," Valetta said, with a contemptuous sniff, "well, she can't hold a patch on you! You should forget him and start dating. Everyone is getting real worried about you, you know." She squeezed Jaymie's shoulder and released, then stalked down the walk toward her brother.

Jaymie felt an unpleasant queasiness in her stomach. It was true, what Becca had said; everyone in town was watching her eat her heart out over Joel, pitying her, blaming Heidi. Jaymie knew there was one thing she did not want in life, and that was to be the object of pity. She rose and strode toward the main table. When she approached Heidi, she could feel the anxious glances of those who knew her best: DeeDee, Becca, even Trip Findley and Mrs. Bellwood.

"That is an absolutely lovely dress, Heidi . . . I mean, Princess Beatrice."

Zell looked put out at being interrupted, but Heidi jumped to her feet and twirled. "Isn't it just beautiful? It cost a fortune, but what's money for if not to splash it around?"

Jaymie smiled, sure the expression would look pasted on, but intent on doing this for those who were afraid to mention Heidi Lockland when she was around. It was ridiculous; she was a grown woman of thirty-two, not a teenager mooning over the cute boy in school. But if all of Queensville was to accept Heidi and move on, the change had to come from her. "It was worth whatever you paid," she said, leaning over the table and examining the silk roses more closely. The costumer had done a breathtaking job. "Beautiful!"

Zell stood up and draped one arm casually over Heidi's shoulders, watching Jaymie with a sly smile on his face.

"Zell was just saying, we should come over and have a look at your new Hoosier cabinet. Have you got it in place yet?" Heidi asked brightly. "Have you had a chance to take it apart and clean it up?"

"Uh, not really," Jaymie replied. "If you want to see it, I'd rather you wait until I clean it up and put it in the kitchen."

"Okay," Heidi said, just as Zell asked, "It's not in your kitchen yet?"

Jaymie shook her head.

"We *should* get together," Heidi said. "I could give you

some great tips on how to make your hair look better, even in that bun."

Jaymie laughed. "Maybe sometime. It would take a miracle worker, but maybe."

"Now, there you go," Heidi said, hands on her hips. "Joel said you'd get offended if I ever said anything about your hair, but you're not the slightest bit standoffish!"

Joel approached, arriving late to the tea party. He flicked a look in Zell's direction, then said, "Heidi, I didn't say she was standoffish!"

Zell tactfully withdrew his arm from Heidi's slim shoulders.

"I . . . I didn't mean you *said* that, I meant . . ." Heidi trailed off and colored a vivid pink, which only made her look prettier.

"She didn't say you said I was standoffish, Joel," Jaymie commented. "Stop being such a pill." Joel had done the same thing with her, criticizing everything she said in public, constantly correcting her and undermining her confidence. It was an unpleasant aspect of his character, but good to remember; she had been mooning for so long about his perfections, she had forgotten the things about him that drove her nuts. "Tell him to calm down when he gets like that," she said to Heidi. "I'd better get back to work. We can't all be princesses, you know. Some of us have to be servants!"

As she turned away, she heard a gasp from someone nearby and realized how that would sound—snarky, petty and cutting, when she had been going for jaunty and humorous—but it was too late to try to amend it, so she just shrugged and walked away. One interaction would not shift public opinion about how hurt poor little Jaymie was. She would just have to grit her teeth, smile and *keep* smiling until everyone forgot about it.

Finally the day wound down. Jaymie found a moment and wandered over to talk to Trip Findley, who, in his Prince

Albert splendor (including a fake mustache, which he twirled quite dashingly) was seated near the wrought-iron fence chomping on his unlit pipe. She observed the pleasantries—yes, it was a lovely day, good turnout, they'd make money for the Heritage fund—then got down to business. "Mr. Findley, the night before last, did you hear anything of the commotion at my place?"

His home backed on the same lane as hers did, only from the other side. His back garden was across the lane from hers, but shielded by a high wooden fence.

He nodded, though. "I did, indeedy. Dogs barking, screams, the whole bit."

"And did you see anything?"

He stared at the sky and chewed his pipe stem, wiggling his fake mustache. "Not a blessed thing. I looked out—my motion detector light had gone on, y'know, but it goes on even if a raccoon wanders through my yard—and still heard the dogs barking. But I didn't see anything. Then the ambulance and police came whizzing down the lane."

"Oh. Okay." She felt let down, but if he had seen anything, he would have told the police, she supposed.

The last customers departed just in time to catch the ferry across to Canada. Jaymie joined DeeDee and Becca, who sat with their feet up on a small PVC table in the shade of the spirea. DeeDee hastily stabbed out a cigarette in the dirt at her feet.

"Dee, stop worrying about getting caught. I know you still smoke!" Jaymie said.

"Only to drive Johnny crazy," she said about her husband, with a wink, as she picked up the butt and stowed it in her flip-top pack. "I just can't seem to give up my three cigarettes a day."

"You guys look tired," Jaymie said, awkwardly sinking down, pushing her small bustle aside, to take a shady spot on the grass nearby.

"I'm bushed," Becca said. She closed her eyes and yawned.

Jaymie watched her sister for a moment, then turned to DeeDee. "I think it's going well," she said. "The tea, I mean."

"Real well," she agreed. "Even you telling Heidi Lockland off didn't take away from it."

"I didn't mean it how it sounded; you ought to know that."

"That sly dig about being a princess?" Becca said, watching her younger sister with concern in her eyes.

Jaymie was about to protest, but stopped and frowned. Yes, she was still a little peeved about Heidi's star turn as Princess Beatrice. If she was to be completely honest with herself, as painful as that could be, the girl's perkiness irritated her, even as she tried to overcome her distaste. "It just popped out," she said, wearily. "I wouldn't change places with Heidi, though; not for anything. Joel can be a bit of a jerk sometimes. He constantly criticized what I said and how I acted in public. He said I was too outgoing sometimes and needed to pull back."

DeeDee nodded. "There you go. Joel's all right, but he is not the be all and end all of men."

Becca put one hand to her back and stretched. "I am going to stow the cups and saucers in the shed after they're washed, then I'm going home to nap. You coming, Jaymie?"

"In a while. By the way, I spoke to the detective this morning, and he said they'll have an officer outside our house for at least another night."

"Good. I heard you up and down all night," Becca said, with a tired smile. "I guess I didn't sleep so well either. Maybe we'll both sleep better knowing there's an officer in the lane."

"I have to take some treats to Mother Stubbs," DeeDee said with a grimace. She rolled her shoulders and lumbered to her feet with a groan. "All I want to do is go home and get into some shorts and sit in the shade with my new Danielle Steele, but Mother naps after dinner, so I'd better go right now with some of the cake and a Tansy tart."

Jaymie leaped to her feet. "Look, Dee, you should go home and put your feet up. Why don't you let me take the stuff?"

"Would you?" the woman asked.

"Sure. I'll leave a note for Lyle, too, to check and see if his missing guest is our dead man. The police aren't going to be able to solve the murder until they know who the victim is." She was anxious to give the police all the information they needed to figure out who the dead guy was and who'd killed him. They parted company, and Jaymie popped a variety of treats, including some of her own Queen Elizabeth cake, into a plastic tub. She said her good-byes to the cleanup committee, and Daniel Collins in particular, and headed through the village.

The identity of the murdered man was nagging at her. He must have family somewhere, friends, relations, people who were worried because they hadn't heard from him. Even if he had been trying to rob her, he was dead now. If they could just learn who he was, that would help figure out why he had been in her home, and why someone had wanted him dead. She shivered, but strode on through the sunshine toward the Inn.

The Queensville Inn had started life as another of the town's Queen Anne houses, but had been expanded into an inn, with a long, modern, two-story addition that ran along Philmore Avenue. Lyle Stubbs, the current owner, had bought it seven years before when he'd retired from life in Detroit as a broker and financial advisor. Local pundits joked that he went from making money hand over fist to throwing it away in the same fashion. Running an inn in a Michigan village was no way to get rich, but the proximity to lots of amenities meant that he at least broke even most years.

Jaymie knew the Inn well, since she had worked there summers when she was in high school, but Lyle had changed it a lot. She went in the front door and approached the desk, which fronted the office; Lyle's new lady friend, Edith, a fifty-something hairdresser from Ohio who he had met on the Internet, came out of the office and up to the desk.

"Now don't you just look as cute as a button!" she said, cocking her head sideways. "That outfit is very neat!"

Jaymie grimaced, then caught herself. It was time to stop being so self-effacing. If people wanted to compliment her, she'd have to learn how to take it graciously for a change. "Thanks, Edith. I just came from the tea with some treats for Mrs. Stubbs. Is she awake?"

"Aw, that's so nice of you! Sure, go on back," the woman said, with a friendly smile. "You know the way? Past our place?"

"I do." She went down the hall to the left of the office and looked around. It had been a while since she'd been there, but at least the hallways had not changed, beyond being repainted to a more neutral tan from the ironically water-stained aqua they had been. Maybe she should have gotten the room number, though, because she was starting to wonder if she knew which room was Mrs. Stubbs's.

Ah, but there was the manager/owner's suite, and just beyond that was Mrs. Stubbs's room, number 107. She tapped lightly on the door and heard a faint "Come in."

"Mrs. Stubbs?" She pushed open the door and entered.

The woman sat in a motorized wheelchair in the sunny window on the far side of the room. She had a large-print murder mystery on her lap; as Jaymie approached she could see that it was an Agatha Raisin mystery by M. C. Beaton.

"Hello, Mrs. Stubbs. Do you remember me?"

The woman squinted through her bifocals and furrowed her brow. "Even in that awful outfit I know you. You're Alan and Joy's youngest girl. Don't look a bit like either of them."

Mrs. Stubbs, she knew, was over ninety, and had a

devoted servant in her oldest son, Lyle. Some whispered that was why he had never been able to sustain a long relationship: "Mother" demanded all his time. Years ago people had called her rude and overbearing, but now that she was so old, folks called her feisty and strong-willed. "How are you doing?" Jaymie perched unbidden on the edge of the nearby hospital-type bed to bring herself down to eye level for the woman.

"Well as can be expected. No one comes near me anymore. Might as well be dead, I suppose, the way folks forget I'm even here."

"But the church ladies visit, and the Reverend Gillis, and the Heritage Society ladies, and—"

"I don't need a list," she said sharply. "Maybe it just seems like no one," she admitted, staring out the window. "Used to be, if I wanted to see someone I could just go, walk anywhere. Went along to the farm market, or to see friends. I went over on the ferry to Johnsonville every week. Haven't been over there in two years."

Jaymie glimpsed a yawning cavern of loneliness in the old woman that touched her heart. And yet Mrs. Stubbs had created some of it herself. DeeDee confessed that she spent as little time with her mother-in-law as she had to because of the woman's constant criticism. She was outspoken and hurt people's feelings sometimes with her bluntness. But Jaymie couldn't help but feel for the once-independent woman now reduced to dependence on the goodwill of relatives, neighbors and those paid to help her bathe, dress, eat and sleep. "Have you asked if anyone can accompany you over to Johnsonville? The ferry ought to be able to accommodate a motorized wheelchair."

"I ask enough of Lyle, and he's the only one who would do it."

Jaymie didn't reply but was determined to either help the woman go over to Johnsonville one day or find someone else who wouldn't mind doing it. Mrs. Stubbs had been a faithful congregant of the Queensville Methodist Church, and surely the church ladies would help. Or Trip Findley; he was every lady's choice escort in the village both for his charming manners and his sprightly goodwill.

"How is your grandmother doing?" Mrs. Stubbs asked.

"She's good. I was there just a couple of weeks ago, and we went out to lunch and shopping. She's using a cane these days, but still not doing too badly."

"Well, she's just a youngster. I remember looking after her and her younger brother when she was little Lucy Armitage, in braids. Mischievous little imp."

Jaymie smiled, saving that tidbit to tease her grandma with. A mischievous imp in braids! Mrs. Stubbs was not that much older than her grandmother, but when you're in your teens any age difference seems vast. Time had flowed on, but not Mrs. Stubbs's perception of little Lucy Armitage, she guessed. "We knew you had never missed the Queen's Tea before," she said, presenting the plastic container. "We can't make up for that, but DeeDee sent me over with some of the treats we're serving this year."

The book slid, forgotten, from the old woman's lap as she reached for the treats. She awkwardly pulled the lid off with gnarled, arthritic fingers and surveyed the contents. "One of Tansy Woodrow's tarts," she sighed in happiness. "That child can bake! Always could. And some Battenberg . . . looks a little dry. And what's this?" she asked, poking one knobby finger at a slice of cake.

"That's my own rendition of Queen Elizabeth cake, Mrs. Stubbs," Jaymie said, picking the book up off the plush maroon carpet and putting it on the nightstand. "I'd be interested in your opinion. I found the recipe in an old cookbook, but I'm not sure it turned out right."

The woman broke off a piece, popped it in her mouth and chewed thoughtfully. She nodded. "About right, young lady. A little dry; let the dates soften longer next time. But not bad. Takes me back. Your grandmother must be proud of you! Most girls your age are too busy bed-hopping and taking drugs to cook!"

Jaymie bit her lip to keep from laughing. "Actually, cooking and home arts are making a comeback. Most of us—people my age—just want a good life, and some of that includes remembering the best things about the past." It sounded a little stilted, but it was true.

At Mrs. Stubbs's bidding, Jaymie made her a cup of tea at the little kitchenette counter along the far wall and brought it over to wash down the treats. Surprisingly, Jaymie found a kind of soul mate in Mrs. Stubbs, a kindred spirit. The old woman was able to fill her in on how some of the cookware from previous generations was used, and what some mysterious cooking terms from old recipes meant. Her grandmother had been able to tell her much, helping with the progress of *Recipes from the Vintage Kitchen*, but Mrs. Stubbs was older, even, and knew things from *her* grandmother that would truly help with old pre–World War I recipes. Jaymie checked her antique watch pin and found she'd been there almost an hour. "Mrs. Stubbs, if I have questions in future, can I come to you?"

"Just as long as you don't come when I'm napping, after dinner. Woman my age . . . it's not good to be woken up suddenly." She smiled, a wry crinkling grin that rucked wrinkles around her mouth.

"I've got to go," Jaymie said, standing. "Enjoy the treats, and I'll come back for the container later tomorrow or Tuesday."

Mrs. Stubbs chewed on another piece of Queen Elizabeth cake. "You can try out your old recipes on me, too. I miss good home cooking."

Jaymie left knowing that, though she had known Mrs. Stubbs her whole life, now she had made a friend. The woman's bluntness didn't hurt her feelings—she had told Jaymie that she looked plain and frumpy in her maid's outfit—and in return she felt just fine about saying no to the old woman's excessive requests. Mrs. Stubbs had wanted her to come by the very next morning to pick up the container, but Jaymie knew she'd be too busy.

The woman was full of complaints, it was true. Living in an inn meant she never got home cooking, she had no private patio, she couldn't garden because a landscaper took care of everything and the people upstairs were often noisy. Lyle purposely put the noisiest guests directly above her, just to spite her, Mrs. Stubbs said, then admitted she knew it wasn't true. Lyle did his best, but he was busy.

Jaymie made her way along the passage to the main desk, wondering about the fellow who was missing from the Inn, last name McIntosh. Common enough name, she supposed, but was he related in any way to Daniel's friend Zell McIntosh?

"Edith, may I ask you a question?" Jaymie asked, pausing at the desk.

"'Bout what?"

"You have a guest, last name McIntosh . . . is he back in yet?"

"Lachlan McIntosh? Mmm, lemme see . . ."

The door opened and a couple came in as Jaymie waited. She recognized them. It was the pair from the estate auction, the Fosters; they had bought a painting but nothing else.

"I just can't imagine where it went," the woman said to her husband, adjusting the binoculars slung around her neck. "I can't have just dropped it somewhere."

"Stop fussing, Lynn," the man said.

"Easy for you to say!"

Both stared at her in her maid's uniform as they approached the desk. She must seem like a ghost from the Inn's past life as a Victorian mansion. She smiled, and the man smiled back and nodded.

"I'm one of the servers at the Queensville Tea with the Queen," Jaymie offered. "It's an annual event to raise money for the heritage committee. We're continuing tomorrow afternoon, the Canadian Victoria Day holiday; are you coming out for tea?"

"We hadn't heard about it," the gentleman admitted. He asked for any messages for room 207. Edith rustled around and said there were no messages. "Would you like to go to this tea, Lynn?" he asked his wife.

She shrugged, shifting her black suit jacket from one arm to the other. "If you want to, darling. We don't have anything planned, I don't think, until Tuesday."

Jaymie plucked a pamphlet from the stack on the desk and handed it to them.

As the couple moved away toward the stairs, Edith said to Jaymie, "Found him, that McIntosh fellow you're looking for! He's still out, but it's only been a couple of days. He's been gone for a week at a time before, since he's been staying here."

"When did he arrive?"

Edith squinted at her. "You got a reason for asking? I think I'd better let Lyle answer your questions."

"It's not important," Jaymie said. Her feet were now killing her and she wanted flip-flops or, better yet, slippers. "I need to leave a message for Lyle; can I have a pen and some paper?"

As she wrote a note to Lyle, telling him to check in with police about his missing guest right away, Edith grilled her about the murder and gasped in ecstatic horror at the few details Jaymie was willing to share. She had already been through the tale a dozen times.

"Just like a Stephen King movie, or something."

"Except no giant rats or killer mists," Jaymie joked. "Edith, it's important that Lyle get this message right away when he gets in," she said, waving the message paper around. "His missing guest might be my dead guy."

That was the best tactic she could have used to make sure Edith passed her note along to Lyle. Her eyes widened until they were round, white showing all the way around her blue irises. "Really? I'll make sure he gets this note right away."

Jaymie turned and saw a shadow move on the stairs, but her jumpiness was unwarranted. It was just the woman from the older couple coming back down the stairs. She was now wearing the suit jacket of unrelieved black, its severity suiting her forbidding expression, and had left behind the binoculars. She ignored Jaymie, sailing right past her, heading toward the coffee shop, through the glass doors off the foyer.

"Bye, Edith; make sure Lyle gets that note," Jaymie said, then rustled out of the Inn.

IT WAS A short walk, and her beloved home welcomed her. She still checked the whole house the moment she got in to make sure there were no intruders, but hopefully, in time, the horror of the night of the murder would ease. It would help if they found the murderer. She let Hoppy out, changed into shorts and a tank top, and sat out in the garden for a while, with Denver slinking under her chair to glare out at the world.

It had been an exhausting couple of days, she thought, staring up the lawn at her summer porch. She had kept busy, avoiding thinking about the grim occurrence on her property. She suspected Becca had been handling it by being busy, too, with DeeDee and other friends. But that wouldn't do for Jaymie. She lived in their beautiful old family home, and had to make her peace with the brutal occurrence. She'd give herself a free pass tonight, but tomorrow she would tackle the boxes from the auction and try to regain her excitement over the goodies she had purchased, the Pyrex and cookbooks.

But tonight she had a hot date lined up; three loads of laundry and her Mary Balogh romance novel.

❊ Nine ❊

JAYMIE PEEKED OUT her back window before turning off her light for the night, and saw a police car sitting behind the house in the back alley. From her window she could see Trip Findley wander down his backyard, his motion detector light going on as he did so; he exited through his wooden gate, then leaned into the police car to talk to the officer. Jaymie had a much better night's sleep and awoke refreshed.

It was another beautiful morning, an excellent harbinger for day two of the Tea. Jaymie took a steaming cup of coffee to the officer in the car, a young African-American woman this morning. The officer, Bernice Jenkins, thanked her, and Jaymie told her just to leave the empty mug by the back gate.

Jaymie bathed and slipped on fresh clothes. Letting Becca sleep, she retrieved the pavé pin she had found in her garden from her jewel box and slipped next door, down the back walk and through the gate—the officer had left by then, and the coffee cup was in the grass by the wrought-iron fence—to the bed-and-breakfast. Anna was sitting with a cold cup of coffee, head in her arms, weeping, when Jaymie came in.

"What's wrong?" Jaymie asked, sitting down beside her friend.

Anna looked up. "I just don't know if this is right," she said, tears rolling down her freckled cheeks. "I don't know if I'm cut out for this. Clive has to go back to Toronto today, and Tabby misses him *so* much when he's gone all week, and . . . and I miss him, too!" She choked back a sob.

Jaymie got her a paper towel to blot the tears. "But you knew it was going to be like this when you bought the place, didn't you?" she asked, trying to understand how Anna could be so unprepared for that aspect of her new life. She made herself a cup of coffee and sat down.

Tears drying, Anna gazed down into her coffee cup and sighed. "Clive works long hours. Sometimes he doesn't get home from the office until eleven or so. I just thought being separated all week would be no big deal, but . . . but I miscalculated. You know, when we lived together in Toronto, even if he got home at eleven, at least we had those night hours together, and breakfast in the morning."

Jaymie nodded, finally getting it. You don't know what you've got until you don't have it anymore. Those few precious hours every day had been underestimated. "So what are you going to do?" she asked.

Anna shrugged. She turned her coffee cup around and around, sloshing a little over the edge. "Stick it out, I guess. We've sunk a lot of money into this, including my inheritance from my grandfather. And I made a commitment."

Clive entered then, and sweeping her red curls back, dropped a kiss on his wife's forehead. He poured himself a cup of coffee and sat down with them.

He was a handsome man, Jaymie reflected, examining his dark, smooth skin and chocolate eyes. But there was something more that made him attractive, beyond even his good looks, the faint Jamaican accent that flavored his speech and his elegant manners. He was attentive to Anna, even after several years of marriage, and demonstrated an unwavering support for her venture. How would he feel if he knew Anna was having doubts?

Which reminded Jaymie that the couple didn't have much more time together before Clive had to go back to Toronto. It was a holiday Monday for Canadians, but he had a border crossing and a long drive ahead of him, so Jaymie should leave them alone. She jumped up, turned on the oven and scooped some of her premade Morning Glory muffin batter into a muffin tin. "Pop these in the oven once it's preheated, Anna," she said. "I'd better get moving." She tossed the remnants of her coffee down the drain and put her mug in the dishwasher. "Did Tabby enjoy the tea yesterday?"

"Completely!" Clive said, as his wife set a cup of steaming coffee down in front of him. "We took photos of her against that hedge of white flowered shrubs, wearing her fairy wings."

"And today she wants to come back again," Anna said. She glanced down at Clive, her hand on his shoulder. "I told her maybe. If you're leaving early, it might distract her from that."

He put one hand over hers, and said, "You *know* I have to go on the early ferry. I've got an eight a.m. meeting tomorrow morning and I still have work to do to prepare."

"The tea it is, then!" Anna said with a bright and fake smile. "Tabby and I will see you later," she said to Jaymie.

"All right, I'm off. One thing, though," Jaymie said, pulling the pin out of her pocket. "Did either of you lose this in my yard?" She handed it to Anna.

The young woman looked it over and shook her head in the negative. "What is it? An earring?"

"No, it's a pin of some sort, like a tack pin, or a tiepin."

Clive shook his head, too. "Not mine! I don't go for jewelry, except this," he said, moving his wedding ring around his finger. "It looks real, though, and valuable."

"It does, doesn't it?" Jaymie said, watching how the diamonds sparkled in the morning sunlight.

SHE RETURNED HOME and found a note from Becca; her sister had gone with Dee to pick up some junk left over from local garage sales. They'd spend the rest of the morning sorting through it for saleable gems. Dee's online business had grown, so she needed a constant stream of new sixties and seventies kitsch. Jaymie knew Dee would keep her in mind if she found anything kitchen related.

Since they had been a relative success the day before, Jaymie baked a couple more Queen Elizabeth cakes and set them to cool on the counter. But she couldn't avoid forever facing the bad associations she was beginning to have with the summer porch and the items she had bought at the auction. The poor man's death, while awful and violent, would not keep her from living fully in the home she loved so much.

If only the weapon hadn't been the grinder! Even if she got it back, would she ever be able to look at it again without remembering?

She took a deep breath and opened the door to the summer porch. Hoppy heard and scooted after her, awkwardly bobbing through the repaired back door, as Jaymie held it open for him. She turned and examined the sunny room. Luckily, the rag rug had sopped up most of the spillage from the deceased, and DeeDee had done such a good job of cleaning the rest that not a bit of the blood was left.

Who *was* the murdered man? What had he wanted in her home? Who had killed him? Those questions plagued her, but she would face them without fear. She was strong, she was capable; that was her mantra, and she repeated it as she surveyed the porch. It stretched the width of the house, with a wicker sofa and chairs beyond the Hoosier cabinet on the one side, and tables with wintered-over plants at the other end; scarlet geraniums thrived through the winter in the cool shelter of the summer porch.

She moved the boxes aside and examined the Hoosier cabinet. Could there be something inside of it that the dead guy had been looking for? The detective had said there were fingerprints on the Hoosier, but then there were fingerprints on everything, he admitted. She tugged on the tambour roll-top door, but it still would not budge. There was no way there could be something hidden in there that the thief would have wanted. That tambour had not been opened for many a year, so she didn't even know yet if the cabinet had its original sets of glass jars and rolling pin.

She opened the cupboards again, and the drawers, searching for something, anything, that would explain the murder. Nothing in them. Not a *thing*. She even pulled the stuck flour sifter bin forward to peer down into it, but there was nothing in that, either. Tearing apart and cleaning the Hoosier would have to wait for another day, when she had more time. She should at least go through the boxes of things she had successfully bid on, the cookbooks, vintage Pyrex, and sewing odds and ends.

Sewing. Buttons. She stood, staring down at the boxes, her mouth open as the conversation she had overheard came back to her. Why hadn't she thought of this before? Those two people at the auction were concerned about a valuable button. Could a button be valuable enough to risk breaking into her home to steal? That didn't make a bit of sense, not when she had gotten the sewing stuff for fifteen bucks, but it was worth a try. She pulled the sewing box off the Hoosier and sat cross-legged on the floor with the back door open, warm spring air wafting the scent of fresh cut grass from a neighbor's yard over her.

She pulled open the cardboard flaps and sorted through the box. There were cards of rickrack trim, lace, bobbins and spools of thread, the old wooden kind. There were a couple of old patterns, cards of metal snaps, a few random zippers and some plastic cases of sewing machine needles, along with an old tomato-shaped pincushion. But among it all was a large Mason jar full of buttons; she spilled the contents into a tea towel across her lap. The buttons were vintage, no doubt about that; a few looked like they might be Bakelite, some were most definitely mother-of-pearl, but nothing caught her eye as being particularly valuable. There wasn't a single one she could even suspect of being diamond or some other jewel, and none that looked older than the turn of the last century.

But would she know a valuable button if she saw it? Sometimes, in the vintage and antique business, the ugliest old cast-iron toy or a dirty woodworking tool could be worth more than a pristine piece of Depression-era glass. An unschooled eye might never catch the worth of something in the esoteric world of antique junk.

Information was power, so she took the best ones and went to her computer, upstairs in the spare room—that was where *Recipes from the Vintage Kitchen* had been born—and Googled "valuable buttons." She found out there actually was a national button society for collectors, and loads of useful information, but frankly, none of the buttons she had seemed of particular value. Even the so-called pearl buttons—mother-of-pearl, of course—were worth only a buck or two each. She shut down the computer and went back downstairs to rummage through the rest of the box of oddments to see if there were any political campaign buttons, which apparently could be even more valuable than sewing buttons, but came up empty-handed.

Stymied at last, she decided to stow the whole box of sewing items up in the craft room and move on to take care of the rest of the items. The cookbooks were easy; she carried the whole lot to her cookbook shelf in the kitchen, a small wire shelf that had once been a display unit in a store. There just wasn't enough room, so she had to find a new way to stack them, and place a few more above on top of the cupboards. Sooner or later she was going to have to winnow the wheat from the chaff and get rid of some, but that would be after the Queen's Tea, when she had more time to really look through them.

Rummaging through the box of vintage Pyrex and other cookware was pure joy. She carried the box into the kitchen and opened it up. Luckily, it had not been disturbed in the break-in, so the items were as they had been left two nights before. Jaymie had done a little research, as her appreciation for vintage cookware grew to obsession, and knew that the ingenious wife of a Corning Glass Works engineer, who asked her hubby to bring home a dish made of the heat-resistant glass the company was working on, was in a sense the mother of the casserole dishes, mixing bowls and refrigerator dishes that would become the ultimate in modern convenience. Recognizing a growing market, Corning Glass Works began manufacturing a line of mixing bowls and glass containers to store leftovers in the icebox.

The first refrigerator dishes, in primary colors to match the mixing bowl sets, had glass lids and came in a set of three sizes: a large one that many mistook for a casserole dish, a medium one that looked about the right size for a pound of butter, and two smaller ones. Jaymie already had a couple, but there was always room for more. She spread the goodies out on the trestle table and examined her treasure trove. There were a couple of the small red refrigerator dishes—only one had its lid, but the finish was in remarkably good condition, better than what she had—and one of the medium blue ones. She now only needed the largest yellow one and some glass lids to complete a set.

One could buy a complete set online, but a lot of the fun in collecting, for Jaymie, was in finding lonely pieces for next to nothing and creating a complete, valuable set. That was how she had built her Primary Colors Pyrex bowl collection, one piece at a time. She frowned as she examined her treasure. The lid of the red dish was unlike the one she already had, the grooves differently spaced. She'd have to research that later. Perhaps the company had varied the design over the years.

The rest of the box contents consisted of some canning utensils, knives, old mason jars, canning rings and one large, clear glass Pyrex mixing bowl, too modern to be interesting to Jaymie. She'd foist that off on someone else, probably Anna. She took the box back to the summer porch and sat on a stool to sort through the utensils, deciding which to keep and which to pass on. Hoppy—in the backyard, of course—started barking, and a male voice called out her name. Her heart started thudding erratically, but it was just Joel coming up the stone walk from the back lane.

"Geez, Joel," she said, one hand over her heart, "you scared the bejeebers out of me!"

"Only you, of all the girls your age, would use the word *bejeebers*," he said, smiling as he came up the two steps and sat down at the top. Hoppy had followed him and jumped into his jean-clad lap, gazing up at him adoringly. The breakup had almost been harder on Hoppy than Jaymie. The little dog loved Joel so much.

"I get it, I get it . . . I'm just an old-fashioned gal." She said it with what she hoped was no rancor, while wondering what had made him show up on her doorstep. He hadn't set foot on her property since he'd left on a cold, rainy December day.

"It's a charming kind of anachronistic quirk, that's all."

As her heart slowed back down to normal, she finished what she was doing, then looked up to find him regarding her solemnly.

"What?"

"I never apologized or explained, did I?" he said.

He thought of that more than six months after walking out? Six *months*? She said, "Do you want coffee or tea? I was just about to make some Earl Grey, and then I have to get moving for the Queen's Tea. It takes a while to climb into that hideous maid's outfit."

He nodded at her offer of tea; it was one of his charms, that he would drink tea, unlike most guys she knew who wrinkled their noses in disgust. "Y'know, I didn't think you were being snarky yesterday," he said, "when you made that comment to Heidi about princesses and servants."

"You didn't?" She got up and went in to put the kettle on.

"No," he said, raising his voice so she could hear him. "Maybe other people don't know you as well as I do, but I know it was just you putting your foot in your mouth. I explained it to Heidi, too. She didn't get it at first. I don't think she even realized it could have been construed as an insult."

Jaymie poked her head back out and glared at Joel, who had stretched his legs out along the top step of the summer porch stairs. "Thanks so much for explaining to your new girlfriend that I insulted her but didn't mean to."

"She was bound to hear about it from someone," he said, equably. "Better I explain it to her properly than let someone else, who would put an unkind spin on it."

"Explain it to her? You are such a pompous jerk sometimes," Jaymie said, eyeing him with surprise. "How did I never see that before?"

He smiled, the dimple in the corner of his mouth winking at her. "Smitten by my many charms?" He scruffed Hoppy under the chin and the little dog trembled with joy and whined.

"That must be it," she rejoined, her tone dry. It was impossible to insult Joel Anderson, a trait she shared with him, as her feelings weren't easily hurt either. Except by being dumped with no notice given. She went back as the kettle boiled and poured water over the Earl Grey tea leaves in her favorite Brown Betty teapot. Her hand was only shaking a little, and the urge to throw an ice pick at him had lessened with her realization that he was now inflicting his "wisdom" on Heidi, poor girl. What had she done to deserve that? Jaymie made up two cups and carried them out to the garden, slipping past Joel, down to the flagstone path. "I've made you some; you can drink it or not, as you like. I don't know how you feel about Earl Grey. It seems to be a 'love it' or 'hate it' proposition."

He sat down in the other Adirondack and accepted the cup. "I didn't come here to argue. I came to thank you."

"To *thank* me? For what?" Jaymie looked away; looking directly at him still hurt. Why, even now, when she didn't think she would take him back if he wanted her, did it hurt? Maybe it was because she didn't give herself away easily. She had committed body and soul to their relationship, but he up and left so quickly, and she still didn't really know why. One day they were making love on a rainy Sunday afternoon, laughing and sharing intimate jokes, and literally the next day he was gone, to his new love.

How could anyone turn his emotions on and off that quickly? It still didn't make sense to her, how he could make love to her and then leave the very next day. She read romance novels; she should have been prepared, she supposed. But she had thought Joel was the hero of her tale, not the heartless villain. She wanted to ask him why, and it seemed he wanted to explain, but something held her back; she didn't think she could handle the truth, which she suspected was that he just didn't love her like she loved him.

He frowned down into his cup. "I saw your face yesterday afternoon, when you made the decision to be kind to Heidi. I know you, Jaymsie," he said, using his pet name for her, as he looked over to gaze steadily into her eyes. "I know it took a lot. You feel things deeply, and I should have known better than to leave you like I did, without giving you a chance to yell at me, or . . . or something."

She breathed deeply, and said, "The *or something* being throwing an iron skillet at your head?" It was those moments, when he was being sincere, that he was most attractive, but she deflected lingering warm feelings with a dose of black humor.

Denver wandered out the open back door and down the lawn toward them, picking daintily through the rapidly growing grass. But unlike Hoppy, who was basking in the glow of Joel-love, the tabby took a sentinel position near Jaymie's leg and glared a hole through Joel's forehead in his determined cat manner. *You are dead to me, since you hurt Jaymie*, his penetrating green eyes seemed to say.

Joel hadn't answered her sarcastic response; he just continued to massage the scarring where little Hoppy had lost a leg as a pup, before Jaymie had adopted him. She considered his words, sipping the fragrant brew, which she drank from a chipped china cup that she couldn't bear to dispose of, since it was her grandma's favorite. *Did* she feel things more deeply than others? She didn't think so. Joel's behavior would have been hurtful no matter who she was. She glanced at him as a thought occurred to her. Was he . . . no, it wasn't possible. Was he *enjoying* the notion that he had the ability to hurt her so deeply?

The idea, once conceived, would not vanish. If it was true, it meant he really was a selfish jerk. *Was* it true? She mined all her intimate knowledge of Joel, and found nothing to contradict the idea. He did like the sound of his own voice and could be astonishingly self-involved, blind to the effect of his actions on others unless it somehow boosted his ego.

What the heck was it she had loved about the guy? That notion was the dash of icy water she needed to cool her warming feelings toward him.

Joel, perhaps sensing the unflattering direction of her thoughts, scuffed his feet in the grass, shifted uneasily, and said, "I see you've got that Hoosier cabinet you bought at the auction on the summer porch. You feeling okay after that guy was found dead?"

"Oh, yeah, I'm just peachy," Jaymie said. *Her new grinder covered in blood.* She closed her eyes, willing herself to forget the image.

"Sorry," Joel said, reaching out and touching her arm. "I

didn't mean to make light of it. Funny how those other two guys got in a fistfight over the Hoosier, though, at the auction."

Jaymie's curiosity was piqued, and she asked, "What did you see?"

"Well, first there was a scuffle, but that ended quickly. The two guys separated. I only got involved because one guy was yelling obscenities at Les Mackenzie. Really disrespectful. I poked one in the nose, when he pushed Heidi. Then before I knew it, two guys were hollering at each *other* and trading blows."

"What did they look like?"

He shrugged. "You know me; I have lousy recall."

"Oh, come on, Joel. You poked one in the nose and you can't remember what he looks like?"

"Not too old, not too young, fairly well dressed. They broke it up and left, as far as I know. There was nothing outstanding about either of the guys, except the one I poked would have had a bloody nose!"

Jaymie pondered that for a moment, considering if it was possible that the fighting guys at the auction had something to do with the break-in. What were the chances? Probably slim. Some guys could fight over anything, and auctions brought out the competitive spirit in dealers and collectors. It wasn't the first time a fistfight had broken out at an auction. "Did Heidi get a look at the guys fighting?"

"I don't know. She might have. She's more observant than I am."

"Everyone seems to be more observant than you," Jaymie responded.

"Well, one of them did shove her, the one I poked in the nose. I don't know if he meant to push her, or if he was just trying to get at the other guy. I'll ask her, if I think of it." He gently set Hoppy down on the grass, put his cooling tea on the table between the chairs and stood, shaking dog fur off his jeans. "So, for future reference? Earl Grey, not for me.

I've gotta go, and I know you're busy for the rest of the day. I've got to leave on business today and . . . look . . ." He hesitated for a moment and stared down at Jaymie. "Can I ask you a big favor? Will you keep an eye on Heidi for me? She's such an innocent, and she doesn't really have any friends in Queensville. I don't want anyone taking advantage of her, you know?"

Jaymie was dumbfounded; he wanted his ex-girlfriend to look after the current model, who was too young and innocent to fend for herself? In usual Joel fashion, he took her silence for acquiescence, leaned down to pet Denver, who hissed at him and turned his back, and then left with a quick wave, strolling down the stone pathway toward the back alley.

After he was out of sight, Jaymie shook her head. "Wow. Just . . . wow."

But she didn't have time to marvel, because as Joel drove away, a dark sedan pulled down her back lane, and from it emerged Detective Christian. She watched him enter her gate, carefully pull it closed behind him and stroll up the walk. How did he manage to look like a hero from a romance novel even with dark circles under his eyes and a grim set to his mouth?

And what could he possibly want?

❧ Ten ❧

"MS. LEIGHTON," HE said, as a greeting. "I'd like to have another look at your summer porch, if you don't mind."

Hoppy barked and danced around him in a wobbly pattern, while Denver hissed and slunk under the holly bushes.

"Sure, Detective," Jaymie said, and led the way.

He hunched down in her summer porch, the floor creaking as he moved. She watched for a moment as he eyed the piece from different angles, then said, "I've been thinking about this a lot, and wondering not only who the guy is—"

"We know who he is now. Kind of."

"Really?"

He looked up at her. "Lyle Stubbs came into the station and said that you left him a note to tell us about his missing guest, Lachlan McIntosh. Turns out his missing guest and the victim are one and the same. How did you know that?"

She felt a little thrill of nerves rush down her back, and she sat down on the top step of the summer porch. "I didn't, but

Dee Stubbs—Lyle's sister-in-law and a friend of ours—mentioned at the tea yesterday that Lyle was supposed to go through his guest list and then talk to you, so when she mentioned that there was one guy missing, it made sense. If she'd said the same thing to anyone else they would have got it, too."

He nodded, then went back to examining the legs of the Hoosier, then scanning the room and the door.

"What are you looking for?"

He didn't answer for a moment, then shrugged. "Anything. I'm wondering if the killer was all the way up on the summer porch when he—or she—killed the victim, or whether they were still outside."

"I'm assuming the murderer must have been up in the summer porch if they grabbed the grinder, wrenched it off the work top and hit the fellow with it."

"That's what we figure."

"But why the grinder? Why not whatever was used to pry the hinges off the summer porch door?"

"You ask a lot of questions."

Frustrated, she continued. "Oh, I have a lot *more* questions, Detective. Why was he breaking into my house? Was he with anyone? Dee said the guy at the Inn had been gone a lot since he came to town; what's he been doing since he got to Queensville?"

He looked up and a slight smile tugged up the corners of his mouth. "Want me to tell you everything I know?"

"That would be great!"

"Sure. I'd lose my job and taint the investigation, but what the hell, right?"

"Oh." She sighed.

"What I want to know is, why your house? As you pointed out, the house on the other side of you is unoccupied right now, an easy target for a random thief. But this guy's been in town for weeks, and as far as we know, hasn't broken into any other place. What did he want from your house in particular? Did he get it, and his killer took it from him? That's what we're wondering."

"I started wondering the same thing," she said, and as he looked at her with a skeptical expression, she added, "No, really. I bought a lot of stuff at the auction the other evening, and I wondered if there was something in the Hoosier or one of the boxes. I've searched the Hoosier . . . nothing. I've looked through the boxes, but unless it's something I'm just not recognizing, there's nothing there. But I hadn't thought that he may have found what he was looking for, and the killer took it from him."

She examined his eyes, which held no clue of what he was thinking. "Look, I thought of something later that I maybe should have brought up before, but I didn't even think of it in reference to the break-in and murder. I overheard a conversation at the sale that night about a valuable button. I bought a whole box of sewing stuff, including a bottle of buttons, out of curiosity. I looked at all the buttons, but can't find a single one that looks valuable."

His expression turned thoughtful. "If you still have the bottle, I should take it to the station and we'll look through it, see if there's anything 'off' about it."

"Okay. Have you notified Mr. McIntosh's relatives yet about his death? That must be the worst part of the job. Where is he from?"

"That, Ms. Leighton, is an excellent question," the detective said, standing up. "He seems to be from nowhere. In fact, there is no Lachlan McIntosh, or at least, not one that is missing and fits the deceased's description."

"So it's not his real name." Another dead end! She rose, and said, "I'll get you that bottle of buttons."

She had to go up to the spare room to retrieve it, since that was where she kept sewing and craft supplies. As she passed her room she thought of the pavé pin on her dresser and fetched that, too. When she came back down, he was looking around her kitchen with an odd expression on his face.

As she handed him the bottle, he said, "If I had to guess, I would have imagined this room as the kitchen of an eighty-year-old woman."

Her chin went up and she said, "I decorated it all myself. This is my collection." She swept her arms around, indicating all the tins and bowls and kitchen implements. She paused for a moment, then said, "I'm a cookbook writer." It was the first time she had said it out loud!

"I guess it makes sense, then, all this old stuff."

And there she was again, feeling out of step and out of time with the world. No wonder she liked to read historical romances. "Detective Christian, there's one more thing." She held out her hand, palm flat, the pin in it. "I found this in my garden the day after the murder."

He looked it over. "Could it have been there before the murder?"

"Sure. I suppose it could have been dropped there anytime in the last few weeks since I planted the holly bushes. I just thought . . ." She shrugged.

He took it and examined it, but then shook his head. "I'll make a note of it," he said. "But I don't imagine it's connected at all." He strode down the walk, but turned halfway down, walking backward, the buttons rattling around in the bottle. "I'll have someone drop off a receipt for this. Thanks for your cooperation. We'll get this guy, whoever he is."

"Is there going to be a police car out back again tonight?" she called out, wrapping her arms around herself and hugging.

"We can't do it forever, but I'll make sure there is, at least for tonight."

Jaymie returned inside and glanced at the clock in the kitchen. After two unexpected visitors, she was going to be late if she didn't hustle. Today the tea would be busier than ever, since they had a couple hundred Canadian tourists—they would be bussed to Johnsonville, on the Canadian side of the river, then come over by ferry—scheduled. It might be a long, busy afternoon if the Heritage Society was lucky.

* * *

THE HERITAGE SOCIETY was very lucky indeed! The
weather was perfect, even better than the day before, and
the ferry made extra runs to carry all the eager, elderly
Canadians, busloads of geriatric tea drinkers and staunch
royalists fascinated by an American town's take on high tea.
It required everyone's attention and quick moving to keep
a watch and aid those who were using rollator walkers over
the rough grass. Daniel was especially helpful, and Jaymie
noted his thoughtfulness with appreciation. If she was looking for the polar opposite to Joel, she may have found him.

The Queen's Tea was not the only popular spot, because
once they had tea, and while they were waiting for the ferry
back, people strolled through the village and checked out
Jewel's Junk, Queensville Gems, and the Knit Knack Shack.
The "Shack," a posh parlor in one of the ubiquitous Queen
Anne mansions along Main Street, sold wool and patterns
for knitters, the ideal pastime for many the age of the tea
drinkers, but also for the younger crowd among whom knit-
ting and other handcrafts were becoming popular. Jaymie
did not knit, but she did frequent Jewel's Junk. It was a shop
that specialized in "repurposed" vintage finds; Jaymie rec-
ommended it for those not knitting- or jewelry-inclined.

Anna and Tabby attended, and Jaymie was pleased to see
her friend looking a little more cheerful, as many of the old
folks fussed over her beautiful daughter. Tabby preened and
fluttered her wings, dancing around the tables like a tiny fairy
among a party of elderly gnomes. As the day wore on and the
tea organizers began to run out of some of the most requested
delicacies, like Tansy's tarts, Jaymie found herself serving
more and more thin wedges of her Queen Elizabeth cake. It
was a surprising hit, especially with the older Canadian
women who found butter tarts and Battenberg cake too sweet.

"You, girl!" one called out, waving to her.

Jaymie came over, teapot at the ready. These women

could drink gallons of plain black tea, and demanded infinite refills, so that was what she expected, but she was in for a surprise.

"That girl," she said, pointing over at Heidi, "said you made this Queen Elizabeth cake."

"I did," Jaymie said, sketching a wave at Heidi, who bounced in her chair, grinned and waved back.

"This, my dear, is the real deal, as you young people say," she said, waving her fork in the air. "It's delicious! Moist, full of flavor . . . wonderful."

Just that moment a wandering reporter, who had come over with the latest group from Johnsonville looking for colorful Victoria Day photos, paused and listened in as the woman praised Jaymie's accurate rendition of the old recipe.

"Hey, can I take some photos?" he asked, eyeing her. He was armed with an intimidating-looking camera and various camera bags over his shoulders, but appeared cheerful and had an engaging smile. "You look like the most authentically dressed maid here, and your cake is a good angle." He then interviewed both the tea drinkers and Jaymie—which she actually enjoyed, oddly enough—and asked for her phone number "to check on details later," he said.

When he walked away, the elderly ladies exchanged looks. "You have a new suitor, it seems," one of them, with a distinct English accent, said.

Of course Jaymie blushed—curses on her too-easily embarrassed physiology—then said, "Oh no, he was just being nice!"

"It was more than being nice, my dear," the original lady said. She nodded past Jaymie and added, "and I think that young man was not too pleased about the reporter's interest. You have more than one anxious beau!"

Jaymie glanced in the direction the woman was looking and saw Daniel just turning away. If he truly was interested in her, he was being low-key about it, but that was okay. Jaymie wasn't sure how ready she was for dating and men, since she was just beginning to come to terms with Joel's desertion.

The couple that Jaymie recognized from the Queensville Inn took a seat at one of the empty tables, and Jaymie went to serve them. Once they had given their order, she said, "I'm glad you came today! Did you find anything interesting at the auction Friday evening?"

"Yes, as a matter of fact," the man said. When he smiled, it creased his seamed cheeks into friendly lines. He was faultlessly dressed in brown tweed dress slacks and a butter-yellow Oxford-style shirt, and had a sweater slung casually over his shoulders. "We went there thinking there were to be antiques, but we ended up acquiring an oil painting that may be an unknown Cropsey. If so, it is a most fortuitous find!"

Jaymie looked at him, and wondered. Should she have heard of Cropsey?

"Jasper Francis Cropsey," the woman explained, watching Jaymie's face. She had a low pleasant voice, throaty, a "whiskey" voice, Jaymie's grandmother always called it. "He spent some time in Ann Arbor, a painter from the Hudson River School."

"Of course, *that* Cropsey," Jaymie said, and rushed off to get their tea and treats. She canvassed DeeDee and some of the others, but they had never heard of Cropsey either, so she didn't feel so bad. When she returned to the couple to offer a plate of goodies, they introduced themselves as Lynn and Nathan Foster. She didn't mention that, as it was a small town, she already knew their names.

But she did remind them that she had been the one who suggested the tea to them, the day before, which they acknowledged, thanking her. "I hope you're enjoying your time in Queensville?" Jaymie said, moving from one foot to another. It was late in the afternoon, and the black shoes were beginning to pinch again.

"It is a delightful village," Nathan said, beaming with gentle good humor. "We've extended our visit here indefinitely. Quite the relief after some of the tourist traps, you know, places that have no real interest, but are built around some spurious claim to fame."

"Queensville has no claim to fame at all," Jaymie deadpanned, then told them if there was anything else they wanted, to let her know.

"By the way, what did *you* buy at the auction?" Lynn Foster asked, with a polite air of interest. She was what would be called a handsome woman, fortyish, dark hair pulled back into a chignon, and wearing a gorgeous gray suit—Chanel, or something like it—with a sparkly pin on the lapel.

"I bought a lot," Jaymie admitted, shifting her tea tray to her hip. "A box of kitchen stuff, cookbooks, a box of sewing stuff with a bottle of old buttons in it and a Hoosier cabinet."

"Buttons?" Lynn glanced over at her husband. "What kind of buttons?"

Nonplussed, Jaymie paused, then said, "Uh, sewing buttons." What other kind of buttons were there?

"A Hoosier? I know what that is!" Nathan Foster said. "It's a type of kitchen cabinet, is it not?" As Jaymie nodded, he went on, "In fact, I think my grandmother had one at the old farmhouse. You know, the old homestead in upstate New York," he said to his wife, who nodded, but appeared to have lost interest in the conversation.

Jaymie moved on to serve others. Another couple of hours and she'd be done. As she served and chatted and cleared, she noticed Detective Christian circulating among the tables and glancing around. She turned away; all she needed to be completely humiliated was for the elegant detective to see her in her awful maid's outfit. His comments in her kitchen about it being the room of an eighty-year-old wasn't the first time she had felt out of step with the world. Joel had always said she was a homespun girl in a polyester society, but sometimes Jaymie wished she were a little more like the effortlessly elegant Heidi.

After another half hour, she saw that Nathan Foster was alone at his table reading a book. That was not the point of the tea; they were not Starbucks, for crying out loud! She approached and asked if he was done with his tea. He nodded absently and went on reading as she cleared his dirty cup, saucer and cake plate.

"Mr. Foster, we have other guests waiting for a table." Determined to defeat the blush that was even now beginning to creep up her neck, she said, "Would you object to sharing?" She looked pointedly at the three empty chairs.

"Oh, *oh!*" He rose and bowed, formally. "I do apologize, young lady. I did not realize there were still those who had not had tea. I will depart, if I can find my wife. You didn't happen to see Lynn in the last half hour, did you?"

"No." Jaymie signaled to DeeDee to let another group have the table.

But Nathan Foster only walked a little way away. He looked around, blinking.

"Is everything all right, Mr. Foster?"

"I don't know where my wife has gone," he said, his tone plaintive.

"Perhaps she went to find a bathroom?"

He shook his head. "She's been doing this lately, leaving and not telling me where she's going. I've even awoken in the middle of the night to find she's gone. For a walk, she says."

"I'm sorry," Jaymie said, not sure what else to say.

He sighed heavily. "Perhaps I can sit for a while and wait for her?"

Jaymie took pity on him, and dragged one of the lawn chairs to a shady spot, and there he sat, reading and waiting for his wandering wife.

❧ Eleven ❧

FINALLY IT WAS over. Lynn Foster had retrieved her befuddled husband, and the last guests, Canadian and otherwise, had straggled off to their homes, or the ferry, or the public parking lot behind the community center on the edge of town. Quite a few of the tea lovers would be stopping at Tansy's Tarts on Heartbreak Island to buy a dozen pecan or butter tarts, because they were, as everyone expected they would be, the hit of the tea. Jaymie was more than satisfied with the compliments on her "authentic" Queen Elizabeth cake.

The Heritage Society ladies were all gone, dragging off looking exhausted and gray, to drink tea on their own front porches. The indomitable Mabel Bloombury, eighty if she was a day, had volunteered to take all the linens with her to wash and put away for another year. As Rebecca had suspected, not a single person had said a thing about the napkins, though Jaymie had seen quite a few of the older ladies fingering the polyester suspiciously.

DeeDee and some of the other women had stayed to help clean up, and some had even roped in their menfolk to stack tables on the porch. Becca and DeeDee were laughing together as they piled teacups and plates into a tub to take home and wash. Jaymie unpinned her hair from the atrocious bun and shook it out just as Heidi shyly approached.

"Your Queen Elizabeth cake was a hit, Jaymie. I wish I was more like you. You really contributed, and everyone appreciated it."

Not quite knowing what to say, Jaymie shrugged. "You played a wonderful Princess Beatrice," she said.

"That just involved dressing up and acting a part. I've done that all my life. Do you think . . . could you teach me how to cook sometime?"

Jaymie was saved from answering when Zell McIntosh, who had been looking around with a frown, caught sight of Heidi and trotted over to them.

"There you are!" he said. "I told you not to get lost. I'll take you home."

"Oooh, thank you," she said looking up at him. "My feet hurt so bad!" She lifted her frothy skirt to show off ivory buttoned shoes, very Victorian looking.

"I'll rub them for you, shall I?" he said, with a playful leer.

She giggled and batted his arm playfully. "You are so *bad*!"

And Joel had worried about her being alone and defenseless?

"Zell," Daniel said, strolling toward them. "You going to stay and help me get these tables up to the attic?"

"It can wait a few, can't it?" he said, his dark eyes gleaming, as he slung his arm casually over Heidi's shoulders. Heidi shrugged, and he pulled his arm away.

"A few what, minutes? Hours?" When Zell didn't answer, Daniel sighed and said, "Yeah, I guess. What's up?"

"I'm just escorting la princesse home," he said, with an exaggerated sweeping bow.

Jaymie rolled her eyes and Daniel caught it, grinning at her in conspiratorial glee.

"Okay. Take Heidi home." He started to turn away, but then looked back at his friend, and said, "Did Trev text you? I just got another message from him, and he said something about a 'big score' and being tied up, and it seemed like he thought I'd know what he meant. What does *that* mean?"

"I haven't a clue, old man. You know Trev . . . always on some scheme. That's what's holding him up, I guess."

"I guess. So you'll be back?"

"In a while." He walked away, down the path, with Heidi.

"I'll see you, Jaymie," she threw over her shoulder.

Wiggling her aching toes in their black-leather prison, Jaymie watched them walk away. McIntosh scooped Heidi up and carried her down the path while she laughed and playfully struggled. Joel had told her to look out for Heidi. Did that include protecting her from wolves?

"Will you stick around for a while?" Daniel asked. "I've got to help tear down, but I'd like to talk to you."

"Sure," she said. She joined Dee and Becca up on the porch where the last dishes were being dumped into plastic bins. Her sister was on her cell phone, and Jaymie could tell by the set of her shoulders that something was wrong. "What's wrong, Becca?" she asked, as her sister closed her phone.

"That was the retirement home. Grandma Leighton fell in the bathroom," Becca said.

"Oh no!" Jaymie cried.

"She's at the hospital in Emergency; they think she's broken her kneecap. I have to go!" Distracted, she looked around, her gaze unfocused. "What am I going to do with all the teacups and stuff?"

Jaymie grabbed her arm. "Becca, is she okay?"

Her older sister nodded. "I just talked to a nurse. They said she's fine, cracking jokes and telling stories. But still . . . I've got to go." Grandma Leighton was special to Jaymie, but it was Becca, as the closest family member and living in the same city, who took most of the responsibility for her finances, her living arrangements and any needs the elderly woman had.

"Poor Grandma! You're not going to worry about any of this," Jaymie said, waving her hand at the tubs of dirty dishes. Her heart thumped and she felt ill. It flashed on her that she had underestimated, perhaps, how much thought and care her big sister put into her responsibility for their grandmother. Jaymie visited once a month or so, but Becca looked after everything so well, there was little for Jaymie to do. "I'll look after everything here. Unless you want me to go with you? I can be ready to leave in twenty minutes; I'd just have to go home, change and arrange for someone to take Hoppy for a few days and come in for Denver."

"No, Jaymie, stay here," Becca said, one hand on her sister's arm. "There's no head injury or other more serious damage. She'll be all right. It'll be faster if I go alone. But I do have to go right away."

"Yes, of course. If you go now, you won't catch much traffic on the Blue Water. You can be in London in an hour and a half." Grandma Leighton, in her mid-eighties, was fragile but feisty, and Jaymie couldn't bear the thought of her in pain. It was good to hear she was well, but she would still need her essentials brought to the hospital, and other details taken care of. "Call me when you get a phone in her room so I can talk to her."

"I should *not* have left London this weekend," Becca fretted, putting her cell phone back in her shoulder bag. "I had a feeling—"

"Stop it! You can't be there all the time," DeeDee said, grabbing her elbow and shaking her best friend. "Jaymie's right. Just go, and don't worry about *any* of this. You know we'll be fine. Just take care of that precious woman."

"But the murder . . . and who did it, and . . ." Becca, normally unflappable, looked teary-eyed.

"Jaymie can stay with me, if that's what's got you worried," Dee said.

"Just go!" Jaymie gave her sister a shove. "Everything will be fine. Call me when you see Grandma!"

Becca trotted away, down the walk and back toward the Leighton house, where she'd pick up her car. More folks filtered away, and Jaymie sent a weary-looking Dee home, despite her protests. Finally there was just Daniel and Jaymie left at Stowe House.

He stood on the porch staring at the stack of tables, scratching his head. "I guess I'll wait until Zell comes back to help me get these tables back to the attic."

"How about you keep them in the cellar instead?" Jaymie suggested, thinking it would be easier to take them down there than up the winding stairs and then up a ladder into the attic.

He shook his head. "Basement leaks."

"Really? You ought to do something about that."

"I've already talked to Bill Waterman about it. I plan on spending a lot more time here this summer, and that's on my list." He gave her a significant look and smiled.

He had a pleasant face, she thought; not spectacularly good-looking, but he had kind eyes and a mobile, interesting mouth. Could she picture kissing that mouth? Her thoughts made her blush. "It won't do them any good to sit outside, not with how damp it gets overnight, this early in the spring," she said, briskly looking away. "I can help you get them into the house, anyway, then when—or rather *if*, considering he's captivated by Princess Heidi—Zell comes back, he can help you get them up into the attic."

They carried the tables into the front hall, leaning them against the wall. It took a while, since there were fifteen or so, and one long one used for the royal family. When they got them all in and lined up, he looked over at her in the dim hall and said, "You know, for what it's worth, I think Joel Anderson is an idiot for letting you go. He traded down, if you ask me."

She looked away, embarrassed, and said, "I didn't mean anything by that crack about Princess Heidi. She seems like a nice girl, but . . ." She shook her head.

"But holy catfish, is she needy!"

"Yeah, I know. She is kinda clingy." And flirtatious and pretty and sweet natured. A person could have worse attributes, Jaymie thought. But did she want to be Heidi? She was stronger and more independent, a tiger to Heidi's kitten. Or at least, that's how she saw herself. She'd better start acting like it, though, instead of letting everyone think she was still going all drama queen over Joel's dumping her. "Hey, I haven't seen the inside of Stowe House for a couple of years," she said. "Have you done anything to it?"

"Have a look around, if you want," Daniel said. "I haven't been here much, as you know."

Jaymie walked from the front hall, with the stained-glass sidelights surrounding the door casting colorful bars of light across the dark wood floors, to the central hall, from which the stairs ascended, and were adjacent to the parlor and dining room. The rounded turret room, which had been a library in the Stowe family days, was directly off of the parlor, so she walked through the parlor to the unusually shaped room, windowed on four sides of an octagon. It looked exactly as it had a few years before, since Daniel had bought it intact, with the books and furniture in place. The walls that didn't have windows had bookshelves that stretched to the fourteen-foot ceiling, with a sliding library ladder attached to a brass bar, to reach the upper shelves.

"Do you read these books?"

He shook his head. "I'm not much of a reader, except technical manuals and stuff like that."

She noticed that he had added a few of his own items, including a table of photos in ornate frames. "These your family?" she said, looking them over.

Daniel approached and stood just behind her, looking over her shoulder at the photos. "Most of them," he said.

"That's my mom and dad," he said, pointing to a picture of an older couple by a pool, surrounded by palm trees.

"I don't think I've ever known where you're from, really," Jaymie said, her heart beating a little erratically. It seemed a kind of intimate moment in the dim library, no one else around, looking at his family photos. But what was she feeling? Did she really like Daniel, or was she just flattered that he so clearly liked her? Was it attraction or gratitude that she felt?

"Cali," he said. "I was born in California, near Bakersfield. My parents live in New Mexico now, though; that photo was taken in their backyard."

"Any brothers or sisters?" She idly picked up another photo of a younger Daniel with a couple of other guys in front of a big, dilapidated house. Daniel, yes, and the tall geeky one was surely Zell McIntosh. But then her eyes riveted on the remaining one of the three. She didn't hear his reply to her question, as her heart thudded sickly in her chest. "Who . . . who is that?" she asked, pointing to the shortest fellow in the photo.

"That is the guy who is holding up the party," Daniel said, with a laugh. " 'The late Trevor Standish,' Zell and I always call him."

"Late . . . why? Why do you call him that?" she asked, turning swiftly and gazing up at him, searching his smiling face.

"Because he's always late for everything." His smile died. "Jaymie, what's wrong? You look like you've seen a ghost."

"Um, well," she said. "I think I just may have."

❧ Twelve ❧

"WHAT DO YOU mean?" Daniel asked. "Jaymie, are you okay? Tell me!"

She swayed. So now she knew who the mysterious Lachlan McIntosh was. But how could she tell Daniel that his buddy, his friend, was the murder victim found in her home? *Hey, Hoosier dead guy?* DeeDee's joke replayed in her mind, but this was neither the time nor the place. It never would be, now that she truly knew who the dead man was. "Daniel," she said, and put her hand on his arm, looking up at his perplexed expression in the dim library light. "I think that Trevor Standish might be Lachlan McIntosh, the guy who was murdered on my summer porch."

"What do you mean?" He stared at her for a long moment, then, his half smile dying, he said, "Okay, so I said 'the late Trevor Standish'. I get it, haw haw! Joke's over."

"No, Daniel, I mean it," she said, touching his arm.

"Look, Jaymie, you're way off base with this one. I just got a text message from Trev not more than an hour ago."

"Then someone is playing games, Daniel. I wouldn't joke about something like that; you have to believe me. The fellow they identified as Lachlan McIntosh is really Trevor Standish. I saw his body; I ought to know. Do you have a more recent photo than that?"

"Of Trev? Sure."

He dashed over to the desk, grabbed his iPad and brought up class reunion photos from the year before. One showed him and Zell McIntosh and Trevor Standish at a bar, toasting. It was him, the fellow she had seen, all right, down to the same slacks and shirt.

Daniel watched her face anxiously, and when she looked up at him her certainty must have showed, because his face twisted, and he whispered, "No! Not Trev!"

"I'm so sorry! We've got to call the police." She did so while Daniel sat down in a leather desk chair and stared into space, tears gathering in his eyes. He squinted, took off his glasses and knuckled one of his eyes, then cleared his throat. The police said they'd send someone right away. Jaymie hung up, returned to Daniel and took his arm. "C'mon, let's go into the kitchen and sit. I'll make some coffee."

The kitchen was expansive but old fashioned, and not in a good way. But she found coffee in the freezer and put the pot on as she looked out the back window at the well-kept gardens. When the victim was a stranger it had been hard enough to figure out the mystery, but it seemed even weirder now that she knew it was a friend of Daniel's. Why had Trevor Standish broken into her home? It didn't make any sense that this stranger, who was only coming to have a reunion with his frat buddies, would wind up murdered on her summer porch.

"What was he like?" she said, returning to Daniel's side.

He had recovered some, and he talked, telling her about his buddy's college days, how they met as fraternity pledges, how they got along, even though they were as different as two guys could be. She made him a cup of coffee as he told her how Zell McIntosh was the third musketeer in their oddball gang; they'd gone through all four years together as the best of friends. Trevor Standish was the son of a tenured history professor at Ball State, and so naturally fell into history, but Daniel said he'd had a genuine passion for it, too.

"What kind of history?"

"American. Trev loved the Revolutionary War. He even had a bit part in *John Adams*, that HBO series a few years back." He brought up a picture on the iPad of his pal in knee breeches and a periwig. "He was one of the rabble-rousers at the Boston Tea Party!"

"What did he do after college?"

"The year after his dad retired, Trev became an associate professor of American history at Ball State."

It occurred to Jaymie at that moment that "Hoosier dead guy?"—her silly joke with DeeDee—had a double meaning neither of them could have foreseen; the dead man truly was a Hoosier. "He must have been in his glory: loving history, the college you all graduated from, his dad's old job, practically!"

Daniel's expression darkened, as if a storm cloud was passing, and he turned away to look out the back window. "He lost his position a few years ago and started working as a historical document dealer."

"Lost his position! That's too bad." She frowned down at her hands, thinking things through. "How can you have received two texts after Trevor died? Could they have been sent before he died, and just got through now?"

"I don't know, that's weird," he said. "Maybe some time delay in the messaging? Or maybe he set it to send later?"

Jaymie shrugged. She wasn't big on technology. She had a cell phone, but hadn't used it in weeks. It was buried in her purse somewhere, the battery probably dead. "Do you still have the message?"

He shook his head. "I don't keep stuff like that. I delete 'em as soon as I read 'em."

Silence fell between them; what could she say? She considered what she had learned about Trevor Standish. Jaymie had thought academic jobs were pretty secure, but with the uneven economy, who knew? Did colleges have cutbacks like normal jobs? She guessed it depended on whether the fellow had tenure, a concept she didn't exactly understand, but knew equated with some measure of job security. "Why *did* Trevor lose his position at Ball State?" she suddenly asked.

Daniel was about to answer, but just then someone knocked on the door. It was the police, Sergeant MacAdams and a compact deputy of Asian heritage, introduced as Deputy Ng. Jaymie explained why she thought the dead man was Trevor Standish, and Daniel showed MacAdams the photos. The officers didn't commit themselves, but Jaymie could see that they were as certain as she was.

"Would you come with us to identify the body, Mr. Collins?" MacAdams asked.

Daniel nodded curtly.

"Detective Christian will want to speak with you," the sergeant added. "And we'd like a copy of the most recent clear photo you have, too. You can bring your device with you, and our tech staff can grab the pictures. We'll need to find out about his latest movements. Also, if you know his family, we'd like those names and any addresses or phone numbers you may have."

"It's all on here," Daniel said, patting the gadget. "He's not married, no kids, no girlfriend that I know of. His dad is dead, but his mom . . . she's going to be devastated." His voice broke on the last word.

Jaymie waited for Daniel to say something about the after-death text messages, but he didn't. She knew enough now to know that it was bound to come out in questioning.

He went with the police, and Jaymie went home. She approached by the back lane, as she usually did when she walked.

"Jaymie, Jaymie!"

She turned, as Trip Findley opened his wood gate and beckoned her over.

"Yes, Mr. Findley?"

"I got to thinking about what you asked yesterday, about seeing anything."

"Yes?" she said, eagerly.

"Well, I still didn't see anything." His wizened face was pinched in thought, his beaky nose hovering over his pursed lips. "But there is something odd."

"Yes," she said, trying not to hop around in her eagerness.

"There were lights on at that bed-and-breakfast next door to you. I saw 'em when I looked out, before the commotion."

"When was that, exactly?"

"I don't know. Didn't look at the clock. But before. My motion detector light was already on, though."

Well, that probably didn't mean a thing, Jaymie thought. "Which window?" she asked.

"That one right above the back deck."

"Thank you, Mr. Findley," she said.

She went through her wrought-iron gate and up the stone path to her back door. Keys in hand, she paused and looked at the new lock. Were those fresh scratches on it? She got down to examine more closely and realized the scratches were not into the chroming, they were just surface scratches from the use she had already put the lock to. She was letting herself get freaked over nothing.

She unlocked the door, let Hoppy out and gratefully shed her ugly maid's outfit for another year. She called Becca and left a message to call her the moment she found out anything about Grandma Leighton, and told her that she thought she knew who the murder victim was. Then she phoned her parents, but there was no one home there, either. She felt alone and walked through her beloved old house like a ghost. Her faithful little dog, who had come back in after his necessary business, followed, looking up at her as they ambled.

Every squeaky floorboard of the dear old place was familiar, every creaky stair. Sometimes she felt like the stable center of a whirlwind: her parents moved among their condo in Florida, a rental in London and the cottage on Heartbreak Island; Becca split her time among her house in London, the cottage and the Queensville home and traveled extensively for her china-matching company to conventions and sale events.

She moved, on automatic, toward the kitchen. Jaymie, unlike her sister and mother, was a dedicated homebody, a putterer, a grateful small-town girl. She moved through the kitchen and to the summer porch, then stood and looked out at the backyard; the roses were just now bursting into bud. A hundred years ago no one would have thought twice about a young woman who didn't "have a career," but looked after the family home. A modest inheritance and income from the cottage rental and her management of it, along with her own thrifty ways and numerous temporary and part-time jobs, made it easy for her not to have a career, so she could, as some said, "waste" her life doing what she wanted.

But what *did* she want? She had spent a lot of time pondering that topic in the last few months. Maybe being dumped by the man she had thought was the love of her life had a salutary effect. It had made her wonder what she was going to do with the next sixty-or-so years. The answer was something that both connected her to her home and her family, something that she felt passionately about: a cookbook using the wisdom of the past to enrich the present. The past was not meant to be a mystery to those alive now, it was meant to be a school, a lesson book where one sought answers. That's exactly what the cookbooks she wanted to write and publish would do, refresh collective memory about the wisdom of the past.

Losing Joel had made her focus on things other than her

love life; digging out her family cookbook and rewriting it for the modern cook had been a lifesaver. But still, she was vaguely unsatisfied. Others did so much, and she seemed to do so little. She relished the peace and quiet, the sedate pace, the time she had to help others and to create this oasis of calm. It wasn't "normal," but then she never had fit in with the stream of life as her friends—most of whom had moved away from Queensville and their roots—lived it. Had her ease been purchased by the hard work of previous generations, though, and did that mean she owed it to them to work harder at life?

She hugged herself, feeling teary and depressed. It was all catching up with her, she feared, the death, the blood, Grandma Leighton's injury and now this. When the man was an unknown victim, it had been easier, but the buddy of a friend . . . She shook her head and swiped away the welling tears. It was moments like this that she missed having someone around all the time, someone to talk to and lean on. The year she had spent with Joel had been lovely at times, difficult at others.

The phone interrupted her contemplation. It was Daniel, and his voice was downhearted: "Hi, Jaymie."

She cleared her tear-clogged throat, and said, "It's your friend, isn't it?"

"Yeah, it's Trev all right."

"Daniel, I'm so sorry!"

"It's okay. He looked kinda . . . peaceful. I couldn't see . . . that is . . . the wound." He paused, then said, "He was hit on the head with something, but it was the back of his head, and I couldn't see that. But the room . . . it was so cold, and I hated . . . hated leaving Trev there."

"Oh, Daniel, I'm so, *so* sorry!" she repeated, not enlightening him as to the weapon. He sounded odd, but it must have been an awful shock. "Daniel, why was he staying at the Inn as Lachlan McIntosh?" There was silence on the other end of the line. Finally she said, "Daniel?"

"Yeah, I was thinking. I don't know."

"Okay. Just wondering. And the text messages . . . did you tell the police?"

"Yeah. They figure someone must have his cell phone. They may be able to triangulate its location from his calls, but what good that will do, I don't know."

It would tell them if the calls had been made locally, and if his killer was still around, or had been when the last call was made. But who would use the dead man's cell phone to send that particular message, the one she had heard Daniel relay to Zell? It was so particular, and seemed to come from someone who knew Trevor. What was he involved in, and with whom, and what was he after on her summer porch? Now was not the time to plague Daniel about it. "Can I do anything? For you, or . . . or anything?"

"I don't think so. I've talked to his mom in Indiana, and she was upset, but Trev's brother was there, so she's in good hands. Zell and I are going down to the Thirsty Fox to get wasted, in Trevor's memory. We'll cry in our beer, then we plan on staggering back here and passing out."

"Sounds like a fitting tribute for a frat brother," Jaymie gently said. "You know where I am if you need anything. And I mean that; it's not just a platitude. If you need a shoulder to cry on or someone to talk to, I'm here." As she hung up, she murmured a prayer for Trevor Standish. She wasn't sure where she stood on the whole "God" issue, but a prayer for his soul's peace, and that of those who loved him, couldn't hurt.

Dee called to offer her a bed, but with a cop in the back alley, Jaymie figured she'd be all right. Even as tired as she was, though, sleep was elusive. She got up several times to look out over the dark back alley and Trip Findley's shadowed yard. The puzzle of Trevor Standish and his death on her summer porch seemed more tangled than ever, but the next morning she awoke with a new determination to get to the bottom of it all. This was her home, and it had been violated by a murderer. She was not going to be the passive victim.

The morning started with a good phone call from Becca. Grandma Leighton had indeed broken her kneecap, but it was stable and would not require surgery to correct. She'd be in the hospital a few days, and would be released wearing a knee brace, back to her comfortable retirement home, where, with some physical therapy, she would heal. Becca asked her to pass the news on to their parents. Jaymie did so, talking to her mother for just a few minutes.

Jaymie helped Anna out, then came home and washed all the Pyrex and other items she'd bought and carefully put them away. She stood staring at the old wood kitchen cupboards for a long moment; they were getting overfull, as Becca had pointed out. The tops of the cupboards were crowded too, and sooner or later she would have to thin out the herd of bowls, tins, utensils and bric-a-brac.

The extra storage in the Hoosier cabinet sure would be welcome. She could display some of her vintage kitchenware on it, but it was meant to be a useful piece, too. Cookbook number two, *More Recipes from the Vintage Kitchen*, would be another collection of forgotten vintage recipes, like the Queen Elizabeth cake, reimagined for the modern kitchen. People longed for the past and were nostalgic for simpler times, but it didn't mean they wanted to use all the old methods. There was nothing wrong with modern when it meant better or faster or more efficient. Or tastier!

It might be a while before she heard back about her first cookbook, she had learned from her online perusal of publishing websites, and until then, she had to keep busy.

Every year the Heritage Committee sent the extra goodies from the Tea with the Queen fundraiser to a different retirement home, and this year the selected home was Maple Hills, near Wolverhampton. When the ladies were looking for someone to deliver the tubs of frozen treats, Jaymie had volunteered. She had remembered something she had over-

heard from one of the auctioneer's grandsons. He'd said that
Mr. Bourne, the owner of the Bourne estate, was now living
at Maple Hills. Maybe the elderly Mr. Bourne would be able
to tell her if there was anything especially valuable about
her Hoosier that would inspire someone to break into her
home the very night she bought it.

She fired up her rattletrap van and headed over to the
Queensville Emporium. They had commercial grade freez-
ers, and so had volunteered to freeze and store the treats
until they were delivered to the home. Valetta, who virtually
ran the store for the elderly owners, met her at the back-alley
entrance and helped her load the goods.

"How are you? I heard about your grandma; how is she
doing?" Valetta asked once they were done loading the big
plastic tubs of treats in the back. She searched Jaymie's eyes.

"I'm fine," Jaymie said, slamming the back door of the
van. "Things are a little better. Grandma Leighton is going
to be okay, the murdered guy has been identified—"

"Yeah, how weird is that?" Valetta said. She had heard
all about it, of course, via the Queensville telegraph, also
known as the Emporium front cashier, more efficient still
than texting or Facebooking. "He's been in Queensville this
whole time, and under an assumed name. I wonder why? I
heard he's a friend of Daniel's. You don't suppose . . ." She
eyed Jaymie. "Daniel Collins couldn't be involved, could he?"

Jaymie thought back to her conversations with him. The
text message he brought up with Zell McIntosh still nagged
at her. "I don't think so. Daniel's too good a guy, and this
was an awful shock to him. Whatever Trevor Standish was
doing in Queensville might be the reason he was killed, and
I sure would like to know who did it." She shuddered. "I get
the creeps every time I think about it. Someone killed, on
my doorstep, and now knowing it's a friend of Daniel's . . .
it's just awful." She paused. "I'm hoping the murderer is
long gone by now. Why would he hang around, with all the
fuss? He'd be taking an awful risk."

Valetta nodded as she opened the door to the Emporium stockroom, ready to go back to her post. "He's probably in Canada by now." She waved and went back in to her pharmacy/catalogue counter.

Jaymie left Queensville and followed the highway south along the river, turning inland near where she and Becca had gone to the Bourne estate auction and then turning again down a road to Wolverhampton, a larger town a few miles from Queensville. She passed a Walgreens and a Kroger while she thought about Trevor Standish and why he might have been in Queensville and who may have wanted him dead.

From reading murder mysteries and watching TV, she knew that the identity of the murderer was most easily found if you knew what the victim was up to, and who was in his life. She had a few questions already that she wanted to know the answers to. Was he driving a rental car? And the name Lachlan McIntosh; had he just subconsciously—or consciously—taken the last name of his friend, Zell McIntosh? What was he doing in the time he was in Queensville? Had anyone noticed him in all those weeks?

She saw the sign and stone pillars that indicated the lane to Maple Hills, pulled into the lane and drove around back to the service entrance and unloaded the plastic tubs, hoping the treats, mostly cookies and squares, were still frozen. Once she had signed in and delivered them to a fellow in kitchen whites, she asked directions from him and made her way to the lounge area of the retirement home. Her original hypothesis about the victim's death had been that it had something to do with the stuff she bought at the auction. Maybe Mr. Bourne himself could shed a light on what made something—either the Hoosier or something else—in all that stuff she'd bought at his family's estate auction special.

Maple Hills was not posh, but was above standard. The guest lounge was comfortable, albeit worn, with faded blue carpeting and an electric fireplace, framed paintings and a courtesy table loaded with a coffee urn, tea carafe and foam cups. Jaymie glanced around and found herself being regarded with some curiosity by a young African-American woman in a cheerful outfit of scrubs with playful kittens cavorting across it as a pattern. "Do you know Mr. Bourne? He just moved here a few months ago."

The nurse nodded. "He's in 22C North, here on the main floor. You going to visit him? He loves having visitors."

"I bought some things from his estate auction last week, and I'd love to know more about the stuff."

"Oh, he'll tell you. He'll tell you *all* about it. Be prepared," the young woman said with a laugh, pushing her medication cart toward the elevator.

Mr. Bourne was not in his room, but Jaymie was guided to where he sat in a motorized wheelchair at a sunny window in the library/lounge, literally twiddling his thumbs and looking out over the green lawns. Jaymie introduced herself and asked if she could sit down in the patterned wing chair opposite him.

"Mr. Bourne, I went to your estate auction last week and bought the old Hoosier kitchen cabinet. Do you remember it?"

"'Course I do. 'Member every detail o' that cabinet. I'm old, but I'm not senile."

Jaymie bit her lip to keep from smiling. It seemed to be her week for cranky oldsters. She could imagine being touchy about one's mental faculties, though, because far too many people assumed anyone over seventy was lacking. She had the example of her grandmother to guide her and would never make that mistake. "Of course not, sir. I was interested in finding out more about the cabinet, when it was bought, if it was bought new, that kind of thing."

"I remember the day the damn thing was delivered, clear as a bell, as if it was yesterday. That's the day my father said Momma was trying to kill him."

❧ Thirteen ❧

"TRYING TO KILL him? What do you mean?" Jaymie asked.

The old man chuckled, which led to a coughing fit; he dragged a tissue out of his cardigan pocket and held it over his mouth. A nurse came over, gave Jaymie a sour look and got some apple juice for Mr. Bourne. Through all the nurse's ministrations, the old man had a sly smile on his face, as if he was enjoying making Jaymie wait for the story. When he was better and the nurse had left, with an admonition not to "get him worked up," he winked at her.

"Nurses. Not a sense o' humor among 'em."

"Mr. Bourne, what did you mean, your mom was trying to kill your dad?"

"Now, I didn't say that. I said that's what Daddy *said*. I'll tell you the story of the day the Hoosier arrived, but you gotta promise not to interrupt me."

Jaymie recognized defeat; there was no quick way out of this story. He had a visitor and a story to tell, and he was in no hurry to be done with either. Even though she also wanted to ask him about some other things, she nodded, recognizing a strong-willed personality when she met one. She'd have to let him do this his way.

"Okeydokey. It was 1927. Depression time." He swiveled his gaze and glared at Jaymie. "You know about the Great Depression?"

She nodded. Grandma Leighton was a Depression baby, born when times were at their toughest.

"Momma was a nurse in the great war . . . the first one, you mind. That's where she met Daddy; he got hisself gassed in France, and she nursed him back to health at a convalescent hospital in D.C. He was a fair bit older than her, but they got married and he brought her back here." He paused, his eyes misty with remembrance. "She was from Indiana originally, you know."

"A Hoosier," Jaymie said. Lately, she had been inundated by Hoosiers, it seemed.

"Yup. She missed home, I think." He gazed off out the window at a sparrow hopping from branch to branch on a flowering crab.

Jaymie glanced at her watch; it was getting on. She still had a lot to do. "Mr. Bourne—"

"She'd get this look in her eyes," he continued. "And then she'd say something like, 'They'd be doing this, that or the other thing in Indiana right then'."

"What about the Hoosier cabinet and your mom trying to kill your dad?" Jaymie put in, trying to get to the meat of the story.

"Slow down, or go away," he said grumpily, slewing his gaze over to her, his rheumy eyes watering.

She took a deep breath and sat back. He'd warned her. "Of course, sir. I'm sorry."

While he spoke about his family, she forced herself to relax and listen and wait, thinking about her grandma, sending her healing thoughts and wishing she was with her right then. Maybe she should have gone with Becca, but at the moment, it had seemed best to send her sister on alone, since she could speed there while Jaymie took care of things in Queensville. As soon as she was free, Jaymie would go and visit, check in on the sweetest lady in the world.

She brought her mind back to Mr. Bourne and his tale of the good old, bad old days. He was an interesting-looking fellow, almost bald, with wisps of gray hair sticking out from his liver-spotted dome, deep pouches bagging under his eyes, making him look like a hound dog. He had gone back further, now, back to his father's family, the Bournes. He told her about how they had originally emigrated from England to America after the Revolution, and how they had kin in Georgia somewhere. "Came over with a bundle o' letters talkin' 'bout how pretty Georgia was. Coulda gone to live there, but my daddy's folks didn't like slavery. Immoral, they said. Said it would cause trouble later, you see, and weren't they right?"

Jaymie nodded, and said, "The Civil War." She was anxious to get back to the story of his mother wanting to kill his father, but now knew better than to rush him.

"Anyways, 1927," he finally said. "I was six. My momma's only surviving child. Momma worked like a dog: kept chickens, sold butter from the Jerseys, did anything and everything to keep us goin', while Daddy sat in the corner by the fire and carved pipes out of meerschaum. You know what that is, meerschaum?"

She didn't, but she nodded, not willing to ask. The last thing he needed was an excuse to go off on a tangent.

"You're lying, but I don't care," he said with a wink. "Meerschaum is some kinda seafoamy stuff found floating on lakes in Germany. I guess it's some kinda mineral. Anyways, don't know how much you know 'bout the old days, but in those days houses didn't have kitchen cupboards."

"I live in a family home, Mr. Bourne, in Queensville. My great-grandmother was one of the few who had cupboards installed when they remodeled the kitchen in the twenties, but I've always been fascinated by Hoosier and other brand cupboards. That's why I bought yours."

"Well, then you know money was scarce. Work was hard. Any bread we 'et, Momma made. Jam, the same. Butter, too. She had an acre garden and canned the vegetables. Kept chickens. She did everything she could to keep us afloat while my daddy sat in the corner and carved his pipes outta that stuff he ordered from Germany. Strange, him ordering that crap from Germany, when it was the Krauts that gassed him, but he was hard to figger out. Secretive bugger. Anyways, he said when the economy was back on its feet, those pipes would sell for a fortune."

Jaymie was lost for a moment, imagining the loneliness and hardship his mother had suffered. Unlike the Leighton home, Bourne House was in the middle of nowhere even now, and in the twenties they probably didn't have phone lines out that far, and likely didn't even have a car. Vintage cookbook two tugged at her mind. "Did you keep her recipes? I'd be interested in seeing them."

He eyed her, and his expression softened. "Momma wrote everything down. I'll ask m'grandson. He's the one looks after everything, since my daughter died of the cancer. Might have 'em. Might not. He tossed out a mess of papers and books when he emptied the house. No one has time for the old stuff anymore." He was solemn for a long moment, staring out the window at the cheerful scene. Sighing, he turned back to her. "Everything changes," he said.

"Some of us still have time for the old stuff," she said gently.

He shifted in his seat, cleared his throat and continued. "Anyways, my momma worked like a dog, and my daddy never gave her so much as a kind word. He was a hard old sonuvabitch. Nowadays they'd say he had that 'PTS' or whatever y'call it."

"Post-traumatic stress from the war?"

He nodded. "Back then they called it shell shock. And

he oughtta've gotten over it. He treated Momma like she was his housekeeper. Then one day Marvin's Cartage pulled up; Marvin, he had this big Morgan horse, size of a truck, and that horse pulled a heavy cart. He pulled up in the yard behind the house with somethin' in a big old crate. Daddy tried to send him away, but Momma came out in the yard, arms crossed over her chest, and said it was for her. She was shakin' when she said it, but still . . . even at the age o' six, I could tell that she was determined to have her way, for once.

"She'd ordered the Hoosier cabinet from some traveling sales guy a few months before, and now it showed up. Daddy went sky-high, face turned the color of a beet pickle, asked how much it cost. Momma said a dollar. A dollar, he said! She was a damned liar, he said, and I thought he was gonna hit her. But then she said a dollar a week for two years. That's when Daddy clutched his chest, fell backward onto the ground, writhin' and a'wrigglin', and said Momma was trying to kill him."

Jaymie laughed at the picture. "Served him right," she said. "It was about time she got something for herself."

"Daddy was right in one way, though. Dollar a week for two years was a lot! But Momma loved that Hoosier; said it cut out hours of work for her. She'd polish it and clean it, croon over it like it was a baby. I was damn near jealous of the thing . . . like a brother to me, it was."

Jaymie laughed out loud, and some of the other elderly guests looked over, as if surprised to hear laughter.

Mr. Bourne grinned, but then continued. "Ladies came from miles around to see it too, and plagued their menfolk for one like it. Momma was likely damned in more than one home that day. She became the queen of Bourne County, and wasn't lonely no more." He leaned over, tapped her hand with his knobby finger, and said, "Glad you got it. You'll 'preciate it. I can tell."

"Did your father ever come around? See its utility?"

"Funny thing about that," the old man said. "Think he respected Momma for standin' up to him. Got to be a joke, in a way, between 'em. He used ta hide things in it, y'know?"

"Really?" Jaymie asked, curiosity piqued. Finally, they were getting somewhere. "What kind of things?"

He shrugged. "That was way back, honey. I don't remember."

"Oh," she said, deflated.

"He went a little loopy toward the end. Lived with me an m'wife, y'see, at Bourne House, long after Momma died, right 'til he passed. One night he got to laughing, I remember . . . this was when he was starting to go, you know . . ." He circled his finger around his ear several times. "Cuckoo. And he said, 'Let's play "Button, button, who's got the button?" ' "

"What did he mean?" she asked, breathlessly, moving to the edge of her club chair. The button conversation! Was she finally going to learn what that was about?

The old man shrugged. "It's a kid's game. You form a ring and one o' you has the button; whoever is 'it' has to guess who."

"I know, but why did he say it?"

"Don't know." He yawned widely.

"Did it have a grinder with it when she bought it?"

"It sure did. She used that thing to make sausage and hamburger, relish, lots o' stuff."

So the grinder with it was likely original. "Mr. Bourne, I bought a bottle of old buttons at the same time as the Hoosier. Do you know if any of them are valuable? Is that what your father was talking about?"

"Not likely. Them was from my wife; she liked to sew."

"But—"

"Nap time. You can go now." He hit a button on his chair's control pad, and turned, using the joystick.

Jaymie stood as he moved a ways away. "Mr. Bourne, did he ever say anything *else* about a button?"

"Young lady, he said a lotta crazy things," he said, over his shoulder. "Used to quote from some old Frost poem 'bout a witch. He was nutty as a pecan."

"Can I visit again sometime, Mr. Bourne?"

He turned back toward her. "No one your age comes here, y'know." He stared at her, his blue eyes watering. "No one. Or hardly no one; one feller, a writer, was here a while back. But I'll tell ya, my grandson, he's almost fifty, and I barely see *him*."

"I'll come back," she said, gently. "I promise."

It was all a jumble in Jaymie's head, as she bid him good-bye. A button. The Hoosier. She watched as he rolled away, down a hall off the lounge. On the drive home she sorted out what she had learned. All the stuff about the Hoosier's history was fascinating, but the "Button, button" comments had thrown her. The detective now had the jar of buttons; would he give it back to her, or should she tell him about Mr. Bourne?

But it might not mean anything at all! She'd look like an idiot, phoning Detective Christian to tell him about a conversation with a ninety-year-old about his whackadoodle daddy and the kid's game "Button, button, who's got the button?" That was so many years ago, and how many other buttons could have been thrown out by the Bournes, given away, whatever? No button on earth was *that* valuable, to inspire murder!

Maybe this valuable button really was in the Hoosier. She'd have to search it more thoroughly, really take it apart. She acknowledged, though, that even if there once was something in the Hoosier, it didn't mean it was still there.

She had to help Anna again, in preparation for the coming Memorial Day weekend, the real official test of her ability to run the Shady Rest Bed-and-Breakfast. Duty first, her grandmother had taught her. And if you promise something, follow through.

When Jaymie got home from that, she checked her

e-mail; there was a message from Becca with a bunch of photos from the auction and the tea. She then did a search for a witch poem and Robert Frost. She came up with "The Witch of Coos," and read it; the poem had a line about the game of "Button, button, who's got the button?"

Strange and stranger. It all came back to a button somehow, but other than that she was no closer to solving the mystery. She'd definitely search the Hoosier again, but had a feeling she wouldn't find any button in it. Even if it was once there, Mr. Bourne's father had probably retrieved it and sold it decades ago. She fed the dog and let Denver and Hoppy both out into the yard. Dinner was a sandwich eaten while contemplating her empty garden. When she brought her plate in, the phone was ringing. It was Heidi. She still wasn't sure how she felt about Heidi. On the one hand, the girl seemed harmless enough, but on the other, she was an unrelenting flirt, and Jaymie wondered if she could be trusted. Did Joel know what he was getting into? And why did Jaymie even care?

But Heidi got to the point quickly. Her voice breathy with haste, she said, "Jaymie, the dead guy . . . the one who was murdered . . ."

As if there was another dead guy, Jaymie reflected, and then decided she was just being mean.

". . . I think he was one of the guys who was fighting over the Hoosier you bought. Joel said to think about it, and I did. He's the guy Joel had to tell to shut up, and the one he decked, I'm sure of it! Is that important? Should I tell the police? Joel's not home yet . . . should I tell the cops?"

Trevor Standish was one of the men fighting over her Hoosier? "Why are you sure it's the same guy?"

"Well, first, Zell told me about his friend, the dead fellow, wearing a cable-knit cardigan, and I noticed that sweater on him at the auction. I knit. I thought maybe I'd try the design I saw on the sweater. When I thought about it . . . it has to be the same guy!"

"Well, they do already know who he is, and that he was in town for a couple of weeks, but yeah, you should tell the police. It establishes that he was definitely at the auction, at least." *And* bidding on the Hoosier. She needed to take the cabinet apart and examine it more closely. She moved out of the kitchen onto the summer porch and eyed the piece. She couldn't believe she hadn't done so already, but now it was urgent, and she was anxious to get Heidi off the phone.

"Jaymie, I'm scared! Can I come over after? Can we talk about it? Do you *really* think I should call the cops?"

"Yeah, sure, of course," Jaymie said. Heidi should definitely tell the police about Trevor being at the Bourne auction. "Hang up and do that right away."

Heidi hung up.

Trevor Standish had wanted to buy her Hoosier cabinet, and so had someone else with whom he'd fought. Coincidence? Could Trevor have just been one of those guys who hopped in to the bidding on anything that seemed to be heating up?

But Jaymie didn't think so, because that very same night he had broken in to her place, and then been murdered by someone else. The guy he'd fought with, maybe? Since he could not have thought that he could steal her Hoosier, he must have planned to search it. And that meant there was something valuable in it. It *had* to be that button. It was a great place to hide things. Mr. Bourne had said his father had hidden things in the Hoosier.

It was definitely time to get to know her purchase a little better.

❋ Fourteen ❋

As TWILIGHT GRAYED the sky and the neighborhood quieted around her, Jaymie dragged the looming cabinet away from the porch wall, the feet screeching on the wood porch floor and pulling up some of the gray paint. She had to be careful to not let the unsecured upper cabinet fall over in the move—it rocked a little and made her nervous, but stayed on—then she began at the top and worked down. Her hands were trembling, so she forced herself to calm down and pay attention to what she was doing. There may indeed have been a valuable button inside, but where?

Now that it had occurred to her that the item of value in the cabinet could have been hidden there many years ago, it changed everything. A Hoosier cabinet, Jaymie discovered, truly was a dandy place in which to hide things. Lots of nooks and crannies!

First, she got on a step stool and checked the top and back of the upper cabinet. Lots of dust, but nothing else. The top cupboard, with two square doors that latched in the center, held nothing, but it was interesting nonetheless. She had a book about Hoosier cabinets—she had lusted after one of the antique kitchen centers for a long time—and she knew that the smooth white paint in the interior surfaces of the cabinet was called "milk paint." It was used because it was nontoxic for shelves or other surfaces where food was stored or prepared. That fact amazed her, considering the lead that makers had used in paint on children's cribs and toys in the past.

The long left cupboard still had, as she had discovered right away, the flour sifter, a long, large hopper made of tin. She had already searched it, forcing it to make it tilt out. It still stuck as she did it again, despite the obvious signs of wear, an arc on either side of the cabinet wall marking where it had been tilted out by two generations of Bourne housewives. Originally the hopper could be filled with flour, then the baker could just put her cup measure under the sifter and pull a lever to fill it. There really was nothing in that part, no mysterious button, no hidden valuables, nothing glued or taped behind it or in it.

She knew that Trevor Standish having thought there was something of value in the Hoosier did not make it so. He could have died for nothing. She wasn't sure what would be better, to find what he had been looking for, to discover that there never was anything in the Hoosier or to figure out that whomever had killed him had taken whatever it was he was looking for.

Now to the cranky tambour door. This was the one she had been anticipating, because it would tell the tale of how original the piece was. This lowest cabinet in the upper section originally held all the glass spice jars, but much could have been lost or broken in almost ninety years. When they had lifted the upper cabinet onto the lower, she had thought she'd heard something clinking around inside, but she wouldn't know until she opened it up.

She pushed and pulled the tambour, but it wouldn't

budge. She tapped it, then got a butter knife from the kitchen and put it under the bottom and gently pried it up a fraction of an inch; from there it slid up with a whack that caused the butter knife to fly out of her hand, clattering down onto the porcelain top. Hoppy came to the back door and barked at her. Darn!

"Sorry, buddy. Scared me, too." She peered into the interior and, lo and behold, the original spice jars on a carousel mounted to the top of the interior were intact, as were two larger jars that would have held sugar and tea or coffee. "Wow," she breathed, almost forgetting about the treasure she was hunting for in her rapture over the beauty of the Hoosier. She turned the carousel of spice jars and examined the other jars, but there was not another thing in that section.

Hoppy limped over to the cabinet and sniffed, curious as always, nosing the lower drawer.

"Something in there, m'boy?" she asked the intelligent little dog, and he looked up at her with a quizzical look. Wouldn't that be a story to tell people, if the valuable button was in the drawer and her little Hoppy found it?

She started searching the lower cabinet, the bottom tin drawer first; she pulled it right out and examined it. Tin had been used to make the bottom deepest drawer because it would have stored bread or other baking; metal kept the wee beasties out. Originally, it would have had a sliding tin lid, but that was gone. Contrary to Hoppy's "pointing," there was absolutely nothing in the drawer, so maybe he was just sniffing the ghost of long-dead mousies. The other drawers were almost empty, but one did hold some of the other discs for the grinder. The sliding breadboard was intact, and the largest bottom cabinet held only the memories of baking pans and pots from long ago.

There was nothing else inside: zip, zero, zilch. No button of any kind. She sat back on her haunches and looked it over. So what was it about the Hoosier that made it such an object of interest that the murdered man had come to blows over it at the auction? She stood up, stretched and regarded it, mystified, then opened the flour sifter cabinet again.

The cabinet still had what looked to be the original table of weights and measures stuck to the door, but one corner was loose. How had she missed that? Her heart thudded. Could there be something *behind* it? She gently peeled back the corner and tried to see, but it wouldn't come far enough away. Darn it. She didn't want to damage it with no cause. She pressed gently on the cardboard poster; there could not be a button behind it, nor anything else, because it was completely flat.

There was *nothing* in the Hoosier.

"I may as well clean it properly, then, Hoppy, before it goes into the kitchen, right? Who knows, if I take it apart, maybe something will pop out at me!" The little dog yapped happily in reply. "First things first; how to get this upper cabinet off the base without killing myself?" It was heavy and awkward and teetered perilously when she moved it. She pictured the heavy upper section falling on top of her and shuddered. Lifting it down would require some strength, but it was more the awkwardness of the piece. She tried to move it, and it rocked; maybe she shouldn't try it alone.

"Hey, let me give you a hand."

She jumped and whirled around at the voice behind her, her heart thudding against the wall of her chest. It was Daniel at the summer porch door.

"I'm sorry," he said, "I shouldn't have spoken up like that!"

"It's okay, I was just startled. You have great timing," she said. Thinking suddenly of Trevor, she watched his face. "How are you doing? You okay?"

He shrugged, took his glasses off and looked down at the floor as he wiped the lenses on his shirttail. "I'll be all right. It's been a shock, and seeing his body . . . Zell met me there. At least he was some help. Then I had to talk to Trevor's mom. She's really upset."

"Oh, Daniel, that must have been so hard!"

"Yeah. She hasn't seen Trev for a few months. Said he had some project under way that he wouldn't tell her about, but it was connected with his dad somehow."

"That's too bad, that he never got to finish whatever it was. Unless he did. Maybe he did." She considered mentioning her musings about Trevor Standish and her mysterious Hoosier cabinet, but hesitated.

"I told her I'd help with his stuff back in Indiana, help his brother clear out his apartment. Maybe I'll be able to figure out what the mysterious project was from that."

"That's nice of you," she said, putting one hand on Daniel's shoulder. She squeezed and was surprised that, as slim as he looked, there was still some muscle in the guy. "Did you tell her in what circumstances he died?"

He shook his head. "What would be the point? The poor woman has been through enough in the last few years. She had breast cancer, then Trev's trouble . . . it's not fair. I'm glad she has Trev's little brother to stay with her. He was always the responsible one in the family."

"What about Zell? Has he seen Trevor lately? Does he know what your friend's project was?"

He shook his head. "Zell's been working in Kuwait for the last year or so, until his employer's company went bust. That's what made this get-together so great; we hadn't all seen each other since our fifteen-year college reunion two years ago."

"But you've talked to them both, right? On the phone?"

"Yeah. But Trev's been distracted lately. I've been thinking a lot about him the last coupla days, and some things keep nagging at me."

"Like what?"

"Well, about six months ago or so, he called me up out of the blue. We talked for a minute, but then he asked me to invest in a venture." Daniel grimaced. "Last time I invested in anything of my friend's I lost a bundle. Zell may run Trevor down for his get-rich-quick schemes, but he's had his share of them himself."

"It may have been legit, though," she said.

"I hate to say it, but that was unlikely. Trev's moral center was always a touch off. He was fired because of an incident at Ball State. Plagiarism."

"You call plagiarism being a touch off, morally?"

"No, no, that's not what I meant. I know that's real bad, especially for a professor."

"Yeah, that's for sure. He's supposed to be teaching his students that plagiarism is wrong."

"Anyway, after that I gave him some money. He was dead broke and in trouble. He had borrowed money from the wrong people, and they wanted it back. He called it a loan, but he was in such bad shape financially, I didn't expect it back. And I didn't get it." He shrugged. "No big deal, but I wasn't going to give him more. It had already affected our friendship."

"What kind of a venture was it that Trevor wanted you to invest in this time?"

"That's the thing, he wouldn't tell me." Daniel shrugged and looked away. "I thought he was just looking for another handout, and I told him all my money was tied up in stock. I think . . . I'm *sure* he knew I was lying. He didn't call me for a few months after that. I feel so bad that that's how we left it."

"Don't feel bad. You didn't do anything wrong," she said, putting her hand on his arm. "He organized this reunion; that shows he wanted to see you again. *That* should be your last real memory of him."

He nodded, but looked thoughtful, his brow furrowed. He swept his lank hair off his forehead. "That's a little weird too, now that we know he was in Queensville for a while. What was he doing here? Zell says when they last talked, a few weeks ago, Trev told him he was going to be rich. Said he had some scheme that was going to pay off big, he just had to finesse the details. People were trying to cut him out of the big money, he said, but they couldn't."

"Couldn't?"

"I guess Trev said he was going to 'get to it first' and leave them in the dust."

That didn't make a whole lot of sense, unless . . . the valuable button was still a possibility. "Do you think it's associated with why he was on my summer porch?" she said, still not willing to talk about the valuable and elusive button.

"Maybe, but if it was someone who was after Trevor for some other reason—I loved the guy, but he did have a knack for getting himself in trouble—that could be just incidental. Somebody could have followed him here, if they wanted to knock him off."

"I guess," she said. Trevor was involved with some folks he thought were shady, people he didn't trust, so why go looking for some motive apart from that? "I hope they catch whoever did it soon."

"So do I, for your sake, and for Trevor's family. But it's up to the police now."

"What if they never figure it out?"

"They will, Jaymie. They know what they're doing. That detective has been talking to everyone in town, and sooner or later they'll figure it out."

Meanwhile, there was a murderer wandering around out there, and she was angry that he—or she—was still on the loose.

"Anyway, can I help you?" he said.

"Sure. I'd appreciate it." She told him what she wanted to do: take the upper cabinet off the bottom so she could take the porcelain work top into the kitchen to clean it properly.

"Can you do that?" he asked, bending over and examining the side brackets. "Isn't it all attached?"

"No, the upper cabinet sits in these metal brackets; they hold it in place," she said, pointing out the rusted brackets.

"The tabletop slides out from under it a foot or more so the cook can have more workspace. It's completely removable. Normally the brackets would be screwed to the upper cabinet, but the top part was taken off to move and hasn't been screwed back into place. I don't have to take the top cupboard off to remove the work top—I could lift and pull it out—but the whole thing is a little unstable because the screws aren't in place, so I want to lift that off first."

"Okay, let's do it."

They grunted a little and got the upper cupboard down onto the floor and shoved it to the free space on the other side of the summer porch. Then he helped her lift the porcelain work top; it was more awkward than anything. When she turned it over, something fluttered and flapped.

"What's that?" Daniel asked, pushing his glasses up and peering more closely in the yellow light that spilled out to the porch from the kitchen.

There was a paper package taped to the underside with decades-old cellophane tape, yellowed with age and crumbling. She pulled it off and turned it over in her trembling hands. The outside of the package just looked like lined foolscap of the kind used many years before in schools. She unwrapped it in the dim light of the porch and saw that the paper was only a blank wrapper for something much older.

Much, *much* older.

She swallowed hard. This *had* to be the valuable treasure that was hidden in the Hoosier. It was high-quality rag paper, probably the only reason the letter had survived. Remnants of red sealing wax were stuck to the edge, and she opened it carefully so it wouldn't flake off. It was from, if the date at the top could be believed, 1776. "Wow," she said, holding it up so Daniel could read it, too. "Do you think it's real?"

"I don't know. I'm no document expert. Now is when we need Trevor; he'd be able to tell us in an instant."

Jaymie felt a shiver pass through her, and she met her companion's serious gaze. "Daniel, you do realize that this is what Trevor was after, don't you? *This* is why he broke into my house. *This* is why someone killed him."

"We don't even know what it is yet. And how would he know about this?"

She wasn't about to go through all she had already established, the Bourne family history and the "button" chase she had been on. "*Is* it valuable? How are we going to know?"

"Well, I suppose a letter from 1776 could be; I think it really depends on who it's from."

"The ink is kind of faded. Let's look at it in better light." They moved into the kitchen, and Jaymie put on the overhead, an old pendant light still remaining from the 1920s remodel of the kitchen. She sat at the table, and Daniel looked over her shoulder as she flattened the paper. She was a quick reader and got to the bottom. "It's about stuff going on after the Revolutionary War," she said, with growing excitement. "How cool! But—" She stopped dead at the signature. "This signature . . . Button Gwinnett!" Button. *Button!* She gaped in astonishment; it was a name, a *person*, not a thing! The "button" was this letter!

"Button Gwinnett!" he said, his voice hollow.

Jaymie looked up; Daniel appeared stunned too, and put his trembling hand to his head, reflexively pushing back his floppy bangs.

"Do you realize what we have here?" he asked, his lenses glinting in the light. "It's a Button Gwinnett letter."

"Should that ring a bell?"

"Well, *yeah*!" he said, with heavy emphasis. He clutched his forehead with both hands and scrunched his sandy hair. "Button Gwinnett was the representative from Georgia to the Continental Congress," he said, rapidly. "He . . . he became the governor of Georgia, and so he was one of the men who signed the Declaration of Independence!"

Jaymie's eyes widened, and she stared at the letter, her hands truly shaking now. Anything connected to the Revolutionary War and the Declaration of Independence was of historical value, but often monetary value, too.

"Not only that," Daniel continued, sitting down heavily in the chair next to Jaymie, "but he is the rarest of all signers, because he died a year after the signing, from a wound he got in a duel with Lachlan McIntosh."

They looked at each other, in stunned disbelief. "Lachlan McIntosh," Jaymie whispered. "That was the name Trevor was staying at the Inn under."

"How did I not recognize that name?" Daniel shook his head. "So this letter, this is the whole reason Trevor came here."

"If it's real—"

"—it could be worth hundreds of thousands of dollars. Maybe even a million."

"Enough to murder someone for, if you're that kind of guy." Her mind was whirling, from fact to wild supposition. It made sense that Trevor would want the letter; he was, as she had learned from Daniel, a historical document dealer. But how did he know it was in the Hoosier? And who else knew about it and had killed him? And why *before* he had the letter? That, in particular, beyond all else, made not a bit of sense.

"I have to tell you something, Daniel. I think I overheard Trevor at the auction talking to someone else, a coconspirator, about the Button letter." She explained, finally, about the "button" mystery. "And Heidi phoned earlier to tell me he was one of the ones fighting over the Hoosier," she added.

"What did the person Trev was talking to sound like? Did you recognize the voice?"

"That's just it, I can't even tell you if it was a man or woman. The person was whispering."

"Shoot. Whoever that was either killed Trevor or may know who did."

They reread the letter together. It was from Button Gwinnett to his in-laws in England, the Bourne family. So that explained the connection to the Bourne estate. Jaymie remembered the conversation she'd had with Mr. Bourne, about his father's "Button, button" game joke, and the packet of letters the Bournes had brought with them when they emigrated to Michigan. This might be the only surviving relic of that time, a single, solitary, valuable letter.

The tragedy of Trevor's murder closed in on her. He had been so close, his hand stretched out to search the Hoosier, and then he had been struck down by someone. Why? Why, when the letter was still to be found? Or was that the point?

She asked those questions of Daniel—he didn't have answers any more than she did—and then told him the rest of the backstory, all she had learned so far. It was late, and Jaymie was overwhelmed with weariness suddenly. She laid the letter down on the oak table. "This has all been too much. In the morning I'll figure out what to do with the letter. It should go to Mr. Bourne, but first, I guess turning it in to the police is the best thing. Or at least telling them about it." She was torn; which was the best thing to do? "I'll do that first thing in the morning, when my mind is clear."

Daniel appeared troubled and took off his glasses, wiping them again on his shirttail, which was looking increasingly rumpled. "This is an awfully valuable letter, Jaymie," he said, tapping it with one long, bony finger.

"I know that."

"I don't want to tell you your business, but I really don't feel comfortable with you having it here. Someone *killed* Trev for this thing."

She was silent, watching his troubled expression. What was he getting at? She supposed she could call the police now, but why would it matter if she did that immediately or in the morning? There was not a thing they could do about it at this time of night.

"Look, why don't I take it and put it in my safe overnight," he said. "No one will know it's there."

"Then what's the point, Daniel?" she said. "If no one *knows* it's there and not here, then it makes no difference."

"Except no one can steal it from you if it's in my safe."

She shrugged and tried to ignore the moment of suspicion that sent a trill down her back. Daniel was Trevor's friend; could he have been involved, even somewhat innocently? No, she couldn't believe that. He could not possibly be a good enough actor to have feigned ignorance when they'd found the letter and identified it.

"This explains the 'venture' Trevor wanted you to invest in," she mused.

If he'd known about the existence of the Button letter, but not exactly where it was, it might have taken him that long to track it to the Bourne family estate. And if he was as perennially broke as Daniel said, then he needed money to live on while he searched.

"I didn't hear from him again, so he must have found someone else to give him money," Daniel said. "The sad thing is, he didn't trust me enough to tell me exactly what the investment was."

"He knew you wouldn't fund him trying to steal a national treasure like that, or theft of any kind, for that matter. You guys are clearly different men."

"True. I would have . . . I don't know . . . told Mr. Bourne about it, I suppose."

"So I must have overheard him talking to his investor. Maybe that's who killed him?" If Trevor had been in Queensville for weeks, he had likely been tracking down the letter. What a panic he must have been in when he discovered that the entire contents of the house were going on the block, she thought, and how relieved when he figured out that the letter must be somewhere in the Hoosier! He *must* have been the "writer" who'd talked to old Mr. Bourne. If Mr. Bourne had spun the same tale of his father, the "Button, button" references and the old Hoosier, it all probably came together for Trevor. He'd figured out exactly where the letter was.

How much had he told his investor? She recalled the conversation she'd overheard. "He wasn't willing to say exactly where the letter was," she told Daniel. "But it would have become apparent that it was in the Hoosier as soon as he began bidding on it. That explains the opposing bid, and the fight. Maybe his coconspirator was trying to cut him out of the loot." He had already told Zell that people were trying to cut him out.

"Heidi and Joel said the fighting at the auction was with a man, right?" Daniel said.

"Yeah. That narrows it down a little," she said, with a half smile. "Though I wasn't really thinking a woman bashed him over the head anyway." She put her hand over her mouth, realizing how indelicate her phrasing was when she saw the look on Daniel's face. "I'm sorry! I didn't mean to put it that way."

He shrugged. "I know. Please reconsider keeping the letter here, Jaymie. Someone killed Trevor to get their hands on this."

"I know, but I can't believe that the murderer would stick around Queensville with the police presence now. It was different before, when nobody else knew." She was still stuck on why the killer had murdered Trevor *before* he had the letter. "Maybe the killer thought Trevor had found the letter, and searched him after hitting him on the head, but didn't have time to look in the Hoosier because of the ruckus it was causing, Hoppy barking, and all that."

"You can't be sure they won't try again."

"We'll leave the Hoosier out on the porch, but I'll hide the letter." She grabbed the book on Hoosier cabinets she had been perusing earlier, while eating dinner, and stuck the letter in the book, then put the book up on her cookbook shelf.

He was watching her when she turned back. "I didn't mean that I was worried about the letter."

"I know." She stretched. "I'll turn it over to the cops in the morning and tell them everything, I promise. Come on, help me put the Hoosier back together, and then I'm going to bed. To sleep."

He took the hint and headed back to the summer porch. She slid the countertop back into place, then they put the top cabinet of the Hoosier back up on the base unit. He turned before he stepped down from the summer porch. He put his hands on her shoulders and she could feel the warmth through her T-shirt. "You be careful, though. I don't like this, not a bit."

She looked up into his worried eyes, and said, "It's just one night, Daniel. It'll be all right. I promise I won't keep the letter here after tonight."

"Okay. As long as you promise."

He looked like he was undecided about something, and she half expected him to kiss her, but he firmed his lips, nodded and dropped his hands to his sides. "Talk to you tomorrow, then." And he was gone.

"C'mon guys," she said to Hoppy and Denver, who had been hiding under the Hoosier as long as Daniel had been in the house, but now slunk out to glare at Jaymie. "It's time to hit the hay. I'm so tired I can't think straight."

She locked up thoroughly, then eyed the bookshelf for a moment. "It'll be safe there. Won't it?"

Hoppy watched her and gave a sharp yip.

"Right. I'm just tired and imagining things," she said, shrugging her shoulders. "I can't help feeling like I'm being watched, but that's just stupid. I need sleep." In the clear, calm light of morning, she would look at the letter one more time, before turning it over to the police.

❧ Fifteen ❧

HER MARY BALOGH book couldn't hold her interest—
a rare moment indeed, when that happened—the bed
felt lumpy, and her pillow wasn't the right shape. She just
couldn't get comfortable, no matter how hard she tried. As
cool night air puffed in the open window, ruffling the dotted
Swiss vintage curtains, and Hoppy sighed and groaned in
his sleep, turning around and around on his pillow under
her night table, she thought about Daniel. Was he the good
guy he seemed to be? She'd been wrong before, and it left
her wondering about her radar where men were concerned.
Daniel liked her, she could tell, but why?

Deliberately turning her mind away from her love life,
or lack thereof, she shivered as she thought of the letter. The
Button. Who had she heard talking about it at the auction?
One of the speakers was Trevor, but who was the other
person? Denver jumped onto the bed and curled up at her
feet, one forepaw flung over her ankles. Hoppy groaned and

whimpered, chasing Denver in his dreams, probably, something he didn't dare do in real life.

She thought back to the auction; one of Lesley Mackenzie's muscular grandsons had said he'd been hired as security because someone had broken into Bourne House and rifled through everything before the auction. Had that burglar been looking for the Button letter? Given its extraordinary value, that seemed logical. So was the burglar Trevor Standish? Probably, but not absolutely. It could have been his untrustworthy coconspirator.

She turned on her side, and Denver grumbled. "Sorry, fella," she whispered and scratched his head.

When Trevor and whoever had bid against him lost out on the cabinet because of their fight, Standish had to go to "plan B": break into her summer porch and search the Hoosier. But it still nagged at her; why had someone—his untrustworthy partner or someone else—killed him before he'd found the Button letter?

As she lay wide-awake, she remembered sweeping the porch and finding a corner of some kind of paper. She meant to have another look at it, but had forgotten completely. It hadn't seemed relevant until now. Where had she put it? She sat up and turned on the light, found the torn corner of paper in her jeans pocket, then sat on the side of the bed and examined it.

It was old paper, yellowed and with faded courier print from a typewriter. Since it was just a corner, though, it was hard to tell what it was, or had been. She squinted and blurred her vision. Sometimes that helped. Hmmm. A receipt, maybe? Part of a line of an address? But what was it doing on the floor of her summer porch? It was probably just the product of her exhausted mind that she connected it in any way with the murder. It could easily have fluttered out of one of the cookbooks, since they had been spilled across the floor during the fracas.

She turned the light off and lay back down. Now she had an even longer list of questions, for which she had no answers. That was an uncomfortable state, and left her nowhere to go but finally, blissfully, to sleep. It was some time later when her bedside phone rang and she grabbed for it reflexively, her mind instantly going to her grandma or her parents, as middle-of-the-night phone calls are never good news.

"Jaymsie? Is Heidi there? Did you see her?"

"Wha—?" Jaymie put her legs over the edge of the bed and sat up in the pitch-blackness, scrubbing her eyes and holding the phone receiver to her ear. "Who is this?"

"It's Joel! I woke you up?"

She squinted blearily and looked at her clock radio. Two-thirty-seven . . . and he had to ask if he'd woken her up? "Why are you calling me, Joel?"

"It's Heidi. I just got back—I wasn't supposed to be back until tomorrow—but she scribbled down your name and address on a notepad by the phone. I thought maybe . . . look, did she talk to you tonight?"

"Last evening?" Jaymie shook her head and sat up straight, clearer. She turned on her bedside lamp and flexed her shoulders. "Yes, I spoke to her." She had a vague memory of the conversation, but hadn't been paying complete attention because of the information the girl had just given her. Heidi had asked if she should call the police, and Jaymie had said yes. That was it, right?

Jaymie told Joel all that, then said, "I don't know . . . she *may* have asked me if she could come over, and *may* have interpreted what I said as a yes. But she never arrived. She could have gotten sidetracked, or went over to another friend's place instead."

"She doesn't *have* any friends in Queensville, Jaymie. I told you that. Folks have been standoffish."

Jaymie winced. Loyalty will make people do strange things sometimes, even cut someone out of a social circle just so it won't hurt someone else's feelings. "She didn't come here," Jaymie repeated. "Call the cops if you're worried."

"I already did. They said to give it a while, that she'd be back. She's an adult, they said."

His tone implied that if they thought that, they clearly didn't know Heidi, and Jaymie was reminded of some of Joel's less admirable qualities, one of which was a sometimes unbearable condescension. When he hung up, Jaymie felt antsy and went downstairs to the kitchen. She turned on the back light and looked around the yard, letting Hoppy out to piddle, but trotting out and firmly grabbing him before he could hare off in the dark. "Oh no, m'boy," she said. "I am not going to let you have another go at the skunk, like you did last month. I can still smell Pepé Le Pew on you."

She sent him upstairs, looked around the kitchen thoughtfully, did a couple of little tasks, then went back up to bed and to sleep. When Hoppy started barking, Jaymie was once again hauled out of a deep sleep; she groaned and turned over. "Hoppy, go to sleep!" she yelled. "You are *not* going out after that skunk!"

The only response was a noise in the kitchen, and Hoppy kept barking.

"Hoppy, will you . . ." Jaymie hoisted herself out of bed and clattered down the stairs and through the dark house, intent on telling the little dog that a four a.m. wake-up call had *not* been ordered! But as she approached the kitchen, she heard the back door slam. It was too late to stop herself; she launched into the kitchen, terrified of what she would see, but there was just a flashlight on the floor and nothing else.

No dead body, but the kitchen door open, the summer porch door open, and her dog barking. From outside.

"Hoppy!" she shrieked, and pelted out of the back door without thinking, just in time to see the last of a hooded someone as the figure ducked through the gate and around the hedge. She raced barefoot into the yard, grabbed Hoppy, and stomped back in to the kitchen, slamming the door shut behind her, and picking up the phone. She dialed 911, breathlessly telling the operator that there had been a break-in and she needed police. No, the perpetrator was not still in the house, and yes, she was sure of that. Her dog would have chased down whoever it was in the house, if he or she were still there, she told the operator, and she thought she had seen the would-be thief leave.

The police arrived quickly, and she set Hoppy down to let them in the back door. The little dog tore outside as she let in the two uniformed officers, Deputy Ng and Officer Jenkins. The Yorkie-Poo started barking again almost immediately, but Jaymie still tried to answer the officers' questions. Did she think anything had been taken? Her stomach clenched; she looked over at the bookshelf. The Hoosier book was gone.

Confused, shaken to the core, she couldn't think in that moment, and just muttered, "I . . . I d-don't think so. M-my dog must have scared them off before they got anything. Whoever it was dropped the flashlight and took off. I ran out back after my dog and saw someone just going around the hedge at the back gate." Her mind whirled with questions and suppositions and fragments of thought. The only person in the world who knew what was in the Hoosier book was Daniel.

Daniel Collins. No! She needed to think about this.

They asked a few more questions and fingerprinted the door, photographing the broken window on the summer porch that had allowed the thief to unlock the door. They also photographed the damaged lock on the kitchen door, and bagged the flashlight as evidence to be processed at the police lab. There wasn't a whole lot more they could do. All of that took some time, but Hoppy was still barking on and off. Finally, the dog trotted up the back steps as the cops were about to leave. The little Yorkie-Poo stared at Jaymie and barked again, his black button eyes snapping with intelligence, then raced outside.

"What is up with him?" she said out loud, and followed him down the path to the back gate, and when she opened the gate, he bolted through it and around behind the shed/garage that let onto the back lane. She followed, and by the yellowy illumination of the ancient light on the post near the garage, she saw a figure lying on the ground in the overgrown weeds. "There's someone here!" she cried.

The police pushed her aside, and went toward the person, guns drawn. When they checked the form for signs of life, Jaymie squeezed between them.

"Heidi! It's Heidi Lockland!" Jaymie knelt down beside her, and Heidi looked up, her beautiful eyes fogged with pain.

One tear squeezed out of the left eye, and she said, her voice muffled but audible, "I came to see you, and someone hit me!" Then her eyes rolled back, and she fainted.

They called for an ambulance, and as it pulled away Jaymie told the police she would call Heidi's boyfriend to meet her at the hospital.

"No! Don't do that, ma'am," Deputy Ng said. "We'll take care of everything, if you'll just give us his name and address."

She rattled it off, and said, crossing her arms over her chest and shivering with the night chill, "He called about an hour and a half ago, and said she was missing. He said he'd called the police, too."

"We'll take care of it," the young cop said, sternly adding, "Please don't call him! We appreciate your cooperation."

She should go stay with someone, Deputy Ng advised her. If she was going to try to sleep more, she probably would have gone to Valetta's or Dee's, but the officer told her that, in any case, they would have a cruiser stationed in the back alley and circling past her front door the rest of the night. If she wanted to go somewhere, all she had to do was tell one of them.

"You know, none of this would have happened—not the break-in, nor the attack on Heidi—if one of you had still been in the back alley," she said, a sick feeling in the pit of her stomach.

"I wish it were that easy, ma'am," he said, with a polite, regretful look. "Unfortunately, the resources of the Queensville Township Police Department are not unlimited."

It only occurred to Jaymie a few minutes later, after he'd left and she was shoving a chair under the doorknob of her busted door, that they probably wanted to ask Joel "a few questions," as the cop shows always had investigating officers say.

She thought of something else in that moment, too. Trevor Standish had broken into her summer porch, using something to bust the lock and break the door open. What had he used, and where was it? If the killer had used the grinder to murder him, whacking him from behind, then why did that person carry away the other thing? Whatever it was must be somewhere, and might have fingerprints on it.

The first glimmers of dawn were showing on the horizon. *Way* too much excitement for one night. She circled the kitchen restlessly, eyeing the bookshelf every time she passed it. She should have told the police about the missing book, but if she called them back now and explained about the letter, it would look weird. Someone, the murderer likely, had been in her home rooting through her belongings, and that someone had known to go for one book in particular, from all her cookbooks: *Hoosier Cabinets* by Philip D. Kennedy. She shivered and rubbed her arms. How had the thief known?

No one but she and Daniel Collins knew that she had put the Button letter in that book, and now the book was gone! He had arrived that night just *after* Heidi had called her and asked if she could come over. If Jaymie hadn't been so darned preoccupied with what Heidi had just told her about the fight at the auction, she would have heard correctly!

She had to reason things out. If Daniel was involved with his buddy Trevor's scheme, how would it have impacted last night? Say Daniel found Heidi snooping, or coming to see her, and bashed her on the head. But why would he do that? Why wouldn't he just wait until she went away? Unless . . . could *Daniel* be the other guy who had been fighting with Trevor Standish over the Hoosier cabinet? Then he wouldn't have been able to risk Heidi seeing him again.

Except, that didn't make one bit of sense. Not a single one! Joel would have recognized Daniel at the auction if he had been the one fighting with Trevor. And Heidi saw Daniel at the Tea with the Queen. Still, even if he wasn't the guy Trevor had been fighting with at the auction, Daniel *could* have been involved with Trevor's scheme as his mysterious investor, and could have told her just enough to exonerate himself and get her to trust him.

Jaymie definitely needed to talk to Daniel, to ask him where he was and what he was doing. It didn't seem possible that she could be so wrong about his character, but how well did she really know him? She climbed the stairs, Hoppy bouncing up ahead of her, and went to her room, sitting down on the side of her bed. She picked up *The Love Thief*, another historical romance, from her side table and opened it. She took out her plastic-covered "bookmark," turning it over and over.

Whoever had stolen the Hoosier cabinet book would now have the old, mimeographed copy of the recipe for Queen Elizabeth cake, but they wouldn't have the Button Gwinnett letter, she reflected, looking down at the valuable piece of American history in her hands.

❧ Sixteen ❧

SHE HAD TAKEN the Button Gwinnett letter out of the Hoosier cabinet book in the middle of the restless night, put it in a Baggie and brought it upstairs with her, sticking it in her romance novel. The thief would be the only one who knew that she had removed the letter from *Hoosier Cabinets*, though. She'd have to decide what to do: confront Daniel, or not. Was he involved somehow in the attempted theft of the letter? She couldn't condemn him until she knew for sure, because he *could* have told Zell McIntosh, or someone else, for all she knew, about the letter and Jaymie having put it in the book.

Zell McIntosh: who was more likely to have been in on something with Trevor Standish? And his arrival was so precisely timed, the very night Trevor had died. Who was to say Zell hadn't been lingering somewhere, in another village, waiting for the word from his partner, Trevor? It was more than possible, given the connection between the two men. And if that was the case, and he killed Trevor and took his cell phone, who more likely to know what to text Daniel?

She needed to talk to Daniel, but not yet. And before sundown the Button Gwinnett letter had to be out of her home, and it had to be *known* that it was out of her home for the sake of whoever was trying to steal it. How she was going to manage that, when she didn't know who had broken in, was going to be a challenge. It was too dangerous to keep, that was for sure.

The morning got busy really early, once villagers learned of the break-in and the attack on Heidi. As Jaymie cleaned fingerprint dust off her back door for the second time in a few days, she received half a dozen phone calls, all before eight a.m., and most expressed concern and sympathy for Heidi, as they should have. Being bashed on the head and left for dead was an easier way to the villagers' hearts than just being a nice—if vacuous—young woman, because the universal response seemed to be "poor little thing."

The second response among callers was to make sure Jaymie hadn't taken out her "rival" with a baseball bat. It was not mindless wondering, in that case, apparently; there was a rumor going around Queensville that she had beaten Heidi unconscious, then gone inside and had tea. Folks didn't really believe it, each person claimed, but they still called, "just to check."

"Who would say something like that, Valetta?" Jaymie asked her friend, who had dropped in to check on her before she had to be at work at the Emporium.

The woman gazed at her quizzically, then said, "Kathy Cooper?"

Jaymie sighed. It *had* to be Kathy Cooper, her one and only enemy in Queensville.

"What has she got against you, anyhow?" Valetta asked, wrapping her bony hands around a blue mug. "I have never seen anyone so bound and determined to destroy someone's reputation. Good thing we all know you well, 'cause she paints you as a catty, jealous, spiteful old maid." She paused a beat and cocked her head. "Kinda like me."

Jaymie laughed, knowing it was a joke, but then said, "I wish I knew what went wrong. We were friends as kids." That soured somehow, and now Kathy persisted in regarding her as an enemy and badmouthed her whenever she had the chance. It was puzzling. Jaymie had tried to discover what was behind it, and had attempted to make amends for whatever had come between them, but there didn't appear to be a rational explanation, so she had just learned to live with it.

"You know, you'd better call Becca and tell her everything, or she'll hear it from someone else," Valetta advised. She had gone to school with both Becca and DeeDee, but had never become close friends with either. Instead, she and Jaymie had become close pals over the years. "She's gonna want to know why you didn't go stay at Dee's place after the break-in last night. Why didn't you, anyway?"

The easy answer was that she didn't intend to go back to bed, and hadn't. But there was more to it. "Ever since I turned twenty or so, it seems like as much as I see myself as a competent, intelligent adult, I've got ten people telling me I'm just a kid, and not a very bright one at that. I'm thirty-two; when is that going to stop? If I ran over to Dee's every time something bad happened, it would just confirm that impression that I can't look after myself. It's ridiculous."

"It's the 'woman alone' syndrome," Valetta said sympathetically. "My brother still figures he needs to step in and run my life for me, and I'm forty-two." She was really forty-seven, but shaving five years off her age was a long-ingrained habit. "It's only gotten worse since his wife died. Brock figures I should move in with him and his kids, but that," she said with a shudder, "is a fate worse than death. I don't mind helping out sometimes with them, but to live there? I'd rather be steeped in boiling tea."

It was comforting to talk to someone who knew how she felt, but Valetta was right about one thing. Jaymie had to call Becca and tell her all, so she didn't hear it from Dee or some other well-intentioned Queensvillian just looking out for Jaymie.

"So . . . what is this all about, Jaymie? Why two break-ins? You hiding Lazarus Stowe's missing fortune in here or something?"

It was on the tip of her tongue to tell Valetta, but the woman was the gossip pipeline to the rest of the village. She may as well hire a town crier and tell the world, if she told Valetta. Instead, she shrugged and said, "Whoever it is, is looking for something."

"But what?" Valetta peered at her directly. "Give it up, girl. You know something, I can see it in those baby blue eyes of yours."

"I've got to get going to help Anna next door, and so do you have to get a move-on, if you're going to open the pharmacy on time. Isn't there something in your contract about your hours of operation?" Jaymie said.

"Yeah, yeah, so after all these years you still don't trust me," she grumbled, rising and putting her coffee cup in the sink. "Speaking of Anna Jones, talk about a woman needing help," Valetta said dryly. "She takes the coffee cake in the helplessness department, and she's got a handsome hubby to boot. Why she thought she could run a business on her own, I'll never know."

Moved to defend Anna, Jaymie said, "She's not stupid or helpless, Valetta; she's indecisive. There is a difference. Indecisiveness seems to be part of her personality." They left the house together, Valetta striding off toward the center of town to open up the Emporium, and Jaymie next door to help Anna.

Anna was wide-eyed and fearful. "I lived in Toronto for years," she said, as they sat in the kitchen with coffee, "and always worried about crime. Then I move my little girl to a small town to get away from the worry, only to wind up next to a murder, a violent attack and a couple of break-ins!"

"You can't treat them like separate incidents, though," Jaymie responded. She got out a recipe for lemon cranberry muffins and rooted around in Anna's freezer for a bag of frozen cranberries she knew was there. "I think they're all tied in to the same thing."

Anna shrugged, clearly not really buying it. "What are we making?" she asked, sitting at the table and sipping coffee.

Jaymie told her, as Elaine Carter came into the kitchen to ask Anna a question about local wineries. Anna turned to Jaymie, who supplied the names of a couple that also had cafés that served dinner. When the woman left, Jaymie asked, as she chopped walnuts for the muffin batter, "So, has Brett's boyfriend, Ted, returned yet?"

"Not yet," Anna said, getting down the tub of flour and a bottle of oil.

"It's strange that he hasn't gone looking for him. Wouldn't you, if you had a fight, and Clive stormed off?"

"Clive would never do that," Anna said placidly.

"Never? Doesn't he have any temper?"

"Not with me. I've seen him chew out a coworker who didn't get something right, but he has never raised his voice in our home."

"Isn't there anything about him that irritates you?" Jaymie asked, sidetracked by her friends' marriage. "I just can't believe that." She tossed the walnuts in the flour; that would keep them suspended in the muffin batter so they didn't sink to the bottom.

Anna shrugged. "We've been married for years, and have never had a real fight. We've bickered a little, I guess, but no actual fights."

"I guess Ted and Brett can't say that, after the fight they had the night of the murder."

"Now that you mention it, it's odd how Brett just doesn't

seem upset. I mean, he did at first, but now he's just going about his business. Whatever that is."

Jaymie thought back to what Brett said. "After they fought, Brett said Ted stormed out, but he just went to bed and to sleep. I have never in my life been able to sleep after a fight. I always lay awake for hours going over what I should have said, what I'm going to say next time and wondering where he is." She realized that she had forgotten or blocked out all those fights with Joel. It was so clear to her now that their time together had not been as idyllic as she had once thought.

"Their car was parked down by the marina," Anna said. "Brett *says* he figures Ted went over to Johnsonville and is waiting for Brett to come looking for him."

"But he hasn't yet. That we know of, anyway. Wonder why? And why is he even in Queensville? It's not like there's a lot here to see, much as I love the town." Jaymie shook her head. "Not our business, I guess." But still, it gave her pause and deserved some thought. Brett had been at the auction, and knew exactly where the Hoosier was, on her summer porch. In fact . . . putting it on the summer porch had been his suggestion. Was he, perhaps, Standish's coconspirator? But then, who was Ted in all of this? And why had the fellow disappeared? "What does Brett do all day?"

Anna shrugged. "I haven't a clue. He goes out every day, but he's back every evening."

Jaymie thought about that as she finished whipping up the muffin batter. Why was he still in Queensville? She told Anna that she could leave the batter in the fridge until the next morning, then bake it like the Morning Glory muffins. She gave her friend a hug and headed home.

She paused at her front door before going in, though, and examined the façade. Looking after a home as old as theirs was a constant battle to ward off decrepitude. The paint on the trim had begun to crack and peel from years of lashing rain and blistering sun. It was time to have it scraped and painted, but not until the fall. The place was looking a little empty and bleak. She would definitely need to get on top of the gardening, maybe even today. Memorial Day weekend was her deadline to have the outdoor baskets and beds fitted out with annuals, so that meant getting to work.

She glanced over past the B&B and saw Brett Delgado down the block, talking to someone who was in a big black car, a Lincoln or Cadillac, from the looks of it. If she knew cars better she'd have been able to tell. He leaned in the open window, having what looked from a distance to be an intense conversation. She supposed it caught her attention because she had just been thinking of Brett and Ted. If it was all on the level, and Brett was really who he said he was, then why was he in no hurry to go after Ted Abernathy, who he was supposedly marrying within days? Of course, if Abernathy was already in Canada, maybe the two had talked on their cell phones, or maybe they often had this kind of quarrel and took a few days to cool down and reconcile.

She shrugged; it was irritating being in the middle of so many mysteries, major and minor, and not having the answers to any of them. The cops could already have a suspect in mind, and she would never know until they made an arrest. Her stomach twisted again as she thought of the Button letter; what was she going to do about it? Was the killer the same person who had broken into her house the night before? Did Daniel Collins have anything to do with it? He seemed to be so fortuitously on the scene last night as she was dismantling the Hoosier.

Brett straightened and headed toward the B&B, and so did Jaymie. He appeared deep in thought and didn't see her until she was standing in front of him.

"Hi there. How are you?" she asked.

"Jaymie, how are *you*?" he said. "I hear there was another commotion at your place last night. What was that all about?"

"Someone broke in. Again."

"What were they after? Did they get whatever it is?"

"Actually, they did," she said. Mendacity came surprisingly easy to her after all she had been through.

"Really?" he said. His eyes narrowed. "They got what they were after?"

"Yes." She examined his expression and wondered if she read consternation in his shifting gaze. He seemed surprised, that was for sure. She was suspicious of everyone now. His lack of concern over his boyfriend's disappearance allied with his being at the auction, but not buying anything, made her wary of him. "So, have you heard from Ted? Did he call you after all?"

"Actually, no. I'm beginning to get worried," he replied.

"Who was that you were talking to? In the big car?"

He raised his brows at her direct questioning. "That? Someone asking directions. Why?"

She wasn't very good at subterfuge after all, it appeared. She shrugged. "I thought I recognized the car, that's all." It hadn't looked like a simple conversation about directions.

"It was a woman driving. I recognized her. I think she was at the same auction we were at the other night, but I didn't catch her name."

"I wonder if that was Lynn Foster?" Jaymie said. She was the only woman Jaymie had seen at the auction who was staying in Queensville. Odd that she had stopped to ask Brett directions.

He shrugged. "Like I said, I don't know her name."

"What did she want directions to?"

"Uh, Wolverhampton. I have to go in now," he said, and opened the front door of the Shady Rest.

The phone was ringing as Jaymie entered the house; it was DeeDee, checking up on her, berating her for not coming to stay with her after the break-in, and asking about Grandma Leighton. They talked for a while, but Jaymie was still distracted by thoughts of the tangled mystery of the Button letter, so when DeeDee said something, Jaymie caught just part of it.

"What did you just say about your brother-in-law, Dee?" she asked.

"Lyle's in a tizzy. That Lachlan McIntosh, who it now seems was really Trevor Standish, tricked Lyle into charging another guest for his room."

"Another guest? Who?"

"You know that tall couple at the auction, the Fosters? You saw them again at the Queen's Tea."

"I know who you're talking about."

"Well, it seems that this Standish—or McIntosh, or whoever—told Lyle that the Fosters were to be billed for his room on their credit card. Lyle made an inquiry—this was before the Fosters arrived—and it came up all right. But now they're saying they don't know the guy from Adam. Told Lyle they don't know who he talked to to confirm, but it wasn't them."

The Fosters again! "Wow, what a mess. Lyle must be beside himself."

"He's in a bind, all right. The guy ran up quite a bill. Now he's going to have to charge the guy's estate. He'll probably never see the money."

After hanging up, Jaymie puttered in the kitchen, trying to clear her mind. It was all such a muddle. The list of those she didn't trust was now as long as her arm. The Fosters, who kept popping up in a multiplicity of spots, were now on her list, as were Ted Abernathy and Brett Delgado. Trevor Standish seemed to have connections to all of them, in one way or another.

And then there were Daniel and Zell McIntosh. Could Daniel have done something so dastardly as break in to steal the book? It was pretty powerful evidence that he was the only one who knew about the letter, and the book in which it had been hidden disappeared that very same night. Could he, Zell McIntosh and their friend, Trevor Standish, *all* be mixed up in the tangled mess? Was a frat brother reunion their cover story?

Daniel Collins, she deeply felt, could be trusted, and it wasn't just because she liked him. He had an aura of calm competence. He was solid, dependable, and she wanted to believe he had nothing to do with the Button letter mess. If Trevor had organized the reunion as an excuse to be in Queensville, he could have dragged Zell into it as a fall guy or coconspirator, and Daniel could have been left out of the loop. As she hid the letter in the Hoosier book, she'd had a feeling she was being watched, the uneasy sensation lifting her neck hair and creeping down her spine; had Zell followed Daniel, and had he been watching the house? Was *he* the one who'd knocked Heidi out and stolen the book? If that was the case, then he was probably the murderer, too, intent on getting all the money for the Button letter. Still . . . she couldn't rule Daniel out entirely. She had a definite sense that he was interested in her, but she wasn't sure how she felt about it yet. She just knew she wanted time to figure it all out, and she didn't want to be wrong about a guy this time. It was vital that she not let her interest in him mislead her about his character or motives. He could be feigning interest to get close to the Button.

She sighed, then sat down at the kitchen table and called Becca, who, as she expected, chastised her severely about not going to stay with Dee. Her sister was distracted, though, when she told her about the Button Gwinnett letter hidden in the Hoosier.

"So the most valuable thing about that piece is something you can't even keep! That just about fits with you, Jaymie." Becca had always said that her little sister had an eye for making money . . . for other people. She said it every single time Jaymie found a Spode platter or Minton gravy boat in some dusty old junk shop and turned it over to Becca to sell.

Then Jaymie phoned the hospital in Wolverhampton to try to get news on Heidi, but they wouldn't tell her anything. She called Joel's cell phone, but it went straight to voice mail, so she left a message to let her know how his girlfriend was doing. She felt some responsibility; if she had listened more closely to Heidi, she would have been looking out for her. As she did all of that and ate lunch, she moved the Button letter several times. She was uneasy about it, but undecided.

She was going to *have* to take it to the police station. It was most definitely not going to spend another night in her house, even if a cop was sitting in her lap. She finally took it out to the van with her, sticking it in the glove compartment, then starting up the ancient vehicle. How she was going to present the letter to the police, without admitting she had held it back, was what was troubling her now. And so she procrastinated a bit, knowing she couldn't put off the unpleasantness forever.

Her first stop was a garden center out on the highway, where she loaded the van with annuals and a few new perennials. She was going to try bee balm in the corner near the garage, both for its beauty and for its other properties, as an attractor of bees and butterflies. Bee balm, a kind of bergamot—though not the same as the flavoring used in Earl Grey tea—had pretty red flowers that, as its name suggested, attracted bees. She was tempted by a tall, feathery bamboo plant, but decided to stick to her planting ideals; in her perennial garden, she would try to keep native plants predominant.

The police station was in the opposite direction from the nursery, though, so she decided to go home first and unload the plants. Procrastinating again, yes, but Detective Christian was a daunting guy: too good-looking by far, enough to make her blush, but with a cool demeanor. She would fuss around a little and work up her flagging nerve.

As she pulled the van around the back, she saw the tattered remains of the yellow police tape that surrounded the spot where Heidi had been found and noted that a couple of locals were eyeing it and even taking photos. One was Kathy Cooper's husband, Craig, and he gave her a sarcastic thumbs-up, and held up his cell phone, taking a photo of her standing gaping at him. Great, now she knew what his new Facebook photo was going to be! Kathy had found the perfect husband, one willing to be as jerky as she could be.

She slammed the van door shut and pelted up the back path and into the house. What was wrong with Kathy *and* her husband? What had Jaymie ever done to her to justify the rumors and ill will? When this was all over, she was going to confront her onetime friend and have it out.

She stared out the back summer porch door and thought about Anna's concerns about the violence that had tainted their quiet little town in the last few days, as Hoppy bounced around, barking at a squirrel on the shed roof and the gawkers near the fence. Delivering the Button letter to police headquarters would give her the opportunity to ask the detective what exactly was being done to catch the murderer of Trevor Standish. Hopefully that *also* meant nabbing the attacker who had hurt Heidi and broken in to her home.

It was late afternoon, but she finally decided she was not going to be intimidated by the occasional lookie-loo. She'd take the Button letter to the police before evening fell, even though she was worried that the first person the cops would look at with suspicion would be Daniel. It was one thing for her to vaguely suspect him, but quite another to see him raked over the coals, when all he had done was to be helpful. Her stomach churned. This dithering was unlike her, but then, this whole mess was like nothing she'd ever experienced.

So first, while she worked up her guts to face the Queensville police with the Button letter and all she feared and suspected about it, she was going to get her plants in. She changed into appropriate clothes for the dirty task of gardening; for her that meant cutoffs and an old T-shirt of Joel's with Green Day's "heart grenade" *American Idiot* album cover on it. Maybe the two of them had never been much of a fit. He liked alt rock; she was into girly Brit pop. He favored local microbrew beer; she preferred tea or wine. But surely being together had been more than the sum of their differences? Even after talking to him, she had no real clue why he had left.

It still hurt a bit, but it was better. Definitely better. At least now she could remember all the things about him that drove her nuts. It wasn't exactly a short list.

She confined Hoppy to the house—one thing she did *not* need was his help in digging—and removed the flats of plants from the van and set them in the shade of the garage; some were wilting after too long in the heat of the vehicle, so she turned on the hose and gave them a good long drink. A week or so ago she had been ambitious enough to dig the garden beds, preparing them for the new perennials and annuals. One stretched the length of the far side of the yard, shaded in mid-summer by the trumpet vine that grew in lush profusion over the edge of the ancient garage. A second narrow bed fronted the summer porch. It would be in full sun most of the day, and needed heat tolerant flowers.

In the hour or so she was gone to the nursery, Bill Waterman had come back and removed the storm windows off the summer porch, including the one smashed the night before; they were lined up along the side of the shed, waiting to be put away. Bill, a lifelong resident of Queensville, was like that, fitting in small tasks for steady clients between larger jobs. The summer people paid a premium for his help, but he never forgot his town people, like Jaymie, Mrs. Bellwood and Trip Findley.

Her lips tightened as she surveyed her backyard. She loved her home so much, but the murder and the attack on Heidi left her feeling uneasy. Just at that moment, though, a Queensville Township Police cruiser edged down the narrow back lane. The driver was a deputy she didn't recognize, but she waved, relieved by the visible police presence. He waved back and chased away a guy with a digital camera, then went back to his observation, slowly driving along, his gaze traveling over each backyard.

She took a deep breath, her anxiety eased. Time to garden. If she worked nonstop, she could have most of it planted before sundown, then she'd bathe, change, and take the letter to the police station and explain.

But right now, gardening. Grandma Leighton always said there was nothing like getting your hands dirty to settle your mind. She had quite a few plants, lots of work ahead. There were also a few boxes for the front windows and two black urns that graced either side of the front door. Those would be planted out in annuals, a few petunias, some ivy and a spike to give height and drama. The first step, she supposed, other than standing and staring at the empty gardens, was to get the gardening tools, window boxes and urn planters out of the shed.

She pulled the creaky door open, and peered into the dark. Once, she had just bolted into the dark, and had stepped on a little mouse. She'd had a shock, but the poor mouse suffered worse, shrieking in terror as her foot almost ended his life prematurely. She was about to step in to the twelve-foot-by-twelve-foot space, but hesitated. Did she really want to start the gardening now? She was tired, and she wasn't sure why. Life had seemed full of upheavals lately. What she really *wanted* to do was make a cup of tea and sit in the garden with the stack of vintage cookbooks.

But that wasn't going to happen. She was beginning to wish she had gone to the police with the Button letter as soon as she'd found it. Until the murder was solved, life could not return to the ease it once had. Oddly enough, she had started out being calm about it all, but as the days progressed, she was getting more and more agitated, uneasy even in her own comfortable home, especially now that she'd discovered what the murdered man and his assailant were after. It would all get better after she turned the letter in, she reassured herself, but maybe she *would* go and stay with Dee or Valetta for a few days.

She took a deep breath, squared her shoulders, and stepped into the dim interior, reaching for the light chain that hung from the fixture in the ceiling of the shed. She found the chain, but nothing happened when she pulled it. "Darn!" she said. What a time for the bulb to blow out.

The shed was as familiar as the house, though, after almost thirty years of living there. The spade was on the left, with the other long-handled implements. If she just felt around . . . she moved cautiously, one hand out, and felt for the long handles of the rake, shovel, spade and hoe. No wood handles, but cloth. What the heck? She batted at it, and felt fleshy firmness under the cloth.

"Don't move, or I'll blow your head off!"

❊ Seventeen ❊

A STEELY HAND GRIPPED her arm, and Jaymie screamed loudly.

"Shut up, willya?" he said, his tone plaintive.

She thrashed about, barked her shin on the potting bench and knocked over the garden tools; they clattered to the cement floor. She tensed to scream again, but he put one rough, smelly hand over her mouth, muffling her effectively; all her struggling accomplished was that he pinned her arms behind her with one strong arm while keeping her silent.

"Stop it!" he grunted. "Stop struggling!"

Had she made enough noise to attract attention? Oh, how she hoped now for one of those sick, murder-obsessed thrill seekers to be lingering. Even Kathy Cooper's husband could be her savior! She seriously considered biting the man's hand, but couldn't bear to put her mouth around his smelly digits. "I'll stop if you promise not to shoot me," she mumbled, her voice stifled and shaking so much it was unrecognizable, even to herself.

"I don't *have* a gun," he said, holding her arms still in a rough grasp. But at least he took his hand off her mouth.

"You said you'd blow my head off if I moved." Her heart was pounding like a machine gun, rat-a-tat-tat against her rib cage, and she took in deep, heavy breaths of dusty air to try to calm herself.

"That was just to scare you."

"Mission accomplished," she snapped. Trying to ignore the nauseating sense of her heart pounding in her throat, she let her eyes adjust to the dust-scented dimness and twisted around to look at her captor. "What do you want?" she asked, afraid of the answer.

"Got a spare hundred thou?" he asked, his voice laced with desperation.

"What?"

"I need money. Why else would I be in this hick town, for my health?"

"So why are you in my shed?"

"I need to see Brett. The asshole isn't answering his cell."

"Brett Delgado!" She twisted more and peered through the gloom at the disheveled man. "Are you Ted Abernathy?"

"You got it in one," he said, his tone glum.

A chill raced down her back, chased by a trickle of sweat. In the close confines of the dusty shed it was starting to feel warm, and the other man's body odor was leaving her faint. She tensed to bolt, but sensing it, he grabbed her arm again, and growled, "Stop it, willya? Why won't you just let me think?"

She could scream, but she didn't relish that smelly hand over her mouth and nose again. Her mind was going a mile a minute: she hoped the police cruiser passed by again and noticed something wrong; she urgently needed to pee; she wished she had let Hoppy stay outside, because he would be going crazy right that moment, like he had when poor Heidi was lying behind the shed.

"Did you kill Trevor Standish?" she blurted, twisting to try to see him.

He plopped down on a stool by the potting bench, and since he had a tight grip on her arm, she was yanked down, too. Her legs folded under her, and her knees scraped on the dirty shed floor. He didn't even pretend not to understand her. "No way! He was dead when I got there."

"To my summer porch. But you knew who he was?"

"Well, yeah."

"Did Brett kill him?"

He was silent for a long moment, then shook his head. "Nah. He didn't do it. Why would he?"

Now that her heart rate was calming—the guy didn't seem terribly dangerous, despite the death grip he had on her arm—she could again reason and figure a way out of this. She needed to keep him talking so he wouldn't have time to plan anything heinous and, in the meantime, plot her escape. "I heard noise and came downstairs and found Trevor dead. Did you see the killer?" she asked.

He groaned. "I saw *something*. Some*one*."

"But it wasn't Brett?"

"Brett wanted the . . . the thing we came here for."

An oblique answer. Was he or Brett the other guy who'd fought at the auction with Trevor Standish over the Hoosier and the treasure it contained? If he knew who Trevor Standish was, and if it was Brett who had pointed the guy out to him, then Ted was deeply involved somehow in the Button search. "I know what you're looking for. Did you get into a tussle with someone at the auction?"

"Aha, so *you* musta found it!" he exclaimed, tightening his grip.

She squirmed. "So you *are* the guy who wrestled with Trevor over bidding on the cabinet!"

"Did you find it, the . . . item we wanted?" He paused and narrowed his eyes. "Wait a minute, you're fishing, aren't you? Do you even know what I'm talking about?"

She twisted and watched his shadowy eyes, barely visible in the dim light that leaked through the tattered curtains from the slanting sun. How much should she say, now that she had spilled the pintos? "How else would I know about the fight at the auction? It's a letter. Really old."

He scratched his scruffy chin. "Okay. For argument's sake, say it's a letter." He was trembling, the tremors vibrating through her body too, where he held her tightly. "Who has it now?"

"I'm not telling *you*! I don't have it anymore. I gave it away. Let go of me," she said, jerking her arm out of his grasp. To her dismay, one fat tear leaked out of his eye and ran down his dirty face, leaving a clean(ish) trail through the grime. "Hey, don't cry!"

"I'm not," he said, swiping the back of his hand across his cheek. "I'm just real tired. And hungry. And I'm sorry for scaring you. I'm not that kind of guy, really." He released her and covered his face with his hands.

Jaymie got to her feet with difficulty and stretched out her cramped legs. "Just tell me what's going on?"

"I wish I knew! I could kill the sonuvabitch who killed Trevor, just for giving me such a scare."

"What about Heidi?" she asked.

"Heidi?"

"She's the girl who was found out here last night, knocked out. Are you saying you didn't have anything to do with that?"

"Look," he said, with pleading in his voice. "I've been hiding out in a boathouse down at the marina for days."

So that explained the car parked in the marina parking lot. The police had searched the marina, but if someone was determined to hide, she guessed he could evade notice. He was dirty enough to have been in the oily water, even, at some point.

"I didn't do any of it, not Standish's murder and not that girl being hurt . . . none of it! Why would I? I don't even know who that is. Heidi? What is she, a frickin' escapee from a kid's book? Look, all I know is, I need to talk to Brett. I've tried to call him but he doesn't answer, and now my cell phone is dead. I can't go back to the bed-and-breakfast. Look at what happened with you! First thing you thought was I killed Trevor."

"I might not have thought that if you hadn't run away!"

"I was scared. Finding a dead body will do that to a guy!" He hung his head and was silent for a long moment. "Look, will you give Brett a message for me if I let you go?"

Jaymie thought for a few seconds. If she said yes, he'd probably let her go, but she might never know any more than he was about to tell her in his message. If she said no . . . well, she still had only his word for it that he didn't have a gun. "Why were you sneaking up to my summer porch? And if you didn't kill Trevor Standish, why did you run?"

He sighed and looked up at the ceiling. "I'm not exactly . . ." He paused and shook his head. "Look, I've been in some trouble. First off, I'm Canadian and I'm not supposed to be down here. I was scared, so shoot me. I'd have left, but I need money!"

"Okay, let's just figure this out," Jaymie said. "You and Brett are clearly not gay lovers intending to marry."

"No."

Jaymie should have listened to Becca about that. Not that it would have made any difference. "You're in a scheme to steal something and get money, am I right so far?"

He shrugged. "I didn't think of it as stealing."

"If you didn't think of it as stealing, you wouldn't all have been sneaking around about it," she retorted. "So you were here to get the letter."

"I gotta get out of here," he said, ducking down to try to peer out the crack between the curtains. "You're gonna call the cops the minute I let you go, and they're gonna think I killed Trevor."

"Not if they solve the murder! I just want to find out who

killed Trevor Standish, and I believe that you didn't do it. But I also know it has something to do with that letter. You were in this with Brett. What's your part?"

"My only job was supposed to be to copy the letter."

"Copy it; you mean, *forge* it!"

He nodded. "I'm the best. Brett was supposed to get the letter, and I was going to make a copy. Or maybe two. Or three. He *said* I could make one for myself, and sell it! I need money."

"What for?"

"I have a sick mother who needs an operation—"

Jaymie made a rude noise. "Don't give me that. You have paid health care in Canada. What did you really need the money for?"

"I took something that doesn't belong to me, and I lost it."

"What?"

He growled and grimaced. "Okay, all right! I got messed up with some people, and I took the wrong briefcase and it had money in it, and then I lost it. In Vegas. Now I hafta pay them back, or . . ." He shook his head. "Sounds like the plot of a frickin' caper movie, but it's true. I don't even want to think about that."

"So you hooked up with Brett and agreed to forge the letter?"

He nodded. "That's *all* I was supposed to do! No risks, Brett said, nothing but a little forgery!"

"But *Brett* was supposed to steal it? So why were you the one who came to the summer porch that night? *You* must have been going to steal it."

"I didn't want to," he whined, wringing his hands. "Brett made me!"

"*Made* you? How?"

"Said I had to earn my share."

"But you were going to forge the letter; that was your share of the work, wasn't it?"

"Yeah, yeah. But we didn't *have* the damn letter," he said, in a tone you use when talking to a slow-witted three-year-old. "Brett was supposed to get it from someone else, but he said we could make a whole lot *more* money if we did it together, just us. 'Cut out the middle man,' he said, then laughed with this weird look on his face."

"You were going to forge it, then, and Brett would sell the copy?"

The man nodded. "*His* copy. He said I could make an extra for myself, and sell it. I need a hundred thou." He was trembling again. "I can't go back to Canada without it, and I'm not supposed to be in the States."

"So you were at the auction; did you know where the letter was?"

"I didn't, and Brett *said* he didn't, but I don't know about that now. Damn double-crosser."

"Double-crosser? What do you mean?" Jaymie asked.

"He was in on this with someone else, but I didn't know that at first, and he didn't tell me who. I figured that out on my own."

"Who was he in on it with?"

"Never you mind," Ted said. "Look, I gotta get out of here. In case you hadn't noticed, someone out there is willing to kill for that letter."

"Ted, if you truly didn't kill Trevor Standish, you really need to go to the police. You could give them valuable information! After all, you did see someone, you said. Tell them that!"

Abernathy got an odd look on his face. "Tell the police I was there and saw someone, but have no proof who it is?" He shook his head, then frowned. "No way. Look, do you still have the Button letter?"

"No. I . . . I turned it in to the police."

"Then I gotta get out of here. I have things to do."

"Find Brett, you mean?"

"Screw Brett," he said vehemently. "I just thought of a way to make some money off of this deal even without the darned letter!" Abernathy pushed past her, opened the shed door, looked both ways, and was gone before Jaymie could remonstrate.

She called the police right away, of course, and was sitting on a kitchen chair cleaning the scrapes on her knees with alcohol when the cops arrived, sirens screeching, for the third time in four days. Hoppy barked and danced around the kitchen as the deputy she had seen cruise by earlier came up to the house, gun drawn.

"Abernathy left," she called out, through the door. "I *told* the dispatcher that!"

The young man holstered his gun and came into the kitchen from the summer porch, Denver hissing and glaring at him from under the Hoosier. "Sorry, ma'am. We thought y'may have been held at gunpoint, y'know, even on the phone."

"Well, I'm not. He's gone." She shook her head and capped the alcohol bottle, tossing the dirty cotton swabs in the garbage. This whole mess was getting old. She wanted to get on with her life instead of worrying about assailants now every time she was alone. It gave her a new, steely determination to get to the bottom of the mess. She was still scared, but now she was scared *and* angry. She looked up at the deputy, and said, "I need to talk to Detective Christian, because this has to do with the murder that happened here. He's going to want to hear it, and I don't want to repeat myself."

Five minutes later Detective Christian strolled into Jaymie's kitchen. He was just as good-looking as Jaymie remembered, but she did her best not to get flustered, despite the inevitable blushing, which thankfully was minor this time. She had a lot to tell him, and she didn't want to get sidetracked. He sat down at the table and took out a notepad. Hoppy danced around and put his one front paw on the detective's thigh, but the detective gently pushed the little dog away. With a disappointed whine, Hoppy wobbled out the back door to watch the police as they searched the shed, dusting for fingerprints yet again.

Jaymie told him what had happened, that Ted Abernathy had grabbed her in the shed. He was not responsible for Trevor Standish's murder, according to him—she believed him, Jaymie admitted—but Brett Delgado might be involved. She related Abernathy's cryptic comment, when he'd called Brett a double-crosser. Christian immediately sent Deputy Trewent, a Welsh immigrant, out to broaden the search already underway for Ted Abernathy, and to look next door for Brett Delgado.

"Now, Ms. Leighton, you told the deputy you had some things to tell us. Is there more than this?" His expression was neutral, but his words were laden with suspicion.

"I haven't been holding anything back deliberately, if that's what you're thinking," she said with some alarm. She gazed into his gray, dark-lashed eyes. She hadn't told them everything, but she would now.

"Why don't you just tell me whatever it is that you haven't been *deliberately* holding back?"

"Okay. Well. I'm going to try to be completely honest," she said, tapping her fingernails on the table surface. "That's more difficult than you would think, because sometimes you don't tell everything because you only figure it out later, or you only suspect something and aren't sure, or . . . well, lots of reasons."

"And that is the difficulty of police work, Ms. Leighton."

She ordered her thoughts while he waited. She was not going to let anyone rush her. "First, I think I know now what the thief was after when he broke into my house, but whether that thief was the dead man, or someone else, I still don't know."

"I don't think I understand."

She held up one hand. "Just wait one moment. I have something to show you." She raced out to the van, retrieved the Button letter, and came back to the kitchen. Her hands trembled as she opened the sandwich bag and carefully extracted the priceless artifact. She explained what it was, and where and how she'd found it as his eyes widened and his thick eyebrows rose.

"Why didn't you tell us this last night, when we responded to the call about the break-in and found Miss Lockland?"

"I don't know," she said wearily, not willing to meet his eyes. "Ultimately, it wouldn't have made a bit of difference anyway, but I really don't know. It was the middle of the night, and I was confused, and scared, and it all just . . . overwhelmed me."

He was silent for a moment, but then said, "You weren't trying to cover up for your ex-boyfriend, Joel Anderson, were you?"

"What?" Of all the things she expected him to say, that was not one of the possibilities. "I don't understand!"

"Please just go on, Ms. Leighton."

But her mind was working on what he had asked, and she realized a couple of things. "Oh!" She met his inquisitive gaze. "The man Joel popped at the auction was Trevor Standish. *That's* why the dead guy had a bloody nose! So you think he knew something, or . . . or was involved somehow with Standish?"

Detective Christian's gray eyes were cool, but a smile lingered at the corners of his nicely shaped mouth. "It's something I've been considering. In any normal murder case, if I find out the victim had an altercation with someone just hours before he died, I've got my lead suspect."

"You haven't lived here long, have you?" she asked.

"What has that got to do with anything?"

"But you haven't, am I right?"

"I just got this job a month or so ago. Moved here from Chicago at the same time."

She was tempted to ask, but didn't, why a man his age would mire himself in a small-town police department after working in Chicago. He seemed cut out for bigger things, but it was none of her business and would just distract from her point. "Queensville is a small town, Detective. Everybody is entangled in everyone else's lives. There are no separate spheres; it's a big Venn diagram of interconnected circles."

"I've never heard small-town life described quite like that," he said, a smile finally breaking his somber demeanor. "Now please, Ms. Leighton, tell me about this letter and why you've connected it with Ted Abernathy."

"Okay. All right." She started at the beginning, but when she got to the part about Daniel Collins coming to her house the night before and how he'd helped her find the letter, which she hid temporarily in the Hoosier cabinet book that was later stolen in the late-night break-in, he stopped writing and looked up at her. She shrugged. "I don't know if they're connected. I really don't. Daniel is a multimillionaire. If he wanted something like the Button letter, wouldn't he just buy it?"

"Some things aren't for sale," he said.

"I think it's more likely he's an innocent party," she said stubbornly. "I think, if anyone is involved, it might be his friend, Zell McIntosh. That guy showed up the very night the murder happened, and he was friends with Trevor Standish, too."

He was silent for a moment, then said, "Excuse me." He got up, paced out to the lawn and called someone.

Jaymie heard Daniel Collins's name mentioned, as well as Zell McIntosh's, and she had an awful feeling they were picking both men up for questioning. But it was not her fault; she had to tell the police everything.

When the detective came back in to sit down, he said, "Anything more, Ms. Leighton?"

"Yes."

He sighed and raised his brows. "Go on, then."

"Ted Abernathy—the guy in my shed—said that he and Brett Delgado, who is staying next door at the bed-and-breakfast, were here to find this letter and forge a copy," she said, tapping her finger next to the Button. "To sell. In fact, he was planning to make multiple copies to sell. Brett had a partner, Ted said, but it can't have been Trevor Standish." She explained why. It seemed to her that there were far too many people involved in the whole caper. It was like an English bedroom farce, with folks popping in and out of the deal.

Abernathy had said he hadn't killed Standish, but a killer wouldn't necessarily tell the truth, would he? Everything he said may have been a lie.

"I don't think Abernathy killed Trevor, I really don't," she said, even though she could not be sure. "He just didn't seem like a killer. He was too scared. If he had killed Trevor, then he'd know there was no murderer to be scared of, right?"

"Doesn't mean he wouldn't be scared of someone else, or paranoid."

The police had finished searching the shed by the time she was done telling Detective Christian everything, but there was no evidence taken away that Jaymie could see. Another deputy, again the young African-American woman, came to the back door and softly said, "Detective? Could I speak with you?"

She and Christian hunched together and murmured, but Jaymie pricked up her ears and heard the woman say something about Brett Delgado not being at the bed-and-breakfast. Had he fled? Was that an admission of guilt? It was all so confusing, and Jaymie just wished it were over. She had flowers to plant and life to live, and as bad as she felt for poor Trevor Standish, and however much she wanted the killer brought to justice, she wanted it done sooner, not later.

Abernathy seemed to have disappeared without a trace, from what she could gather from the police, but Jaymie felt sure they'd find him. How far could he have gotten on foot?

She tried to make sense of what Abernathy had said, about making some money off the deal even without the letter—she had told Christian about that, too—but couldn't figure it out. When Detective Christian came back to her, she slid the plastic bag across the table to him. "I'd feel a whole lot safer if you would take this away and lock it up somewhere. It's a piece of American history, and belongs to Mr. Bourne, anyway."

"Strictly speaking, it's not evidence, since it was never in anyone's hands but yours," he said. "But I think that's a wise choice, Ms. Leighton."

"Jaymie," she said, and smiled.

He stilled for a moment, then smiled back. "I think that's a wise choice, *Jaymie*. I'll write a receipt for this, and have someone drop it off. I don't think you should stay here tonight, at least not alone. We're going to have police here, but still . . . would you consider staying somewhere else?"

"I will," she said. "I've got a couple of friends I can crash with."

He left, taking the valuable letter with him, and after her heart stopped pounding so hard—he had a killer smile—she worried about all she had told him. Was it fair to tell the detective about Daniel Collins's part in her discovery of the letter? How could she have avoided it? She had not said a word that wasn't true. It was still far more likely that the killer was Abernathy—he admitted having been there, after all—or his partner-in-crime, Brett Delgado. Brett taking off was surely some admission of guilt? Or *had* he taken off?

Too many questions and not enough answers!

It was getting late, almost dinnertime, and time she decided what she was going to do that night.

"Valetta, I need a favor," she said, when her friend answered the phone at the pharmacy.

"Shoot."

She explained what had happened that afternoon, interrupted by many exclamations from Valetta, and then said,

"So, it looks like I'm going to need somewhere to stay. I wouldn't admit it to anyone else, but I'm a little freaked. Can I stay at your place?"

"You could." After a pause, Valetta said, "Or I could come and stay at your place tonight."

Jaymie replied, thunderstruck, "You'd do that? Really?"

"Done deal. That way you don't have to admit to anyone that you got chased out of your house, and you don't need to try to take Denver anywhere. I know you'd never leave him there alone, and he doesn't travel well."

Jaymie grimaced. That was the truth. Even his yearly checkup at the vet's was a trial for her independent and suspicious cat. "You are a lifesaver."

"I am indeed a Life Saver, and the flavor is Butter Rum. Have a cup of tea ready at 8:09, because that's how long it'll take me to walk over after I close up at eight."

The cops were still snooping around the shed out back, and the phone rang repeatedly. Finally, after a couple of hours of ignoring it, she dashed to grab the handset off the kitchen table and shouted, "Hello!"

There was silence, but then Daniel said, "Jaymie? Are you okay?"

She plunked down in a chair and put her head in her hand, thinking she might need a good cry. "I'm sorry for yelling, Daniel. It's been a rough day."

"I heard about what happened last night, and then today. I wanted to come over, but then the cops asked Zell and me to come to the station, and we were there for quite a while answering all kinds of questions, and . . . look, are you okay?"

"I'm fine, really," she said, sniffling. "Daniel, did you tell anyone about us finding the Button Gwinnett letter? I don't mean the cops, I mean last night?" She stared at the line of cookbooks on her shelf; the books were still askew from the late-night theft, and there was now some fingerprint dust on the shelf, though the cops didn't find any "latents," as they called fingerprints other than her own.

"No, I would never do that. It was just between us."

"Not Zell, even?" Sometimes one didn't consider telling a friend as telling anyone.

"No, of course not. I didn't say a word to *anyone*. What are you getting at, Jaymie?"

She kind of wished he'd said he'd blabbed it all over the place. What could she say? She turned in her chair and stared out the back window to the yard. Hoppy begged to come up as Denver slunk in from the summer porch. She picked up her dog and cuddled him on her lap.

The silence had stretched to an uncomfortable length. "You don't think I broke in and tried to get the letter? Jaymie! Did someone actually steal the letter, then? And you think I have it?"

So he didn't know that the actual letter wasn't stolen? She was about to say that of course she didn't suspect him, but her tangled mind rounded on itself and pondered if he was being clever by implying he didn't know if the letter had been stolen or not. "I don't know, Daniel, I just don't know!"

"Jaymie, can I come over?"

"No. Daniel, I just . . . I'm confused right now."

He was silent, but then said, "I understand. Really, Jaymie, I do. But please, if you still have that damned letter, get rid of it! Give it to the cops or something. Okay? And don't stay there tonight, please!"

"I'll talk to you soon, I promise," she said, without telling him that she had already turned the letter over to the detective, and without saying that Valetta was coming to stay over. "Really, I'm okay."

She said it, even though she wasn't. Not really. She definitely needed to figure things out, because her head hurt with the confusion. Ted Abernathy, from having been an unknown, had leaped to the top of her list of suspects. She

knew from occasionally reading mysteries to consider
motive, means and opportunity, and he had all three.
Motive: He clearly wanted the letter. Means: Well, the weapon
was right there, attached to her Hoosier. Anyone could hit
someone over the head, right? And opportunity: Abernathy
had already admitted to being at the scene of the crime. If
everything he'd said was true and he was completely innocent, wouldn't he have turned himself in, rather than run,
despite his lame excuses?

But she still had a hinky feeling in her spine about Brett
Delgado. His motive was the same as Abernathy's—he
wanted the letter, and if Standish was in his way, maybe
murder had seemed like the only solution—and he had been
lying ever since he got to Queensville. She remembered,
with a shiver, the night she'd brought the Hoosier cabinet
home. He had helped her, even suggesting the placement of
the cabinet, and all while he'd asked questions that had
seemed innocent at the time, but now, in retrospect, could
be ascribed to sinister motives. When did they all go to bed?
he had asked. Did she have an alarm system? Was Hoppy
the only dog? He could have done the deed and used Abernathy as a shield, implicating him to cover up his own
misdeed.

She could not ignore the other player in this game, Daniel Collins. And with him came an even likelier suspect,
Zell McIntosh. Both guys knew Trevor Standish, and both
had contact with him in the last few weeks. One or both of
them could be lying about not knowing where Trevor was
in the days before his death. A valuable letter was motive
enough. Daniel sure seemed to know a lot about Button
Gwinnett for a tech geek. And Zell McIntosh . . . why had
he shown up so early, when he wasn't expected until the next
day? She had a feeling one of them might be guilty, but not
both, because their stories didn't mesh well enough. If they
were in it together, their stories would be more cohesive.
Neither could truly vouch for his whereabouts during the

murder, because Daniel had said he was on the road, driving toward Queensville, but that was only his own word; and Zell . . . well, who knew if he truly was in his car, sleeping, all night?

And then there was the suspect she had not yet identified. Who had been speaking to Trevor Standish at the auction, having what she now thought of as the "Button" conversation? She tried to recall exactly what had been said; if she remembered right, the dominant voice of the two had said he would bid, but he didn't exactly know where the Button was in what she now knew was the Hoosier. They'd figure that out after the auction. But the secondary voice, which Jaymie couldn't identify as male or female, hadn't trusted the first speaker.

As far as she could tell, every single person involved was out to cheat every other person. Apparently the saying was wrong: there was no honor among thieves.

❖ Eighteen ❖

S HE MADE A late dinner for herself and treats for Denver and Hoppy, chicken pulled off the bone for both animals. After eating, and while waiting for Valetta, she went up to look through the photos that Becca had sent her. Before the ones of the tea, there were a few of the auction, and Jaymie scanned through them, noting all the folks she knew. But she was stopped dead by one. She got closer to the screen and peered at a picture Becca had shot of the Minton she was after, but did not get; in the background, a little out of focus, but recognizable, was a figure that she was almost sure was Zell McIntosh.

She enlarged it and leaned toward the monitor screen, looking more closely. It *was* Zell! What was he doing at the auction? He hadn't said he was there, but she supposed he hadn't said he wasn't either. It could be totally innocent, or sinister. It felt weird, given that Trevor was there, too. Were the two in cahoots? That was a question for Daniel, but it was going to have to wait until she saw him next. One thing she was going to do, though, was send the photo to the Queensville police. She found their site and e-mail address, and attached the photo to an e-mail that explained it.

Valetta arrived, toothbrush and nightie in a little bag, and Jaymie made her tea and some chicken salad. After she ate, they sat at the kitchen table, and Jaymie explained a lot of what had gone on, including the Button Gwinnett letter. She owed it to so good a friend, she thought, and it helped her think it through.

"But Valetta, I'd appreciate it if you could keep this under your hat." She watched her friend with trepidation. She was a gossip, and surely asking a gossip to keep something quiet was an invitation to spread it wider?

"Not a problem," she said, inviting Denver up onto her lap and sharing the last of her chicken salad with him.

To Jaymie's amazement, he ate it right off the end of her finger. She had never tried that before with her own cat. "Really, Valetta, this is serious. I'm not comfortable letting others know about the letter and everything just yet, until this is all out of the way and solved."

"Jaymie, I know you all think I'm a gossip," Valetta said, on a sigh, "but I am also a pharmacist. I know a whole lot that I cannot and will not divulge. If you knew some of the stuff people order via catalogue? And don't get me started on the meds." She winked and smiled. "I only spread what I know is all right to talk about. And I mix in a liberal helping of manure, so folks never know if they can trust what I'm saying. Makes it more interesting."

"I knew it!" Jaymie crowed. "I just knew you were having me on, sometimes. So, if you know so much, what's the scoop on Detective Zachary Christian?"

"Mmmm, isn't he something? He questioned me, and I felt like purring and crawling onto his lap."

Jaymie hooted with laughter at the incongruity of the pinch-faced Valetta Nibley purring, and from there the conversation became mildly salacious, involving many of the local men, until both retired, Valetta to the guest room/ office. Sleep was easier to find, and Jaymie drifted off quickly.

The next morning, over coffee, she remembered something she wanted to ask Valetta about. She fetched the pavé pin—Becca had seen it, but hadn't recognized it—and set it down in front of her friend. She explained where she found it and when.

Valetta picked it up and turned it over. "I think those are real diamonds, and the gold is genuine. It's a tack pin of some sort. Kinda small, though. Strange."

"Do you think it could be a man's tiepin?" she asked, thinking of the black-and-white checked tie Zell McIntosh had worn at the tea.

Valetta considered. "Maybe." She examined it closely. "I swear I've seen this before."

"Where?"

"That's just the thing; I can't remember." She shook her head, doubt filling her eyes. "It was just a glance, if I did see it."

"If you think of where, call me. It just seems so strange that it was in the garden like that."

Valetta left for work, and Jaymie filled the sink and did the breakfast dishes. What was her next course of action? She wanted to find out what Brett Delgado had been doing since he'd gotten into Queensville. She knew *how* he was involved, in the sense that he wanted the Button letter to forge, but who else, other than Ted Abernathy, was involved with him? Just as she was finishing the dishes, the phone rang; Anna called her with the news that Tabitha was not well, and she was taking her little girl to the doctor. The guests had already had breakfast, but could Jaymie come over to answer the phone and keep an eye on things?

Jaymie said she'd do more than that, she'd also clean the rooms. As well as helping Anna, it gave Jaymie the access she needed to Brett Delgado's room, if he hadn't cleared out everything. But Anna would have told her if that was the case.

A few minutes later, she ushered her worried friend outside to her car with Tabitha in her arms, watched while the toddler was strapped into her car seat and waved good-bye to the mother and daughter. As concerned as she too was about the child, she had work to do. The Carters, Anna's only current guests, were already gone for the day over to Canada. Another couple had left the evening before, and their room still wasn't clean, but Jaymie decided to start in Brett Delgado's room. She was curious—very, *very* curious—about the fellow, his possible involvement in Trevor Standish's death and his knowledge about Abernathy's whereabouts over the last few days. If he had been gone from the B&B since the previous day, chances were he wasn't coming back. Was he the thief who had stolen the Hoosier book the night before last?

Cautiously, she opened the door to Brett Delgado's room to find that he was tidy. She hurriedly cleaned, vacuuming the carpet and wiping the surfaces, and then steeled herself to snoop. He had lied about who he was and his relationship with Abernathy, and he was involved waist-deep in the mystery surrounding the Button letter. That much she knew. But could he be the murderer? Ted Abernathy had said he didn't think so, but he was running scared from something.

She kept her eyes peeled and was rewarded by a cryptic note on the phone pad: *Call Queen*, with a phone number scrawled after it. She dusted around it. Queen? What the heck did that mean? Did she dare take it, or would she remember it? The area code was not local, so it was not the Queensville Inn—or *anything* in Queensville, for that matter—but maybe it was a cell phone. She stared at the number, then closed her eyes and repeated it to herself.

She had it memorized. The door tone from below told her she was not alone in the house anymore, so she scooted out of the room, duster in one hand and pushing the vacuum ahead of her to the next room. The Carters, who had left to catch the ferry to Canada before she'd arrived, were just coming in. They had missed the ferry, and so had come back for a brief rest before taking the next. Jaymie told them they were welcome to stay in their room; she would come back later in the day to clean it.

She went directly on to the vacant room and for the next hour vacuumed, dusted, scrubbed and replaced, making the room perfect for the next visitors, due to arrive that afternoon. She replenished the hospitality tray from the store of prepackaged goodies in Anna's larder, and closed the door on a perfect haven of peace and tranquility.

Anna returned soon after and put Tabitha in bed. The doctor had assured her it was just a juvenile fever accompanying a minor cold, but Anna was clearly still worried. Jaymie hugged her and told her she'd be back later in the day to clean the Carters' room, but Anna told her she'd do it herself. It would be therapy for her worries to do something energetic.

Jaymie returned home and stood by her phone, debating calling the number on Brett's pad. The problem with doing that was, she had no clue whom she was calling. If the person had caller ID, they would know exactly who she was, while she still wouldn't know a thing about them. What would she learn from the call if she didn't know what to ask? Nothing.

Taking the stairs two at a time, to the excitement of Hoppy, who bounded after her, she sat down at her computer and looked up the area code. It was a Chicago area number, but when she did a search on a 411 site, it turned out to be a cell phone, and she could not access the owner's name. It could mean something, or nothing at all.

She needed to think things through, and that required fresh air and physical activity. "C'mon, Hoppy. Let's go for a walk along the river." The little dog was ecstatic. The yard was fine, but a walk meant new, though familiar, places, new scents and the chance to catch up on his pee-mail. She pulled on a hoodie—the day had turned a little chilly—and they set off.

What did she know so far about the murder in her home, and what could she surmise?

Trevor Standish had successfully tracked down the Button Gwinnett letter to Queensville, but had only figured out it was in the Hoosier cabinet in time to bid on it at the auction. Someone else—probably either Ted Abernathy or Brett Delgado—figured out the Button's location from Trevor's bidding and joined in, to try to get the Hoosier first. A fight ensued, and Jaymie got the Hoosier.

But there was another possibility she hadn't considered. Say someone who knew her, or knew of her, saw her bidding on the Hoosier. He may then have interfered in Trevor's bidding, knowing that he would have access to her home if she got the Hoosier. She was thinking of Daniel Collins; he knew where she lived and could get to the Hoosier cabinet if it ended up at her house. His recent warmth toward her could all be camouflage. He had expressed an interest in the Hoosier right from the first time he'd seen it, and he had shown up at an awfully convenient time, just as she was taking it apart and found the letter.

She still didn't believe he would have killed his friend. His anguish was real; she'd bet her life on that. But maybe he'd learned about the letter from Trevor, and had intended to cut his buddy out of the Button chase. One of the other conspirators—Brett or Ted—may have been more vicious in their determination to get to the letter first. Or they may have been watching Trevor, following him, even.

All of the facts about Daniel also went for his friend Zell, whom she already knew had been at the auction, though he had never mentioned it. Who knew what Zell was capable of, where a million-dollar letter was involved? He seemed to be willing to use others for money, as evidenced by his willingness to languish in Queensville on his "rich buddy's dime," as he himself had said. In fact, the three men could have started out on the Button quest together, but the partnership could have fractured at some point, leading to the competing bids, and even to the murder.

She shook her head and inhaled the cool air deeply, glancing around. Mrs. Bellwood was sitting on the porch of her stately home—she was on high ground near the river and overlooked it and Heartbreak Island—and waved to Jaymie. She waved back, but Hoppy tugged on the leash, pulling her along. Jaymie never could teach him to walk properly on a leash, but he jerked up quickly at a light post and sniffed, nose to the ground.

Her mind returned to the puzzle as her little dog sniffed his pee-mail. So, in the middle of the night Trevor had sneaked up to the summer porch to find and steal the Button letter. He may have followed her home, and could even have been watching from somewhere. He had used a crowbar or pry bar of some sort to pull the door off its hinges, and he then started to unload the Hoosier, looking for the letter—and then what?

Why did the murderer, if he or she had been looking for the Button letter, not wait to attack until Standish had it in hand? She paused as an idea came to her. Could Standish have had something *else* in his hand that was mistaken for the letter? That was an intriguing line of thought, and something she would have to offer the police.

Hoppy was done, and they moved on.

So, if Standish had something else in his hand that was mistaken for the Button letter, what could it have been? She recalled the corner of a piece of paper that she had swept up from the summer porch in the aftermath of the murder and had looked at a couple of nights before. Possibly that corner was what had been left in his grasp when whatever had been mistaken for the letter was torn out of his fingers as he lay dying. It looked old, and she had already conjectured that it was a receipt of some sort. Could that have been why the table of weights and measures on the inside of the upper cabinet door was loose? Had Standish found this item behind it, and opened it out, trying to find out what it was, just as he was attacked? She would turn that torn corner over to Detective Christian, just in case. If they found the matching piece, as far-fetched and unlikely as that seemed, then it would certainly mean the owner had some explaining to do. It was a stretch, because even if she was right, the person had probably balled up the stolen paper and tossed it in the garbage.

Hoppy tugged excitedly on the leash and yapped his disappointment at Jaymie's sedate pace as they neared the river. Queensville had a long path that edged the St. Clair; it was called the Boardwalk, though it was concrete, because it once had been a true boardwalk. The chamber of commerce had led a fund drive to install park benches and new lighting, making the area a magnet for tourists and locals alike, and named the attached small green space Boardwalk Park. Hoppy loved the smells and watching the boats, and, she suspected, chasing the odd water rat as it slipped along the shore, long tail waving through the water.

Hoppy led her toward the Boardwalk, and from there down toward the docks and the marina, but she was still puzzling out the sequence of events leading to the murder and the aftermath. What exactly was Brett Delgado's part in all of this? He had brought Ted Abernathy into the arrangement with the idea that the forger would make a copy, or copies, of the letter, so he thought he would have it at some point. But could that mean he had planned from the beginning to kill Trevor Standish? She could imagine him sneaking up behind Standish and grabbing the paper out of his hands, but could she imagine him brutally whacking the fellow and leaving him for dead? It was too awful, and he appeared to be so civilized.

And if he had done that, how did she reconcile what Ted Abernathy had said, that Brett had sent him over to steal the letter from the Hoosier?

Brett was certainly one possible suspect, but wasn't Ted more likely? When she thought about it, she only had Ted Abernathy's word for it that he had just come to her garden shed the morning he'd grabbed her. He could have been there the night before, when Heidi got whacked and Jaymie's house was broken into, and if that was true . . . she stopped in her tracks and thought, swiping her bangs out of her eyes and looking off toward the river without really seeing anything.

She remembered, the afternoon before, turning from regarding her cookbook shelf to look out the window at her backyard. What would the reverse view be? Anyone, Ted included, could have seen through her back window as she put the letter in the Hoosier book. She had thought Daniel was the only one who knew, but if someone else knew what was in the Hoosier, her actions that night, even observed from a distance, may have been as clear as if he were standing beside her.

If that was the case, and Abernathy was the one who had stolen the recipe from the book, then he could have lingered to remedy his mistake, intending to break into her home once he knew she was gone, and search her place for the real letter. Except he hadn't even done it when he'd had the opportunity. She had been gone for an hour to the plant nursery, and presumably he had been in her shed the whole time.

Hoppy pulled at the leash and yipped. They walked down the steeply sloped path from the Boardwalk toward the marina, where a crowd was gathered waiting for the ferry to Heartbreak Island and Johnsonville, Ontario. If Abernathy *was* telling the truth, she mused, was it someone else, then, who'd bopped Heidi on the head and was looking in Jaymie's back window while she put the letter in the Hoosier book? If so, who could it be?

As she descended toward the marina, she heard the wail of a siren, and a police car screamed to a stop at the top of the hill. Officer Jenkins threw herself out of the cruiser and scaled down the slope, not bothering with the path. Jaymie, alerted to something unusual going on, trotted the last few feet to where the officer had bolted, at the heart of the crowd that had gathered. What was going on?

She pushed through the crowd, but the officer, with a grim expression, said, "Back up, ma'am."

"But what's going on?" Jaymie said, picking Hoppy up as he squirmed with excitement.

"It's a body!" someone next to her said.

She turned to find Valetta Nibley standing at her side, her eyes snapping with interest behind thick glasses. "A body?"

Valetta nodded and bent to whisper, "Someone came in to the Emporium and said something about a floater, so I took a break and came right down. It's another dead person . . . two murders in a week!"

"Valetta, we've had tragic deaths before," Jaymie reminded her. "Especially in summer. Doesn't mean it's murder. People are always falling out of boats after drinking too much, or in bad weather, or without life vests on. We get at least one or two every summer." It was a sad fact of life. People didn't take their "fun" seriously enough, and too often paid the ultimate price for not being water-safe while swimming, wave running, boating and rafting.

"True. But it's more exciting if it's a murder."

Jaymie shivered. "It's all fine if it's in a book, but real life . . . not so much."

"I'm here with you, Jaymie," Valetta said with sympathy. "I'll stay at your place again tonight, and every night until they catch the jerk."

She squeezed her friend's arm in silent thanks. A breeze came up from the river, whipping the poplars along the Boardwalk, the rustling sound of their silvery leaves carried on the wind. They stood side by side. Jaymie put Hoppy back down and he trotted to the end of his leash to sniff butts with Junk Junior, who was being walked by his daddy, Jewel's current live-in boyfriend, Arnaldo. "Can you see anything?" Jaymie asked the taller Valetta.

"Not really. Not yet."

A gasp rippled through the crowd as the EMTs valiantly lifted the dripping body from the river's edge and hoisted it onto a backboard. As they made their way up the path, they came directly past Jaymie and she looked into the dead, dripping, lakeweed-festooned but too-familiar face.

❧ Nineteen ❧

IT WAS HER erstwhile captor, Ted Abernathy! Jaymie began to shake, and pulled Hoppy's leash, rewinding it in its retractable holder.

Valetta put her hand on Jaymie's arm. "What's wrong with you? You're quivering like a Chihuahua in a draft."

"I know who that is!" She raced off with Hoppy in tow and stumbled up the incline. She reached the EMT and tugged on his sleeve. "I know who that is!" she said gasping and panting.

The police officer had followed, and said, "Are you saying you can identify this homicide victim?"

"Homicide? Didn't he just drown?" Jaymie, against her better judgment, focused on Ted Abernathy's body. His neck had a gaping, flapping, bloodless wound that could only have been inflicted by something lethally sharp. She swallowed hard, and said numbly, "His name is . . . *was* . . . Ted Abernathy, and he was wanted for questioning in the murder of Trevor Standish."

This time she did not need to be told that she had to go to the police station, she just took Hoppy home and went, driving as if on autopilot and parking in the visitor's lot. She was put in a comfortable room alone, and a man in a suit came in and sat down across the table from her.

"I'm Detective Tewksbury, Ms. Leighton. Detective Christian is unavailable at the moment. Why don't you tell me what you told the patrol officer?"

She spilled it all, though it was surprisingly little. The dead man was Ted Abernathy, who had snatched her the previous day and held her captive for a few minutes in her shed. Ted Abernathy, as she had told them the previous day, had been in Queensville at Brett Delgado's behest, by his own admission, to forge a copy of the Button letter, which she had turned over to the police.

Even as she spoke, trying to tell them everything she knew or even surmised, she conned it over in her mind. This most recent event left her puzzled. She had been thinking that Abernathy was perhaps guilty of the murder of Trevor Standish, but now she wasn't sure. Having been murdered himself didn't absolve him, she supposed, but was it possible that there were two killers? It just didn't seem likely.

One more time she toted up her cast of suspects in her head: Brett Delgado, Ted Abernathy, Daniel Collins, Zell McIntosh, and perhaps Nathan and Lynn Foster. The couple didn't seem to have a lot to do with anything, but they kept popping up. In the words of Alice, curiouser and curiouser.

Was she leaving anyone out? There could be others that she just hadn't encountered yet, but she rather doubted it. Whoever it was had been in and around Queensville for a week or more, and strangers were duly noted; even though they were a tourist town, people still saw stuff.

Detective Tewksbury's expression was one of confusion by the time she was done talking, and he flipped through pages of notes. When he looked back up at her with an assessing gaze, he told her he'd be sure to share all her thoughts with Detective Christian. She could go home now, he said, and sent her on her way.

When she got home from the police station, she listened to her messages and decided to follow up on one harmless line of investigation. She let Hoppy out in the yard and sat down on the back step with the phone. Maybe she could shorten her list of suspects by two. Denver climbed into her lap in an unusual display of affection, and she petted him and scruffed his cheeks while she made a call. "Dee?" she said, as the woman answered. "It's Jaymie."

"Hey, how are you? Have you found anything more about how your Grandma Leighton is doing?"

Jaymie told her the gist of a phone message she had just gotten. Grandma Leighton was doing well and moving back to her retirement home already. Becca was relieved, and wanted to know what was going on in Queensville. "I'm going to have to call her and give her the long version, or she won't be happy!" Jaymie said, explaining to her shocked friend some of what had gone on in the last couple of days. She then got down to the purpose of her call, a favor of sorts.

Dee readily agreed to her request, saying, "I'll do you one better than letting you into the appropriate rooms. If you want, I'll loan you my uniform, and you can go into the Queensville as a maid. No one even notices the cleaning crew, trust me! I only work for Lyle when he has someone phone in sick, but that happens a lot, and today happens to be one of those days. You can sub for me this afternoon."

"I worked there when I was in high school, remember? I know the routine pretty well."

"So what are you looking for?"

"Can I tell you later, Dee? I'm probably wrong, but I promise I'll tell you."

"Okay, but *please* don't let Lyle know you're snooping! He'd kill me."

"Trust me, I'm going to be in and out of there in no time flat and do my . . . well, *your* job perfectly. I just want to nose around." The benefit of a maid's job was that some of it was identical to snooping, but what would mean nothing to a maid, might mean something to Jaymie.

Jaymie fed the animals and confined them to the house, promising Hoppy a long walk the next day, since today's had been truncated by identifying a dead body. Then she set out to DeeDee's place, changing into her uniform there as Dee called her brother and told him Jaymie was substituting for her that afternoon.

Jaymie walked over to the Inn, through the parking lot—as always, it was full of luxury vehicles: a black Cadillac, a cream Lincoln, a champagne Lexus—and let herself in the employee entrance with her borrowed passkey. She refamiliarized herself with the routine, pushed the cleaning cart to the service elevator, then slipped down the hall carrying a stack of towels to the room that was her main focus. The occupants were gone over to Canada for the day, DeeDee had assured her, after inquiring in the brief call to her brother-in-law, Lyle. Not that Dee could inquire directly, but a few pointed comments had been enough to elicit the necessary information.

She let herself into the Fosters' suite.

It was the most elegant in the Inn, a double room with a sitting room and private bath furnished in gorgeous antiques authentic to the era of the original home. The bedroom was painted aqua, with one signature wall hung with Seabrook wallpaper. Once in the suite, Jaymie found that "searching" was easier imagined than undertaken. Yes, she was the maid, so she had a right to be there, but it felt like an invasion of the couple's privacy to be looking through their baggage.

So she cleaned first, and as she cleaned she kept her eyes open. Vacuuming was a great excuse to investigate the closets and under the beds. There were a number of suits hanging in the closet and shoes on the floor, but nothing of interest. Making the bed allowed her to check the mattress for anything hidden, and wiping down the surfaces allowed her to search the books on the nightstand. His was a thick biography of President Andrew Jackson, while her reading material was a *Collector's Quarterly* and an art magazine. Lynn Foster had a penchant for showy jewelry: a large art glass pendant, a black-and-white silk flower piece and some gaudy cocktail rings.

As she moved it to dust the side table, the black-and-white silk flower fluttered to the floor, falling apart as it did so. It seemed to be missing a piece in the center, something that would have kept it together and allowed it to be pinned to a piece of clothing. Like the black suit Lynn Foster had worn to the auction. With the black-and-white silk flower on the lapel. Jaymie paused and straightened. She picked up and examined the flower more closely; it did indeed have a pin-hole in the center.

She sat down on the side of the bed and picked up the phone, hit nine for an outside line and called the pharmacy. "Valetta," she hissed, trembling. "Do you remember yet where you've seen the pavé pin I showed you this morning?"

"Not yet. Why do you sound so odd? What happened about that dead body? Where are you, Jaymie?"

"Never mind," she said. "The pin! Focus, Valetta; could it be that you last saw the pin in the middle of a black-and-white silk flower on the lapel of a black suit worn by Mrs. Lynn Foster?"

"That's it!" Valetta said, her shriek piercing on the phone. "That's it! How did you guess that?"

"I didn't guess. I'm sitting here holding the flower, which is falling apart because it's missing the pin. I've got to go." She hung up, her hand trembling. There was no possible reason Lynn Foster's diamond pin should have been in her garden, unless Lynn Foster had been in her yard.

But it didn't prove that she was a cold-blooded killer. Jaymie would need more to believe that. She eyed their luggage, but the bags were locked, and staring at them was not going to elucidate the mystery. She moved on, leafing through the books on their nightstand and the drawers of the bureau. Nothing beyond some sleeping medication with Nathan's name on the label. Her mind was churning with speculation.

Her final cleaning/searching foray was to the bathroom. It was tidy enough, but needed a thorough clean if she was going to do the Queensville Inn proud. *And* if she was going to search properly. She moved the Fosters' personal items—his shaving kit, her nail polish and cosmetic kit, and a collector's magazine—from the room, then removed the soiled towels and old soap, dumping them into the dirty linens bag and the garbage on the housekeeping cart, respectively. Then the tub, tile surround, vanity and mirrors needed a good scrub, on to the sink, and then the toilet.

Nothing. Time to return the Fosters' items to their washroom. As Jaymie picked up the collector's magazine and leafed through it, a piece of folded paper fell to the now-spotless floor. She retrieved it; it was yellowed in places, but the fold appeared new, and the paper, minus a corner torn off, flattened back to its original shape. It was a Sears and Roebuck receipt for a Hoosier brand kitchen cabinet. The date in the corner was March 31, 1927, and the buyer was listed as Mrs. Harold Bourne, Wolverhampton, Michigan.

Jaymie stared at it for a long minute. The full impact of the find soaked in, bit by bit. This sales receipt had been torn from the hands of the dying Trevor Standish. Shivering, she tucked the receipt back where it had come from and set the magazine on the edge of the vanity. Either Lynn or Nathan Foster, or the two of them together, must be the killer or killers. But something was wrong with the thought that Nathan could have been involved. He appeared to be so gentlemanly—but then she remembered his steely grip on her arm. He was stronger than he looked, and more determined.

Still, something nagged at her, some question in her

mind. It wasn't just that Nathan Foster didn't seem the type to commit cold-blooded murder; there was something more that made her question his involvement. She glanced at her watch and was appalled at the time she had taken. If she was going to finish DeeDee's rounds and get out of the Inn, she would have to hurry and clean while she thought. At least she knew the Fosters were gone for the day.

Just a few last-minute touches. As she swiped at the bathroom floor with a clean rag, erasing her own footprints on the damp tile, she noticed that a mascara had rolled under the vanity. How had she missed that? She picked it up, and wondered . . . did it belong to Lynn Foster, or was it from a previous occupant of the room? She couldn't just leave it on the floor, and she couldn't toss it in the garbage. It was an expensive department store brand. If she saw what brand of other cosmetics Lynn Foster used, it might help. Women tended to buy lipstick, foundation and other makeup from a single brand-name line.

She unzipped the cosmetic bag; it was indeed Lynn Foster's brand of makeup, but among the jumbled pots of cosmetics and an empty pill bottle with her husband's name on it she found a familiar-looking piece of paper crumpled up in it. Familiar, because she had put it in the Hoosier cabinet book with her own two hands. It was the old mimeographed copy of the recipe for Queen Elizabeth cake that she had put in the book as a replacement for the Button letter. That placed Lynn Foster in particular at the scene of the break-in and theft of her Hoosier book, and the attack on Heidi! It followed that she was also the one who'd killed Trevor Standish.

Lynn alone, *not* with Nathan! Jaymie sat down on the lid of the closed toilet. *Now* she remembered what it was that was tugging at her memory concerning Nathan Foster. She had been in the Emporium when he was at Valetta's pharmacy window, complaining that he didn't have enough sleeping pills. He was sure he had brought enough, but had run out. Which meant he was either lying and taking more than he should, or someone was taking some out of his bottle for some reason.

If Lynn Foster was sneaking out of their room at night to murder people, then she might drug her husband with extra sleeping medication to aid her in her deception. And thus, the empty bottle of his sleeping meds in her makeup bag. It made sense.

A noise from the bedroom made her jump up and she shoved the folded recipe back in the cosmetic bag, fingers trembling and clumsy. Hoping it wasn't one of the other chambermaids—or worse, Lyle—Jaymie tucked the bag back on the shelf and hurriedly ended her cleaning by folding the end of the fresh toilet tissue roll into a V, like she had been taught years before as a fledgling chambermaid.

A voice behind her coldly demanded, "What the hell are you doing here?"

It was Lynn Foster.

❋ Twenty ❋

JAYMIE TURNED AWAY, hoping the woman hadn't seen her face clearly, and said, "I'm cleaning the bathroom."

"Really?" The woman stared at her for a long moment. Her gaze flicked over the room and then settled back on Jaymie; she tilted her head, looking at her profile. "Do you think I don't recognize you? You're the girl who bought the Hoosier, and you've been snooping," she said, pulling something out of her handbag. "I don't appreciate that. It means you're suspicious, and I don't like suspicious people."

Jaymie looked down at the woman's rock-steady hands to find herself staring at a very small, but lethal-looking pistol. "I don't know what you mean," she said, summoning all her nerve to steady her voice.

Her expression cold, her voice tight with suppressed fury, Lynn Foster said, "Are you going to tell me this is a coincidence, you being in my room, snooping?"

"I work part-time for Lyle, the owner. Look, I'm sorry if

I've upset you. I'm not suspicious, and I haven't been snooping, honest."

"I don't have time for this. Sit!" she commanded.

Jaymie sat down on the toilet again.

"I suppose you've figured it out," she said, her coldly
handsome face set in an expression like granite. The cold
fluorescent light harshened the effect of the mauve lipstick
she wore. "I know for a fact that you still have the Button
Gwinnett letter, and I want it."

Well, of course she knew—or thought she knew—that
Jaymie still had the letter, since she had tried to steal it, and
had gotten a vintage recipe instead!

"You will give it to me," the woman said with a menac-
ing tone, "but I have to figure out a way of getting it that
allows me to get away from here. Those damned cops were
sniffing around here too much, asking all kinds of questions."

Jaymie was silent for a moment. This was a woman who
would kill without remorse, and Jaymie had to be as careful
now as she could be. "All right, I won't pretend I don't know
what you're talking about." She paused, working through it
in her mind. If she could convince the woman she didn't
have the letter anymore, then it would eliminate all reason
to keep her there. It might make her expendable too, but
either way she went into this, she was taking a risk. "Look,
I gave the Button letter to the police after the break-in at my
home."

The woman snorted, the sound echoing off the hard surfaces in the bathroom. "As if I would believe that! You
clearly know how valuable it is, and bought the Hoosier for
the same reason we wanted it. I don't know which of those
undesirables is your partner, but I suspect it's the late Ted
Abernathy."

So she knew about Abernathy, and probably Brett, as
well. Jaymie's stomach turned over. Her mind churning, she
wondered, did she really want to convince the woman that

she no longer had the letter? As she'd already realized, not having it would make her expendable. Lynn Foster was cavalier about dispatching human life, so maybe it was better if she thought she had something to gain by keeping Jaymie alive.

Okay, so Jaymie was not going to go out of her way to convince the woman she no longer had the letter. She stared at Lynn Foster, who was pacing in the narrow confines of the space between the bathroom vanity and the door. Had this elegant woman really killed two men? Was it possible? "You might think I know more than I do," she said, slowly. "I stumbled across the Button letter. Really, I *did*!" she emphasized, as the woman snorted again in derision.

Lynn Foster stopped and stared down at Jaymie. "You didn't know what was in the Hoosier when you bought it?"

Jaymie shook her head. "I fell in love with the cabinet. I collect early and mid-century kitchen stuff."

Lynn Foster chuckled, then began to laugh, guffawing until tears ran down her cheeks. "Good God, I'll give you some money and you can buy me a lotto ticket!"

A momentary urge to lunge for the gun seized Jaymie, but the impulse disappeared as the other woman sobered and maintained her iron grip on the pistol. The bathroom was not a good place to tackle Lynn; too many places to hit one's head and be knocked out. She was going to have to be smart about this. She had stumbled into it on her own, and she'd have to get herself out of it the same way. "Yes, I'm a very lucky person," she said, staring at the gun.

Lynn Foster's expression darkened. "If people would just stay out of my business, I wouldn't end up having to be so nasty!"

"So . . . you knew Trevor Standish, already, right?" That was something she had just figured out; there had been no mistake about the hotel bill for "Lachlan McIntosh," nor had he been swindling them. That was just a tale told to Lyle Stubbs to separate themselves from the murdered man. They must have had some kind of agreement for him to find the Button letter. "You knew him from before. Standish was a historical expert—I know that from his buddy, Daniel Collins—but was his specialty signers of the Declaration?"

Lynn Foster nodded. "And he was as crooked as a pawnshop owner," she said, with a twisted smile.

So, finding and stealing the Button letter was the venture Trevor had wanted his frat brother, Daniel, to invest in. But he couldn't tell his honest buddy the truth. She *knew* Daniel wasn't involved in anything underhanded! And it looked like Zell was absolved, too. Ted Abernathy and Brett Delgado were still involved somehow, though how, she had no clue. Jaymie's thoughts returned to her perilous situation. "How did he find out about it in the first place?" she asked. Keep her talking, she thought, until she figured a way out of her dilemma.

"He was looking for either a customer or a partner when he joined the collector's group Nathan and I belong to. It wasn't long before he approached us with his wild tale of an undiscovered Button Gwinnett letter floating around out there somewhere in some little podunk town in Michigan."

"There actually is a Podunk, Michigan," Jaymie said, helpfully, then bit her lip as she saw how the woman's face tightened in fury. Her insides quivered with nerves, but she needed to focus on getting out of this situation alive. A gun poked in her direction was distracting. *Focus, Jaymie!* she admonished herself. "How did he find out about the letter?" she asked again, genuinely curious, but also hoping to distract Lynn Foster, getting her to let her attention stray long enough for Jaymie to do something about it.

"Trevor's father—he was a professor of history at Ball State—got a call back in the early sixties from the old man who owned it; it was some kind of family heirloom. He acted like he wanted to sell it, but he was probably fishing, to see if it was worth anything." She looked at her watch, then back to Jaymie. "Nowadays he could find out in five minutes on the Internet, but back then it wasn't so easy."

Mr. Bourne's eccentric father! Even in the sixties a Button Gwinnett letter would have been considered valuable, but he must have decided to squirrel it away. Then, as he went senile, he kept making jokes about it, the "Button, button" suggestions and "The Witch of Coos" poem mention. Strange that he never told his son or wife about the letter, but then he sounded like he'd been an odd kind of guy, secretive and off-kilter, enjoying taunting his family and laughing at them. "But Trevor Standish didn't know *exactly* where it was," Jaymie said. Old Mr. Bourne had died without ever telling the truth.

"No. His dad used to tell the story about the phone call . . . cocktail party chitchat among the town-and-gown set. But the old guy either didn't say exactly where it was, or Trevor's father never mentioned it. If Standish had known where it was, he would have just marched up here, broken into the house and stolen it!"

"But he couldn't very well sell a stolen letter, could he?"

Lynn gave her a withering look and waved the gun, saying, "Oh, come *on*! Surely you're not *that* naïve. Collectors only care that it's authentic, not how it was obtained."

How nice that she was able to speak for all collectors like that, Jaymie mused.

"He didn't have a clue," the woman continued, "other than it was somewhere near Queensville. I don't think his dad ever even got the man's full name, just Horace or Harvey or Harold; something like that. Do you know how many men had those names? So Trevor needed money to come to the area to look around. It took him forever."

It started to make sense. "So that's why you and your husband paid for his room, and why you came yourself." Trevor had gone to them for money when his good buddy Daniel had turned him down.

"It was taking so long that Nathan and I started to think he was going to cheat us. Nathan wanted to keep the letter; he's a 'Declaration signer' collector. But I told him it was going to be too valuable, and he agreed to think about selling it. Our split was going to be fifty-fifty on the auction proceeds, but I suspected if Trevor got that letter without us around to protect our investment, he'd disappear and we'd never find him." She glanced at her watch again.

Time was for some reason important. Was she expecting someone? Did she have an appointment? *Keep her talking!* "But he hadn't given you any reason not to believe he would keep up his end of the bargain."

"He was always shady. I did my background work; Trevor Standish was fired from Ball State for plagiarizing an undergrad's paper on Paul Revere. Anyway, enough talk! Just shut up for a minute!" The woman turned away and murmured, "I need to figure out what to do."

Lynn Foster's voice, muffled like that as she turned away, was familiar. Where had she heard it before? "You're the one I overheard at the auction!" Jaymie blurted. "You were talking to Trevor Standish about the Button!"

Lynn whirled and glared at Jaymie, narrowing her eyes. "You overheard us? Is that when you decided to buy the Hoosier from under us? Did you intend to sell the letter to the highest bidder?"

"I overheard your conversation, but I didn't know what it was about, and I didn't know about the letter when I bought the cabinet," Jaymie explained again, trying not to show her exasperation. "Look, can we move out of the bathroom? The echo in here is giving me a headache."

"Okay, but don't try anything funny," she said, waving the gun.

Jaymie preceded the other woman out to the bedroom and glanced around, looking for a way out of her dilemma. She moved toward the window, but the street outside was deserted. "I really didn't know anything about the letter," she said again, as she feverishly tried to work out how to get out of this predicament.

"I don't believe that."

"It's true! No one else knew about it, not even the owner of the Hoosier!" She paused, then said, turning to face Lynn Foster, "It sounds like neither you nor Trevor trusted each other. You wanted to know where the letter was hidden in the Hoosier, and he said he didn't know."

"He was going to get the letter, then cut and run."

Lynn Foster, like most who were willing to cheat others, expected to be cheated every step of the way, too. She didn't trust anyone because she knew what she would do in a similar situation, and in this case, she could have been right. There were so many people involved, it seemed, and the connections were baffling. "Where does Brett Delgado figure in to this?" Jaymie asked, trying to untangle the twisted knot of mystery.

Just at that moment the door to the suite opened, and Jaymie muttered a quick prayer that it would be salvation. What would she do? How could she take advantage of the distraction?

Nathan Foster entered and started back at the sight of his wife with a gun trained on the maid. "What is going on here?" he demanded. "Lynn, what are you doing with a gun?"

❧ Twenty-one ❧

"**I**THOUGHT YOU were staying in the coffee shop!" the woman said to her husband.

"I needed the facilities, and you know I don't like public washrooms," he said fretfully, picking at a scab on his wrist. He swept his gray hair back and peered at Jaymie. "This is the girl who was playing a maid at the tea, the one who bought the Hoosier cabinet at auction."

"Yes, *yes*! The one who has the Button letter. And she won't give it up."

"But surely a gun is taking things too far, Lynn, dear."

"Nathan, you know how much money we've invested in this," Lynn said, her voice changing subtly, to a softer, almost pleading tone.

Jaymie watched her in horror, thinking it was like watching a snake go from hissing and threatening, reared back in attack mode, to sly and slithery.

"We've been plagued by idiots, my darling! Trevor double-crossed us, and now this . . . this country bumpkin wants to deny us our right to that letter! We've paid and paid; we deserve it!"

Unbelievable, how she had the nerve to cite murder and treachery—oh, and a little money—as somehow earning the right to the Button Gwinnett letter, a piece of valuable American history that belonged to an old man in a nursing home. But Nathan Foster was eating it up with a spoon, smiling fatuously at his wife.

"I want you to have the letter," she cooed, her tone caressing and wheedling. "It was going to be your birthday gift, the crowning glory to our signer collection. You can keep it, the one piece you need for a full collection; I would never deprive you of so much pleasure. I have so *little* I can give you, dearest, but this was going to be the most magnificent present."

A foolish grin twisted his mouth. "Lynny, my dear!" He crossed the floor and took his wife in his arms. "And I thought lately you had seemed so distant!"

"I've been so focused on this. You know how I get, darling."

"Mr. Foster," Jaymie blurted, "your wife has been feeding you sleeping pills while she sneaks out to . . . to . . ." She trailed off at the vicious look Lynn gave her over her husband's shoulder, the pistol still trained on her. She did not want to give the woman any excuse for an "accidental" discharge of the weapon.

"I beg your pardon?" Nathan said, turning toward Jaymie.

"Don't listen to her," Lynn said. "She's raving. She has the letter and she will give it to me. We paid Trevor to find it, and it rightfully belongs to *us*."

Jaymie quickly toted up her options while she tried to look inoffensive and helpless, wrapping her arms around herself. She could throw herself on Nathan's mercy and hope he let her go, but that didn't seem likely, given his infatuation with his wife. He appeared firmly under his wife's thumb. She *could* let it all play out and see where it took her. That was a risky tack to take, doubly so since she really *didn't* have the letter, and thus had no bargaining chip. But Lynn hadn't believed her when she told her she didn't have it. She *could* say she had hidden it, and then, while stalling, plan her escape.

The situation seemed more volatile, somehow, with Nathan there. Jaymie hadn't lost sight of the fact that Lynn was, she knew now, a killer, but it was imperative not to make her desperate. Desperation was what would drive her to use the gun. Jaymie could imagine the court case, with husband and wife standing united: *"I was just showing the maid our little gun, and it accidentally went off! A tragic mistake."*

"I think she's going to be sensible, my dearest," Lynn said, watching Jaymie. "Aren't you?"

"I'm always sensible," Jaymie replied, proud of how steady her voice was.

"She won't even admit she knew the Button letter was in the Hoosier when she bought it!" Lynn declared.

Her husband shook his head and made a *tsk, tsk* sound between his teeth. As she suspected, Nathan Foster would be no help to her at all. But she couldn't let it go without one more try. "Look, Mr. Foster, this is not how you want to get the letter," she said, clasping her hands together in front of her in a pleading way. "I'll gladly *give* it to you, if you just let me go!"

He shook his head sadly. "Lynn, my dear, you were precipitous in pulling out your little gun, it seems."

The woman threaded one arm through her husband's and around his back. "I did what I had to do for us . . . for *you*! I swear, before the end of the day the letter will be with the one person who can appreciate it above all the others."

He smiled and rubbed her shoulder. "Thank you, my dear. You are truly one woman in a million."

Jaymie squinted and thought, trying to take advantage of the tender moment to answer some of the questions she still had. It also kept her calm to force her mind to think logically. "So . . ." she said, slowly, "you both were in it with Brett Delgado and his forger friend, Ted?"

Nathan Foster opened his mouth, but Lynn hurriedly interrupted him, saying, "Let me take care of this, darling," grabbing his sport coat sleeve and tugging him toward the door. "She's just trying to stall, now, but you won't leave here without that Button Gwinnett letter, I promise, and you know I always keep my promises! Go back down to the café and make sure we're not interrupted. If you see anyone headed up here—especially those pesky hick cops—stall them somehow!"

He bumbled out, muttering something under his breath. Jaymie started to second-guess herself immediately. Should she have thrown herself at Nathan and begged his aid? It didn't seem likely that it would have helped. Neither of the murder victims had been shot, but Jaymie didn't want to be the first.

"Idiot," Lynn said, as the door closed. "God, I need a smoke!" She paced around the room, looked up at the clock and feverishly added, "If he thinks I want this letter for him, then he deserves whatever he gets."

She fished a cell phone out of her purse, tossing a set of keys down on the table near her as she did so. When Jaymie glanced down, she saw the Cadillac logo on the keychain. As Lynn Foster flipped open her cell phone, Jaymie felt a thread of unease wind through her. Jaymie now knew how Brett Delgado had found out about the Button Gwinnett letter. She had seen Brett talking to Lynn just the day before, when she had seen him leaning in the window of the black Cadillac, the same car that was in the Inn parking lot. "You're having an affair with Brett Delgado," she suddenly said.

"Brett's a very attractive fellow," Lynn said with a wry grin. "And about as gay as Bill Clinton, despite what he's told the locals. For a while he was entertaining. Especially since we both share a love of money; more, I thought, than any interest in antiques and documents."

"If you and Brett are in this together, what about Nathan?" Stalling was working so far, but it was only a plan if she actually had something in mind, some way of getting out of the room without a bullet buried in her. If she could just get closer to the door . . .

"Don't be so naïve!" Lynn Foster's patrician face looked hard in the light streaming in from the window, the lines around her mouth showing her true age. "Eight years ago Nathan was my insurance policy against old age, but I've paid my premium in years spent cosseting his ego, and he's not shown to be a good return on my investment. I thought with his health issues that he'd be dead in a year, but he got better. Who knew a man could recover completely from a serious heart attack and quintuple bypass surgery?" She shrugged and shook her head. "I'm over forty, now, but I'm not dead."

Jaymie wondered, given what Lynn had done to Trevor and Ted, why hadn't she just murdered her husband? A little overdose of the sleeping meds and she's a widow with a life insurance payoff.

Lynn Foster paced back and forth. "Now, how to get the Button and get out of here?"

"So, you and Brett," Jaymie hurriedly said, trying to scramble for a way out of her predicament. She edged toward the door. "Did you plan to take the letter and leave together?"

"That was the *original* plan. Stop moving toward the door and sit down, right there." She indicated the sofa, while she sat down in a chair near the window.

Jaymie obeyed, not liking that gun barrel pointed in her direction.

"I met Brett in the same collector's group as we met Trevor. Brett wanted me to knock Nathan off and marry him. I think he was under the same misapprehension I was, that Nathan had millions stashed somewhere, but my elderly hubby has been keeping something from me. He's not worth what he used to be."

Jaymie felt a chill at the casual talk of contemplating hubbycide. So there was not enough money left to risk murdering him for, apparently. What, no high-value insurance policy? No double indemnity? That was shortsighted of Lynn Foster.

What to do, what to *do*? How was Jaymie going to turn this awful scenario around? This was decidedly not one of her better ideas, to stay in the room. She should have run, or used poor, misled Nathan Foster as a shield and walked out before him. Above all else, Jaymie knew one thing . . . she needed to *keep Lynn talking.* "You honestly don't sound overly committed to Brett," she said.

Lynn Foster gazed at her in bemusement. "So you're one of those idiots who believe in romance, and that love is forever."

"If you had an affair, you must feel *something* for him!"

"Why would I want to share the money from the letter? Besides, Brett has shown a distressing tendency toward greed," she said, with a huffy twitch to her narrow shoulders. "The minute he brought that miserable weakling Ted Abernathy into the plan, I knew it would be trouble. My plan was to snatch the letter from Trevor and take off, but Brett wanted to keep the original and make a copy to sell."

Or *copies*, Abernathy had said to Jaymie. Brett may have been intending to run a little scam on his ladylove, keeping a couple of copies to sell for his own profit.

"That's dicey business," Lynn continued, rifling through her purse, the pistol sagging and bobbing. She pulled out a pack of cigarettes, jerked one out and lit it, inhaling deeply with a sigh of satisfaction. "It was *always* going to be difficult to sell the Button Gwinnett letter," she said, her tone calmer and more contemplative and the pistol now steady on Jaymie. "I didn't want a buyer who would ask any questions. Even so, though, I felt fairly comfortable selling the original. I mean, who owns something that's been hidden for fifty years? Finders keepers, right?"

"Not really. It's not as if it was found on the sidewalk. You all knew the letter was in that Hoosier, so you should have told Mr. Bourne. He's still alive, after all, and even if he wasn't, his heirs would own it."

"Oh, so you say you didn't even know it was there, but when you found it, you were planning on handing it over to this Bourne fellow?"

The scorn in the woman's voice didn't shake Jaymie's opinion. "I would have, without a doubt. And yet you were worried about Brett wanting to make and sell a forged copy?" It didn't make any sense to her.

"Rich people can be ruthless. If we sold the copy to the wrong rich person, and they found out it was a forgery . . ." Lynn Foster trailed off and shook her head, a grim expression on her face. "It's not worth the risk."

So, it was not a moral issue, but purely self-preservation. Jaymie had heard it said that every person had their own definition of "acceptable risk"; in Lynn's mind, knocking off two people was apparently an acceptable risk, but selling a forged copy of the Button letter wasn't. "Is that why you turned against Brett at the auction, because he wanted to bring Ted Abernathy in to forge the letter and sell copies? You were conspiring with Trevor Standish again, right?"

"Of course! One must be adaptable." She took a long drag on the cigarette, and then stabbed it out in an ormolu dish on a side table as she blew out a thick stream of smoke. "It would have all gone perfectly too, because Brett was clueless. Still is, I hope. But his little copycat, Ted Abernathy, must have seen Standish and I together, and suspected something was up. He didn't trust Standish *or* me, and when he saw Trevor bid on the Hoosier, he realized where the letter was and jumped into the bidding. That idiot, Trevor, lost his cool and the two started to fight. Men! Idiot jerks, all of them. Then some asshole stepped in, interfering and confusing the issue, and you got the Hoosier."

Jaymie didn't think it would be politic to say she knew the "asshole," Joel Anderson. "And Trevor ended up dead." She trembled as she said it, wondering if the woman would excuse her violent solution.

"Served him right!" she said.

"So did Ted Abernathy. End up dead."

"I know," Lynn said with a frown, but then shrugged. "Things happen."

Murder just happens? She was a cold customer! "So, after the auction, didn't Brett figure out that you were going to take the letter and ditch him?"

"Ah, but he didn't see me with Trevor; Ted did! He was suspicious, but I don't think Ted shared his info with Brett." She paused and looked thoughtful. "Or maybe he did. Maybe that's why Brett sent Abernathy over to try to steal the damned letter from under Trevor's nose."

But Abernathy had shown up a fraction too late. Lynn had merrily snatched what she thought was the Button Gwinnett letter out of Trevor's hand as he lay dying. "So, what now?" Jaymie asked, her voice quavering with tension.

Lynn's expression hardened, and her gun didn't waver. "Brett and I have reconciled and made kissy face; that kept him quiet and compliant, anyways. Poor dove; he has a weak stomach and needs a stronger soul to do his dirty work for him. He still thinks we are in some mad love affair, with me in the role of cougar to his man-kitten, I guess. He's been badly frightened by Ted's death. Such an awful thing," she said reflectively.

She seemed so detached!

Lynn sighed and shrugged. "He wants us to keep the original and sell a forged copy. I haven't disillusioned him, so far. Let him think that. But I'm taking that letter, selling it myself, and moving to Italy. The Italians really know how to live. Or Monaco." She smiled and tilted her head. "After a little surgical maintenance, I might catch myself a *real* wealthy hubby."

"It sounds . . . complicated."

"Not so much *now*. It was lovely of you to deliver yourself to me. You're going to give me the letter, and then I'm leaving town," she said, waving the gun at Jaymie. "I'll be out of your hair and out of the country in no time."

"Okay," Jaymie said, standing and stretching out her taut, nerve-constricted muscles. "Uh, so I'll go get it, and bring it back here?"

After a hoot of laughter, Lynn said, "Right, and I'll knit an afghan while I wait. Sit down! What do you think I am, an idiot? Let me think!" She paced and checked the cell phone again, then glanced up at the clock. It appeared that she was expecting a call. "The problem is," she muttered, "I can't risk you telling anyone what's going on, or anyone seeing us together, particularly Brett. And I have a buyer; I don't want to scare him off!"

A musical phrase, Beethoven's Fifth, erupted from Lynn's purse on the table by the sofa, and she dove for it while keeping the gun held up. She dropped the cell phone from her hand, then awkwardly fished another out of her purse as it continued to play the Fifth. She glanced at the call display. "Damn it! Brett again." She flipped it open. "Brett! Sweetie!" she said, with a cheerful tone. "What's up?" She listened, her expression darkening. "I know you're nervous, but calm down." She listened again. "Brett, I've got this under control." She paused, briefly, but then said, "No, you listen to *me*; I'm taking care of it. I will meet you where we discussed!" She flipped it closed and tossed the cell phone into her bag, then picked up the other.

Jaymie processed the conversation, and realized that Lynn Foster's cell phone was likely the phone number written on the pad in Brett's room at the B&B. She was either the "Queen," or it was because she was staying at the

Queensville Inn. Where was Brett Delgado? she wondered. Hiding out from the police somewhere? They must want to talk to him about Ted Abernathy. Did he know that Lynn had killed his coconspirator? It was on the tip of her tongue to ask her captor, but the woman was on the thin edge of reason, and Jaymie didn't want to tip her over that precarious cliff. Instead, she decided to ask something innocuous. "So, when did this happen, that you have a buyer?"

"Just today. Serendipitous, right? I went on to a collector's group online and put out the word—cloaked of course—that I have an extremely valuable first signer's letter that I'm willing to part with, and voila! Instant message, the guy is even local, and he wants to talk. My lovely untraceable cell phone," she said, waggling it. "Bought over the border. No one else knows about it, not even Nathan."

Jaymie decided to take a chance, and said, "It must have been real annoying when you stole what you thought was the Button letter from my Hoosier book, only to find out it was just a recipe for Queen Elizabeth cake."

Lynn's eyes narrowed. "I was pissed off. I was watching your house, birdie binoculars in hand, hoping to sneak in and search the Hoosier myself. Then I saw you and that gangly misfit millionaire find the letter, glad cries and all! I had already hit that bumbling fool of a girl over the head, so when I saw you put the letter in that book, I thought I'd better let things cool off a little. I snuck back here, made sure Nathan was still out like a light, then crept back to steal the book. I'm not without a sense of humor; I *can* laugh sometimes, even if the Botox makes it hard to crack a proper smile. It was a good joke, my dear, the recipe in place of the letter."

She stood and pointed the gun directly at Jaymie as she walked across the room, ending by poking it in Jaymie's ribs. "But the joke is over now. I want that letter, and I want it now, or you will have a hole in your head too big to hang an earring in."

❊ Twenty-two ❊

JAYMIE'S STOMACH CLENCHED, and she felt like she was going to throw up, the glands in her throat spurting water from fear. What was she going to do? Her mind raced in circles; how had she gotten into this mess? Forget that; how would she get out of it? She had no options except escape.

"The letter, yes . . . of course you want the letter." As she stared into Lynn's icy blue eyes, the cell phone in the woman's free hand chirped, just a plain ring tone for business.

Lynn answered it, then said, "Yes, indeed. It is a genuine undiscovered Button Gwinnett letter. It's been in the same family since it was received." She paused, then said, "Well that depends on how much you're offering."

As Jaymie, heart pounding, watched her captor's face, it changed subtly, a look of wonder and greed passing over her handsome, if haggard, features. Now was a time for decisive action; the distraction of the call and the bargaining between buyer and seller might be put to use.

"In cash and bearer bonds?" Lynn Foster paced away,

the hand holding the gun relaxing until her arm was limp at her side.

This was her chance! Jaymie quietly slipped toward the door, just as Lynn turned toward her; the wary woman trained the gun back on Jaymie, put the cell phone to her own chest to muffle her words, and hissed, "You stay put!" Each word was emphasized by a jab of the gun barrel.

Jaymie froze, then obeyed, slinking back to the sofa and sinking down into it.

"I'm sorry, what did you say?" She paused and listened to her caller, glaring at Jaymie with a gleam of rapaciousness in her cold eyes. "No, I was thinking more along the lines of double that."

The beginning of a desperate plan hatched in Jaymie's brain at that moment.

"Okay, so not double, but I will need more than your offer." She paused. "Okay, all right, you won't be sorry. So, you're actually on your way to Queensville at this moment?" Lynn said. "I'm at the Queensville Inn . . . yes . . . but I'll need an hour or so." She listened, then said, "I'll be leaving directly after we make the deal, so I need a little time to pack. I told you, the letter is authentic, but I don't want it known that I have it. You *must* understand. So where do you want to meet to exchange the items?"

While the woman was talking, Jaymie turned her mind to her plan: The other day when she was in the hotel, she had been down this stretch of the Inn, only on the main floor. The Fosters were in number 207, and Mrs. Stubbs was in 107; she was right over top of the elderly woman's room that very moment! "I have to go to the washroom," Jaymie said loudly, jumping up and stomping toward it heavily. Stomping wasn't easy on the carpeted center of the suite's floor.

"Stay! Sit!" Lynn said, holding the cell phone to her chest as she spoke and waggling the gun she still held. "No, not you!" she said into the phone, turning her shoulder to Jaymie.

Lynn wouldn't murder her without having the letter, Jaymie was fairly sure. She needed to summon up every ounce of nerve she had to defy the cold-blooded killer of two men. She edged over to the uncarpeted perimeter of the room near the door and picked up a weighty marble statuette, hefting it in her hand and dropping it "accidentally" on the hardwood floor.

"Oops!" she cried. "I'm so clumsy!" She stomped over, picked it up, only to fumble and drop it again, hoping against hope that Mrs. Stubbs would be jarred awake from a peaceful nap and would be out for blood. She prayed the statue didn't break, but it would be worth the cost of replacing it to save her life. Lyle would surely not have furnished even this most elegant suite in the Inn with costly antiques.

Lynn motioned to Jaymie to stop. Her tone irritated, she said, "Look, how well do you know Queensville? Can't you just name a place to meet?" As she spoke, she stepped over to Jaymie and pointed the gun directly at her heart.

Jaymie stilled instantly. Even through the polyester maid's uniform, the barrel felt cold and hard. Life could be over in an instant; that knowledge hit her hard, and tears blurred her vision. She willed them back, blinking. This was no time to cry. She promised herself a good long sob fest later, but right now, she had to think.

"Hold on a moment!" Lynn said. She put the cell phone to her chest to muffle her words, and said, through gritted teeth, "Don't you move one more time, or I swear, I just don't give a damn. I'll put a freaking bullet through your heart!"

Jaymie shivered, closer to death than she had ever been in her life. "Okay, all right," she whispered, forcing herself to breathe slowly while her heart pounded and the sound of blood rushing in her ears made her light-headed. "I'll stay still."

"You and I are going to have to go to your place and get that letter," Lynn muttered, still holding the phone to her chest. "So help me God, if I lose this buyer because of you, I'll—"

Pounding on the door interrupted her.

"What's going on in there? Mrs. Foster, is everything all right?"

It was Lyle, bless his mama's-boy heart, and he sounded upset. It hadn't taken long for Mrs. Stubbs to roust her son. Now what? How to respond?

"Mrs. Foster, what's going on in there?" he repeated.

"Everything is fine, Mr. Stubbs," Lynn called out, turning toward the door. "I just . . . I dropped something."

Perhaps her only chance had arrived, and Jaymie was going to take it. "Lyle, it's Jaymie . . . Lynn Foster is the murderer! She's got a gun. Get the cops!" As she shouted, Jaymie pushed Lynn out of the way and bolted toward the door.

Everything happened quickly then. The gun went off as Lynn stumbled sideways, Jaymie dived to the floor, screaming, and Lyle shouted something from beyond the door as he banged on it again. The sound of sirens outside the window confused everything. Jaymie crawled toward the door.

"Don't move!" Lynn shrieked, waving the gun in the air.

But Jaymie was done listening. In one swift sequence of movements, she rolled over, staggered to her feet, picked up the marble statue and heaved it at Lynn, catching her in the knee. The woman buckled and fell to the floor just as Lyle, using his passkey, busted in.

"What the hell is going on here?" he yelled.

"Get out, Lyle; she has a gun!" Jaymie cried, grabbing his meaty shoulder as she stumbled past him, yanking him back out to the hall.

As she exited, followed by Lyle, three cops, Deputy Ng in the lead, stormed up the stairs, guns drawn. Jaymie flattened against the wall to let them pass. "Lynn Foster is the killer," she said, panting. "She's in 207, but watch out . . . she's got a gun! She threatened to kill me."

Jaymie descended the stairs two at a time and huddled in the stairwell with Lyle and Edith. Curious guests were coming to the door of the coffee shop to stare, and whispered together in clusters. Lyle was full of questions, but Jaymie just shook her head. It was all a muddle in her brain at that moment. Minutes later, Lynn was led limping down the stairs, handcuffed and teary-eyed, black mascara running in trails down her cheeks. An officer carried her gun.

"Bitch! Why couldn't you just give me the freakin' letter?" she screeched, all illusion of elegance vanished. A string of spittle hung from her lip, and her coral lip gloss was smeared over her chin. "I wasn't going to hurt you!" she sobbed. She lunged at Jaymie, but Deputy Ng jerked her back.

"Like you didn't hurt Trevor Standish and Ted Abernathy?" Jaymie retorted.

Lynn's lip trembled and she pulled up short, her face pale in the dim hallway light, her eyes underlined by smudged mascara. Deputy Ng tried to tug her away. Lynn staggered sideways a little but stood her ground. "I didn't do *anything* to them! Ted killed Trevor and then committed suicide!"

"By slashing his own throat and dumping himself in the river?" Jaymie said. "Good try!"

"Come on," the deputy said, giving the woman a shove. "We'll sort it all out down at the station."

Jaymie followed and watched as the cops marched Lynn right through the crowd by the coffee shop. Nathan Foster was sitting, reading a newspaper, at a table near the door. When he saw his wife in handcuffs, he started up. "What is going on here?" He pushed through some folks standing in a group. "I demand that you release my wife!"

They didn't heed his anguished cries and marched her out the door.

He too would likely be arrested eventually, once she'd told the whole story of what had happened that day, Jaymie thought. He was at least an accessory to his wife's attack on

Jaymie, since he did nothing to help Jaymie escape. But as much as she hoped he would be arrested, she still pitied him; if he truly didn't know his wife was a murderess, he was in for a horrible shock.

"Mr. Foster, you need to call your lawyers," Jaymie said.

"What on earth do you mean? Why?" he asked.

She sighed in exasperation and rolled her eyes. "Oh, come on! You were there, in the room, while your wife held a gun on me. She's a dangerous woman. Maybe you don't realize it, but she didn't want that letter—the Button Gwinnett letter—for you. She was going to dump you and run." He still looked disbelieving. "She killed Trevor Standish and Ted Abernathy while trying to get that letter, so she could sell it and start a new life."

"You, young lady, are not a nice person," he said, his voice trembling. "And you are out of your mind. My wife would never do anything like that!" He turned his back on her and tottered toward the door.

Jaymie followed, out to the parking lot. There, held back by an officer, was Daniel. He broke free and ran to Jaymie, grabbing her in an enveloping hug. "I was so scared for you, Jaymie!" he cried. "I was on the phone with that woman, and I could hear you in the background. I knew I had to keep her talking until the police arrived."

Her voice muffled against his chest, she said, "What are you talking about?"

He released her, but still held on to her shoulders as he gazed down at her, a foolish grin on his plain face, his eyes gleaming behind his eyeglass lenses. "Why do you think Lynn Foster suddenly had a buyer? I was scanning the Internet, trolling the forums where signer collectors gather—I was just trying to get a feel for the culture, you know, like how far these people would go to get a rare piece—and I saw what seemed like a message about the letter. I texted the person, who said they had access to a genuine, undiscovered Button Gwinnett letter. It had to be whoever was trying to steal it from your house. I mean, how many of those are there? And if they were going ahead with trying to sell it, it meant they still thought it was somewhere where they could get at it. There was a chance to lure them out into the open."

"That was you on the phone with her?" Jaymie asked, turning to watch the police put Lynn in a squad car. She never would have thought Daniel so bold.

He nodded. "Yeah. I ran her messages through the Gender Genie, and it said that the author of the texts was a woman, so I knew it had to be Lynn Foster."

"Gender Genie?"

"Online tool," he answered tersely. "Since I *knew* she didn't have the letter, that meant she was intent on doing whatever it took to get it. She was dangerous to you."

"No kidding," Jaymie said with feeling. She shivered, even though the sun was warm on her face. Lynn was staring out the car window at her with a look of such hatred, it was chilling. The car pulled out of the parking lot and sped away, watched by many of the folks who had been in the coffee shop during the excitement. Nathan had gone back in to the Inn, no doubt to call his lawyer, as she had suggested. Once she'd told the police everything, he might be arrested, too.

"I said I would buy the letter, sight unseen and no questions asked. I was a private collector, I said, who didn't care about provenance. But I was publicity-shy, I told her; if anyone was hurt, or if there was a big fuss, it was a no-go." Daniel shook his head and rubbed her shoulder. "If I'd known you'd be right there, I may not have taken a chance. I'd never forgive myself if . . . if she hurt you."

She should have trusted him; if they had worked together, she could have avoided the whole drama. Probably. Maybe. She didn't know; everything seemed so confused right then. There were so many *if*s in the case. Everything would have turned out differently if she hadn't decided to investigate the Fosters' suite: If Lynn Foster hadn't needed to go back to her room. If Daniel hadn't made the call to Lynn exactly when he had. It all could have turned out very badly for Jaymie. She was exhausted.

He offered her a ride to the police station, but she preferred to take her own van, even as shaky as she was. At least Daniel seemed to trust her abilities more than Joel ever had, and simply hugged her and told her to be careful. He'd be going too, to relate his own part in the deception. When he'd figured out what was going on, and that Jaymie was in trouble, he'd called the police just as she was making enough commotion to force Lyle to storm the room. It had all turned out, but it had been a close call.

She was not looking forward to explaining to the police why she was wearing a maid's outfit and how she had ended up in the Fosters' room, but that was not as difficult as she thought. Dee came to her rescue, joining with Lyle Stubbs to say that she was substituting for Dee, who hadn't felt well enough to work that afternoon. It wasn't so far-fetched that it did more than just raise an eyebrow with the cops. Jaymie knew what she was doing, after all, and had worked at the Inn a few years before. Everyone in town knew Jaymie worked odd jobs whenever she could to make a few extra dollars.

The police—Detective Tewksbury again, not Detective Christian—and a police deputy took her statement, which she kept as minimal as possible. If they searched Lynn Foster's room, they would find both the old receipt from her Hoosier cabinet, she told them, and the mimeographed Queen Elizabeth cake recipe stolen from her bookshelf. She hoped that proved Lynn was a determined thief and would not stop there to get what she wanted.

So the next question surprised her.

"Is that why you were in her room?" the detective asked, leaning forward and peering directly into her eyes. "Did you put those items there? Were you trying to incriminate her?"

❧ Twenty-three ❧

"**I**S THAT WHAT Lynn Foster's saying?" Jaymie asked. She saw how it could look, that she'd snuck in to plant the items to make it look like Lynn was guilty. Was she in trouble?

"Do you think she would say that?"

Jaymie watched his eyes, but the detective was expressionless and simply waited with a calmness that was frightening. She sat forward on the padded purple chair. "*I'm* the one who turned the Button Gwinnett letter over to the police. Why on earth would I do something to incriminate Lynn Foster?"

"I don't know; why don't you tell us?"

Her stomach ached, and she was suddenly nervous. She had never been on the wrong side of the law before, not even for a traffic ticket! She paid her taxes on time, didn't litter, and never parked in the disabled zone. But from their aspect, she could see why they'd be suspicious. She had thrust herself into the middle of a murder investigation, dressing up in a maid's outfit to get into a suspect's hotel room. She flattened her palms on her thighs. "I didn't plant the papers. I would never do something like that."

"So if we find your fingerprints on the items what should we think?"

"Well, of *course* my fingerprints will be on things. I handled the Hoosier receipt when I found it in Lynn Foster's room, and the recipe came from my place originally, but I did *not* put them there. As I have already said, the Hoosier receipt must have been taken from the dead man's hand. I found a corner of it, I think, when I was sweeping up the mess. I can give that to you, if you like. I still have it at home." She met the detective's gaze steadily.

"I still find it curious that you were dressed in a maid's uniform and in Lynn Foster's room. It's all very . . . convenient. If you were investigating on your own, Ms. Leighton, please be aware of what a dangerous thing you have done, and that, potentially, you may have ruined any case against Mrs. Foster, if it does turn out that she is the perpetrator."

"I'm sorry," she said. "I didn't mean to make more trouble for you." She was silent for a moment, thinking, but then said, "Would you give Detective Christian a message? I showed him a black-stone-and-diamond pavé pin that I found in my garden. I know how it got there now. It came from the middle of a silk flower that Lynn Foster was wearing on the lapel of a black suit; you can ask Valetta Nibley about that, because she saw it there. If Detective Christian or you can think of any other way it got in my garden except dropping from her lapel, I'd be interested to know!"

The detective's expression was neutral. He wrote a note, then looked up. "You can go home for now, Ms. Leighton, but please don't leave the area."

She left, avoiding everyone else, just too tired to talk, even to Daniel. Once home, Jaymie let the animals out, filled their bowls and sat on the back step of her summer porch watching Hoppy chase squirrels as the sun sank lower in the sky. It had been a confusing, frightening day. She was

overwhelmed with weariness, and yet her nerves were
twitching like Mexican jumping beans. Closing her eyes,
she went through the crimes committed in the last week,
one by one. By Lynn's own admission, she and Trevor had
been conspiring to grab the Button letter for themselves and
leave Nathan, Brett and Ted out of it.

She pictured the Bourne house, remembering her spot
on the trumpet vine–shaded porch, and knowing now that
Trevor and Lynn were along the side wall just feet from her;
in retrospect, if Lynn hadn't wanted to be seen with Trevor
Standish, that side of the house was a bad spot for the schem-
ers to meet. It was within view of some of the auction-goers,
certainly, and apparently they were seen at least by Ted
Abernathy. Heck, her husband and Brett may have seen her,
too! That revelation, that she was scheming with Trevor, had
led to the fight at the auction between Trevor and Ted, both
of whom were vying to purchase the Hoosier. If it hadn't
been for that fight and the distraction it had caused, the bidding on the cabinet would have gone too high, and Jaymie
would have been out of it. One of them would have gotten
the Button letter.

The phone, beside her on the porch step, rang. It was her
mother. They had a vague conversation that meandered
uncertainly, mostly about Grandma Leighton and the Leightons' plans to come up from Florida in August to stay at
Rose Tree Cottage for a week. Jaymie was exhausted after
her stressful encounter, but she certainly did not want to
worry her mother with her near-death experience.

Her mom finally said, "Well, I can tell you have things
on your mind, so I'll let you go. Your father has put me in
a terrible spot! I have to face the bridge club this evening
and tell them that Alan didn't really mean it when he said
they were a bunch of interfering old biddies with too much
time on their hands. I swear, once a man reaches sixty he
changes, and not for the better. I don't even know him sometimes."

She hung up, and Jaymie stared at the phone in her hand. Didn't know him, after forty-some-odd years of marriage? Did anyone really know anyone else, even the ones closest to them?

Jaymie picked at the flaws and assumptions she had made in her reasoning along the way. She had assumed that it was Lynn who'd come along that night, just as Trevor found the receipt that he thought was the Button letter. Jaymie could imagine her whacking him over the head, but is that really what had happened? Did she think that based solely on the evidence of the receipt and the recipe being in the Fosters' suite?

Why had she dismissed Nathan Foster so readily as a suspect? Well, Lynn's pin in the holly hedge meant that Lynn had been in her backyard when she'd had no just cause to be there. Or was that necessarily so?

Jaymie got up and strolled the length of her lawn toward the back lane, eyeing the holly bushes. It was an odd place for the pin to have dropped. Even if someone had snuck up along the line of bushes toward the house, the pin would likely have dropped in the grass. As she had searched the Fosters' suite at the Inn, she had turned toward the theory that Lynn Foster was the murderer, in part because of the pin that had come from Lynn Foster's suit lapel. Maybe that was even what Lynn Foster had been wondering about the other day as they came into the Inn; she had said something to her husband about not knowing where she'd lost something. It could have been the valuable diamond pin.

But why *else* had Jaymie dismissed Nathan Foster as a suspect? The older gentleman's aura of dignity and gentility seemed to preclude any nefarious activity on his part. And there were the missing sleeping pills. She now knew that Lynn had been drugging her husband so he would sleep through her meetings with her boyfriend, Brett, but she had assumed that Lynn had dosed him while she was out killing Trevor Standish, too.

She stopped at the back gate and stared down the quiet road. It was a silent, early evening in the middle of the week; everyone would be inside eating dinner or in front of the TV. A rustling in the nearby bushes was likely a raccoon ambling out to forage for food to feed her babies. She yawned. Queensville would come alive again tomorrow, the official start of summer, the beginning of the Memorial Day long weekend.

Her mind returned to the enigma of Nathan Foster. What if all along he'd known about his wife's affair and her plan to take the Button letter and leave him? What if he'd only *pretended* to take the sleeping pills and pass out? Going to the drug store for more and seeming bewildered about missing so many pills would lend verisimilitude to his obliviousness. But if he secretly had known she was doing all that, wouldn't he have wanted to get rid of her? How better than to have her accused and jailed for a murder or murders that she hadn't committed, all while he was actually the one benefiting by stealing the valuable letter? Lynn was tired of him; well, maybe he was tired of her too and figured if she were in prison he would be rid of her and her scheming.

She could see how it would give him satisfaction to see her marched off to prison, when she had been cuckolding and drugging him. And he was the only other one of their scheming bunch who had access to her silk flower pin. She turned, leaned back against the fence and gazed at the line of holly bushes. If he took the pin out of the silk flower and tossed it into the bushes, he may have expected the cops to find it and trace it to her. Had he even planted the other evidence in their suite? She thought it over; the Hoosier receipt, the empty pill bottle . . . it was possible.

The more she thought of it, the more certain she became. It all added up! "It was Nathan Foster all along!" she muttered.

A strong arm snaked around her neck; she screamed and struggled, but the barrel of a gun was pressed to her temple.

With her peripheral vision, she could see that it was not the cute little toy Lynn had trained on her, but a lethal-looking blue-steel number.

"That's right, my dear," Nathan Foster said, holding the gun against her head with a steady, gloved hand. "It was me, and right now my sweet little wife—who has *not* been charged, and so has been encouraged by the high-priced attorney I retained for her, like a good and devoted husband, to walk out of the police station—is on her way here, thinking she is to meet me by the back gate."

Jaymie looked around wildly, as much as she could while holding her breath. The various backyards were still deserted; no helpful, nosy neighbor to see her plight.

"Now, you are going to turn around and open the gate, and you are *not* going to scream, or you'll be dead before you're done."

He released her, and she turned around slowly, trembling with terror. Gone was the vague expression of befuddlement; instead, Nathan Foster's lined face was twisted with sour triumph. He pushed her, and she staggered away from the fence as he opened the wrought-iron gate. He grabbed her again, and said, "She knows I'm on my way here. She thinks that we'll get the letter after all and sail off into the sunset. Though I'm sure her plans are more along the lines of getting the letter and sailing off into the sunset alone." He grinned. "Instead, she'll find your dead body and the gun, which she will likely pick up, knowing her. If I'm fortunate, it will be just in time for your horrified neighbors to discover her."

"That's never going to work!" Jaymie said, shivering, afraid to move. She had thought Lynn lethal, but all along it was Nathan she should have watched out for.

The melodic twilight song of a robin taunted her with its peaceful sound. She stared longingly up her yard to the porch, where her cordless phone sat on the top step. Hoppy had gone back into the house through the open back door, no doubt to munch kibble and curl up in his basket, and who knew where Denver was? Anna, her closest neighbor, might hear her scream, but might not. And if Jaymie did scream, it would likely be the last thing she did on earth.

"It'll work," he muttered. "I know my sweet Lynn. She's as predictable as most women."

"You killed Trevor," she said, shaking. "And you used the grinder off my Hoosier to do it!"

"Is that what that was? The damned idiot wrenched it off as he went down. I lost my grip on the crowbar and picked that thing up to finish the terrible deed. I did *not* enjoy it, you know, doing that," he said, with a huffy tone. "I'm not a killer. I thought he had the letter in his hand, but the dolt had merely found a receipt. If only I had not been so precipitous!"

She took a deep breath, trying to calm herself. "And Ted Abernathy. Why him?" She twisted, trying to see someone, anyone. But no one was in their backyards, not even Mr. Findley!

"Fool. He tried to blackmail me!" He looked around. "Where should we stage this little drama, I wonder? Here, or closer to the house? Hmm." The evening shadows were long and concealing, and he appeared in no hurry. Yet. Even if someone saw them from a distance, they wouldn't know what they were looking at. "You asked about Ted Abernathy; what a fool that man was! He left a note at the Inn for me to meet him at the marina. Luckily, boathouses have fishing gear and fillet knives, for gutting fish. Knifing is much quieter than a gun, and that particular fillet knife is at the bottom of the river now. Your death, on the other hand . . . I *want* people to hear it."

He grabbed her shoulder with one steely hand and squeezed. Pain shot down her arm. Fear was clouding Jaymie's mind. She needed to clear it, to still the trembling and think. She was *not* going to die.

Nathan checked his watch. Motioning with the gun to

the back porch, he said, "March!" and pushed her up the path, maintaining his unyielding grip on her neck. "This little tragedy will act out on your summer porch, near your beloved Hoosier. There is a certain poetic justice in that. Once my dear wife is found over your body—or running away from the crime—those idiot cops will be able to connect the dots, and Lynn will be up a creek. I won't need to worry about Trevor and Ted's unfortunate demises being laid at my doorstep. I'll be the sadly horrified and misled husband."

If Jaymie had learned anything in the last few hours, it was not to dillydally when faced with a murderer. There was not a moment to waste. She twisted suddenly and managed to get her teeth on his wrist, biting hard while ducking from the direct aim of the gun. He released her and yelped in pain, and she kicked back, connecting with his leg, then tore away from him, zigzagging toward the house, yelling and screaming, hoping her back was not a target. She made it to the porch, and could hear him grunting as he ran after her.

She didn't dare stop to pick up her phone handset, but instead raced through the kitchen. Hoppy, startled, began to bark and ran after her, enchanted by this new game. She could hear Nathan Foster's heavy footsteps behind her on the creaky, wide floorboards, but his unfamiliarity with her house gave her the advantage, and she wove through the shadowy interior, then opened the front door. Instead of exiting, though, she left it open and ducked back into the hall behind the laden coat tree. Hoppy raced outside and began to bark frantically. Bless his excitable nature!

The man lumbered through the house, then paused briefly in the open doorway. Jaymie didn't hesitate, but pushed the coat tree over on him, thinking it might disable him. He thrashed about, flailing through woolen coats. Jaymie grabbed an umbrella from the stand on the other side of the door and began whaling away at him in the doorway, all the while shrieking for help.

Her arms felt like they'd fall off. Nathan Foster grunted, rolled away from her and lumbered to his feet, steadying the gun on her once more. "You little bitch," he said lunging toward her. "I've gotta kill you before Lynn shows up . . . and . . ." He clutched at his heart and turned gray, falling to his knees in her doorway just as Mr. Trip Findley, Prince Albert himself, trotted through her house toward them, cricket bat in hand.

"What's going on here?" he shouted. "Saw him chasin' you up your back lawn from my porch and came to help. Jaymie, you okay?"

Moments later the cops arrived and, since the gun was still in Nathan Foster's hand, even though she had tried to dislodge it, there was no question who the dangerous assailant was. He was cuffed and arrested just as Lynn Foster drove her Cadillac down the block. She screeched to a halt and jumped from the car, staring openmouthed and pale at the sight of her battered husband being led away by two sturdy police officers. He sagged in the officer's hands, though, looking lifeless.

"I think he's having a heart attack!" Jaymie cried.

"That's what it looks like, all right," Mr. Findley said.

"What's going on?" Lynn Foster shrieked. She swatted at one of the cops who held Nathan. "You let my husband go!"

"He was setting you up, Lynn," Jaymie said, loudly.

The police, now aware that something was wrong with their prisoner, gently lowered the man to the sidewalk and started CPR.

"He was going to kill me and make it look like you had done it," Jaymie continued. "You were going down for *murder*, even though he was the one who killed Trevor Standish and Ted Abernathy."

Lynn ignored Jaymie, trotting down the walk and falling to her knees at her husband's side, hanging over him. "I love you, Nathan!" she cried, stroking his face, interfering with the female deputy, who was doing her best to administer lifesaving actions. "We'll get through this. I believe in you!"

Jaymie sighed and shook her head. She had tried, and that was all she could do.

NATHAN FOSTER HAD been about to be charged with murder for killing Trevor Standish and Ted Abernathy, the local news radio chirped the next morning, but he'd died of a massive heart attack, despite all efforts to revive him at the Wolverhampton hospital. He'd admitted the killings in a deathbed confession, so no one else was being charged.

Jaymie had called Becca and filled her in on all the excitement. Her sister was aghast at the danger Jaymie had been in, but claimed to be proud of her courage and resourcefulness. Grandma Leighton was doing so well that Becca was now worry-free. She would be driving down for the weekend, and they could go over every minute of the events of the last week.

For the rest of the day, she didn't do much but answer the phone to calm concerned friends, especially Daniel, who had phoned three times and was on his way over. She ached; whether it was a reaction to the tension and fear she had suffered, or the death grip Nathan Foster had had on her, she wasn't sure. Later in the day, Anna came over to check in on Jaymie. Everyone had the same idea, it seemed, and there were quite a few people already there, and more coming. "Just to drop in," each person had said on the phone.

"Judging from that scene in front of your house, Lynn Foster must have heard her husband had more money than she thought," Anna said, sitting with Jaymie in her backyard while Hoppy frolicked with Tabby.

"By then she knew she wasn't getting the Button letter, and any money is better than nothing, I guess," Jaymie said. She sat in one of her vintage Adirondack chairs. "I will say this; it looked for all the world like she was trying to interfere with the officer giving Nathan CPR. I wonder if she knew what she was doing? I wouldn't put it past her. Those two were a matched set of scheming jerks. I hope they charge her with attempted murder on poor Heidi."

Daniel was sitting in the grass with Denver on his lap, while Valetta Nibley stood nearby, watching Tabby play with Hoppy, a wistful look on her homely face. Joel had even come over with Heidi, newly released from the hospital. The poor girl sported some purplish bruises but still looked pretty. Anna had directed people to go to her deck and bring back the chairs she had there, to allow enough room for folks to sit in the late afternoon golden sun. Dee had just arrived bearing a casserole, and she made coffee, using the huge urn the Leighton family stored in the pantry. Jaymie had already made a big pot of hot tea and put it in a carafe.

"So what exactly happened?" DeeDee said, balancing a melamine cup of coffee on the arm of her folding lawn chair. "I still don't understand. Last I heard from Lyle yesterday, Lynn Foster was in jail, and I thought that was that?"

"I thought she was the one, I really did," Jaymie said. "When I looked in her room at the Inn, I found evidence that pointed directly at her, but I didn't realize that what it really meant was Nathan Foster was setting her up to take the fall for everything he'd done. He even went so far as to toss that diamond pin on the dirt by my new holly bushes, just hoping it would be found and traced back to her. He couldn't have known it *would* be found. It was a sloppy plot, created on the fly, I suppose, as their plan to get the Button letter evolved after the fiasco at the auction. It almost worked, though!"

She detailed much of what she knew, then said, "I don't think Lynn even knew about the Hoosier receipt stuck in the collector's magazine. I interfered in Nathan's plan, but he decided to use even that to his advantage. I had already loudly claimed at the police station that Lynn Foster was the murderer, but they didn't have enough to hold her on. I gather Nathan's lawyer told Lynn to force the police department's hand; she wouldn't talk to them, and told them to either charge her or she was walking out. They couldn't charge her with Trevor's murder based on what they had."

"That is unthinkable," Joel said, indignant. "Why couldn't they hold her?

"Look at the result," Jaymie said. "If they *had* charged her with murder, she'd have a good case against them. And it did look like I had masqueraded as a maid on purpose to plant things in her room. There was enough ambiguity that they couldn't risk a lawsuit for false arrest, so until they had a chance to unravel everything, all they could do was warn her to stay in Queensville for a few days." She squinted into the distance. "The police must have been following Lynn Foster, though, I suppose. That's probably why they arrived so quickly after she did."

Denver had abandoned Daniel to lie in wait for Hoppy, so he could pounce on the dog if he got too close, and Daniel now sat in the grass near Jaymie's feet, legs tucked under him, elbows on his knees. "I sure thought we had it right," he said.

"We didn't know the inner dynamics of their marriage, I guess," Jaymie mused. The sun of late day angled onto her face, and she sighed, relishing the cooling breeze of a May early evening. She was happy to be safe and secure in her home, surrounded by her friends. "Lynn was sick of her husband and planned to ditch him, but he was no idiot, despite seeming kind of gentle and befuddled. That was all an act. Pretty convincing to me. I figure he knew about Brett and her, and he knew she was planning to double-cross him, ultimately, with the Button Gwinnett letter. He didn't have enough money for *her*, maybe, but he was still loaded. At least by all of our reckoning."

Daniel was conspicuously silent, and Jaymie realized, with shock, that he probably had many times the money in Nathan's estate. It made her a little uncomfortable, as Dee eyed her with a knowing smile. To counter the blush that rose in her cheeks—Daniel had made his interest in her plain, maybe *too* plain—she hurried to continue explaining. "If Nathan divorced Lynn, he would have had to give her alimony, but if she was convicted of murder, he may have been able to keep most of it. I'm no lawyer, so I don't know, but I assume he could have made a good case, given that she was drugging him. He might even have been able to claim that she was trying to kill him. Maybe he was setting her up for that."

"Kind of ironic that he almost died with her hanging over him," Dee said. "I wonder if she'll get his money?"

"Probably," Jaymie said. "Why wouldn't she? I suppose she figured her boyfriend, Brett, killed Trevor. She was cold-blooded enough not to care, I guess."

"So how do you figure it happened?" Heidi asked. Joel sat on the other Adirondack, and she sat on his knee, her arm around his neck, looking adorably frail with a bandage on her head covering seven stitches from Lynn's whack.

"It started quite a while ago," Jaymie said, and related what Lynn had told her about joining the collector's group where they'd met Trevor Standish, and then Brett Delgado. The Fosters made a deal with Trevor to fund his search for the Button letter, and they followed him to Queensville to keep an eye on their investment. "When Brett showed up with his forger pal in tow—which Lynn did *not* expect and wasn't pleased about—I think Nathan knew for sure that Lynn was playing him for a fool and, worse than that, had no intention of sharing the Button letter with him."

"That would do it . . . your wife's younger lover shows up in the same village at the same time?" Joel laughed. "Even an idiot would get the not-so-subtle hint that his marriage was over."

Daniel threw Joel an exasperated look. "He must have known about it long before that."

"I think, though, that the final straw was that Nathan

must have seen her at the auction talking to Trevor alone. Nathan really did want the Button, and the thought that his wife and his 'employee' were scheming to deprive him of it just infuriated him."

"But he's dead now," Heidi said.

"Lynn's apparently claiming that she was under her husband's thumb and afraid of him," Jaymie said, shaking her head. She had heard that from a friend who worked in the payroll office at the police station. "Everything she did, she did at his command, she told the police, even holding me hostage. I think she's intent on divorcing herself from any part of the whole thing. It's easy to blame a dead man. And she wants to be sure she's positioned as his heir."

"How can she do that, put all the blame for kidnapping you on Nathan? You can prove her wrong," Valetta said.

"I think she's just trying to confuse the issue. They'll still have her on the attack on Heidi, which she admitted to me."

The conversation turned to other things—it was the first holiday weekend of summer, after all—and her friends headed in to load up plates of the casserole, salad and other goodies laid out on the trestle table in the kitchen. As Jaymie rose from the Adirondack, she looked back to see Anna head down the lawn toward the back gate, Tabitha's small hand in hers.

"Hey, aren't you staying to have a bite to eat?" Jaymie called out, following her.

Anna turned and shook her head, rubbing her stomach. "I'm not feeling too well. I'm just going to go back to lie down for a while. I have guests, and more arriving tonight."

Jaymie walked with her to the back gate as Anna picked up her sleepy daughter. "I'm sorry you're not well." She looked at Anna's face, and suddenly said, "You aren't . . . you aren't expecting, are you?"

Anna's pale cheeks turned pink, and tears welled up in her eyes. She nodded. "I think I am," she whispered, cuddling Tabby to her breast. "But don't tell anyone. I haven't told Clive yet, because I'm not sure. I missed taking my pill a few times."

"Oh, Anna . . . are you happy?"

She hesitated, but then nodded and dashed the tears away with her free hand. "I am. I really am. We always planned on more kids. I just don't know how I'm going to handle the Shady Rest. I had an awful time with morning sickness with Tabby, and cooking eggs for guests . . . it's going to be torture!"

Jaymie only hesitated a moment before saying, "Don't worry about a thing. I'll take care of it as long as necessary."

Anna reached out to her with a sob of gratitude. "Thanks, Jaymie! You're such a good friend."

As the two women hugged, Tabby sleepily patted Jaymie's cheek, and echoed, "Such a good fwiend!"

❊ Twenty-four ❊

IN THE BRIGHT light of day Jaymie could see that the Hoosier still wasn't as clean as she wanted it, so she did it over more thoroughly. *Now* it was truly clean, the drawers sitting out in the backyard in the sunshine drying. It was the Saturday of the Memorial Day weekend, and Becca would be arriving anytime. Jaymie was busier than ever. That morning she had cooked breakfast for all of Anna's guests, and her friend was tearfully grateful. The tearful part was now more understandable, given Anna's "delicate state," as the historical romances Jaymie read would have put it.

Lots of work lay ahead for the summer, because Jaymie had struck a deal with the Emporium owners—for whom she worked occasionally—to fill picnic baskets with vintage melamine and linens for "rental" during the summer. The group would put a deposit on the basket and pay for the food filling it; when they returned the basket and dishes, their deposit would be refunded. Jaymie had scoured a local antiques market for more melamine and a couple more baskets, because it was proving to be a popular idea.

The tourism season was officially in full swing. The Queensville/Johnsonville regatta was coming up on the July First–July Fourth Canadian/American holiday, after which the town would celebrate Founder's Day, and a slew of other special days, not winding down until the autumn events, Harvest Fest, Thanksgiving, and then "Dickens Days," the Christmas festival in Queensville, and New Year's Eve on the Boardwalk. That was the rhythm of life in Queensville, Michigan.

But right now she was at peace with the world and enjoying her Hoosier.

"Jaymie!"

She looked up. Daniel was at the back gate, and Hoppy was leaping for joy, yipping excitedly. He came through and ambled up the long stone walkway to the summer porch.

"It looks great," he said, of the now clean but otherwise untouched Hoosier cabinet.

"I had given it a scrubbing before, but in the light of day I could see how much grubbiness remained, so I just had to give the drawers a better going-over," she said, pushing her bangs off her forehead. "I've finished waxing the tambour door track so it will roll smoothly," she said, stepping over to it and demonstrating the tambour now moving smoothly on its track.

"Looks fantastic."

"So, have you heard from Trevor's mother?" she asked as she shifted the porcelain work top, propping it against the kitchen door.

He nodded, looking a little glum and wiping his eyes, which had welled with moisture for his lost friend. "She had warned Trevor not to get in over his head, she told me. She just got a note from him day before yesterday. It said that if he got into trouble she was to look to Nathan Foster, who, he had a feeling, was a 'bad dude,' in his own words."

"That guy sure got around a lot for a sixty-something man. He had followed Trevor, who was working for Lynn and him, and snatched what he thought was the Button letter before killing Trevor." She still felt a chill down her back at the thought, but shrugged it off. She was not going to let the awful events on her summer porch ruin her summer.

"I still don't understand why Ted Abernathy ended up murdered?"

"Didn't I explain? The day Abernathy attacked me, he said he'd figured out a way to make some money off the deal, even without the letter. Nathan Foster told me Abernathy tried to blackmail him. The guy was desperate for cash—he said he 'lost' some money that didn't belong to him—desperate enough to risk meeting with Nathan in private at the marina. That was his undoing. Nathan killed him to keep him quiet."

"Grim."

"I know. I told Detective Christian all of that." Her heart leaped a little when she thought of the handsome detective, and a blush burned her cheeks, but how silly was that? He'd barely noticed her, and then only as a suspect.

Just then, the man himself, Detective Zachary Christian, strolled through her back gate and up the stone path, carrying a longish box. Jaymie watched him silently, noting his casual garb. No suit today, but jeans and a polo shirt stretched taut over an athletic frame.

"Detective Christian," she said. "What brings you here?"

"Not official business, don't worry," he said with a smile, one foot up on the top step. "So this is the infamous Hoosier cabinet. I looked at it when we were here, but I didn't really get what it was for." He stepped up and moved closer.

Jaymie explained the history of the Hoosier and the starring role it was set to play in her second *Recipes from the Vintage Kitchen* cookbook, then said, "Now I want to get this in place in the kitchen. Can someone help me carry it in?"

Both men stepped forward, then eyed each other.

"We can do it together," the detective said, setting the box aside. "Right, buddy?"

Daniel pushed his glasses up on his nose, and said, "Sure."

So Jaymie was in the novel situation of having not one, but *two* men to direct. They carried the base unit into the house and pushed it into the space she had cleared for it as she carried the tabletop in. She lifted the porcelain tabletop and pushed it into place, then asked them to get the upper cabinet. When they gently lowered it into the brackets, working together better than she would have expected, she got a screwdriver, this time eschewing anyone else's help. Some things she wanted to do on her own.

As she worked, attaching the upper cabinet to the brackets, she wondered anew why Detective Christian had shown up. "So what brings you here, Detective?" she said, over her shoulder.

"Call me Zachary, or Zack." He smiled down at her as she bent to slot the screwdriver into the vintage screw she was using.

The burning spots in her cheeks could easily be explained by her position; the blood was just rushing to her face.

"I just wanted to let you know, we found the real murder weapon, and according to the medical examiner, it wasn't your grinder. Your information helped, what you told us about Nathan Foster's statement to you."

"Nathan said he used a crowbar," she said, straightening.

"That's right. It was probably Trevor Standish's, from his rental car, judging by his fingerprints all over it."

She nodded. "It was what he used to pry my door off its hinges."

"Foster was clumsy; his prints are on it, too," the detective said. "I have a feeling he thought he was so clever, we'd never imagine it was him."

"He told me he lost his grip on it, and since Trevor had

pulled the grinder off the work top when he fell, Nathan picked that up for one last blow." She shivered.

"Where'd you find the crowbar?" Daniel asked. He strolled across the kitchen toward the stove and picked up the teakettle.

"In the trunk of the Cadillac. I think Foster assumed he had gotten all the blood off of it, but luminal shows everything! I don't have the typing back yet from the lab in Wolverhampton, but I have a feeling we'll discover it's Trevor Standish's. Sorry, buddy, I know he was a friend of yours."

Daniel nodded.

"Ted Abernathy's murder is a different matter," the detective said.

"Did you find the knife yet?"

He shook his head. "Not yet. It may wash up, or it may not. In any event, we have Foster's deathbed confession."

Jaymie swallowed and shook her head. So much for leaving it all behind.

"Want me to put the kettle on, Jaymie?" Daniel asked. "You look like you could use a cup of tea."

"Sure. Good idea."

The detective smiled, that gorgeous, quirky smile she had seen only once before. He picked up the box he had laid down and handed it to Jaymie. "This is your grinder."

She backed away. "I don't think I want it."

"I had it professionally cleaned by the lab. No traces of *anything* remain, honest. It really was not the murder weapon, Jaymie. The ME thinks Standish was dead by the time Foster attacked him with the grinder. Keep it in the box, put it away somewhere and forget about it. You may be happy you kept it someday."

She retrieved the bottom drawer from outside, had the detective drop the box in it and pushed it into its slot in the Hoosier. It would stay there indefinitely.

"I have to go," the detective said. "I'll leave you two to . . . whatever."

"Wait!" Jaymie said. "One question I've had all along is, how did Trevor Standish apparently text Daniel, when the guy was already dead?" She wasn't about to say, with Daniel there, that she had suspected Zell based largely on the cell phone usage and text message to Daniel.

"That was another thing we wondered, too. What happened to Trevor Standish's cell phone? We got the records, and could tell someone had used it after he died—to text Dan, here—but there wasn't another single call or text made on it. The phone completely disappeared, and I'd bet it's in the St. Clair River with the knife."

Daniel nodded. "If Nathan Foster knew Trevor at all, then he knew about him communicating with me. Or if Foster read Trevor's text messages, the guy would have been able to figure out about our 'reunion' weekend. He must have known too that I'd be worried if I didn't hear from Trev, so Foster made up that first text and sent it. The second one . . . that was probably part of his plan to keep people from figuring out who the dead man was."

The detective nodded. "That's what we think."

"But why didn't Nathan want people to know who the dead guy was?" Daniel said.

"It would delay things until he got the Button Gwinnett letter, keep the matter confused," Jaymie said.

"With Nathan Foster dead, there are a lot of things we'll never know for sure," Christian added.

"What about Brett Delgado?" Jaymie asked.

"We haven't formally charged him with anything. He's valuable as a material witness, though, and we're in contact with him. He was badly frightened by Ted Abernathy's murder. We'll cut a deal with him, probably."

"Have the police turned the Button letter back over to the Bourne family yet?" Jaymie asked.

"Yes. Mr. Bourne's grandson was of the opinion that they should sell it, but the old guy told him, in no uncertain terms, that two people had died for it, and he was not going to profit from that. He's donating it to the Queensville museum, if they will have it."

"Queensville museum? There is no Queensville museum," Jaymie said, glancing over at Daniel. "Mrs. Bellwood and the others wanted Stowe House for that. That's why she's so frosty toward Daniel. But maybe with something as historically important as the Button Gwinnett letter to protect, the Heritage Society can get some grants to start one."

"I'll contribute to a museum fund," Daniel said. "If I'd known, I would have done that sooner!"

"You'll have to work that out. Quaint little town you have here, I will say that. Lots of . . . unique individuals."

"Well, thanks for dropping by, Detective . . . uh . . . Zachary," Jaymie said. "I appreciate it."

"I never did think you could have done it, you know, the murder," he said, looming over her, his tone gentle. "But I've learned the hard way, don't eliminate anyone until you have an arrest."

"I don't think I helped myself, either. I probably looked guilty as heck."

"You were very gutsy," he said, softly.

His voice sent a shiver down her back, and she was wordless, staring up into his dark-fringed gray eyes.

"Take care of yourself, and don't get in any more jams," he said, chucking her under the chin. "You're too cute to be arrested!" He turned and strode over to Daniel, sticking out his hand. "So long, Dan. I'm sorry about your friend." They shook, and he headed to the back door and out.

She turned away as he left, so Daniel couldn't see her feelings. She was attracted to the detective in a way she was not attracted to Daniel, but ultimately it would come to nothing. He treated her like she was a cute kid, even though she was thirty-two, and he was probably not even ten years older than her.

Daniel made a pot of tea—he had always drunk tea, he

affirmed, because his mom was English—and they chatted. Daniel told her that Zell had left Queensville brokenhearted because Heidi had blown him off, telling him she didn't mean anything by flirting with him and that he should have known that because she told him all along she had a boy-friend.

Daniel shook his head. "Why did she act that way? I saw it; she was definitely flirting with the guy. Zell really thought they had a connection."

"She didn't mean anything by it, though," Jaymie said, moved to defend Heidi. Having talked to her and having watched her with Joel, she saw the subtle differences between how she acted with other guys and how she behaved toward her boyfriend. "Some girls are like that; they just can't seem to keep from flirting with any guy who comes close to them."

"That's not what I'd want in a girlfriend, I can tell you," he said, watching her.

She felt a trickle of warmth in her stomach. Daniel Collins was the real deal, like Clive, Anna's husband. He was a good guy, and he liked her. She wasn't sure how she felt yet, but she really did like him, too. They'd just have to see.

"Can you get me the other two drawers for the Hoosier?" she asked to keep any declaration of interest at bay. She was not going to rush into anything. "By the way, why was Zell McIntosh at the auction on that Friday night?" She had already told Daniel about Becca's auction photo with him in it. She hadn't told him how Zell's flirting with her the first time they'd met had made her suspicious of him and his interest in the Hoosier.

"I asked him about that, because he said something about seeing Heidi first at the auction. He just shrugged. I think he wanders, and sometimes I wonder if he keeps track of the time and dates too well; that's why he showed up early to my place. I don't quite know what to think about my old buddy," Daniel said, his tone sad. "He seems lost. He's not a very happy guy, for all that he's such a joker. I've lost Trevor, but I'm going to make sure I don't lose Zell. I told him to come back and stay at my place if he wants."

"You're a really nice guy, Daniel Collins," Jaymie said, softly, putting her palm to his cheek. "A very nice man."

"Haven't you heard?" he said, staring into her eyes, his voice slightly hoarse. "Nice guys finish last."

"I don't think that's true," she murmured.

"We'll see." He covered her hand with his and smiled. She felt a tremor of dawning warmth toward him.

"You know, I always did like you, Jaymie," he said, still watching her eyes. "But while you were with Joel . . ." He shook his head. "Then I found out you guys broke up. I hate to say it, but I was glad. He was never good enough for you."

"Now, *you* are good for my self-esteem! I should have had you around last December." She smiled up at him, intent on keeping it light.

Once the cabinet was fully put together, she began to choose the display pieces she wanted to store on the Hoosier, while Daniel sat at the table sipping tea. A vintage glass rolling pin and a collection of tin cookie cutters were her first choices for the work top. Then she picked out a wood-handled rotary eggbeater and a copper kettle. Along the top of the upper cabinet she lined up a vintage colander on a stand, a wood spice drawer and a salt box.

It wasn't quite right, yet, but she'd work on it. She got out her digital camera and took a couple of photos. "This will be for the blog, if my cookbook gets picked up." Denver slunk in and rubbed up against Daniel's leg. Jaymie noticed and laughed. "He never does that!"

"I like cats," he said, picking Denver up and cradling him on his lap. The cat didn't hiss or jump down.

"He always hated and *still* hates Joel with a fiery cat passion."

"Cats are more discerning than dogs," Daniel said, his mouth quirking up in an awkward smile.

There was another long pause, a fairly comfortable silence, as Jaymie fussed with her arrangement, then Daniel said, "So, you doing anything tonight?"

"Not really. Laundry, but that can wait."

"Would you like to go out somewhere for dinner?"

She hesitated only a moment, watching him pet Denver, then said, "Sure, why not?" Dinner was just about right. Maybe she needed more time to figure out what she wanted from a guy and a relationship, but dinner she could manage.

HISTORY OF QUEEN ELIZABETH CAKE

by Jaymie Leighton

According to CooksInfo.com, the recipe for Queen Elizabeth cake was sold for fifteen cents a copy during World War II as a fundraiser for the war effort. As Queen Elizabeth (known now as the late Queen Mother, as she was the current Queen Elizabeth II's mother) was a staunch supporter of the war effort, it may have been named in her honor, but it was certainly not a favorite cake of hers.

In fact, according to another foodie website, Astray.com, when the Queen Mother was asked about the source of the recipe, her lady-in-waiting wrote back to the questioner that the source was uncertain, but that it should not be called "Queen Elizabeth cake" but rather "date and walnut cake." Given the rather plain and unexciting nature of the recipe, who can blame her? Perhaps she would have liked something a little more regal named after her!

The modern cook will notice that some assumptions of knowledge were made in this recipe, originally from the

1953 Johnsonville United Church Ladies' Auxiliary Cookbook, that may baffle modern cooks.

First, a "moderate" oven is about 350 degrees Fahrenheit.

Second, what the heck is "top milk"? Cream! In previous years, milk used to be bought in glass bottles with an odd ballooning of the neck. This would capture the cream as it separated from the milk and floated to the top, and thus, "top milk!"

The recipe still seems, to the modern eye, to be a jumble of directions and ingredients. Following this, you will find the deciphered recipe, with baking and serving suggestions!

RECIPES

Queen Elizabeth Cake

VINTAGE RECIPE (FROM COOKSINFO.COM)

This is the original recipe for the cake Jaymie made for the annual Queensville Tea with the Queen event!

Mix 1 cup dates, 1 cup boiling water, 1 small tsp. of soda and let stand while doing the rest. ¼ cup shortening, 1 cup sugar, 1 egg, ½ cup chopped nuts, 1 ½ cup flour, 1 tsp. baking powder, salt and vanilla. Mix cake as usual, fold in date mixture, pour into 8X8 pan and bake in moderate oven for about 30 minutes.

TOPPING:
5 tbsp. brown sugar, ¼ cup cocoanut, 3 tbsp. butter, 2 tbsp. top milk. Boil 3 min. Remove cake from oven and while still warm pour this mixture over cake. Sprinkle cocoanut over and put back in oven to brown.

Queen Elizabeth Cake

MODERNIZED RECIPE

*Feel free to experiment with what is essentially a simple
date nut cake. Perhaps you could change out the "topping"
for a cream cheese icing, or bake it in a round pan, turn it
out and slice the cake horizontally, then fill it with rasp-
berry preserves. It is a very rich, moist tea cake, though,
and doesn't really need any fancying up!—JL*

Makes 16 good-sized pieces.

CAKE:
1 cup dates (I packed the dates down to fill the cup
    measure)
1 cup boiling water
1 tsp. baking soda
¼ cup shortening
1 cup sugar
1 egg
½ cup chopped nuts (walnuts, pecans, hazelnuts)
1½ cups flour
1 tsp. baking powder
¼ tsp. salt (estimated)
½ tsp. vanilla (estimated)

TOPPING:
5 tbsp. brown sugar
3 tbsp. butter
2 tbsp. cream
¼ cup shredded coconut

Preheat oven to 350 degrees.

Mix dates, boiling water and baking soda together and let stand while doing the rest. This softens the dates to let them blend with the batter.

Blend together shortening, sugar, beaten egg and vanilla in large bowl.

Mix together in a *separate* bowl the flour, baking powder and salt, then add chopped nuts.

Mix dry ingredients (flour mixture) with wet (shortening mixture) until thoroughly combined, then fold in the softened dates. (I mashed the dates to make them softer, and it helped the batter blend nicely.)

Spray 8x8 pan with spray oil, pour cake batter in and bake in 350 degree oven for about 40–45 minutes. Test cake with a toothpick for doneness; inserted toothpick should come out clean.

Meanwhile, mix topping ingredients and boil three minutes.

Remove cake from oven, and while still warm pour this mixture over cake. Sprinkle coconut over and put back in the oven to brown. (I put the cake in the 350 degree oven for five minutes, but the coconut was not browning, so I put it under the broiler for two or three minutes—four inches away from the element—to brown the coconut. If you do this step, *watch it carefully*! The caramel glaze on top will bubble.)

Cut into squares and serve with good, strong tea, on your prettiest cake plates! I would suggest, in honor of the Queen Mother's Scottish origins (she spent her childhood at Glamis Castle in Scotland), that you use a tartan-pattern china like Lenox's Holiday Tartan or a wonderful Canadian original, Newfoundland Tartan dishes made by Royal Adderley of Ridgway, though the latter are rare and hard to find! Alternately, in honor of Queen Victoria, you could use the Herend pattern "Queen Victoria," a lovely floral china introduced at the first world's fair, the Great Exhibition in 1851 and actually purchased and used by Her Royal Highness!—*JL*

Victoria Hamilton is a pseudonym for national bestselling author Donna Lea Simpson, who is also a collector of vintage cookware and recipes.

6/12

From National Bestselling Author
CLEO COYLE

M   cha

Clare's Village Blend beans are being used to create a new java love potion: a "Mocha Magic Coffee" billed as an aphrodisiac. Clare may even try some on her boyfriend, NYPD detective Mike Quinn—when he's off duty, of course.

The product, expected to rake in millions, will be sold exclusively on Aphrodite's Village, one of the Web's most popular online communities for women. But the launch party ends on a sour note when one of the Web site's editors is found dead.

When more of the Web site's Sisters of Aphrodite start to die, Clare is convinced someone wants the coffee's secret formula—and is willing to kill to get it. Clare isn't about to spill the beans, but will she be next on the hit list?

Includes recipes and coffee-making tips!

penguin.com

M852T0311